Praise for Shannon K. Butcher's Novels of the Sentinel Wars

Living Nightmare

"[An] action-packed story of the brooding and angry warrior Madoc and his journey to the future. This series rocks!"
—Fresh Fiction

"In the latest chapter of Butcher's Sentinel Wars, two extremely damaged individuals face danger of the body and heart. Utilizing her ability to combine excellent characterization with riveting danger, rising star Butcher adds another fascinating tier to her expanding world. You are always guaranteed generous portions of pulse-pounding action and romance in a Butcher tale!"
—Romantic Times

"Ms. Butcher's written word began to grab hold of my imagination and lead me on a ride unlike anything I have read before."
—Coffee Time Romance

Running Scared

"What an entertaining and thrilling series! The characters are forever evolving, secrets are revealed, powers are found, new details come to life, and love is the cause of it all. I love it!"
—Fresh Fiction

"Superb storytelling . . . I am amazed how Ms. Butcher's intricacies and subplots continue to expand the story without bogging down the overall plot."
—Romance Junkies

"This book jumps right in the fray and keeps you hooked till the end and I was unable to put it down. Emotionally dark, this is a wonderful blending of paranormal romance and urban fantasy [with] many twists and turns."
—Smexy Books Romance Reviews

Finding the Lost

"Exerts much the same appeal as Christine Feehan's Carpathian series, what with tortured heroes, the necessity of finding love or facing a fate worse than death, hot lovemaking, and danger-filled adventure."
—Booklist

continued . . .

"A terrific grim thriller with the romantic subplot playing a strong supporting role. The cast is powerful as the audience will feel every emotion that Andra feels from fear for her sister to fear for her falling in love. *Finding the Lost* is a dark tale as Shannon K. Butcher paints a forbidding, gloomy landscape in which an ancient war between humanity's guardians and their nasty adversaries heats up in Nebraska."

—Alternative Worlds

"A very entertaining read ... The ending was a great cliff-hanger and I can't wait to read the next book in this series ... a fast-paced story with great action scenes and lots of hot romance."

—The Book Lush

"Butcher's paranormal reality is dark and gritty in this second Sentinel War installment. What makes this story so gripping is the seamlessly delivered hard-hitting action and wrenching emotions. Butcher is a major talent in the making."

—*Romantic Times*

Burning Alive

"A wonderful paranormal debut ... Shannon K. Butcher's talent shines." —*New York Times* bestselling author Nalini Singh

"Starts off with nonstop action. Readers will race through the pages, only to reread the entire novel to capture every little detail ... a promising start for a new voice in urban fantasy/paranormal romance. I look forward to the next installment."

—A Romance Review (5 roses)

"This first book of the Sentinel Wars whets your appetite for the rest of the books in the series. Ms. Butcher is carving her way onto the bestseller lists with this phenomenal, nonstop ride that will have you preordering the second book the minute you put this one down." —*Affaire de Coeur* (5 stars)

DYING WISH

THE SENTINEL WARS

SHANNON K. BUTCHER

A SIGNET BOOK

SIGNET
Published by New American Library, a division of
Penguin Group (USA) Inc., 375 Hudson Street,
New York, New York 10014, USA
Penguin Group (Canada), 90 Eglinton Avenue East, Suite 700, Toronto,
Ontario M4P 2Y3, Canada (a division of Pearson Penguin Canada Inc.)
Penguin Books Ltd., 80 Strand, London WC2R 0RL, England
Penguin Ireland, 25 St. Stephen's Green, Dublin 2,
Ireland (a division of Penguin Books Ltd.)
Penguin Group (Australia), 250 Camberwell Road, Camberwell, Victoria 3124,
Australia (a division of Pearson Australia Group Pty. Ltd.)
Penguin Books India Pvt. Ltd., 11 Community Centre, Panchsheel Park,
New Delhi - 110 017, India
Penguin Group (NZ), 67 Apollo Drive, Rosedale, Auckland 0632,
New Zealand (a division of Pearson New Zealand Ltd.)
Penguin Books (South Africa) (Pty.) Ltd., 24 Sturdee Avenue,
Rosebank, Johannesburg 2196, South Africa

Penguin Books Ltd., Registered Offices:
80 Strand, London WC2R 0RL, England

First published by Signet, an imprint of New American Library,
a division of Penguin Group (USA) Inc.

First Printing, March 2012
10 9 8 7 6 5 4 3 2 1

Copyright © Shannon K. Butcher, 2012
All rights reserved

For Mandy, whose optimism and determination never cease to amaze me. Thanks for keeping me sane.

Chapter 1

Jackie Patton was dressed to kill, and if one more of those burly, tattooed Theronai warriors tried to grope her, she was going to do just that.

Her red power suit was far too dressy for the occasion, but it made her feel better, almost normal. The thought sent hysterical laughter bubbling up from deep inside her. Normal was such a distant concept that she couldn't even remember what it felt like.

Two years. That's all the demons had stolen from her. She could never get them back, but she was free now, and determined to live that way.

She smoothed her hands over her suit jacket, ignoring the way they trembled. What little she had was already packed. She'd regained access to her bank accounts. Her house was gone—foreclosed and sold at auction—but she'd find another. She had enough money to live on while she found a job, and despite the tight job market, her résumé was impressive. A good position was just around the corner. She could feel it.

All she had to do now was let Joseph, the leader of this place—this compound—know she was leaving. Today. Right now.

Jackie went to the door of her suite, hesitating with

her hand on the knob. She was safe here. There were no demons roaming the halls, no monsters lurking around the corner. But there were men out there. Suffering, desperate. Dying.

She'd been told she could save one. All she had to do was give up her life and dive into this world of monsters and magic.

They said it like it was no big deal, like she'd gain as much from this bizarre union as the man she chose would. Not true. She was free now. There was no way in hell she was giving up that freedom after having lost it for two years. She wouldn't tie herself to any man. Not now, not while she was still broken and barely holding it together.

Don't think about that now. If you do, you won't leave your suite today. Again.

Jackie sucked in a long, deep breath and focused on her task. Simple. Fast. She'd be on the road within the hour.

That thought calmed her, and gave her room to breathe. She could do this. She had to. No one else could do it for her.

She grabbed what was left of her self-confidence and gathered it around herself like a cloak, holding it close. There had been a time when she could have faced a crowd and spoken to them without breaking a sweat, but those days were long behind her. Now simply leaving her suite made her shake with nerves.

She was a different person now, not the powerful, confident corporate exec she'd once been. She was a refugee.

No, a survivor. That sounded better. Stronger.

She left her suite, feeling moderately less miserable. She had almost made it to Joseph's office when she rounded a corner and came face-to-face with one of the giant warriors who called themselves Theronai. As he towered over her, nearly seven feet tall, his gaunt body seemed to grow taller by the second. A shaggy growth of dark beard covered his wide jaw, and his amber eyes, shadowed with fatigue, lit up with the realization of who she was.

Jackie's heart squeezed hard, flooding her body with adrenaline. Survival instincts honed in the caves where she'd been held captive kicked in. She went still, hoping he'd pass by and leave her in peace, as Joseph had ordered all his men to do. But this man didn't pass. He slowed, coming to a stop only a few feet in front of her.

"You're the one," he said, his voice ragged, as if he'd been screaming for days.

"I'm late for a meeting," she lied.

His long arm reached for her, and she jerked back. "Let me touch you. Let me see if it's true."

Panic exploded in her chest, but she was used to that. She'd learned the hard way to hide her fear and terror, and now that skill rose easily, allowing her to speak.

"Leave me alone," she warned, trying to make her tone as stern as possible. It was a complete bluff. There was nothing she could do to defend herself against him. She was weak from her prolonged captivity, and even if she hadn't been, his overpowering strength was so obvious, it was laughable she'd even consider fighting him.

Angry desperation filled his gaze as he stared down at her. "I don't give a fuck about what you want. Grace is dying. If I claim you, we might be able to save her."

Claim you.

The words left her cold, and sent her careening back into the caves where she'd been held. The monsters who'd abducted her had treated her like a thing—a trough from which they fed with no more concern for her than they'd have for the discarded paper wrapper from a fast-food burger.

She couldn't do that again. She couldn't allow herself to be used or she'd be all used up, with nothing left of herself to salvage.

But what about Grace?

Jackie had heard rumors of Grace. She was a human woman who'd sacrificed herself to save a Theronai warrior who'd become paralyzed. She'd taken on his injuries, freeing him, while she lay trapped and dying, her human body too weak to combat the poison that had caused his paralysis. No one had been able to save her. Not even the vampirelike healers these people called Sanguinar.

"Stay away," she warned, working hard to make her voice firm and unyielding. Sometimes that tone had worked to keep the smaller monsters away. For a while.

She backed up, holding her hands in front of her to push him away if he got too close.

His eyes shut as if he was waging some internal struggle. When he spoke, his voice was gentler, pleading. "I'm Torr. I'm not going to hurt you. But I need you. Grace needs you. You may be her only hope."

Jackie covered her ears before she could hear more. She didn't want to be anyone's only hope. All she wanted was to regain her life. "I can't. I'm sorry."

The man lurched forward and grabbed her arms. He moved so fast, she hadn't even seen it happen until it was too late. Violent, harsh vibrations battered her skin wherever he touched. They shook her bones and made her insides itch.

He stared down at the ring all the men like him wore on their left hands. A rioting swirl of colors erupted beneath the surface of the smooth, iridescent band. Jackie watched as his matching necklace did the same.

The luceria was what they called the jewelry. Two pieces linked irrevocably together by magic she didn't care to understand. They were used to unite couples the way her sisters had been united to their husbands—to channel magic from the man into the woman. While that link allowed the women to do incredible things, Jackie wanted no part of it. This was not her world.

He took her hands in his and brought them to his

throat, curling her fingers around his necklace. "Take it off. I need you to wear it."

The slippery band felt warm. A cascade of yellows and golds rushed out from her fingertips, flying along the smooth band.

"No. Leave me alone."

His lip curled up in a snarl. "I won't. I can't." His grip on her hands tightened until her fingers began to tingle from lack of blood.

"Please," she begged him. "Let me go."

The frantic desperation in his gaze grew until his eyes were fever bright. He backed her against a wall, pushing hard enough to knock the wind out of her. "Do it!"

Jackie couldn't bear to look at him and see his need. She knew he was in pain—all the men like him were—and she wanted to be the kind of person who would help, but she'd paid her dues. She'd been used for her blood, fed on for two years. She'd kept other women and children alive. Not all of them, but some. She couldn't let this man or any other use her now, not when she was finally free.

His body pressed against hers. She could feel the hard angles of bones and muscle, feel him vibrating with anger. She didn't like it.

Fear built inside her, but she was so used to it, she hardly noticed. Her fingers went numb and cold. She tried to shove him away with her body, but it was like trying to push a freight train uphill. He didn't budge an inch, and her efforts seemed only to anger him further.

"Stop fighting me. I told you I'm not going to hurt you."

"Then let me go."

He let go of her hands, wrapped his arms around her, and lifted her off the floor. "We're going to go see Grace. Then you'll make the right choice."

No. Jackie didn't want that. She didn't want to witness any more suffering. She'd had her fill of watching the pain and torture of others.

She kicked him, landing a solid blow against his shins. He didn't even grunt. Instead, he tossed her over his shoulder. His bones dug into her stomach, and a wave of nausea crashed into her. She struggled not to puke over his back while she pounded at him with her fists.

"Put me down!"

A low, quiet voice came from behind them. "I suggest you do as the lady asks, Torr."

Iain. She'd know his voice anywhere. Calm. Steady. It slid over her, allowing a small sense of relief to settle in between the cracks of her panic.

Torr turned around and eased Jackie's feet to the floor. Her head spun, and she reached for the wall to steady herself. A hot, strong hand wrapped around her biceps, and she could tell by the vibration inside that touch that it wasn't Torr's. It was steadier, stronger, more like the beat of a heart than a frenetic flapping of insect wings.

She looked up. Iain stared down at her, his face stoic. The warmth of his hand sank through her suit jacket, spreading up her arm and down into her chest. She stood there, too stunned to speak or move, simply staring and soaking up that warmth as if she'd been starved for it.

His black gaze slid down her body and back up again, as if searching for signs of injury. When he saw none, he looked right into her eyes. The contact was too direct. Too intimate.

Like the chicken she was, she dropped her line of sight until she was looking at his mouth. His top lip was thin, with a deep delineation at the center, while his bottom lip was full, almost pretty.

That thought shocked her enough that her gaze lowered to his jaw, which was wide and sturdy, and then down his throat, where she hoped to find nothing intriguing at all. The luceria around his neck shimmered as it vibrated in reaction to her nearness.

That sight set her straight and reminded her that he was not a man. At least not a human one. None of these men were. Then again, she wasn't human, either. Or so they said.

"Are you hurt?" he asked.

Pride forced her to look him in the eye once more. She was not going to let anyone make her cower, not ever again.

There wasn't a single hint of desperation in his expression, and when his gaze met hers, it was blissfully empty of the same frantic hope she'd seen in so many others.

"I'm fine," she managed to squeak out.

Iain nodded and stepped forward, placing his wide body in front of her, so that she was safely out of Torr's reach. He paused for a second, his powerful body clenching as if in pain. Then he continued on as if nothing had happened. "You can't do this, Torr."

The loss of his touch left her feeling cold and shaky. It was ridiculous, of course, just a trick of her mind or some kind of illusion inflicted upon her by the luceria. At least he hadn't touched her bare skin. She'd learned that fabric muted the effects of contact with these men, and was never more grateful for long sleeves than she was right now. At least that's what she told herself, even as her hand covered the spot his had vacated, trying to hold in the heat he'd left behind.

Torr's voice came out pained, nearly a sob. "I have to claim her. She can save Grace."

"You don't know that," said Iain.

"You don't know she can't."

Iain's tone was conversational, without accusation. "This isn't how we do things. What would Grace say if she saw you throwing a woman around like that? Where is your honor?"

Torr's amber eyes filled with tears. "Grace deserves a chance to live."

"She made her choice. She saved your life. Don't cheapen her sacrifice by being an asshole."

"I can't watch her die."

"Then don't," said Iain, looking the taller man right in the eyes. "Leave. Come back when it's over."

Torr sneered and uttered through clenched teeth, "Abandon her to die?"

"She's in a coma. She doesn't know you're there."

Torr's jaw tightened. "What if you're wrong?"

"Then that's even more reason to leave. If she can somehow sense your suffering, do you really want to subject her to that?"

Torr gripped his head in his hands and bent over. A low moan, like that of a wounded animal, rose from his chest. "I can't do this, Iain. It's too much to ask. I have to save her."

Jackie tried not to listen. She'd already seen so much suffering. She didn't want to witness Grace's, too. It was selfish to wish for the bliss of ignorance, but she couldn't save everyone.

And that, in a nutshell, was why she had to leave.

"You've done everything you can," said Iain. "Let her go."

"Obviously you've never lost the woman you love," snarled Torr.

"Yes. I have. I know what it's like—the pain, the guilt. You'll get past it, eventually." His tone was devoid of emotion, as if he were stating facts from someone else's life.

Jackie almost wondered if he was lying, but something in her gut said he wasn't. Iain didn't look like the kind of man capable of love. He seemed too cold for that, too emotionless.

"There's no *getting past* something like this," Torr nearly shouted.

"You can't see a path forward now, but you will find one. Give yourself some time."

"You're a cold fucking bastard, you know that, Iain?"

"I know. And by the time you're over Grace, you will be, too. For that, I'm truly sorry."

Jackie stood there, unsure of what to do. This conversation had nothing to do with her, and yet she couldn't bring herself to slink away like a coward without thanking Iain for stopping Torr.

She backed up, well out of arm's reach. Torr stalked off, causing her to flinch as he passed by.

"I think he'll leave you alone now," said Iain. He didn't move to touch her again, as so many men had. He stood still, just breathing, watching her with calm, black eyes.

He wasn't as tall as Torr, but still nearly a foot taller than she was. His broad shoulders seemed to fill the hallway. Even though he was dressed in casual clothing, power emanated from him, radiating out in palpable waves. His arms and legs were thick with muscle, his chest layered with it. Faded jeans clung to his hips, the waistband tilted slightly with the weight of his sword, which she could not see, but knew was there.

She could still remember the way her fingers had tingled at his touch the night he'd pulled her from her cage. Every Theronai here who managed to touch her had the same disconcerting effect, but with Iain, it had been different. She wasn't sure what it was about him that had the ability to straighten out her jumbled nerves, but whatever it was, she found herself soaking it in, hoping he wouldn't hurry off as he'd done so many times before during their infrequent, chance encounters.

She looked at the ground, uncertain of what to say. "Thank you. For stopping him. He's obviously not himself right now."

"It's polite of you to make excuses for him, but that's not going to help him in the long run. He needs to face facts. So do you."

Her spine straightened in indignation. She was the

victim here. Who the hell was he to treat her as if she'd made some error in judgment? "Excuse me?"

"You heard me. You go traipsing around here, acting as if you're not a catalyst for violence."

"You think I asked for this? That I did it to myself? Torr was the one who went too far. I just left my room."

"That's all it takes. You're torturing these men, making them think they have a chance with you. If you had any sense at all, you'd pick one of them and get it over with."

One of *them*. Not one of *us*. She noticed the slight distinction and found it intriguing. Why wouldn't he count himself among the rest of the men? He still wore both parts of his luceria, which meant he was available.

Maybe it had something to do with the woman he'd loved and lost—the one whose death had left him a self-acknowledged cold bastard.

She forced herself to look him in the eye while she lied, tipping her head back to make it possible. "I'll pick someone when and *if* I'm ready."

"Yeah? Well, let's hope that no one gets killed while you take your sweet time."

"It won't come to that."

"And just what are you going to do to stop it? These are big, armed warriors you're dealing with, not pansy-assed suits, like the men you're used to."

How had he known? She hadn't told anyone about her former life. She didn't trust anyone enough to risk giving away more information than was necessary. "Did you check up on me?"

"I Googled you. I thought someone here should know who you really were, rather than daydreaming about who they wanted you to be."

"And?"

"And what?"

"Did you find a bunch of skeletons marching out of my closet?"

He crossed his arms over his chest, making his shirt stretch to contain his muscles. The tips of several bare branches of his tree tattoo peeked out from under his left sleeve. "You're smart. Educated. A barracuda when it comes to business. People respected you. Feared you."

"You say that like it's a good thing."

"In our world, it is. Of course, I don't see any sign of the woman you used to be. All I see is a scared little girl who would rather hide than do the right thing."

"I've been through a lot these last two years," she grated out through clenched teeth.

"Who hasn't? Life's hard. Wear a fucking cup." With that, he turned on his heel and left her standing there.

Jackie shook with anger as she watched him walk away. And there was only one reason she would have been as infuriated by his words as she was: He was right. She was merely a shell of her former self, and she didn't like who she'd become. She didn't like being afraid all the time—not just of the monsters, but of the people who lived here. And of her future.

She gathered herself and marched the last few yards to Joseph's office. It was time to take back her life.

Chapter 2

Normally, once Iain walked away from someone, he put the conversation behind him and let it go. He simply didn't care enough to carry around other people's baggage. But this time was different.

He couldn't get Jackie out of his head. She lingered there, in the back of his mind, like a puzzle left unsolved.

His monster—the dark, enraged beast that lurked within him, always threatening to break free and kill— had perked up, its ears twitching with interest.

Even through the layers of clothing, he'd felt something when he touched her. Some deep, resonant vibration that seeped into the coldest parts of himself. His hand still tingled, and the pain pounding through his body—which had eased slightly upon contact with her— had now returned with a vengeance.

He was used to pain. It was part of his life. He accepted it the way he did his own skin, but since meeting her, he noticed it more.

Jackie had the ability to affect him when no one else could. Not that it mattered. She couldn't save him. He'd stopped Torr from making a mistake. There was nothing left to think about.

And yet there she was, haunting a small corner of his mind with the memory of how warm she'd been, how delicate her arm had felt under his fingers. When he'd touched her, there had been something there—some subtle change inside of him. He couldn't tell what it was, and even if he could, it wouldn't have made any difference.

He was damned. Soulless. No one knew of his dangerous state but him. Even his luceria hummed when he got near Jackie, as if hoping for a reprieve from death. The thing apparently didn't accept that it was too late for him.

But there was someone else who still had a chance: Cain.

Iain couldn't save his brother's soul, but he could sure as hell slow its death.

The black ring burned his hand with cold as he carried it through the hallways of Dabyr—the fortified compound that protected nearly five hundred humans and Sentinels. He could have shoved the ring into his pocket, but the pain reminded him of the danger of what he was about to do. One false move, and he and four other men—men he considered brothers—would be sentenced to death.

The Band of the Barren was the only refuge for soulless warriors, and Iain was the only man who knew who was in it. He'd recruited them all. And now there was one more he had to recruit, before it was too late.

He found Cain in the antechamber outside the Hall of the Fallen, staring at a worn sword mounted on the wall. A delicate band of shimmering gray was woven around the well-used grip.

Angus's sword. Gilda's luceria.

The couple had died a few weeks ago, and while Iain was beyond feeling any sort of grief for his friends, he remembered what grief felt like—how it crushed the breath from a man's body and sapped his will to live. He remembered feeling like that after his betrothed had died at the hands of the Synestryn. The pain had been much worse than anything he had experienced in his long, long life, and yet somehow it hadn't killed him.

For years, he'd wished that it had.

A sliver of the man he'd once been yearned to feel like that again, if only because it would mean some minuscule part of his soul was still alive. But the only emotion he seemed to have left was rage—the only thing that had survived the death of his soul.

Cain lifted his dark head in surprise as Iain entered the place of mourning and remembrance. The room was silent except for the crackle of a fire. The dark walls, soft carpet, and comfortable furniture were designed to make the room welcoming, but there was no happiness here. No hope.

Cain's deep voice was gravelly as if from a prolonged silence. "I'll leave so you can have time to mourn alone."

Iain kept his expression neutral, hoping the other man would take it for some form of grief. He couldn't let Cain know his secret—not until he was sure of what his instincts were telling him. "I was looking for you."

Cain was a giant of a man, even among Theronai. Years of battle had hardened his body and etched themselves into his very skin. Small scars dotted the backs of his hands, as well as a few places on his face. Muscles bunched under his turtleneck as he shifted to face Iain.

A turtleneck was a bad sign among their kind. Each Theronai warrior's chest was marked with a living image of a tree. As they grew, so did the lifemark, branching out and growing stronger each day as the magic inside them swelled—magic that could be accessed only by a female of their kind. A couple of centuries ago, their enemy attacked, killing nearly all their women. The men were left alone, struggling to contain the magic that continued to grow inside them with no outlet. As the power they housed grew, their souls began to weaken and die. Leaves fell from their lifemarks, each one marking a loss of what made them who they were.

The warriors became darker, angrier. The pain was too much for some, and they took their own lives.

Iain had considered doing the same more times than
he could count, but one thing kept him holding on: He
was the answer to the prayers of his brothers. He could
save them.

He'd found magical artifacts that slowed the decay of
their lifemarks and allowed them to cling to their souls
for a few more years. His efforts hadn't saved everyone,
but he'd saved Madoc, who was now happily united with
a woman who could wield his power and take away his
pain. Nika had saved Madoc's soul, but Iain had made it
possible.

He hoped to offer Cain that same chance for survival.

The signs were all there. Cain had grown darker over
the past month, quieter. His clothing had changed. So
had his habits. He no longer dined with others. He sat
alone, ignoring the rest of the men who offered to share
his company.

Those were all signs that his lifemark was nearly bare,
and that his time was almost up. He was distancing himself from the others, doing what he could to make his
death easier on his brothers. Iain had seen it all before.

"Why were you looking for me?" asked Cain.

This was always the hardest part. Iain had to offer
Cain a chance to slow the fall of leaves from his lifemark
without betraying the fact that there were others like
him—others whose souls were nearly dead. "I was worried about you. You seem . . . different lately."

Cain's face tightened with skepticism. "Did Joseph
send you?"

"No."

"Bullshit," spat Cain. "He won't listen when I tell him
I'm fine, so now he has you spying on me."

"You're not fine, and we both know it."

Cain backed up and his hand moved to the hilt of his
sword. A bit of magic made it invisible to the naked eye
until it was drawn, but Iain knew it was there. He also
knew that a man close to the end would have no trouble

drawing a blade to use on someone he had once considered a friend.

Iain slipped the ring into his pocket and lifted his hands in surrender. "You don't want to do that."

"What I want doesn't seem to matter anymore. My best friends are dead. Their daughter—the little girl who has been like my own child for centuries—has grown up literally overnight and no longer needs me. No longer wants me meddling in her life. That's why she left." His voice broke at the end and his throat moved as he struggled to regain his composure.

The man's pain would have had Iain aching a few years ago. Now it was simply more data used to gauge his brother's decaying status.

"Your duty to Sibyl was what you lived for. Now that she's no longer a child, you feel lost. I get it."

Cain glanced up, meeting Iain's gaze for the first time since he'd entered the room. There was pain and desperation there. Mountains of agony crushing the soul from his body.

"I want to help," said Iain.

"There's nothing anyone can do. It's too late. I'm done pretending. I'll let Joseph know my intentions before I leave tonight."

"You're going to kill yourself." It wasn't a question.

Cain swallowed hard, and his big body shook with fear and regret. "I don't want to die, but I'd rather walk calmly to my death than risk hurting Sibyl—which I will do if I follow her to Africa like some kind of overbearing father. Even if I pretend I'm only there to help rebuild the ruined stronghold, she'll know the truth."

"What if I could offer you another alternative?"

Cain let out a long, resigned sigh and then stripped off his shirt. His lifemark was nearly bare, with only a precious few leaves clinging precariously to the empty branches. "There are no other alternatives. It's too late for me."

Iain showed no sign of horror or surprise. It was just as he'd thought. "I've found another way, but before I tell you more, I need your vow of silence."

Confusion wrinkled his wide brow. "What?"

"You must promise me that you will never speak to anyone of what I tell you here today."

"I don't understand, Iain. What the hell are you talking about?"

"I'm offering you your life in exchange for your silence. Do you want to take the deal or not?"

Cain hesitated, but he wasn't the first to do so. And Iain knew exactly which buttons to push to get the result he wanted. His brother's life was worth more than the rules by which they lived.

"Think of Sibyl. She just lost her parents. What will it do to her to lose you so soon?"

Cain's eyes slid shut and his mouth tightened in anguish. "She asked me to leave her alone. She left me behind when she went to join Lexi and Zach."

"She didn't ask you to die, did she?"

"There's nothing anyone can do about that. Not even you."

"What if you're wrong? What harm is there in hearing me out? Worst-case scenario, you turn in your sword and go fall into a nest tonight if you don't like what I have to say. Best-case scenario, you live long enough to see Sibyl united with one of our men, protected."

Cain hesitated for a long moment. His gaze moved to Angus's sword, where Gilda's luceria was woven around it.

"Let me try to help you," said Iain.

"No one can help me, but I'm fool enough to listen all the same."

"Swear to me that nothing we speak of here and now will ever pass your lips."

There was a long silence before he finally said, "I do so swear."

The weight of Cain's promise barreled down on Iain. He braced himself, suffering through the heaviness of his brother's vow. It passed quickly, but the magic holding Cain to his word would not soon fade.

Iain looked right into Cain's eyes, willing him to know that what he spoke was the truth. "There are a few of us, like you, who have come to the end of our time. Years ago, I began seeking out a way to save them. I discovered artifacts that had the power to slow the process."

"Artifacts?"

"Magical trinkets. Gilda's mother spoke of them once when I was a boy. She didn't know I'd overheard. I thought they might simply be a myth, but then I found one. It worked." For a while. Nothing could hold back the flow of time forever, and Iain's last leaf had long since fallen, but he'd bought himself enough time to learn what he needed to do to hide his barren state. He'd learned to pretend he had a soul, to pretend he had honor. Everything he did now was a carefully choreographed set of lies meant to fool everyone around him. And it had worked.

He'd passed this knowledge on to those who allowed him to help, just as he'd passed on the artifacts he'd found.

The black ring had been the first.

"How can that be? I've never heard of anything like this."

"Those who created these devices didn't want their existence known. If what they'd done had been found out, the people they were trying to help would have been put to death."

"How do they work?"

Iain pulled the black ring from his pocket, ignoring the frigid burn of it, and held it out in his palm. "This one slows down the rate at which your leaves fall. It won't save you forever, but it will buy you time to find the woman who can save you."

Perhaps Jackie. She hadn't chosen a man yet, but she would. Cain was a good man. She might choose him.

A low swell of anger rose up inside Iain, distracting him for a moment. He didn't understand where it had come from, but it was there, burning deep in his gut.

The urge to draw his sword and lop off Cain's head slammed into him. In his mind's eye, he could see his brother's blood arcing across the wall as he fell to his knees. He wanted that. Needed that. Cain couldn't touch Jackie if he were dead.

Iain's fists tightened as he fought back the bloodlust. His hand ached to draw his sword.

Cain was his friend, and while he felt nothing more for the man than he did the leather armchair to his left, he had once felt something. A fondness, perhaps. It was hard to remember now, especially with anger pounding at him to act, to kill.

Pretend you have honor.

That was what he told his men. It was all he had to do now. It wasn't that hard. He'd done it a thousand times before. He'd been a good man once. It was his duty to behave as if he were that same man now. Perhaps he'd kill Cain later, but not right now.

The thought eased him somewhat, giving him the strength to take control of himself. He shoved down the last flickering embers of his rage with a force of will, returning his focus to his brother and what had to be done.

Cain flashed him a skeptical look. "How many of you are there?"

"You don't need to know that. Only I know, and if you agree to join our Band of the Barren, I swear I will never reveal you as a member, just as I will never reveal who the others are to you."

Cain stared at the ring, hope plain on his face. "What do you ask for in return for saving my life?"

"Only that you live by the code I set for all of us. Our lives depend on secrecy. If Joseph were to find out, he'd have us sent to the Slayers for execution. We must lie well, my friend. You must act as though you are fine, as though you have honor, no matter how dark your thoughts become."

"What's in this for you?"

Iain wasn't sure anymore. At first he'd simply wanted to save his brothers, but now even the satisfaction he gained from that was a distant memory. His actions were merely habits now—doing things because he'd always done them, without thought of why.

But that answer was not what the members of the Band needed to hear. They needed hope so they could hold out for a while longer, fighting back evil as they were sworn to do.

"What wouldn't you do to save one of your brothers?" asked Iain. "We're in this together."

"It's against the rules."

"We need all the warriors we can get if we're to have even the slightest chance to win this war, even if it means breaking a few rules."

"You said it slows the progress?"

"Right."

"How do you know when it's too late? How do you keep yourselves from hurting others because you wait too long to give up the fight?"

"I keep a careful eye on everyone. If you're too far gone, or if you do anything to jeopardize the others, I'll kill you myself."

So far that last resort hadn't been necessary. Even Madoc, who had been worse off than most, had managed to find salvation in time. Only Iain had held on too long, and there wasn't enough of the man he used to be left for him to care that he should have gone to his death long ago.

If he died, who would recruit those nearing the end of their time? Who would watch out for them? He couldn't give that burden to someone else. He alone was strong enough to resist his darker urges. His absolute commitment to his brothers had kept him going for years. His devotion to rules he created for himself had hidden his condition, even from the other members of the Band. None of them knew his soul was dead, only that he was nearing his end.

One day he'd go down fighting, but he refused to give up. He might not have the gentler emotions that made up what passed for a conscience, but he had his honor. He remembered what it was like to love someone so utterly that nothing else mattered.

Serena was long gone, but his brothers had filled the void, giving him a purpose to replace the hope he'd lost so long ago.

Cain nodded and held out his hand. "Okay."

Iain extended the ring. "It burns like hell."

"I'm used to pain."

"When you find your woman, be sure to take it off and return it to me. You won't be able to bond while wearing it. You may not even be able to detect compatibility." Madoc had worn that ring and had learned that bit of information the hard way.

"I understand."

Cain slid the ring onto one thick finger and clenched his hand into a fist. If he felt the cold burn coming off the metal, he hid it well.

"Good. Now sit down and let me tell you what you need to do—what will keep you from being sent to the Slayers."

Chapter 3

Torr stood at Grace's side. She'd grown so thin, so pale. All the beauty and vitality that had once filled her every movement was now gone. With every passing day, she slipped further away from him.

The machine that breathed for her hissed quietly, breaking the silence of the room.

Torr held her hand, refusing to voice his anger at her actions. She'd done this to herself. She'd saved him, thinking he was more important.

She couldn't have been more wrong. The world was full of people, but few had souls as pure and good as Grace. Her limitless kindness was now gone, and the world was a darker place for its loss.

Logan came into the room with his woman, Hope, at his side.

"What did you find out?" Torr asked.

Logan's bleak expression said it all. Even the unearthly beauty of his kind couldn't mask the ugly truth. "I was unable to locate help. I'm sorry."

"What do you mean?"

"Tynan is the strongest healer among us. There are only two more in the world whose skills surpass his. One died a few days ago. The other is sleeping."

"Then wake him up."

"It's not that easy, Torr. He went to sleep because he was too weak to continue."

"I'll give him my blood. He can have it all." He didn't care if he died, so long as Grace lived.

"It's not enough. I'm sorry. You have to let her go."

Torr's grip on Grace had grown too tight, and he had to consciously relax his hold on her delicate fingers. "No."

"It's cruel to leave her hooked to these machines. She gave you a gift—one which you are squandering with your thoughtlessness."

"I want her to live."

"She's human. Even if the device hadn't paralyzed her, she would have died in a heartbeat of time."

"A lifetime."

"A brief, human lifetime. Your suffering is inevitable. The sooner you let her go, the sooner her pain can end and your healing can begin."

Torr was never going to get over what he'd let Grace do to herself. Even if she survived, he'd live with his guilt until his last breath. It was his job to protect humans. He'd taken a vow, and yet she'd been the one to risk her life to save *him*.

Torr barely kept control over his anger, keeping it out of his voice in deference to Grace. "You sound like Iain. You act as though she's a thing I can easily toss away. You're wrong. If I lose her, I won't survive it."

Logan's mouth bowed with pity. "You will. You can't see clearly now, but I've seen it before. This is the nature of things."

Torr sprang up, balling his hands into fists to keep from wrapping them around Logan's pretty neck. He stared at the new woman. "I've heard you can see auras—that you can read people."

"I can," said Hope.

"Is she in pain?"

Hope's gaze moved past him to where Grace lay on the bed. "She's confused. Sad."

"So she is still in there?"

Hope nodded, making her blond ponytail sway. "Barely. She's weak."

"She's a fighter. She'll make it through this. We just have to find someone strong enough to heal her."

Logan sighed. "What if there is no one? How long will you force her to stay here, tethered to this place?"

Determination rose up inside him, like a fortified wall no one could tear down. He gave Logan a hard stare, warning the leech to back off. "As long as it takes."

As soon as the door shut behind Logan, Hope pulled him to a stop. The sorrow haunting her eyes was nearly too much for Logan to bear. He wanted to wipe it away, to make her smile again. He wasn't quite ready to reveal his surprise for her, but perhaps it was better to tell her sooner rather than later. Anything to see her happy.

"You mustn't do this to yourself," he told her. "Promise me you won't come back here and witness Torr's suffering."

"I want to help. I *need* to help."

"There's nothing anyone can do. We'll console Torr when Grace has passed. He's going to need us."

She shook her head. "It's just so sad, you know? So unfair."

Logan pulled her into his arms and held her tight. Seeing Torr reminded him of how lucky he was, how precious Hope was to him. If anything ever happened to her . . .

He couldn't even think about such things. They made dark, evil feelings swirl deep inside of him, threatening to break free. Hope was fine. She was his. All was well.

"I've been thinking about it for a long time," she said. "I didn't want to say anything in front of Torr, but I think I might have an idea."

Logan pulled back enough to peer down into her lovely face. So sweet, his Hope. He'd never tire of looking at her. "What do you mean?"

"My memories of Temprocia have continued to come back."

Temprocia, the world where she'd been born and raised. Her memories of the place had been removed for her protection, but they'd been returning slowly ever since she'd taken his blood.

"How does that help Grace?" he asked.

Her blond brows drew together in concentration. "I don't remember everything, but I remember a woman, a healer. I can't recall her name, but I can see her face. She had no wrinkles, but there was a wisdom there—a kind of timeless intellect, as if she knew all the secrets of the world. I remember looking at her and *knowing* she could do anything. What if she can help Grace?"

Warnings sounded in Logan's head. Hope had proved she was more than willing to put herself in harm's way to save another. He didn't want her anywhere near danger ever again. "Perhaps she could, but since there's no way of reaching her, it's best if we don't mention this in front of Torr."

Hope pulled her gaze away from his and stared at the floor. "What if there is a way?"

"The fact that you won't look me in the eye when you say that tells me that it's far too dangerous to even consider. Grace is dying. We have to accept that and move on."

"I can't. I have so much. My life is full and happy. What kind of person would I be if I didn't try to give that chance for happiness to someone else?"

That was just one more reason why he loved her.

Despite the fact that he knew he'd regret asking, he did anyway. "What were you thinking?"

"I came here through the Sentinel Stone in the Tyler building."

"The one I had relocated here, just in case any more women like you come through." He desperately hoped that they would, too. His fellow Sanguinar were starving, and there was something special about Hope's blood that took away that hunger. At least it had for him.

She was what his kind should have been if they hadn't been cursed before their birth. She had no thirst for blood. She could walk in the sun. And while Logan wished that he, too, had such freedoms, there was no other person he'd rather see happy than Hope.

"What if we can somehow get a message through the Stone? We could call for help."

"Assuming we can, how would that help?"

"I am having flashes of a memory—just little bits that keep teasing me. There's something there, and if I can uncover it, I think I'll know how to operate the Stone."

"Gateways are tricky things. Dangerous things."

"I can do this, Logan. I just need your help."

He didn't like it. He didn't like anything that put her in possible danger. But he knew better than to deny her. If he didn't help her, she'd find someone who would. She wouldn't let this puzzle go—not while Grace's life hung in the balance.

Logan nodded. "If you wish, I'll help you, but you have to promise me that you won't do anything without me."

She smiled, and Logan's entire world brightened. "I promise."

Her vow settled gently over his shoulders, comforting him. "Mention this to no one. If Torr gets even a hint of our purpose, he will be relentless. I won't have him pushing you beyond what's safe."

"I agree. We'll do this alone. If it works, then we'll tell him."

And after they determined the outcome of this attempt to save Grace's life, he'd tell her what he'd done and give her what he hoped would be her wedding gift.

* * *

Jackie entered Joseph's office, and he immediately rose to his feet. She averted her gaze, seeking out anything that would distract her from the hope she saw spring into his expression with her mere presence.

The room was cluttered with maps and papers, photographs, and a stack of unopened letters. Weapons hung on the walls, and she was certain that they were for more than mere show. A cluttered conference table had been pushed against a wall, the chairs filled with rolled maps, cables, and a few spare electronics. The large window behind his desk offered a clear view of the grounds outside, including the outdoor workout area where several men lifted ridiculous amounts of weight. Judging by their size and the trees marking the bare chests of some, she guessed them to be Theronai.

Jackie stopped dead in her tracks, freezing as she caught sight of them. If they could see in, they might come here and demand things of her that she wasn't willing to give.

Joseph must have realized her problem, because he turned and lowered the blinds, blocking out the possibility of being seen.

"Thank you," she managed, despite the tightness in her throat.

"Sure. Please, have a seat."

She did, perching on the edge of the chair on the opposite side of his desk.

"You look nice," he said.

Suddenly, her suit felt more like a costume than something she had always been comfortable wearing. "Thank you," came out polite and automatic.

"Is there something you need?" he asked. "Has someone been bothering you again?"

She wasn't about to tattle, so she kept what had happened with Torr to herself. "No. I'm fine. Thank you."

"Then . . . what can I do for you?"

She pulled in a breath for courage. "I'm leaving. I just came to tell you."

"Who's going with you?"

"No one. I need to rebuild my life. Alone."

Joseph began shaking his head before she'd even finished speaking. "No. We've discussed this. I'm sorry, but that's out of the question. It's too much of a risk for you to live outside of these walls."

"It's not your decision."

"Is this about Samson? Because if it is, I can make some kind of arrangement."

An ache radiated out from deep in her heart. Samson was a half-demon baby that Iain had delivered a few weeks ago. The child's mother had died giving him life, and despite the odds, he'd lived more than just the day or two that most children like him survived.

She'd grown attached to him in a short time, but he'd been taken away to live with foster parents outside the walls of Dabyr. Joseph had claimed that his presence was too much of a risk to the other children here, that there was no way to know if he'd turn evil and attack.

Some of the less human offspring of the Synestryn demons had done just that. She'd seen it happen.

"He's just a baby," she told him for what felt like the hundredth time.

"He's half Synestryn. Until we know what that means, I'm not taking any risks with the people under my care. We've been through this, Jackie. I'm not changing my mind."

She understood. She missed the little guy, but she couldn't blame Joseph for being careful. There were so many people—so many children—here who depended on him and the decisions he made. Having been in a position of power herself, she understood how difficult that balancing act could be.

"This isn't about Samson. I need to leave. I'm stronger now. I need to find a life. A real one, not one filled with monsters."

Joseph seemed to bow under some unseen weight. "You can never go back to the way things were before you were abducted."

"I can try."

"All you'll do is get yourself killed, and I'm sorry, but I can't let you do that. We need you too much."

Anger spiked through her, making her tone sharp. "You need something from me that I'll never be willing to give."

"I think you're wrong. I think that once you get to know us better, once you've healed, you'll change your mind."

"I am healed." It was a lie, but one she would keep on telling until it was the truth. Despite her weakness, despite the nightmares and the scars left behind, she would be fine. Eventually.

He lifted a skeptical brow. "Really? Is that why you've been hiding in your suite for weeks?"

"I don't like the way the men look at me. The way they touch me."

"There's only one way to stop that. Pick one."

"No."

He let out a long sigh. "If you leave, the Synestryn will come after you. They'll find you. You'll be right back in a dark cave somewhere, hoping one of us comes to the rescue. And that's if they don't simply kill you outright."

Bleak, violent memories threatened to steal her breath. Fear crushed her lungs. Her vision dimmed, and she swayed in her seat. All those poor children being hurt. Used. She couldn't face that anymore. She'd rather die.

It took Jackie a moment to beat those memories back, and the effort left her shaking and weak. She'd come a long way over the past few weeks, but she had a long way to go to get back to the woman she'd once been. If she didn't stand on her own two feet now, she feared she'd never be herself again—that she'd end up depending on these people for the rest of her pitiful life.

She couldn't meet Joseph's eyes. "What choice do I have? I can't live here. I don't want to be a part of your world."

"I'm sorry, but what you want is irrelevant. You *are* part of our world. You were born into it—you just didn't know it until now. Whatever natural protection your ignorance afforded you is gone. If you leave the safety of these walls, the Synestryn *will* come for you."

Denial rose up in a swift, hot wave. Her words came out through clenched teeth. "I'll fight them. I won't let them take me alive."

"So . . . what? You're ready to die?"

"Of course not, I just—"

"You're just willing to let a good man go to his death because you're too selfish to do the right thing." His biting tone took her aback.

"It's not like that."

"No?" he asked, rising to his feet. "That's the way it looks to me. We saved you. We sheltered and fed you. All we ask is that you step up and do what you were born to do."

"I wasn't born for . . . this." She waved her hand at the weapons and maps.

Joseph shrugged. "You're making it hard for me to have any sympathy for you. My men are dying. You can save one. I really don't care whether it's what you wanted to do with your life."

"Is it really that simple for you?"

"Yes."

She let out a frustrated sigh. "You saw what happened when I tried to go out and lend a hand with Paul and Andra. That didn't exactly go well."

"You weren't bonded then. You had no power. And despite that, you found Samson."

"No, Iain found Samson, or should I say he found a thing he was willing to kill. There's not a bit of warmth in him anywhere."

"He's possibly the best warrior I have. I don't ask for warm and fuzzy. I ask that he gets the job done."

Jackie was certain he did that. She'd seen him in action the night he'd pulled her and the others out of those caves. She'd seen the lethal violence that he was capable of. And when he'd stood between her and the monsters, she'd never felt safer.

"You don't want me to leave. I don't want to hide in my suite all the time to avoid being pawed by strange men. What am I supposed to do with myself?"

Joseph crossed his arms over his chest and leaned back in his chair. "Pick one of the men. Then I'll let you go out. You can even go see Samson if you like."

She stared at him for a long, shocked moment. "You'd really play dirty like that?"

"I'm not playing."

She could see that. His posture was closed, his expression hard, and there wasn't so much as a hint of a smile anywhere.

"Why are you doing this?" she asked.

"I need you to give the men hope. They're good men. Whoever you pick would give his life to keep you happy and safe. Hell, even the ones you don't pick will."

"It's not what I want."

"I thought I'd made it clear that I don't give a fuck about what you want. We saved your pretty little ass and kept it safe for weeks now. I'd say it's time to pay up."

"I didn't realize my rescue came with strings attached."

"Damn it!" He scrubbed his hand over his head, mussing his dark hair. When he spoke, he sounded exhausted and used up. "I'm sorry. I didn't mean it the way it came out. You're welcome here for as long as you like, no strings attached."

"But you won't let me leave."

"No. You're too precious to risk. If you want out, you go with a Theronai—one you've chosen."

"I'm not picking."

"You will. Eventually, you'll get tired of men fighting over you. I just hope that they don't kill each other in the process."

The thought horrified her. "They wouldn't do that," she breathed.

He moved around the desk and got too close. She surged to her feet and took a step back, putting the chair between them.

He scowled at her action, but didn't try to get closer. "You can't possibly understand what these men are suffering—what they'd do to make the pain stop."

"Don't tell *me* I don't understand suffering. I spent two years in caves at the mercy of those monsters while they tortured and killed innocents."

"I'm not trying to diminish what you've been through, but at least now your suffering is over. Ours isn't. You can't change that for all of us, but you can change that for one man, save one soul. Is that really too much to ask?"

It wasn't. She knew deep down that her hesitation was more about fear and selfishness than about doing what was right.

"What if you're wrong? What if I pick the wrong man? How can you ask me to choose whose life to save, knowing that the others may die?"

"You still don't get it, do you?" he asked. "You may choose only one man, but your decision will give hope to all the others. It will help them hold on longer. Keep fighting. Resist giving in to the pain."

"How can I give anyone hope when I'm so messed up?"

Joseph shook his head. "I don't know. All I ask is that you try."

She'd fail. She wasn't cut out for this kind of life. She really only had one option.

Jackie sighed in defeat. "If I do as you ask and pick one of the men, will you stand aside and let me leave?"

"I will."

"Promise me." She knew their promises were binding, and that once he gave his word, he couldn't go back on it.

Joseph looked her in the eyes. "I vow that if you choose one of the men to be your partner, I will allow you to leave."

A heaviness bore down on her and she scrambled to grab the desk before she collapsed.

She could hear the smile in his voice. "I'll gather the men right now. You won't regret this, Jackie."

She already did, and as soon as he figured out what she was up to, so would he.

The moment word got out that Jackie was choosing a man, Dabyr descended into a state of chaos. Men ran through the halls, pushing and shoving to get their spot in line. Iain made sure Cain and the rest of the Band had a front-row seat to the ceremony, hoping Jackie would choose one of them. He found himself a nice, empty spot in back, and settled in to watch the show.

The velvet-draped auditorium was rarely used, but the formal setting was fitting for what was about to take place.

Helen led Jackie onstage and whispered a few quiet words to her sister. Now that they were standing together, Iain could see a resemblance in the women—proof of the Athanasian father they shared.

Whatever Helen had said, it had made Jackie's face go pale. Her wild, gray eyes roamed over the crowd, and he could see the fine trembling of her hands.

Helen stepped up to the microphone, and flipped her twin braids over her shoulders. "You all know why you're here, so I'll be brief. My sister Jackie has agreed to choose one of you. I want you all to remember that she can only pick one, so most of you will be disappointed." She pointed a finger in stern warning. "Do not let that turn any of you into jerks, or I'll be forced to take action. I doubt you'll enjoy the outcome. Understood?"

There was a general rumble of assent among the thirty or forty men present. Iain didn't recognize all of them—men had been coming from the far corners of the world after hearing rumors of Jackie's presence.

"She's going to accept a vow from each of you, and then make her decision. So please file up in an orderly fashion."

Drake, Helen's husband, stood guard at the stairs, doing crowd control. His sword was out and visible, as a warning to any who might consider causing trouble.

On the opposite side of the stage stood Andra. Her black leather, combat boots, and readied stance didn't fool Iain. If the green tint to her skin was any indication, she was nervous about these proceedings. Paul was at her side, his hand low at her back in a protective gesture. Apparently, he was worried about her as much as she was worried about Jackie.

Madoc scowled at the men from his post near the rear doors. Nika stood in front of him, staring off into space, her head cocked to the side as if she were listening to something no one else could hear. A faint smile curled her lips for no obvious reason.

One by one, each warrior filed up to offer Jackie his vow. The first man in line was Nicholas, his horribly scarred face so full of hope that it almost made Iain wince. He was a good man, but he wasn't exactly the most handsome man around, and Jackie didn't have a whole lot to go on. Looks would matter, if only in a small way.

The moment Nicholas stepped up, bare chested and smiling, Jackie looked up and flinched. It was a small movement, covered up in milliseconds, but Iain saw it and knew Nicholas was out of the running. Poor bastard.

Still, he knelt, sliced a shallow cut over his heart, and offered her his vow. "My life for yours."

Jackie's gray eyes widened as she saw the blood. She swayed on her feet, and Helen put an arm around her shoulders to steady her.

Cain was next, and Iain hoped that the leaf tattoos he'd given the other man—the ones that would help disguise his lifemark's lack of leaves—were no longer red and swollen, thanks to their natural ability to heal fast.

No one seemed to be looking at Cain's chest. All eyes were on Jackie. Good.

"Nice ring he's wearing," muttered Madoc from behind Iain.

"Leave it alone," warned Iain. "You owe me that much."

"Yeah, yeah. My fucking lips are sealed."

Iain nodded, letting the matter drop.

The line progressed, and with each man who bled for her, she seemed to lose a bit of color. The weight of all those promises seemed to crush her until her breathing was fast and shallow.

Iain made his way to the end of the line, pretending like he wanted this as much as the rest of them. No one knew it was too late to save him, and he had to keep it that way, even if it meant going through this ridiculous charade.

Samuel was in front of him, and he took his turn kneeling at her feet and offering to die for her. The ring portion of his luceria was pristine against the scarred flesh of his left hand. As he neared her, the colors in his ring began to move, swirling with yellows and golds.

Iain's ring no longer contained any discernible color. It had faded to a pale, snowy white with age. So far he'd found no way of disguising it, but several of the older men's rings were also washed-out, so he simply pretended that it wasn't a problem, and everyone else took their cues from him. As long as he kept his monster in check, didn't try to hide his lifemark, and pretended his honor was still intact, no one would question his soul's status.

Samuel rose and moved away, his face alight with hope.

Iain could find none. He couldn't even find the sorrow that his hope had died long ago.

Shrugging away the thought, he stepped up to Jackie. Her eyes were wide, and her pupils had shrunk to reveal paler gray rays among the darker ones. Her hair was shiny and clean, unlike the first time he'd seen her. She'd cut away the dirty, matted clumps, and styled it so that it curled around her jaw. A pale scar bisected her left eyebrow, and he found himself wondering how she'd been injured. Had it been some childhood accident, or had that been done to her during her captivity?

A slow, feral rage expanded beneath his ribs at the thought of her being hurt. The monster inside of him rumbled in warning, rattling the bars of its cage as if testing for weakness. Iain tightened his control on the beast and pushed thoughts of her injury aside before he lost control. With an audience like this, there could be no mistakes.

Instead, he focused on her mouth, which she'd colored the same deep red as her suit. Her lips were full, the bottom one wavering the slightest bit in trepidation.

"What are you staring at?" she asked.

"Nothing. Just committing this moment to memory," he lied.

Before he could raise any suspicion, he drew his sword, knelt in front of her, and cut himself. "My life for yours, Jackie."

She stumbled, but Helen held her up. Iain waited until the weight of his vow evaporated before he rose to his feet and left the stage without looking back.

As he made his way to the back of the room, he saw dozens of faces staring up at her. So much hope. He didn't know why they bothered when they knew that all but one of them were going to be disappointed.

"Take your time," he heard Helen say to Jackie.

He wanted to slip out, but that was too risky. He'd have to explain why he was willing to walk out on the best chance of living any of them currently had. It was better not to draw attention to himself. Pretend he cared. Pretend he had hope.

"I don't need any time," said Jackie. "I just want to get this over with."

"Okay. I understand. Which man do you choose?" asked Helen.

Iain swore he could hear the men draw in their breaths in anticipation.

He settled in his seat as Jackie's wavering voice filled the auditorium. "I want Iain."

Chapter 4

Jackie tried to still the panic rioting inside of her. What the hell was she thinking picking the coldest man of the bunch?

At least she wouldn't let him down. Everyone else had looked at her with such hope. She knew she'd crush their spirits. But not Iain. He had simply looked at her, accepting of whatever she decided. There was no hidden agenda in his gaze, no dreams for her to destroy. He was the only man here who wasn't asking something from her that she knew she could never give.

The room fell silent at her announcement, then exploded into shock, anger, and disbelief.

"That's it," shouted Helen over the noise. "It's done. Clear the room."

Iain hadn't moved from his seat. He hadn't so much as flinched. He continued to stare at her with those calm, black eyes that registered no emotion.

Finally, he stood. Her panic deepened. She was crazy to do this. Certifiably insane.

He took a step toward her, and she bolted, like a scared little rabbit. She pushed through the crowd to the nearest door, ignoring the frantic buzzing of her skin as she accidentally touched the men, and ran through the hall to her suite.

Jackie scurried inside, slammed the door, and then

leaned against the wood, panting. Her heart was racing so fast, she could barely hear. The wood at her back vibrated with a loud banging.

Her heart lodged in her throat again, stealing away what little calm she'd managed to regain.

"Open up," said Iain. "We need to talk."

"Later," she called through the door.

"No. Now."

He was right. The longer she put this off, the worse it was going to be. She was already shaking and numb from suffering through that ceremony. Best to get it over with now.

She opened the door and moved away from it as if it were on fire. Iain stalked inside, shutting and locking it behind him.

"What the hell was that?" he demanded. His mouth was drawn tight, and his body shook with anger.

She'd seen that look before. It was the same one he wore when he killed.

Jackie struggled to find her voice. "I thought you'd be happy."

At least until she left, like she was planning to do. He'd be pissed then, and now that she was facing that anger, she wasn't sure she wanted to be on the receiving end of it.

His voice grew quiet, but that made it no less cold. "There are dozens of men who need you more than I do."

"I can't be what they want me to be."

"What the hell is that supposed to mean? You already *are* what they want you to be."

She shook her head. "No. They think I'm some kind of savior. That I'm what they've been hoping for all their lives. It's too much pressure." She swallowed, forcing herself to stand her ground. "But not you. You have no hope."

His black eyes narrowed and he moved forward, his smooth gait menacing and predatory. His voice was lethally quiet and he looked at her with unveiled suspicion. "What do you mean by that?"

She backed up until she ran into the couch, which kept her from retreating farther. "The others . . . they all looked at me like I'm the answer to their problems. I'm not. You get that."

"So you picked me because you can't save me?"

She shook her head. "Because you don't seem to want to be saved. I figured that when I fail to be what all these people think I'll be, that my failure would be easier on you than the others."

"You're wrong. Take it back. Pick someone else."

"Why?"

She heard muffled voices through her door. Someone said something about remotely unlocking it, and her door flew open. Joseph stood there, with Drake and Helen behind him.

"What are you doing here?" asked Iain.

"You looked angry," said Joseph. "I wasn't about to let you do something stupid."

A calm facade covered Iain's face. Gone was the anger that had been there only a moment ago, as if he'd simply willed it away. "Of course I'm not angry. I'm simply anxious to complete our union. I didn't think it would be kind to do it in public—rubbing it in, so to speak."

"There will be no *union*," said Jackie.

Every head swiveled her way, and four sets of eyes rested on her.

"What?" asked Joseph as he moved forward. Behind him, Drake shut the door.

Jackie was done being intimidated. She didn't like it. She squared her shoulders and smoothed her hands over her suit to remind herself who was in charge of her life. "Our deal was that I pick a man, not that I do anything else. I've picked. Now you have to let me leave. Alone."

"Like hell," said Iain. "You go out there alone, without any powers, and you'll be eaten before sunrise."

"Joseph promised," she said, then looked at Joseph. "Didn't you?"

His face contorted with frustration and he glared at her. "You tricked me."

"You should have done a better job with the fine print."

"You can never have a normal life," he told her.

She flinched, feeling the blow of his words all the way to her toes. "I can, and I will."

"He's right," said Helen. "Please, just think this through."

She had to get out of here. This place was killing her with all the expectations and pressure. "I've spent weeks thinking about it. All I want is for my life to go back to something resembling the way it used to be. I want a job, a career, a home." A family. Baby Samson had given her a taste of something she'd never thought she'd want, but now she did. But there was no way she was going to raise a child in this place. Her child would have a normal life.

"It's not safe," said Helen, her tone gentle.

Jackie looked at Joseph. "You promised. Tell them."

His lip lifted in a sneer of frustration and anger. "She's right. I promised her she could leave if she chose a man. She's done her part, and despite the fact that it's stupid, reckless, and insane, we have to let her go."

"I don't," said Iain, his gaze fixed firmly on her. "I made no promise."

"You wouldn't," said Jackie.

"Do I look like a man who jokes around? If you go, I go, too. Like it or not, you picked me. Now you're stuck with me."

"I won't ever put on your necklace."

He shrugged. "Fine. Don't. I'm still not letting you die out there. I gave you my vow, and I intend to uphold it."

Kind and gentle were not words she'd use to describe

Iain. She'd picked him because he was cold—because he seemed to have no expectations of her—but now she was beginning to see the error in her decision. That coldness wasn't going to gain her any favors or understanding. The best she could hope for now was that eventually he'd figure out she wasn't worth the effort, and go find some other woman.

"Fine," she snapped. She went to where her suitcase was standing and raised the handle to wheel it out. "But I'm already packed and ready to go, and I'm not waiting."

Iain took the handle from her grasp. His fingers grazed hers, and the result of his touch was immediate. A string of bubbles slid through her veins and burst into pinpoints of warmth. It felt shockingly good, startling her with the force of it. She had to fight the urge to simply close her eyes and enjoy the sensation, letting it fill her up. It made her forget all about the chill of the caves and the things she'd endured. Her entire focus was on the small patch of her skin that made contact with his.

It wasn't right. It wasn't even real. She had to remember that and not let whatever magic he possessed sway her from her path.

Jackie jerked her hand away, already regretting the loss of contact.

His body clenched tight, like he'd just taken a punch, but he continued to stare at her without blinking.

Jackie rubbed her skin in an effort to rid herself of his touch. She didn't want to feel anything magical, no matter how good it may have been. All she wanted was for everyone to keep their hands to themselves.

Joseph opened his mouth, but Helen grabbed his arm, stopping him before he could speak. She leaned over and whispered something in his ear. Joseph nodded, then stared at Jackie in speculation.

"We'll see you when you get back," said Joseph.

"What was that about?" she asked, looking at her half sister.

"Nothing," said Helen. "You two go do what you need to do. You'll always have a place here if and when you want it."

Jackie wasn't sure what they were up to, but she doubted she'd like it if she knew. "I don't plan on coming back."

"I know," said Helen. "But I hope you change your mind. I'll miss you while you're gone."

Jackie couldn't bear any emotional farewells. Helen was her sister by blood, but that was all. They didn't know each other. They had no connection, no shared history. All they had was a similar affliction—a magical disease that drew these men to them—one Jackie hoped she could either find a cure for or come to live with eventually.

"Where will you go?" asked Joseph.

"South," she lied. "Florida, maybe."

Beside her, Iain grunted his disbelief. "Daylight's burning. If you're serious about leaving, we need to put some miles behind us before dark."

Jackie looked at Helen, seeing her hazel eyes fill up with tears. "I'm sorry I can't be what you want—what any of you want."

"I don't want you to be anything but happy," said Helen.

Jackie wasn't setting her sights nearly that high. She'd be satisfied with simply being free.

Tori pulled the hood up over her head, shoved stolen sunglasses on her face, and walked through the halls of Dabyr as if she belonged there. She kept her head down, looking at no one while she made her escape.

She heard voices of children as she passed through the large open dining and recreation area. The smell of coffee— something that reminded her of her dead mother—filled her nose, giving her a pang of grief. Mama had been gone a long time now. The demons had killed and eaten her when

Tori was eight—the night she'd been stolen by monsters and her old life had ended.

Light seeping in under the glasses burned her eyes. Or maybe it was tears. She couldn't tell. It was too bright there for her. All those years underground had made her eyes sensitive. Sadly, these people were so blind they needed to light this place up like the surface of the sun just to see their own feet.

It didn't matter. She wouldn't be there long. She only had to tolerate the light for as long as it took to get to her sister Andra's car. The sun was setting. It would be dark soon, and the searing behind her eyes would ease.

Zillah—the Synestryn lord who'd caged and tortured her for years—was asleep now, hiding like a coward, but she could still feel him coursing through her veins, laughing at her with every beat of her heart. He was weak now. Nearby. She could find him and capture him before anyone even realized she was gone.

The bag on her shoulder was heavy, slowing her progress toward the garage. Over the last few weeks, she'd collected everything she'd need, gathering up knives, rope, matches, and other tools she could use to turn Zillah's life into the living hell he'd made of hers. She'd spent a lot of time thinking about just how she was going to torture him before she let him die. Finding him, making him pay, was all that mattered.

Pain was not enough. She had to cause him fear, too. Oceans of it—as much as he had caused her and the others during her childhood. Since her rescue, she'd spent nearly every waking moment thinking up different ways to make him scream. She didn't just want him to hurt—she wanted him destroyed, broken, and begging for his life. Then and only then, after his last scream's echo had died out, would she be able to rest. Finally. He'd leave her dreams and never return. She'd truly be free of him.

Capturing Zillah was going to be hard, but she knew he and his guards were weaker during the day—trapped underground, away from the sun. She could sneak into his caves unnoticed. After all the years of him forcing her to take his blood, shoving it into her veins, making her drink it, she even smelled like one of them. Tynan had said so to Logan when they'd thought she was sleeping.

At first she'd tried to scrub herself clean, but no matter how many times she washed, no matter how many cleaners she used on her skin, the stench was still there, seeping out of her pores.

Now she realized it for the gift it was. Who else could sneak into a Synestryn cave without being detected?

Zillah probably hadn't realized what he'd done, and now it was going to come back to haunt him.

A slow smile of excitement pulled at her mouth as she hurried her pace. Tynan would come to see her as soon as he woke up, and she had to be long gone before then.

No matter how hard he'd tried, no matter how many times he'd come to her with soft words and kind eyes, all his efforts to clean her blood had failed. She'd left him weak and shaking, his mouth blistered from her blood.

She was one of them—one of the monsters. A Synestryn. Their blood was inside of her, burning her veins and calling her back to them.

Part of her wanted to answer that call.

Tori turned the last corner and nearly ran into one of the Theronai. Fear lurched into her chest, and she started to turn and run, her instincts screaming at her to flee. Before she took even one step, he moved to block her path.

"Whoa," he said. "Slow down there."

Words lodged in her throat. Her heart was pounding fast, and she heard herself panting. By now she should have been better at hiding her fear, but he'd surprised her, and she couldn't seem to keep control of herself since coming there. These people were all too nice. She wasn't used to it, and it left her confused and suspicious.

At any moment, she knew they'd turn on her, and she was sick of waiting for it to happen.

She looked up and saw scars crisscrossing the man's face. He was trying to smile at her, but it pulled his skin, twisting his mouth. He had bright blue eyes and hair the same dark blond as Andra's husband's.

"Where were you going so fast?" he asked, his voice quiet and gentle as if he was trying not to scare her.

"I was just getting some exercise."

He pulled a phone out of his pocket and started playing with it, his thick fingers flying fast. He watched her and not what he was doing. "The only thing down this hall is the garage. You wouldn't be trying to sneak out, would you?"

He'd caught her. She was cornered. Trapped. Panic raked her skin and she realized there was only one thing she could do to escape.

Tori moved fast, giving him no time to react. She pulled a steak knife from her bag and stabbed it into his chest.

Nicholas stared down in disbelief at the knife buried in his chest. Pain radiated out from the wound, but it was nothing compared to the pain he endured every day as his power grew. Nothing compared to the betrayal he felt.

Tori had stabbed him. All he'd wanted to do was stop her from leaving and getting herself hurt or killed. Hell, he hadn't even touched her, despite his urge to see if she was the one who could save his life.

Jackie sure as hell hadn't wanted him. Not that he blamed her.

Tori's small hand was still wrapped around the wooden handle of the knife. When he felt her tug on it, likely to pull it out and stab him again, he covered her hand with both of his, holding the knife in place.

The pain his growing power caused seem to dull. The

edges rounded, and the bulging pressure behind his eyes
eased. Everything within him went still and quiet—even
his heart stopped for a few, timeless seconds.

Tori was compatible with his power. She could save
him.

He hadn't been this close to her before, but now that
he was looking at her, he realized she was just a child. A
feral, deranged child.

Her blue eyes went wide with shock, and then a rabid
snarl contorted her face and a low growl of warning
spilled from her lips.

In that moment, he realized that her compatibility
didn't matter. He couldn't ask anything of her. He'd
been there the night she'd been rescued. He knew what
she'd gone through. It wasn't fair to ask her to do anything more than heal and grow strong.

Nicholas ignored the pointless surge of hope, shoved
aside the pain of his wound, and showed no weakness.
His tone took on the same disappointed, lecturing qual-
ity his father had used on him too many times when he
was a child. "What the hell do you think you're doing?
You don't go around stabbing people like that."

She tried to pull her hand away, and it wiggled the
knife, burning like fire. Her lips pulled back, baring her
teeth. "Let me go!"

"Not a chance. You're staying right here until Andra
shows up."

"She thinks I'm sleeping. I snuck out while she was in
bed with Paul."

"Sorry to break it to you, kiddo, but I texted her. In
fact . . ."

The heavy beat of footsteps came pounding down the
hall. Andra raced around the corner, her face pink and
her shirt on inside out. Paul was only a couple of steps
behind her, and he was shirtless and barefoot.

Tori let out a scream of frustrated outrage.

"Thanks for coming," said Nicholas. "Now that you're

here to deal with her, I can have this knife removed. I suggest you figure out something to do with her before she hurts someone for real next time."

He didn't wait around to see how Andra dealt with her deranged sister. It was none of his business. As much as he wished otherwise, as much as he would have gladly altered his life to help Tori heal, all he could offer her was the added burden of saving his life.

It was just as well. She was too young for him to think of her as anything but a child, and she was too unstable for any kind of relationship, even if he could overlook her age. It didn't matter how patient or gentle he would be if he didn't live long enough to help her. Tori was obviously the kind of girl who would stab a man in his sleep. The Synestryn had turned her into that, robbing her of the life she could have had.

He hoped that Andra figured out something soon. Tori was a danger to herself and others, and unless they wanted people to get hurt, they were going to have to lock her up. She'd spent her childhood imprisoned by Synestryn, being tortured and fed their blood. He didn't think captivity was going to sit well with her.

Just the thought made him sick.

She could be his. In a few years. When she was older and had healed.

He wasn't sure he had that much time left. His life-mark was dying. The rate at which his leaves were falling had increased recently. There was no way to know how much time he had left, but he was fairly sure it wouldn't be enough for Tori to truly heal.

Pain throbbed in Nicholas's bones. It was worse now than it had been only a few minutes ago. He could barely even feel the knife sticking out of him. Putting one foot in front of another took all his concentration. He wanted to run back to her so she could make the pain stop.

What if he couldn't control himself as his pain grew? What if he forced her to make it stop?

Nicholas had seen what happened to his brothers as they reached the end of their lives. They became darker, angry and desperate. He'd seen good men do bad things. What if he did the same with Tori?

There was only one thing he could think to do—only one way to keep her safe from himself.

As soon as Tynan was done healing his stab wound, he was going to bargain with the Sanguinar—give him anything he asked for—to have his memory of the last few minutes removed. If he didn't know Tori could save him, she'd be safe. It was the only way he could be sure.

Chapter 5

"Where are we really going?" asked Iain once they were in his truck and driving out through Dabyr's gates.

The sun was still high in the sky, but Jackie could feel its descent, like sharp fingernails raking over her back. "To see Samson. I want to see him one more time before I cut ties with your world."

"So you lied. I figured as much. Not that it matters. They'll know where we go. Tracking devices in all the vehicles."

Of course there were. "Great. Nothing like an electronic leash to make a girl feel free."

"I don't get you. If you'd stayed, you could have had anything you wanted. You would have been safe. After two years of being locked up, I'd think safety would be at the top of your list."

How was she going to explain anything to him? He didn't live in her world—or at least not in the one she wanted to inhabit. "I didn't feel safe there. I felt caged. Stagnant."

He said nothing, his eyes on the road. His hands were fisted around the steering wheel, and she noticed a faint scar on the back of his right hand. It was jagged and pale with age.

"How'd you get that?" she asked, looking for a way to get the conversation off herself.

He stared at his hand for an extended moment, as if he had to think about it to remember. "Six against one. Little vicious raptor demons. One of them flew in from overhead and I didn't see it until it was too late."

"What happened?"

"I killed it before the poison in its talons felled me. By then Liam had made it to my side. Saved my life."

He said it so calmly, as if he were talking about what he'd had for dinner last night.

"When was this?" she asked.

"A couple hundred years ago. Right after the big attack."

"The big attack?"

"We'd thought the Synestryn were nearly extinct—that we'd wiped them out. We were all feeling pretty proud of ourselves. Overconfident. We spread out and tried to lead normal lives. We let our guard down, which was what they'd been waiting for. They coordinated a massive attack near every homestead and Sentinel compound they could find. All of us rushed to help and save the nearby towns from massacre. The Synestryn had planned on that, too, and were ready. They launched their real attack, which was designed to kill our women. It worked."

Jackie stared at him, her mouth hanging open in shock. There was no emotion in his voice, no grief, horror, or regret.

"We lost hundreds of women that night, and dozens of men. On top of the killing, they sterilized every male Theronai with some kind of magic—though it took us a while to figure out what they'd done. Without the ability to have children and refill our ranks, we've never recovered from that attack. Couple that with the painful deaths of many more men who can no longer house their growing power, and it was likely a killing blow."

"You think they've won?"

Iain shrugged as if it didn't matter. "I don't think. I fight. I get up every day and kill as many of them as I can before they kill me."

"And you're happy with that?"

He turned his head, gazing at her. His black eyes held only faint confusion. "It's not my job to be happy. I do what I need to so others can be."

"But what about what *you* want?"

"It's irrelevant. I realized it's easiest not to want things, so I just stopped doing it."

"Stopped? How do you just ... stop?" She would desperately like to learn that skill, because right about now, she'd really love to stop wanting what she was afraid she could never have. Her old life was a dream, a distant memory. As hard as she tried to reclaim it, she feared it would always be out of reach.

That didn't mean she wasn't going to keep trying to make it happen. She was way too driven to simply give up.

"This topic is clearly distressing you, and it's my duty to see to your comfort. Let's talk about something else. Or better yet, just not talk at all."

That suited her just fine.

The landscape slid by them, the hope of spring hovering over everything. It was as if the world had just pulled in a deep breath and was holding it in anticipation.

Jackie lasted for all of ten minutes before she couldn't stay quiet any longer. "Do you hurt? Like the others?"

"Hurt?"

"Helen said that holding in all that power hurts you." That thought had haunted Jackie the most—knowing these men were in pain. Helen had said Jackie could make it stop.

"Helen talks too much."

She took that as verification of what she'd suspected. Iain was in pain, like the others. She'd only seen a couple of flashes of it—always after he'd touched her, as if she somehow made it worse. "How do you manage it?"

"Just fine, thank you."

She turned in her seat and stared at him, hoping her silence would force him to speak. His grip had tightened on the wheel, but other than that, his posture was relaxed. She wished she could do the same, but the tension riding between her shoulder blades never seemed to leave, even when she slept. Not that she did much of that these days. Nightmares of her time in captivity made it hard, and after she woke up a few days ago to one of the Theronai standing over her bed, watching her with desperate hope in his eyes, sleep had not come easily.

Why, of all the dozens of Theronai she'd met, was Iain the only one who looked at her differently? Jackie stared at him, trying to figure him out.

His luceria was paler than the other men's, so pale it was nearly silver. She couldn't see enough distinction between the colors to tell if there was any movement in the band, as there was in those of the other men like him.

For a moment, she wondered what it would be like to put it on and wield the kind of power her sisters had. Would it hurt? Would it feel good? Would she feel anything at all?

There was only one way to find out, and she wasn't curious enough to try it.

She stole glances at Iain as he drove, doing her best to hide it. She couldn't help but stare. He intrigued her with his impassive expression, leaving her to puzzle out what he was thinking.

He had nice features—high cheekbones, a wide jaw and strong chin with a slight cleft. His beard had grown out just a bit, shadowing his jaw. There were a few paler spots where scars dotted his skin, and she wondered if he'd gotten them in the same attack that had scarred his hand, or if there had been others.

Jackie reached out to trace her finger over that scar before she realized what she was doing. She snatched her hand back and shoved it under her thigh to keep it where it belonged. Touching Iain was not an option. It made her feel strange, tingly and warm.

She remembered that warmth from the night he'd rescued her. She'd been so cold for so long. The heat of his skin felt like sunlight spreading through her. Shock and weakness had numbed her, but that heat had penetrated through the haze, giving her something to focus on so she could hold herself together for just a little longer—long enough to see that the children were all brought out safely.

It occurred to her that she didn't think she'd ever thanked him for that. He'd gone after the kids alone, risking his life to save them. She owed him for that. But was her debt large enough to do what these people wanted and give up her life?

Iain's seat was pushed all the way back to make room for his body, and despite the cool temperatures outside, his arms were bare beneath his short sleeves. Corded muscles wove their way up over his shoulders, and she could see just a bit of his tree tattoo peeking out from his sleeve and creeping up his neck. What branches she could see were all bare—not a good sign among his kind, according to Helen.

"How much time do you have left?" she asked him, before she thought better of it.

"As much as it takes," he answered a bit too quickly.

"How many leaves?"

He turned and gave her a steady stare. "If you want to know that, you'll have to count them."

The idea of getting his shirt off sent a little trill of something shooting through her. Fear? Excitement? She couldn't really tell. It had come and gone too fast for her to make any sense out of it.

"I think I'll pass."

He grunted. "That's what I thought you'd say."

The sun burned her eyes, and she'd just now realized how low it had gotten in the sky. She'd been staring at him for way too long. Sunset was only a few minutes away. "We need to find a safe place to stop."

"I thought you wanted to see Samson."

"I do, but I don't want to go there at night. I can't risk drawing any of the monsters to him."

Iain accepted that without argument. "There's a Gerai house not far from here."

"No. That's part of your world, not mine. We'll find a hotel."

"Suit yourself. But just so we're clear, we're sharing a room."

"I don't think so. I may have picked you, but that's as far as it goes."

"I'm not going to fuck you. I'm not even going to touch you. But if you think that I'm going to leave you unguarded so that you can be taken again, you're wrong. One room, Jackie. I'm not negotiating with you on this."

"Two beds," she demanded.

"If that makes you feel better, but I won't need one. I won't be sleeping."

"Why not?"

"Because I don't trust you not to run off. That's not happening on my watch, even if it means I invest in a nice pair of handcuffs."

Jackie didn't doubt for a second that he'd do it. While some of the other men might have hesitated to do anything to upset her, Iain didn't seem to suffer from that same soft spot. For some reason, that was part of what she liked about him. He wasn't pretending. This was who he was, and he wasn't changing himself to try to entice her. As inconvenient as it was that he wasn't bowing to her every wish, she had to respect that.

They pulled into the first hotel they found, just as the sun was setting. It was a bit dated and run-down, but as long as the beds were clean, she didn't care.

Jackie grabbed her suitcase from the bed of the truck, and hurried inside, not waiting to see if Iain was keeping up.

She checked in and headed right to their ground-floor room, which wasn't nearly large enough now that she was standing in it with Iain right behind her. She could feel the heat coming off his body, hear his slow, even breathing.

He dropped a duffel bag on the floor and went directly to the window. He shoved the sheers back and pressed against the glass.

"What are you doing?"

"Testing to make sure it's airtight. I don't want the Synestryn to smell you in here."

"Smell me?" She did not like the sound of that at all.

"It can happen, especially if you bleed. Since I didn't think you'd want me inquiring about your menstrual cycle, I thought I'd be safe rather than sorry."

That news left her standing there, going numb from the feet up. "You're telling me that once a month the monsters can smell me?"

"At least that often. Unless you'd like to actually pick a man whose luceria you *want* to wear. You could use magic to mask your scent, and to protect yourself if one of the demons did find you."

The way he'd said that made her blink in confusion. "How did you know I didn't want to wear your luceria?"

"You're not exactly a master of subterfuge, Jackie. Any more than I'm a fluffy white bunny. You picked me because you knew you wouldn't like me, so you wouldn't be tempted to take pity on me and do the one thing you don't ever want to do: become a part of my world."

He was a lot more astute than she gave him credit for. "That's not exactly right."

Iain went to the door and engaged both locks. Then he opened his bag and began pulling out items. "No?"

"I picked you because you were the only one who knew the score."

"And what score is that?"

"I'm not like you. I'll never be like you."

"Wrong. You don't want to be like us. You are, but you're going to fight it, kicking and screaming, every step of the way."

"You make me sound selfish."

He shook his dark head. "No, just childish. But you're young. You have centuries to grow up and do the right thing. I just hope you do so before any more of my brothers die."

Jackie stood there in shock, reeling from his talk of death, his insult, and the thought of living that long. He'd worded it so casually, so matter-of-factly, that she had to face it.

He grabbed a change of clothes, a toothbrush, and razor. "I'm going to shower while the sky is still light. You should be safe for the few minutes it will take me to clean up. Then I'll stand by and guard you while you sleep."

She watched him disappear into the bathroom, her feet rooted to the same spot.

He was right. She was so concerned about what she wanted that she hadn't really spent any time considering how her decision would affect others, beyond her certainty that she'd let them down. Her pain had blinded her. She was so wrapped up in getting over what she'd endured that she didn't stop and think about what the men who'd saved her had endured every day. For centuries. Only there was no rescue for them unless she was the one doing the saving.

It wasn't what she wanted. This world. The demons and magic.

Did that matter? It didn't seem to matter to Iain. He did what needed to be done and didn't even bring his wants into the equation.

Could she do that? Could she truly be that selfless?

She'd already given up two years of her life. How

could they ask her to give up the rest of it as well? Especially now that she was starting to realize just how long that was going to be.

Then again, how could they not ask her to do it? She was special, as much as she hated that fact. She was the only woman they'd ever found who could partner with any of the men. She hadn't asked for this burden, but she'd always been responsible in the past. Could she really turn a blind eye to so much need?

Iain came out of the bathroom a few minutes later, a cloud of soap-scented steam following in his wake. His hair was damp, and the shadow of stubble was gone.

"You haven't moved," he stated.

She wasn't sure how he knew that, but she let the words pass by. They were unimportant to what he'd say in response to her next question.

"All the unbound men need me. All of them want me—with the apparent exception of you. They all think I'm some kind of miracle. How in the world am I supposed to live up to those expectations? And how do I pick who gets to live?" And who had to die.

Iain was going back through his conversations with Jackie, trying to determine how she'd realized he didn't want a union with her, while he formulated the answer to her question.

Anger at his carelessness gathered in a swirling mass behind his eyes. If anyone found out that he didn't want her the way he should, it could compromise the Band of the Barren. He couldn't betray them, even unknowingly. He had to keep up the ruse and figure out exactly where he'd gone wrong so he wouldn't do it again. And he had to make sure she told no one what she suspected.

He stared at her, calculating his next move. She was more perceptive than he would have guessed, and if he didn't convince her to drop this line of questioning, he might accidentally reveal something crucial—something that could get his brothers killed. The real question was, if it came down to a choice between the Band or Jackie, who would he choose to live? She could save only one man, but she could cause the death of many.

Just the thought was enough to make the monster inside of him rear its head and howl in rage. He wouldn't let her hurt his brothers. He wouldn't let her curiosity send good men to die at the hands of the Slayers.

"This partnership is a long-term thing," he told her carefully, keeping his anger in check. "Permanent in most cases. You need to pick a man you can stand to spend eternity with."

"And how the hell am I supposed to know that? I don't even know what I want for breakfast tomorrow."

It didn't matter what she wanted. It was her duty to save one of them, and he was going to make sure she did it. "You're an intelligent woman. You'll figure it out."

"And if I want you?" she asked, her voice quiet and uncertain.

"Don't," he snarled before he could stop himself. His beast pounded at its confines, demanding to be set free. Just for a moment. Just long enough to force her to do the right thing.

She took a step back, fear flickering through her expression.

Iain fought the urge to follow her up and use his bulk to intimidate her, scare her. It didn't matter how he got her to pick Cain or one of the others, so long as she did. "I'm not the kind of man you want to spend eternity with."

Her brows lowered over her gray eyes, hiding her fear. "So, you're just going to let yourself die?" she asked.

"I have no intention of dying anytime soon."

"Then why aren't you falling over yourself to convince me to be with you, the way the others have?"

"I've made promises."

"To another woman?"

He'd been thinking about how he couldn't fail the men who looked to him for survival, but her question gave him the excuse he needed. "Serena," he said, trying to sound sad. "She died the night of the attack. All I found of her was a pile of severed hair and part of her skirt." There hadn't even been any blood, as if she'd simply been picked up and carried away, never to be seen again.

To add veracity to his story, he went to his duffel and pulled out a golden locket. In it was a miniature portrait of Serena and a small braided lock of fiery red hair. He carried it now more out of habit than sentimentality. He hadn't grieved for her for a long time—one of the few blessings of his soulless state.

Iain handed the locket to Jackie. She opened it and pulled in a shocked breath. "She's beautiful."

"Yes," he agreed.

"And you miss her, even after all these years?"

"I loved her." And now he couldn't even remember what that had felt like. Sorrow, joy, eagerness . . . all of those he could remember, but love had been lost to him for a long time.

"I'm sorry," she whispered as she closed the locket and handed it back to him.

Her bare skin accidentally brushed his, and his constant pain fled for that single, brief moment. And there was a flash of something else—something he couldn't quite recognize—as if a curtain had been parted for a split second, only to fall back into place before his eyes had time to focus. Then her touch was gone, and agony came crashing back.

He braced himself for its return, but it was always worse than it had been before. Every time he stopped touching her, the pain was more intense, more demanding. It sliced through his skin, cutting deep. It ground at his bones and crushed his organs. His blood caught fire, scorching his veins as his entire world lit up with agony.

It took every ounce of discipline and self-control not to draw his blade and lash out at the one who'd hurt him. Jackie. He could kill her so easily. It wouldn't even take any effort at all to break her slender neck so she could never again hurt him.

The monster in him cheered at the idea, banging at its bars. One moment of freedom. That's all the beast needed to make the pain stop.

He locked his knees, gritted his teeth, and tried to remember to breathe through the pain, but with lightning bouncing around inside his skull, thought was nearly impossible.

Jackie gasped. "I keep forgetting about that," she said. "I'm so sorry."

Her words were a hollow echo at the end of a long tunnel. The pain bore down on him, making everything else inconsequential. All he could think about was making it stop. Forcing *her* to make it stop.

He reached for her blindly, knowing that only she could end this torment. His fingers found smooth fabric. Her sleeves. He quested up until he found the warmth of her neck and face.

Instantly, the agony eased, as if he'd been doused in cool water, washing it all away. He was left feeling buoyant, light. The monster that was his constant companion quieted, no longer screaming and pounding at his insides. He felt ... at peace for the first time in years, perhaps decades.

He couldn't let her take that away, sending him spiraling back inside the pain. If she did, he wasn't sure he could remember not to kill her.

Iain's vision had not yet returned, so he couldn't read her face. He pulled her tight against his chest, spearing his fingers through her hair to hold her in place. He could feel her rapid breathing washing out over his arm, feel her frantic heartbeat beating against his chest.

He'd scared her.

Something faint fluttered inside of him—some feeling he'd lost long ago. He didn't like her fear. He liked even less that he'd been the one to cause it. He wished he could take her fear away and give her some sense of happiness and safety.

"I won't hurt you," he said, hoping it was true. He couldn't think of what else he could say to make her feel better. He couldn't stop touching her. Not yet, not with his pain lurking, huge and terrifying.

"Let me go," she said, but it wasn't a command. Her voice was weak and breathless.

"I will. Just give me a minute. Please." He needed time to regain control and ensure that his beast was safely caged.

He felt her give a tentative nod. He could smell the shampoo she'd used, along with something else. He dragged the scent into himself, trying to figure out what it was, and why he found it so compelling.

Slowly, his sight returned. At first it was only gray, but then the color returned, too, as his field of vision expanded.

He spotted their reflection in the mirrored closet doors and froze. She was leaning into him, as if he'd pulled her off-balance. Her cheek was pressed to his chest, and her whole body was shaking. One hand was splayed on his shoulder, and the other was wrapped around his biceps, against his bare skin. Her fingers tightened, kneading his muscles. Tingling heat bubbled out from everywhere skin touched skin, and the only thought he could muster was what it would be like to get the two of them naked and rubbing against each other.

He could see her face clearly in the mirror. Her lips were parted, and her gaze was focused on where her hand met his skin. Her eyes were huge and dark, haunted by a look of such longing that he instantly wanted to give her whatever it was she needed. A deep blush stained her cheeks, spreading down to her throat.

He'd been with a lot of women over the years, and he knew what they looked like when they were aroused. And Jackie was definitely that.

Iain felt his cock stir, twitching beneath his jeans. Shock hammered into him, stealing his breath.

He hadn't gotten hard in decades.

And then he realized something else. Since the moment he'd touched her, he'd begun to feel again. Regret, lust, surprise. Those things had been long dead in him, but one touch from Jackie and those lost things began to come back.

Hope. Blessed, vital hope budded inside, barely flickering with life. Maybe she could save him.

She caught his gaze in the mirror. A look of horror crossed her face and she shoved herself away, breaking contact.

Pain exploded in a fiery blast. Those fleeting emotions he'd felt were incinerated in a split second, and all that was left was the enraged monster breaking out of its cage, ready to kill.

He took a step toward her, but fell to his knees as the agony bore down on him. Then suddenly, it all went away. Everything went away.

Chapter 6

It was not even sunset, and Tynan was already over-whelmed. Nicholas's stab wound hadn't been bad, and he'd paid for his healing and the removal of his memory in blood, but Grace's condition had deteriorated in the past few hours, and now Tori had seemingly become homicidal. And all of it was his problem to fix.

He had to make a quick stop by Grace's room before going to see to Tori. When he entered, he found Torr bowed at her bedside, cradling her hand in his. The man rarely left her, and his guilt was beginning to hang on him, eating him away bit by bit. Tynan could sense the decay of his condition, both in his appearance as well as in each sluggish movement of his body.

"You should go and rest," said Tynan.

Torr turned around, his eyes rimmed with red and sunken with fatigue. "Don't," was all he said.

"Fine. If you want to throw away the gift she gave you, then so be it. It's your life to discard as you see fit."

"I'm staying with her."

Tynan didn't bother checking the output of the machines breathing for Grace. He simply laid his hand on her head and let her body speak to him.

She was still in there, fighting. She hadn't given up. Neither had Torr. If sheer force of will could keep someone alive, then perhaps Grace could hang on for another day or two.

There was no way to make this easier on the Theronai. "I've done all I can."

Torr shot to his feet. "No. You can't give up on her."

"I haven't given up on anyone. I've tried everything I know to do for her. I swear I have. No human medicine or Sanguinar magic is going to sustain her for long. Her body is simply too weak. You have to let her go. She's holding on for you, protecting you from your grief."

Torr's mouth moved as if struggling not to spit out something vile. "I'll go find the demon that caused this. Then you can create some kind of antivenom."

"You've looked. Others have looked. No one has seen even a hint of the creature. And even if you did find one, it wouldn't matter. She's too far gone."

"She's still here. That's all that matters."

"She's here because of you. Do you really think she can rest in peace if she knows you're suffering? She gave her life to save yours. That kind of love is rare, and it's the only thing keeping her alive now."

Torr swallowed and tears brimmed in his eyes. "You're telling me that I'm prolonging her suffering?"

If Tynan sugarcoated it, Torr would never listen. The man was beyond stubborn. Infuriatingly so. "Yes. She's clinging to life for you. You must let her go. Holding her here, forcing her to take breath after breath from that machine so that you don't have to feel guilty, is selfish."

Tears slid down Torr's face. He didn't even try to hide them. "I can't lose her."

"You already have. There's nothing anyone can do. I'm sorry."

"I can't," said Torr, backing away, holding his hands up as if to ward off an attacker. "I can't let her go." He sounded uncertain, as if he was finally beginning to accept the eventuality of Grace's death.

"One of us will do it. We'll turn off the machines."

Torr surged forward, taking a threatening step toward Tynan. "No! I will fucking kill anyone who does that to her. Do you hear me?"

Tynan knew when it was time to back off. He didn't need his neck broken twice for that lesson to set in. "I understand. No one will do anything without your permission, but neither will I expend any more precious blood on her behalf. There simply isn't enough to go around."

Torr nodded tightly. "Go. I want to be alone with her. While I can."

Tynan left, grieving for what they were about to lose. Not only Grace, but Torr. He was no longer the man he'd once been. Grief had weakened him, drawn him thin enough to snap.

One more casualty of war—one Tynan had no time to dwell upon. It was Tori's turn for his attention, and she was the one he had to save. Theronai women were far too precious to lose, even ones who had no hope of happiness. Or possibly even sanity.

He locked his dark thoughts away and did what needed to be done, just as always.

The door to the suite Paul and Andra shared with Tori was open. The moment he neared, he smelled blood. Fresh. Powerful.

Hunger rose within him, widening its jaws. There wasn't enough Athanasian blood left on Earth to feed his kind. The path between Earth and Athanasia had once been wide-open, allowing passage between worlds. But now the gate was shut and Earth was cut off from the Athanasian blood that fueled the Sanguinar. Small traces of ancient blood had been passed down from one human generation to another, leaving behind the blooded humans from which he fed, but their blood alone wasn't enough. The healing he did, his work to restore the fertility of the male Theronai, drew too much power from him, leaving him in constant, aching hunger. The only time he could remember being truly full was when one of the Athanasian princes had come through the gate and shared his blood.

That gift had been a miracle—one that had saved Tynan from sending himself off to sleep for decades. It had allowed him to continue his work, but he couldn't keep it all to himself. There were others of his kind, helpless and asleep beneath Dabyr, depending on him and his brothers to provide for them. Most of what he'd received he'd given to them, saving only what was necessary to complete his work.

The smell of that blood now drove him forward, his mouth watering for a taste of that power. He entered one of the bedrooms and found Paul holding Tori in his lap, his arms and one leg pinning her body against his. His shoulder was bleeding from a set of ragged teeth marks left in his skin. That was the blood Tynan had smelled.

Andra knelt in front of her restrained sister, trying to talk some sense into her. "You can't leave, baby. They'll find you and take you away from me."

Tori thrashed inside his hold. Her pale skin was flushed. Too-dark veins beat at her throat and in her temples, proving that the blood of her captors still coursed through her. She bared her teeth, which were coated with Paul's blood. "I will kill you if you try to make me stay here. Zillah has to die. I have to kill him."

"We'll find him for you. I'll kill him myself."

"No! He's mine! I want to hurt him. I want to make him scream."

Tynan had heard enough. Tori was unwell. She'd been with the Synestryn for too long. They'd changed her, fed her their blood. Zillah had tortured her and raped her and forced her to bear him a child. That child—her child—had died. No one could come through something like that unscathed.

Her suffering beat at him, making him forget all
about his own paltry problems. He had to end her suffering. Somehow. He'd thought that if she found a man
who was compatible with her, one whose power she
could wield, it might save her, but now he was beginning
to think differently. If this young woman had any kind of
power at all, she might well use it to kill the people inside this stronghold.

Tynan couldn't let that happen.

Nicholas had been right to have Tynan remove his
memory of the encounter with Tori. He'd done it for
reasons different from Tynan's, but the result was the
same. Tori would not gain access to Nicholas's power
unless and until it was safe for her to become a deadly
weapon. No one could know that they were compatible —
especially Andra, who would do anything to save her
sister.

Tynan strode up to where Paul held her, and touched
Tori's forehead, willing her to sleep.

She went limp in Paul's arms, and he let out a long,
relieved breath. "Thanks. She's strong for such a tiny
thing."

"I'm so sorry," said Andra, as if all of this were somehow her fault.

Paul laid Tori on the bed and pulled Andra against his
bare chest, hugging her close. The look he gave Tynan
was filled with demand. "You've got to make this stop.
She stabbed Nicholas today."

"I know. I was the one who removed the knife and
mended his flesh."

"I'll give you whatever blood you need," said Paul,
"but you've got to help her. She's not getting any better."

Andra turned, wiping tears from her eyes. "She's getting worse. More violent."

"No, she's always been this violent. It's just that now
she's getting strong enough to act on those feelings. You
must let me put her to sleep in the way of my kind. She

will rest in peace until I can find a way to remove the taint of Synestryn blood from her body."

"Can't we get some kind of dialysis machine?" asked Andra.

"Machines cannot filter out magic, though I wish it were possible."

"You can't give up on her."

"I haven't. I won't. You know how much she's needed. But there's no other way."

"I can't make her go to sleep," said Andra. "She says that Zillah is in her dreams. Hurting her." She swallowed and when she spoke again, her voice shook with emotion. "He rapes her in her sleep, Tynan. Every night. She wakes up screaming, crying. I can't make her live through that for as long as it takes you to find a cure. At least now she has some time awake. Away from him."

Paul stroked Andra's back. "We'll cage her before we let you put her to sleep. We've already decided."

"Then we cage her, because there's no way we can let her roam free after what she did today."

"I'll talk to Joseph," said Andra. "I'll see if he'll let us put bars on her door and windows so she can stay here."

It wasn't going to end well. Tynan could already tell that much.

Tori began to writhe on the bed, making pitiful sounds of pain and terror.

Tears spilled down Andra's face. "Don't let Nika know how bad she is. It would kill her."

"The two of them are connected. Nika probably already knows."

Andra shook her head. "No. Tori still protects her, even though she's barely human. Nika was the one who was with her in her mind for all of those years of captivity. Tori won't repay that by making Nika suffer. I don't want you to, either."

"I agree. We'll keep this to ourselves." Not only was it the right thing to do, but it would garner good faith with

Andra as well as keeping Nika's mind free of worry. Tynan wanted Nika happy and content so that nothing interfered with her ability to become pregnant.

A few weeks ago, he'd given Nika's husband a serum he hoped would cure his infertility. With any luck at all, Tynan's tireless efforts would pay off and Theronai babies would once again be born. It was the only hope his people had for avoiding starvation.

He moved to Tori under the guise of checking her pulse. Andra was protective of her younger sisters, and he didn't want to do anything to anger her.

Tynan sent his power streaming out through his touch and found the seething, rotting pain of Tori's nightmares. He couldn't shield her from them, but he could blunt their edges for a time by taking them into himself. It was difficult to do, and taxing on his already dwindling power, but Tori deserved a bit of rest after what she'd been through.

He gathered up her nightmares, allowing them to flow into himself. The images hit him hard, nauseating him. He refused to look directly at them for fear of driving himself mad. There was too much torment there, too much agony and hopelessness. If he looked at it for too long, it would suck him in and destroy him.

Tynan shoved all of it into a corner of his mind and locked it away. It was still there. He could feel the fetid edges of it trying to creep out, but this wasn't the first time he'd done something like this. It took all his willpower, but he managed to take control and face Paul and Andra as if nothing had happened. "She'll sleep peacefully for at least a couple of hours. Don't wake her."

Andra nodded, sniffing. "Thank you."

"I'll walk you to the door," said Paul.

He left his wife behind, and as soon as they were out of sight, he stopped Tynan. "Take my blood. I know you need it after what you did for her."

"I wasn't able to do anything."

"Liar." Paul lifted his wrist. "Go ahead. I owe you."

Tynan was too weak to resist such an offer. He was ashamed that he wasn't stronger, but that changed nothing. His actions were the same. In the end, his actions would always be the same.

He'd do whatever it took to survive—to keep his people alive—no matter who had to bleed to make it happen.

Zillah trembled with fury as he stood before his peers. Synestryn lords lined the cave, each seated upon a throne carved from the surrounding stone. Tiny crystals twinkled along the walls of the cavern, and in the center of the space was a large fire, casting flickering shadows over everything.

He'd been summoned. Like a dog. And like a dog, he knew better than to ignore the call. He was powerful, controlling a vast swath of land, but no one was powerful enough to ignore the might of several of the other Synestryn lords combined.

"Why was I interrupted and forced to come here?" he asked.

Raygh—one of the other Synestryn lords present—had apparently been instrumental in the summons, for he was the first to answer. He was tall and skeletal, his bluish skin hanging on his bones, so loose, it looked like it might simply slough off at any moment. His nostrils were flat holes in the center of his face, each one leaking mucus onto his lips. He hunched over like an old human man, but there was nothing frail about him. His slit eyes glowed with power. "We question your ability to protect your holdings. And your loyalty."

Fury blasted through Zillah, and he gripped the hilt of the stolen sword at his side. "How dare you question me?" he demanded.

"We granted you land and all the humans on it. You were to cultivate them, separate the meat from those with power, and find breeders. And instead, you allowed the breeders to escape. At least two of them carry our young, and they are now in Sentinel hands. You failed. Even worse, you allowed the Sentinels to learn of our plans too soon. Your failure has ruined what we have spent years creating. Because of that, your lands are revoked. The question we're here to settle is one of loyalty— whether or not we should spare your life."

He was too shocked to speak for a long moment. Yes, the Sentinels had invaded his territory and stolen his breeding stock, but that didn't give the lords gathered here the right to take away what was his. Those lands had been his for years. He'd earned them, working his way up in power until he was strong enough to kill the Synestryn lord who'd held them previously.

"You can't do that," growled Zillah.

"The decision is made," said Raygh. "We will hear your defense if you have one."

"I don't have to defend myself to any of you. You are my equals."

Another Synestryn lord behind him snorted in derision.

Zillah whirled around to face him. His head was too large for his body, fleshy and bulbous, with protruding bug eyes and thick, scaly lips. He looked less human than the others gathered here, covered in fur, with talons instead of fingers. When he spoke, the words were barely understandable. "You are weak. Too human. Food."

"I'll show you weak," promised Zillah as he drew his sword. An instant later, he became immobile, his body frozen.

"That answers the question of loyalty," said Raygh, spinning Zillah around with a wave of his hand. "You will be put to death for your crimes."

Fear swelled in Zillah's mind, leaving room for nothing else. He couldn't move. He couldn't speak. He couldn't defend himself.

"No. I have a better idea," said a man from the shadows. Zillah thought he recognized the voice, but couldn't place it exactly. "He may yet be of use if he can learn some humility."

"What do you suggest, son?" asked Raygh.

"Lock him up. Use him for blood, rather than meat."

Zillah's muscles clenched as he tried to fight his way free. He couldn't allow himself to be treated like a human.

High, strained sounds vibrated from his chest, but his mouth would not move.

"What say you?" Raygh asked the gathering. "Meat or blood."

"Blood," said the lord on Raygh's left.

"Blood," said the next.

"Blood."

On it went, around the room, until the last voice echoed out, "Blood," sealing Zillah's fate.

Chapter 7

It had felt so good. So right.

Jackie had been sucked in by whatever magic Iain had. She'd fallen for it. She hadn't meant to, but when he'd pulled her up against his hard body and wrapped her up in bubbling warmth, she'd been powerless to resist.

In that moment, she'd given in to his need and let it wash over her, giving her purpose. No one was around to see her weakness, and it had been so long since she'd been held like that.

Not that she'd ever been held quite like that.

There was no comparison between Iain's powerful body and those of the men she'd been with before. They were like scrawny preteens next to a professional athlete. At first it had been a shock, but then her body had a mind of its own and began to relax into his embrace, enjoying it.

The pleasure trickling through her had grown with each passing second, until she was sure that she couldn't hold any more. He'd made her want things she'd thought she'd never want again. He'd almost made her believe that maybe her life wasn't beyond repair.

She could picture the two of them, together. Touching. Even kissing.

The thought made her toes curl in her shoes and her fingers dig into his skin. She was driven to try it. Just once. She needed to feel his lips on hers and see if the crazy desire was real or imagined.

She'd lifted her head in search of his mouth. That's when she'd seen his face.

She'd thought he was different, but that had been a lie. That look of hope she'd seen in all the men was there, on Iain's face, mocking her.

She'd panicked and pushed hard enough to break his grip, but it had been a mistake. She'd hurt him.

Iain fell to the ground, gurgling and shaking, like he was having some kind of seizure. And then he went still.

Jackie panicked. She didn't know what to do or how to help. All she knew was that she was afraid to touch him again, even to see if he was breathing. Her touch had done this. She didn't know how, but it had.

Hating what she knew she had to do, she rushed to her purse, fumbled for her phone, and called Helen. In a voice that sounded panicked even to her own ears, she told her sister what had happened.

"It's okay," said Helen, her tone steady. "You can fix it. Just put your hand on his skin."

"No. That's what made this happen."

"No, it didn't. That only happens if you pull away suddenly. He's strong. He'll be fine. Just do what I say. Trust me. I've been right where you are."

Jackie held her breath and took Iain's hand in hers. His thick fingers were limp in her grasp. "It's not working," she told Helen.

"Give it a minute."

Maybe she wasn't touching him enough. She set the phone down, scooted close, kneeling over him, and then put her other hand on his face. His skin was smooth from his recent shave. He was warm, and now that she was closer, she could see his pulse, strong and steady, in his neck.

Iain's eyes opened. His fingers twined through hers and he covered the hand on his face with his, holding it in place.

"Are you okay?" she asked.

His powerful chest heaved with each rapid breath. Sweat dotted his forehead. His dark gaze slid over her face, then to where their hands joined, their fingers threaded together.

He was so warm, sinking into her skin and spreading out to drive away even the memory of a chill. His silence stretched on, making her wonder if he'd heard and understood her question.

What if he was still in too much pain?

"Iain? Are you okay?"

He hadn't moved, and she didn't dare try to get away again for fear of what it might do to him a second time.

Her hands broke out in a nervous sweat, and her gaze moved down to the broad plane of his chest. She couldn't look him in the eye right now. She was too far out of her element, too off-balance. If she got another glimpse of the hope she'd seen shining in him, she knew she'd freak out.

He sat up, bringing his head close to hers. Their mouths were only inches apart, making hers water. She hadn't even thought about kissing a man for years, and yet she was doing so now. In fact, she could think of little else but how his lips would feel against hers, how he'd taste. His fingers slid across the back of her hand. Spirals of heat wove their way into her skin and up her arm, expanding inside her chest until they reached every part of her. A shiver shook her spine.

Dark, compelling need gathered low in her belly, conjuring images of things she knew she shouldn't want. Her skin heated, and the vibrations coming from his hands seemed to engulf her entire body. All she had to do was let go, and she knew that he'd take care of her. Give her the kind of pleasure she'd been denied for far too long.

Having a lover was normal. She could let herself do that. Here. Now.

His gaze moved to her mouth, and he swallowed. A dark look of need filled his eyes. "I want you," he said, as if it surprised him.

A thrill of victory shot along her spine. Yes. That was what she wanted. She knew she shouldn't want it, but logic was not getting a vote. Not this time.

"Jackie?" came Helen's voice from what seemed like a long way away.

Suddenly, Jackie became acutely aware of the cell phone lying only a foot away from them.

She tugged on her hand so she could deal with the phone, but Iain didn't let go.

She raised her voice and spoke so Helen could hear. "Iain's fine now, Helen. Thanks for your help."

"Okay. Bye," she heard Helen say, a bit too cheerfully. Then the phone's screen displayed the length of the terminated call.

Iain captured her hand from his face and leaned forward, burying his nose against her neck. He nudged the high collar of her shirt, trying to move it out of his way.

Panic gripped her before she could catch herself. He wasn't a demon. He didn't want her blood. Still, she didn't want him to see the scars there—the rough patches of skin left behind from the constant feedings she'd endured. They were ugly reminders of her captivity. Even she could barely stand to look at them.

She managed to pull one hand free and hold her collar in place. "Don't." Her voice was cold, final.

He stopped, lifting his head. His black eyes studied her face. A slight frown creased his brow. She couldn't tell if he was upset, confused, or both. And then all emotions vanished from his face as if they'd never been there. It was as if he'd flipped a switch and simply turned them off. "I need to take you back to Dabyr."

"No."

"This isn't right. If I stay with you, I'm going to forget that."

"What if I don't care?"

"You will. When it's over. You'd care. I can't do anything to knowingly hurt you. I have to retain my honor."

His honor? That's what this was about? "Sleeping with me isn't honorable?"

He looked at her mouth again and she saw dark need flicker in his eyes. "Not if I know it's not what you really want."

The heat inside of her began to dissipate, allowing her to think clearly. He was right. They couldn't do this. As much as she'd enjoy a few fleeting moments of pleasure, she had to live with herself once this was over. This was her chance to make a break from these people, not tie herself to one of them. "You should leave me. I'll be fine on my own."

His nostrils flared in anger and his grip on her hand tightened. "I won't let you die, which is what would happen if I leave you alone. We're going back. You can pick someone else to escort you."

"Someone else who won't do exactly what you're doing right now?" she asked. "Is there a man there who will let me live my life in peace? Because if there is, just name him, and I'll happily go be with him."

His lips flattened, and she swore she saw a flash of something dangerous lurking in his eyes. She knew he wasn't human, but what she saw reminded her just how far away from human he really was.

"I don't want you to be with anyone else," he told her. "But you can't save me. When I touch you, it's hard to remember that."

"Then don't touch me." Even as she said the words, she hoped he would ignore them. As much as she didn't want to be part of his world, she didn't want to lose the way she felt now, with those warm strings of bubbles bursting inside of her. Feeling want, desire. She'd felt so horrible and cold for so long, and he made even the memory of that frigid terror fade.

He gave her a resigned look. "Hold still," he ordered. "I'm going to move away. Slowly."

She nodded her understanding and let her fingers loosen in his grip. He leaned back, then scooted his hips away, and then slowly, painfully, he disengaged their fingers until he made contact with only the tip of her index finger.

He pulled away and instantly went pale. A low, pained moan erupted from his chest, and his brow beaded up with sweat.

Jackie sat utterly still, biting the inside of her lip to keep from reaching for him. A metallic hint of blood hit her tongue. Her gut twisted with worry, while the warmth inside of her fizzed away until it was all gone. She hated seeing any living thing in pain, and despite her desire to have nothing to do with him, that didn't mean she wanted him to suffer.

He clutched his stomach and panted. His eyes were scrunched closed, and his powerful body trembled like he was freezing.

She gathered a blanket from the bed and tossed it over him, making sure she didn't touch even his clothing.

He looked up. His eyes were red and his skin was pale. Dark bruises hung beneath his eyes, marking his exhaustion. "I need to meditate. Recover. When I'm done, we'll go back."

"But I—"

"Do *not* argue with me right now. I'm warning you."

She'd hurt him. She hadn't meant to, but his agony was obvious. The least she could do was let him suffer in peace. She wished like hell someone would offer her the same courtesy.

Jackie nodded, picked up her phone, and shoved it into her pants pocket. The golden locket gleamed on the dingy carpet. She picked that up, too, and tucked it back into his bag. "I'll be ready to go when you are."

Iain knelt, drew his sword, and laid it in front of him.

The blade gleamed. Delicate vines made of metal wove their way around the hilt and over the cross guard, coming up to cradle the blade and hold it in place. Those vines had been worn from use, nearly gone in the places where his hands gripped the weapon. She wondered how long he'd been fighting with the sword to make that happen.

He yanked the blanket from his shoulders and tossed it onto the bed. One thick arm reached over his head and grabbed his T-shirt. He pulled it off and laid it beside him. He didn't look her way. He stayed facing away from her, but she had a nice view of his splendid back, reminding her of exactly what she was missing.

A deep groove ran down his spine, the muscles on either side of it corded and tight. His wide shoulders tapered to a slim waist, and all the muscles in between were covered in smooth, tan skin. A few bare branches of his lifemark reached over his left shoulder, and as he breathed, they seemed to sway.

His body was even more powerful than she'd imagined. He seemed to fill the room with his presence, dwarfing everything else. That warmth that he'd given her with his touch came back all on its own, lighting her up inside. A slow, liquid heat coalesced between her thighs, making her tremble.

She wanted to reach out and touch him, but that had already caused enough problems for one night. Instead, she dragged her gaze away and forced herself to think about what she needed to do next.

Her journey to find a normal life hadn't gotten her very far, but she could hardly ask Iain to do more for her. As it was, he looked like he was barely hanging on, struggling to deal with the pain she'd inadvertently caused him.

They were only a few hours away from Dabyr. She would let him take her back and find someone else — someone she would not touch. Ever.

Jackie rummaged in her suitcase for a pair of gloves and a scarf. It wasn't nearly cold enough to need them, but as soon as Iain was ready, she'd wrap herself up tight so there were no more accidents.

Once she had them ready to go, she settled down at the table by the window and opened her laptop. Joseph hadn't even hesitated when she'd asked for one. He'd had it delivered within an hour of her request. Of course he hadn't known then that she'd intended to use it to find herself a new place to live and a job.

She pulled up her résumé to work on it while she waited for Iain to finish meditating. The two-year gap in her work history was painfully obvious, glaring at her from the screen. She didn't know how she was going to explain her disappearance without sounding like a lunatic.

Her only option was to lie, which she hated doing. She'd have to invent an aunt and say that she'd left work to care for her during a prolonged illness. If anyone checked into her story, she'd be found out, but she didn't know what other choice she had. She wasn't about to claim she'd been in rehab or sick herself, for fear of not getting hired, and there was no way she could say she'd been abducted by demons and kept alive for her blood.

With a sigh of frustration, she closed the laptop and laid her head down on her folded arms.

She hadn't really thought through all the details yet, but the more she did, the more problems she ran into. Her foreclosed house was a huge black spot on her credit. What if she couldn't even find a place to live? And if she did find a home, how was she going to protect herself from monsters every time she got a paper cut?

A faint sound made her lift her head. She looked at Iain, but he was motionless except for the slow expansion of his ribs as he breathed.

She heard it again—a soft scratching sound. Coming from outside.

Fear made her freeze in place. The last time she'd left Dabyr, she'd been attacked by clawed monsters who'd tried to scratch through a car to get to her. If it hadn't been for a magical barrier Andra had erected to keep them out, she would have died that night.

The sound came again, louder this time. "Iain," she said, but it came out as little more than a shaky whisper of sound.

She heard another noise. A thump against the glass, only a foot from her elbow.

Jackie yelped and jumped from her chair, scrambling away from the glass. "Iain." His name was louder this time and filled with the same panic skittering around in her chest.

From the corner of her eye, she saw him turn his head. Then there was a flash of motion—a blur of skin and steel—as he leaped toward her.

She continued to back up as he placed himself between her and the danger.

"It's just a bird or something," she said, trying to convince herself.

"Let's find out." He jerked back the curtains and right there, not ten feet away, were two glowing green eyes set in the head of a monster.

It stood on two legs, nearly as tall as Iain. Its body was fish-belly pale, covered in random patches of black fur. Pointed teeth filled its mouth, and fluorescent yellow saliva wet the front of its body. The thing was heavily muscled, its jaw sloping down to its thick shoulders, totally forgoing the need for a neck. Each finger was tipped with a black claw at least two inches long, and it used them to scrape at the glass.

Its eyes—disturbingly human—landed on her, and a sickly green light flared within them, as if it recognized her.

"That's no bird," said Iain. "We need to get you out of here."

Fear had a tight hold on her. She'd been fighting it ever since her rescue, but her system seemed to go back to that terrified state so easily, locking up her body so that she couldn't act.

"Now, Jackie!" bellowed Iain. "Move!"

His command cut through her fear, and she scrambled toward the door, grabbing her purse and suitcase handle.

"Leave it. There's nothing in there worth your life."

She let go of the suitcase, but her purse was already strapped to her body. Besides, that's where she carried her gun, and she wasn't about to leave her only weapon behind.

He drew the curtains shut and raced across the room, grabbing a leather jacket from the top of his bag. She was already at the door, fumbling with the locks, failing to open them.

"Move your hands. I can't risk touching them right now."

Right. The pain could incapacitate him, leaving her to defend herself.

What a laughable thought that was.

She did as he asked, moving out of the way so he could open the door. A moment later, he peeked out into the hall. "It's clear. We're going to run to the exit at the end of the hall, okay? Head straight for my truck. Don't look back." He pulled the keys from his jeans pocket and dangled them. "If anything happens to me, leave without me. Don't stop driving until you're back at Dabyr."

"Nothing's going to happen to you," she said, as much for her own benefit as his.

"Take the keys. Put this jacket on. It will protect you."

"You take it. You're the one who has to stay alive to fight."

"Do what I say, and we'll both be fine. I saw only one of them. It's probably just a scout. I won't even break a sweat taking it out."

Jackie took the keys and the jacket, being careful not to touch his skin.

He gave her a satisfied nod. "Stay close."

He didn't need to tell her twice.

Murak was not going to fail his father, one of the most powerful Synestryn lords on the continent, the way his brother had. The way Zillah had. His father, Raygh, was not known for his tolerance or his mercy, so when Raygh ordered Murak to hunt down Zillah's stolen humans and bring them back, Murak jumped to obey. Two of the females were carrying Synestryn offspring, and the theft of their young could not be tolerated.

Murak drove down the narrow street, blending easily among the humans. Unlike his ancestors, he looked more human than monster, with only a few exceptions that the proper clothing hid. The cattle moving past him, sitting behind him at a stoplight, were none the wiser, completely oblivious to the fact that soon all of them would be either food or slaves.

The stink of their bodies burned his nose, but he drew deeply of the night air, seeking for some sign of a trail.

This backwater town was the closest one to where the captives had escaped. Certainly one of them had to be here, reeking of fear. And if some brave little soul wasn't afraid, the distinct scent of Synestryn blood would be seeping out of their pores.

Find them and I'll grant you all of Zillah's holdings.

That's what Murak's father had promised, and there was nothing more he wanted than to expand his domain and fill it with his offspring and enough food to stuff their bellies. Zillah's holdings were expansive, and a good start for Murak's kingdom.

He'd already dispatched his hunters, giving them the items he'd recovered from the caves. Clothing, blankets, hair—whatever he could find that still held the scent of those who'd been stolen. Between their efforts and his, it wouldn't be long before they'd reclaimed their property.

The cattle seemed to be converging on the center of town. He'd passed a school there earlier, and seen the sign outside lit up, streaming with balloons and announcing tonight's special performance. Based on the rush of traffic, a large segment of the population would be in attendance.

Perfect. He could slip in, check for escaped prisoners within the large gathering, and begin recapturing what Zillah had lost. He didn't need to find everyone, just the humans in which they'd invested precious time and blood. It took years to create a vessel for their offspring, and Zillah's mistake was going to be Murak's gain.

He entered the school, paid for his ticket, and went to the back of the auditorium. The curtains were drawn and the cattle milled around, greeting one another with smiles and conversation. No one paid any attention to him, which suited him fine.

He pulled their stench into his lungs, seeking for a hint of prey.

A young human rushed by, stirring the air.

There. Right there was the scent of the blood of his kind. Sweet and metallic.

He rose from his seat and followed the trail. It led to a young girl in the second row. She was skinny and pale, with bruises under her eyes from lack of sleep. Much of her hair had fallen out, and what was left was pulled back with a cheerful yellow bow.

Murak summoned his power and concealed himself from all those present. He moved closer to the child, seeing the bony knees protruding out from under her skirt. She was ten or twelve, perhaps, and nearly complete. Years of work and gallons of their blood had gone into her so that she could perform her duties. Another year of alterations and they'd be able to breed her.

The child began to tremble, as if she sensed his presence. She looked around and reached for the hand of her father, sitting beside her. The man wrapped his arm around her and looked at his wife with sunken eyes filled with despair.

"We should go," he said. "She's not ready to be out in a crowd yet."

The woman nodded sadly and stood, gathering her purse.

Murak moved out of the way, letting them pass. It was a simple matter to follow them home. Once the girl was alone, he'd take back what was rightfully his.

Chapter 8

Iain's body was still throbbing with the pain of losing Jackie's touch. So much that it was making him slow. He could feel the slight lag in his thought processes—only a split second, but definitely enough to make him hesitate and die in a fight.

Whatever that thing out there was, he'd never seen anything like it before. It was new, and he wasn't looking forward to finding out what surprises it had in store.

He bolted down the hallway, keeping tabs on the steady pounding of Jackie's feet behind him. She stayed close as he slammed out through the door and into the cold night air.

His truck was about two hundred feet away. There were only a few cars in the parking lot of the run-down hotel, and with any luck, the inhabitants weren't spending any time looking out of their windows.

Iain moved fast, keeping watch around them, searching for signs that there were any more Synestryn where that one had come from. The area was dark, quiet. There was little around except for a restaurant and gas station on the far side of the interstate.

He heard a noise to his left and spun around to face it. The demon was crouched next to a bush in a decorative landscaping bed. Its eyes flared bright as it spotted them, and it let out a wet, gurgling hiss. Yellow saliva cascaded from its mouth, sliding down onto its chest.

"Keep moving," said Iain. "I'll hold him off."

To her credit, she didn't waste time asking questions. She sprinted toward the truck, leaving Iain in a much better position to kill this thing without worrying about her getting hurt in the process.

Iain took a firm grip on his sword. The monster within him beat at its cage, demanding to be set free. It liked killing. It was good at it, but with Jackie so close, he couldn't risk it. He couldn't risk not being able to shove all that rage and violence back to where it belonged. It was better to stay in control. Do this with frigid efficiency of logic, rather than the searing release of anger.

He lifted his blade and moved in. The demon sprang toward him, claws extended. He ordered his body to move, but the slight lag caused by the pain made him clumsy. Instead of stepping cleanly out of the way the instant he should have, he hesitated, ducking at the last second.

One claw parted his hair as the demon passed overhead. Iain felt no pain, no sting of poison entering his system, but he couldn't take any chances with Jackie only feet away. He needed this thing dead. Now.

Iain spun around and followed the demon up, slicing a shallow cut on one of its arms. It howled in pain and then spat at Iain.

With his chest bare and no face shield or armor of any kind, Iain was a sitting duck for a poisoned attack. And the thing knew it.

He lifted his blade, letting it take the brunt of the barrage of glowing yellow demon spit. Some of it landed on Iain's arm.

He whipped his sword to discharge the poison onto the ground, and moved forward, closing the gap between them. This thing was clearly going to keep spitting from a distance if Iain let him, so he angled his body, forcing the demon to circle back toward the wall where it would be pinned.

It wasn't smart enough to figure out what Iain was doing, but that hardly mattered. The poison on his arm began to tingle, telling him that he was running out of time. It hadn't entered his bloodstream yet, but it was sinking through his skin too fast for him to do this slowly and methodically.

As soon as the angle was right, Iain leaped forward and went in for a low strike, cutting across the demon's thigh.

It screamed in pain and crumpled down to hold its leg.

To his left, a set of curtains parted, letting the light inside spill out. The humans inside couldn't see the demon from where they were, but that noise was going to bring company.

Letting humans witness a fight was a risky thing. Knowing that Synestryn existed could open them up to attack. Most humans didn't possess enough ancient blood for the demons to bother them, but those that did—the blooded humans—were at risk of being captured or killed for food.

Iain was honor-bound to protect all humans to the best of his ability, which meant ending this fight now.

While the demon was crouched, Iain moved in for the kill. Before he could cross the small distance, the beast gobbled up some of the landscaping stones and spat them at Iain.

He dodged.

"Behind you!" shouted Jackie.

Too late, Iain spun to face the new threat. Another demon charged, barreling toward him with claws extended and yellow teeth bared.

The first demon now had access to his unprotected back.

Iain maneuvered to get himself out of the vulnerable

flanked position even as he prepared to meet the demon's charge. At the last possible second, he stepped sideways, dropping down into a spinning arc. His sword slashed through the beast's face, lopping off the top of its head.

Black blood, glowing spit, and bits of brain splattered onto the wall of the hotel with a wet slap. The whole thing had taken only seconds, but in that time, the first demon had moved closer—close enough to be a real threat.

Its cheeks bulged, barely containing what it held in its mouth.

Iain moved in for the kill before it was too late. The demon drew in a huge breath and propelled soggy chunks of gravel from its mouth. Glowing yellow rock sailed toward him.

He jerked, midstride, dodging as much of the rock as he could, but some of it grazed his chest and arm. A cold burn hit his skin, and a second later, a wave of dizziness slapped him out of nowhere as the poison entered his system. He hadn't meant to lose control, but it was too late for that.

Rage detonated inside him as he realized what had happened. He let out a bellow loud enough to shake the glass and charged.

His first attack was sloppy. He was slower than normal, the pain and poison weighing down his limbs. It took him a moment to realize that he'd misjudged the distance and swiped through thin air. He stumbled, struggling to regain his balance. His vision extended, tunneling out, like he was looking backward through binoculars. Everything seemed too far away.

But he knew the demon was there, laughing at him. He just had to get in one good hit and take it down—make it scream as it died.

Iain swung blindly, cutting his way forward toward the demon, who appeared to be a tiny speck on the horizon. The thing moved, as if dodging a blow, and Iain was sure hc had to have nearly hit it.

He swiped again, and the drag on the tip of his blade told him he'd made contact with something. The demon? The building? A bush? He couldn't be sure.

Sweat trickled down his brow and into his eyes, burning them. His body began to shake, and his sword felt heavy. He forced his arms to lift it up, but the effort made him tremble.

The demon hissed in anger, and the sound got closer as he did so. Iain swung again, tracking that sound.

A cold, insidious weakness started to spread from his chest into his limbs. His muscles began to tighten, clenching down involuntarily. He didn't have much time until his body gave out, and before it did, he had to kill the demon so it couldn't touch Jackie.

Just the thought was enough to make the monster inside of him howl in rage. His blood pumped faster, sending poison careening through his veins. He was out of time. He had to finish this.

Tires squealed nearby. Jackie was leaving. She was safe.

His monster hissed at her loss, demanding that his legs move so he could go after her. She was *his*. He needed her. How dare she leave him?

Iain tried to take back control before his inner monster did something irrevocable. And then his knee buckled, and he realized that the demon's poison prevented him from doing anything.

Jackie was gone. He couldn't go after her. All he could do now was finish off the last Synestryn so she stayed safe.

The demon seemed so far away now it was merely a glowing speck of light in the darkness. Or maybe that was a landscape light. Iain could no longer be sure. He kept his sword moving, spinning and cutting so that the thing couldn't get close without taking a hit.

"Hold still," ordered Jackie, her tone imperial. She was close. Too close.

His monster cackled in victory, staking a claim on her as the spoils of battle. Iain tried to beat the beast back, but he was weak now, growing weaker by the second.

A gunshot went off, so loud it had to have been only a few feet away.

"Run, damn it!" he shouted.

The gun barked, over and over.

Iain's legs went numb, and he feared that if he took even one more step, he'd topple to the ground.

"It's dead," she said, her voice a thin strand of panic.

"I need to cut off its head. Just to be sure." He fell over, feeling nothing but the sudden stop of his body as it hit the ground.

"What's wrong?" she asked.

"Poison. Don't worry about that. Take my sword and cut off its head. If you don't, it will follow you."

Her voice was unsteady, uncertain. "I don't think I can do that."

In the distance, he heard the faintest scream of a police siren. "Cops are coming. Hurry."

"They'll see it. I need to drag it into the woods."

"Don't touch it!" If she had so much as a hangnail, she could end up just like him, blind and vulnerable.

"Someone saw us through their window. We need to go. I'm sorry, but I'm going to have to touch you."

"Leave me here. There's no time." His words slurred together.

"Shut up, you contrary bastard. I'm doing this."

Rather than waste his breath, he did what he could to help her lug his contrary ass into the truck. He wasn't sure exactly how she managed the feat. Then again, he kept fading in and out of awareness, so he wasn't sure about much of anything right now.

All he knew was that he was freezing, and being tugged into the black.

His monster screamed in rage, demanding that Iain grab her and hold her so she couldn't run away. He didn't bother wasting effort trying to fight it. His body was too weak for him to cooperate, effectively thwarting his monster's plans.

"Call for help," he mumbled. "Joseph." He could barely hear himself over the hissing rage within him.

And then suddenly, it stopped. Everything went quiet, as if she'd somehow lulled the monster to sleep.

"Hush. I'm driving with only one hand. I don't have another for a phone right now."

He vaguely wondered what she was doing with her other hand, but after a few seconds of grueling thought, he gave up the effort. The struggle to remain conscious was taking too much of a toll, sucking away his strength. But he couldn't black out and leave her alone. She'd be completely unprotected.

The cold numbness crept up his neck. "Call Joseph," he insisted, before he could no longer speak. The words were slurred, and he hoped she could understand them.

"Don't you dare die," she ordered him.

He could no longer move his mouth. He couldn't even feel it. A few seconds later, he couldn't feel anything at all.

Iain was dying.

Jackie tried not to panic. She kept reminding herself that she'd been through worse and come out alive. She could do this, too. It was just one small crisis—one she would overcome, getting Iain the help he needed before it was too late. Unfortunately, that help was going to have to come to her. She wasn't going to make it back to Dabyr in time. Iain was deteriorating too fast.

She'd passed three police cars driving on the far side of the highway since leaving the hotel, and she didn't think getting pulled over with a loaded weapon that had just been used to kill a monster would do her job prospects much good. Oh, and the unconscious, bleeding, half-naked man sprawled across the seat wouldn't help, either. She didn't think the police would accept her explanation that she needed to keep touching him so he wouldn't be in pain. She couldn't even bear to think what might happen if they pulled her away from him right now, after all he'd been through tonight.

She kept the speedometer in control, searching for a place to stop and call for help.

Iain had quit talking, which wasn't a good sign. Her hand was on his thick wrist, and she could feel his pulse beating against her fingers. That steady beat was the only reason she hadn't completely flipped out. But his pulse had slowed more with each passing minute. Another bad sign.

She saw a rest stop up ahead and took the exit. A trucker was parked on one side of the facilities, so Jackie went to a spot as far away from him as she could. She locked the doors, hoping that if any more monsters came their way, that would hold them off long enough for her to flee.

Iain's skin was frigid, so she turned up the heat as far as it would go. Being careful not to break contact with his skin, she fished her cell phone from her pocket.

He'd told her to call Joseph, but she really didn't want to hear a lecture right now. She was already dealing with too much. Her fingers scrolled through the contacts, and landed on the name of the only person she could stomach calling.

Helen answered on the first ring. "How's Iain?"

"Poisoned."

"What?" gasped Helen. "What happened?"

"Demons found us in our hotel room. Iain got poisoned. I don't know how. I didn't see it. I was running for the truck, but he said that's what happened."

"How long ago did he get poisoned?"

"Maybe five, ten minutes. It's hard to say. I'm a little freaked-out here—not really watching the clock."

Helen's tone was confident, giving Jackie a bit of relief. "I'll send help, but you need to do what you can to slow the poison."

"How?"

"Magic."

"I don't have any. I keep telling you that."

"You have to take his luceria."

Jackie closed her eyes, seeking for some reason to deny her sister's advice. "I can't do that."

"He could die, Jackie. I know you don't want that."

"Of course I don't, but this is too much to ask."

"There's no time to argue," said Helen. "It doesn't have to be permanent. All you have to do is promise him you'll wear it for a little while. Tap into his power and hold off the poison until help arrives. The Sanguinar can patch him up, good as new."

"You really think this is possible."

"I know it is. You can do this."

There really was no other choice. Iain was dying as she spoke. His pulse had slowed even more since she'd stopped the truck. "Okay. Tell me what I need to do. And then send help. I may not be able to do anything for him."

"It will all be fine. I know it will."

Jackie wished she were half as sure as her sister.

She listened to Helen's instructions, then hung up the phone. She could do this. It was only a small thing—not even as hard as most of what she'd had to do in those caves to keep the kids alive. By comparison, this was going to be a walk in the park.

Her fingers shook as she reached one hand to his throat, where the shimmering band lay close to his skin. She could feel it humming, leaping toward her as she neared.

It really was beautiful. Simple. Elegant. The slippery length felt warm. She hadn't worn a necklace since before her capture. The ugly scars around her neck made it seem silly. Why bring attention to something she wanted to hide? She used to wear them all the time, and she suffered through a momentary, ridiculous flash of mourning for what she'd lost.

Helen said she had to want it to make the luceria come off, so she closed her eyes and pretended that her throat was lovely and smooth, and that the pale iridescence of it would glow against her skin.

The luceria opened, coming loose from his neck easily. She held it for a moment, marveling over whatever magic made the thing function, feeling the slick heat of its surface as it draped between her fingers.

She just hoped that this worked, for Iain's sake.

There was no way she could put it on without both hands, and she didn't dare stop touching Iain for fear that she'd hurt him more. The only option she could think of was to tuck his hand in the waistband of her slacks, hoping the contact worked both ways.

As soon as his thick fingers were lodged at her waist, she slowly removed her hands from him. She saw no sign that there were any ill effects of her solution, and breathed a sigh of relief.

The luceria went around her neck, the ends snapping together like magnets. She opened her collar enough that it could lie close to her skin, then went on to step two—the one she dreaded the most.

She had to cut him. Helen said there was no other way. Normally, the man would cut himself, but that wasn't going to happen here. So, Jackie was left with no choice but to get the distasteful task over with as fast as possible.

She cleaned his sword with an alcohol wipe she found in the first aid kit under the seat. Cringing, she drew the sharp steel across his chest, barely nicking the skin. A few drops of blood welled up, and she used her finger to smear some across the luceria.

Now for the tricky part. Somehow, she had to get Iain to wake up and give her his vow. He'd already done it once, but Helen said she wasn't sure if it would work, so it was best not to risk messing things up.

She leaned over him and patted his cheek. "Iain. Wake up."

He let out a moan, but that's all she got.

"Iain," she said louder, adding a bit of force behind her pats against his smooth cheek. "I need you. Wake up."

His eyes fluttered open, but she could see that he wasn't aware of what was going on. His gaze slid around as if he couldn't focus and his eyes started to close again.

"Give me your vow," she ordered. "I need it. Give it to me."

He blinked a few times, confusion plain on his face. "Jackie?" Her name was barely recognizable.

"That's right. My life for yours. Say it."

"No. Too late."

She grabbed his jaw and gave it a shake. "You listen to me, mister. You're poisoned. I just cut you, which means the demons can smell your blood. If you don't give me your vow, I won't be able to help you." She swallowed hard, forcing herself to say the rest. "They'll take me again, Iain. They'll take me back to those caves. I can't let that happen."

His eyes widened. Then rage painted his features, hardening them into a snarl. "No!"

"They're coming. Give me your vow. Now, before it's too late."

His nostrils flared, and his lips twisted as he struggled to get the words out. "My life . . . yours."

Relief wrapped around her, making her sway. Now there was only one thing left: her vow to him.

She'd had little time to think about her promise with all that had happened, and her mind raced now, trying to think of exactly the right thing to say. She knew this was binding, and she didn't want to mess it up. But she also didn't want the luceria to fall off too soon—before the Sanguinar showed and he had a chance to fully heal. She wasn't sure he'd be up to another round of this. She was certain *she* wouldn't be.

Jackie pulled in a deep breath. Iain was staring at her, but his eyes were closing under their own weight. There was a warning there, but she didn't have the time or mental space to translate what it might be. He was hardly even conscious, mostly incoherent, so whatever warning he gave, she'd likely already considered it herself.

"I won't let you die, Iain. I promise to stay with you until you're as good as new." Just like Helen had said.

The luceria slid against her skin, shrinking to fit close. His eyes opened wide, and she swore she saw fear reflected in his gaze. And then she saw nothing at all, as the world dissolved and melted away.

Jackie tried to figure out what had gone wrong. She'd done everything Helen had said, but somehow, she'd been flung away from Iain, landing inside an old farmhouse.

She stood there for a long moment, trying to get her bearings. She spun around, not recognizing anything. Where was she? Where was Iain?

Lanterns lit the space, showing her she was in an old kitchen. On a small table was a single candle flickering over a simple meal. Some kind of soup steamed in the bowls, and a loaf of bread sat between them.

The back door opened and Iain walked in.

Relief settled over her, making her sag. "You're okay." But how could he be? She hadn't done anything yet.

Iain said nothing to her. His clothing was different. Old-fashioned. His hair was longer. He removed a hat and set it on a bench by the back door. He didn't even glance at her.

"Serena? I'm back," he called.

"Coming!" said a woman's voice from upstairs.

"What's going on, Iain?" asked Jackie. "Where are we?"
He said nothing, completely ignoring her.

"How did you get rid of the poison?" she asked.

The woman came down the steps and Jackie turned around. The breath left her body and the whole world seemed to grow dim by comparison.

Serena was the most beautiful woman Jackie had ever seen. She was almost ethereal, so perfect that there was no way she could be real. Her red hair fell in loose curls to her tiny waist. The dress she wore was also old-fashioned, but accentuated her curves perfectly, especially her bust, which rose up from the tight bodice. Her skin was flawless, her features feminine and elegant, and her mouth was a deep, rosy pink.

She raced forward as if Jackie wasn't even there. Jackie tried to move out of the doorway, but there was no room. She braced herself for an impact, but none came. Serena moved right through her and threw herself into Iain's waiting embrace.

Serena had passed through Jackie, as if she were some kind of ghost.

Jackie was distracted by shock for a second before she realized that this wasn't real. This was a vision. Helen had mentioned it, but Jackie had been so busy memorizing the steps to tap into Iain's magic, she hadn't really digested every last detail.

Jackie forced herself to relax. All she wanted was to get back to the real Iain and try to find a way to slow the poison. She didn't have time for visions or dreams, especially of Iain alone with a woman too beautiful to be real.

Iain pulled back from their hug, smiling down at Serena as if she were the center of his universe. And that smile made him simply gorgeous. He had a dimple in his left cheek—one Jackie had never seen before. Jealousy hit her before she had time to realize it had happened. Iain was hers now. She'd dragged his heavy body into the truck, done that stupid ceremony, and tied herself to him. How dare he go hugging another woman like that? *Smiling* at her? He'd never smiled at Jackie. Not even once. And he sure as hell had never looked at her the way he was looking at Serena. If it hadn't been so sweet, it would have been nauseating.

"Tonight?" he asked her, eagerness clear in his voice.

She nodded, grinning up at him. "Tonight. We've waited long enough, don't you think?"

"More than," he agreed, and stepped back, pulling his sword.

"Oh, no. You're not going to ruin this for me by rushing things. First dinner. You haven't eaten all day."

"Dinner can wait. I want to see you wear it now." He traced a finger over Serena's neck. "It's going to look so pretty here."

It took Jackie a minute to catch up, but she realized they were talking about Serena taking his luceria. This was all in the past. That explained the old clothes and lack of electric lighting.

Iain bowed his head and kissed her. She rose to him as if she'd been dying for a taste of him. His hands slid around her.

A sour churning started in Jackie's stomach.

Serena pressed her palms against his chest. "If we don't stop, we'll ruin all of my plans."

"*Your* plans? I've been trying to get you to do this for three years."

"You know how Mother felt about us. But I shall be worth the wait. You'll see."

He set her back down with a begrudging sigh. "I want this to be perfect for you—a night you'll always remember with fondness."

"Then sit and eat. I don't want you swooning with weakness later."

He grinned and shook his head. "I've never swooned in my life, woman."

"There's always a first time for—"

"Did you hear that?" he asked, his body going tense and alert.

"It was just the horses."

Iain lifted his blade and went to the door. "Stay inside. I'll go check."

"I'm sure it was nothing," she said, but the frown marring her smooth brow gave away her concern.

He gave Serena a long look so full of love that it nearly brought Jackie to her knees. She'd never much thought about finding true love. Her education and then her career had been more important. She'd always thought that there would be time for romance later, after she'd accomplished the things she wanted to do with her life. But now, watching this, she began to wonder if her priorities had been all wrong. Not only had she not done what she'd wanted, but she also had no one in her life to love.

"I won't risk your safety," said Iain. "Especially not while you're still vulnerable."

Serena followed him to the door, peering through the window. Jackie went to the closest window, which was on the adjacent wall. She couldn't see Iain, but what she did see was several spots of glowing green.

Fear sliced through her and she began to shake. "There are demons out there. Synestryn," she warned Serena.

Of course, Serena couldn't hear her, because Jackie wasn't really here. This was just a memory—a past event from Iain's life. It had all already happened. She couldn't do anything to change that. Could she?

Only one way to find out.

Jackie reached right through Serena to get to the doorknob. Her hand passed through the brass knob, too. Holding her breath, she stepped forward and went through the door and was standing outside.

The glowing green eyes had come closer. She could see Iain's broad back headed toward a barn. He scanned the area, but a wagon was blocking his line of sight.

Jackie raced forward to warn him. She called his name, but he couldn't hear her. He couldn't sense her presence.

Finally, Iain went past the wagon, turned, and saw them coming. Serena burst out of the back door, shouting. He saw her and started sprinting back toward her, his face a mask of anger and fear.

"Get back inside!" he yelled.

The demons broke through the brush and came at them, running on all fours. Their powerful legs ate up the distance, sending chunks of dirt and weeds up behind them.

Jackie crouched behind a tree trunk, desperately working to combat her fear.

This wasn't real. It wasn't happening. She wasn't even here.

But Iain was. He made it to the doorway just as the first demon attacked. His sword was raised, his mouth open around a vicious battle cry. He swung down, hacking at the demon's furry back.

It let out a hissing scream, and black blood splattered out from the wound. Iain kicked the monster away, sending it crashing into the next one behind it. He backed up a couple of steps into the doorway so he could take on the demons one at a time.

There were at least six of them. Their black, furry bodies melted into the dark landscape. It was only when Jackie saw their eyes that she was able to tell how many were truly there.

Iain continued to fight, lopping off the head of one demon while another leaped over its back to go for his head. He ducked just in time, but the demon went sailing though the doorway, into the little farmhouse kitchen.

Where Serena was.

Jackie went racing across the ground to warn her, but by the time she neared, it was too late. The demon was inside and Serena was facing off with it, wielding a sword of her own.

She was fast—faster even than Iain was. There was less power behind her swings and thrusts, but she kept the demon at bay while Iain worked to kill the last two outside.

In the distance, Jackie saw a new set of lights approach and heard the rumbling of something big coming closer. The lights were yellow, not green, and as the sound grew louder, she could just make out the shape of people. Some were on horseback, some were in a wagon.

They were human, and, based on the swords many of them carried, Sentinels. A woman in a pale green gown stood in the back of the wagon as it slowed. In one hand she held a globe of fire. She flung it toward the fight. White fire spilled out over the demons and Iain. It slid off his skin, leaving him untouched, but the demons screamed as their fur ignited.

Iain turned before they'd even finished falling, and charged inside to deal with the demon fighting Serena.

Jackie could see only motion—Iain's big body moving and flashes of black fur and a pale gingham skirt. She held her breath, walking closer to the house, where at least a dozen people were speaking in hurried voices.

A second later, the demon's head came flying out through the door and passed through Jackie's body. She swallowed down a wave of nausea.

Iain came out, his arm around Serena. Her face was pink from exertion, which seemed only to make her even lovelier.

"We're under attack," said a man on one of the horses.

"Where did they come from?" asked Iain.

"Everywhere. We need to take shelter here. More are on the way."

"More Synestryn or more Sentinels?"

"Both," said the woman in the green dress. "Serena,

your mother is doing what she can to slow them down so we could warn you."

"Come inside," said Serena.

"There!" shouted another man. "They're here!"

And they were. Dozens of demons broke from the tree line in the distance and began their charge.

"Inside," Iain ordered Serena. "Lock the doors and windows."

"Where are you going?" she asked.

Iain grabbed the reins of a horse and mounted it. He gave her a look of regret. "I shouldn't have waited."

"It was my decision."

"I should have changed your mind. When I get back—"

She nodded. "Yes. Now go, and don't you dare die."

Ten men formed a line and held back the advancing horde of demons. Another two stayed behind in the house, along with both women. Jackie watched the battle, unable to believe her eyes. This was the kind of thing that happened in movies, not in real life. And then one of the men fell and three slavering beasts descended on him, tearing his body into pieces. It took all of three seconds, and that's when Jackie realized that this was not make-believe. This had really happened.

Overhead, a harsh blue light streaked through the air. No one seemed to notice it—they were all too busy fighting. But Jackie saw it.

The light hit the house. She braced herself for some kind of explosion, but none came. A second later, the light bounced back up into the night sky and sprang away, as if it had been attached to a rubber band. It was dimmer as it left.

There were no screams from the house. The outline of the woman in the green dress was easily discernible on the porch. A man stood nearby, watching the far side of the house as if he expected more company.

The men fighting finished off the last of the demons

and retreated toward the house. They carried what was left of the dead man with them, their faces grim.

Jackie raced ahead, unable to look at the dismembered parts without feeling sick.

"Do you see any more?" Iain asked the man standing watch.

"Not yet," answered the woman. "But they're coming. Gilda just sent me a message that they're under attack as well. We're not alone."

Iain frowned. "Where's Serena?"

"Inside. She's safest there."

Iain pushed past them and went inside. Jackie saw him come to a dead stop. His body became unnaturally still. Then he took a slow, measured step forward and fell to his knees. A low moan of anguish vibrated out of him, getting louder as it went on. Pain echoed in his voice, quieting everyone around.

"Iain?"

Jackie knew how this ended. Serena died. Iain had already told her that much. But he hadn't expressed how much he'd loved her, or how much her death had hurt him.

She stepped through the crowd, unable to stop herself from getting close to him. She knew she couldn't comfort him, but she also couldn't simply stand there and do nothing but listen to his pain.

She saw the fiery mass of curls lying on the floor of the kitchen, next to a small puddle of fabric—the same fabric Serena had been wearing. Both the hair and the fabric had been cut cleanly away, leaving a slight singeing around the edges.

"Where is she?" asked the woman.

"Gone," said Iain, his voice tight with emotion.

"What do you mean?"

"I can't feel her anymore. There's just . . . emptiness where she used to be."

The group's faces told Jackie what that meant. Once

the shock faded, grief took over. A heavy sadness hung in the air.

"What happened to her?" asked one of the men.

"She went to fight. You know how she is," said the woman as if trying to convince herself.

"No," said Iain, rising to his feet. He tucked a lock of hair into his pocket and drew his sword. Gone were his smile and the single dimple she'd seen earlier. All that was left was a cold, dark anger that seemed to snuff the light from his eyes. "She's dead. They killed her. And now I'm going to make them pay."

This was the man she recognized—this harder, darker version of Iain. He'd been born that night—the night the woman he loved died.

Sympathy for him gathered inside her chest. He wasn't the kind of man who would want pity, but it was hard not to feel something for his loss.

She closed her eyes to block out the sight of his suffering, and when she opened them again, she was back inside the truck. Iain's hand was still tucked inside the waistband of her slacks, and he'd grown even paler.

Jackie had seen enough death for one night. She was not going to witness Iain's as well. Whatever magic she now had, it was time for her to find it and fix him. Fast.

Chapter 9

The monsters wouldn't let Beth die. She was so weak, she fluttered in and out of consciousness, sometimes waking to find herself in a different place than when she'd passed out. This time when she woke, there was a brick building towering over her. She could smell garbage nearby, as well as the oily stench of exhaust fumes.

Beth knew what was coming, but she was too tired to be afraid. She simply didn't care anymore what they did to her as long as they let her die. Maybe this time the thing that fed on her blood would take too much and end it, giving her peace.

She couldn't remember her life before the caves, before the monsters. It seemed so distant and unreal, she questioned whether it had ever existed outside of her dreams.

A clawed hand gripped her by the arm and hauled her to her feet. She didn't fight. There was no point in fighting. At first she'd tried, hoping she could get away, and later she'd tried, hoping they'd kill her. Neither had worked, and she only ended up weaker and sicker than before.

Acceptance was easier. Shut down. Go away to a quiet, still place where fear and pain could not reach her.

Your blood is the key to your escape.

The phrase had been going through her mind for a

long time now, resonating as if she should know what the creature had meant. He'd seemed genuine, though she had no idea why he'd want to help her escape when that would mean his meal ticket would vanish. He'd said other things that night, shaking her so she'd pay attention, but she'd been so weak and afraid, she hadn't been able to hold on to more than those few words.

The monsters used her for her blood. They'd also used her for other things, but her blood was the root cause of her captivity. If it hadn't been for her dirty blood, the creature growing in her belly would never have sparked to life.

She didn't know what it was she carried—human or something else—but she wanted it out.

The demon that had brought her here held her on her feet. Its face was vaguely human, but more long and angular. There were scales covering its head and reaching down around its eyes. Below that was bluish skin.

She'd seen this thing before. It was one of the demons under Zillah's command.

A screaming rush of hatred lanced through her at the mere thought of his name. It was his child she carried, and he'd nearly killed her putting it there. The violence raging inside of him could be caused only by pure evil, and if she could have one wish granted, it would be to see his eyes fixed in death, his mouth gaping open from screaming in pain.

The demon holding her up sniffed the air as though it had smelled something wrong. It pushed her down onto a stack of wooden pallets and hissed out a barely understandable, "Stay."

Beth swayed as it left. Her head spun, but that was nothing new. Being alone outside, however, was a novelty.

She looked around. It was some kind of building with several big doors for trucks. The lights on the outside had been smashed, and the pavement was cracked and caked with dead weeds. There was a high chain-link fence surrounding the area, mocking her for her inability to scale it. She could hear traffic passing by not far away, but saw no headlights.

She tried to stand. It took three tries, but she managed to get to her feet and not fall over.

The fence was only a few feet away. If she could get over it, maybe she could escape. And if she fell off, then the fall might kill her.

It was a win-win situation as far as she was concerned.

Beth staggered forward a few feet. She lost her balance and slammed down into the concrete, skinning her hands. Blood seeped from her skin, and she stared at it, knowing what it would mean.

Every time she bled, demons came running. It was like they could smell it and rushed in for a bite.

She was too weak to fight them off. It was easier just to fall to her side and let them take what they wanted.

The pavement was cold against her cheek. Her matted hair fell across her eyes, blocking out her sight. She didn't have the strength to push the grimy strands away, and if she did, she wouldn't like what she saw coming for her.

Beth waited for the attack, for the searing pain of teeth digging into her flesh. When the seconds passed and no demons came, she became confused.

The sound of a fight erupted not far away. She gathered her strength enough to lift her head, and saw the demon that had brought her here fighting a man. A gleam of metal flashed between them, but in the deep shadows, that's all she could see.

If ever there was a chance for her to escape, this was it.

Beth forced herself to crawl on her hands and knees toward the fence. It seemed impossibly far away, but she had to try.

She didn't know if she'd been brought here to feed

the man and something had gone wrong, or if he'd simply stumbled upon them, but she wasn't going to wait around to find out.

The grunts and the ringing of metal continued to sound behind her. She reached the fence and gripped the cold metal, pulling herself up.

Her muscles trembled with the effort of simply standing. She had no idea how she was going to climb up all eight feet.

Beth shoved her bare foot into an opening and pushed her body up with everything she had. Sweat broke out on her skin, chilling her. The metal bit into her flesh, but pain was nothing new. She could take the pain as long as her body didn't give out.

She rose a few inches, found another foothold, and did it again. After what seemed like an hour, she looked down. She was less than two feet off the ground, with so much more to go, she wanted to give up.

The sounds of fighting stopped suddenly, and she cast a quick glance over her shoulder. The demon was crouched over the man, drinking his blood.

A futile sense of loss filled her. The man wouldn't live. Unless he was special like the other men the demons kept for blood, he'd be used up and thrown away.

She couldn't save him. All she could do was try to save herself.

Her fingers slipped on the wire, making her yelp. She barely caught herself before she fell. A small bit of skin had been ripped away in the slip, making her finger slick with blood.

Footsteps sounded behind her, too fast to be human. She looked and saw the demon headed straight for her, its eyes glowing an angry green, its teeth coated in the man's blood.

Fear gave her a burst of strength. She scrambled up. Her hand settled on the top bar, and then her body was

ripped away from the fence as the demon jerked her
down.

She was crushed under the weight of failure. The air
was squeezed from her lungs. Spots formed in her vision,
and the world went sideways. She could see the man on
the ground, lying in the shadows. The gleam of his
leather coat shifted, as if he'd moved.

Not that it mattered. He was getting farther and farther away with every passing second as the demon
sprinted, carrying her.

She didn't know what her punishment would be for
trying to escape, but it didn't really matter. They couldn't
do anything else to hurt her now. She was drifting off
into her quiet place where no pain or fear could reach
her. With any luck, she'd stay there until they killed
her.

Ronan woke up, wondering why he was still alive. The
demon had been guzzling down his blood so fast Ronan
was certain it had intended to drain him dry.

He closed his wounds and gathered up the remnants
of poison in his bloodstream from the demon's saliva,
forced it out through his own saliva glands, and spat it
onto the ground.

Hunger roared inside of him, but that he could handle. There was something more important here. Something vital his spinning head couldn't seem to recall.

Blood. Powerful blood. He'd smelled it before—a
faint hint of it in the air. That's why he'd come. He could
still smell it now, though not as strongly as before.

He pushed to his feet, gathering up his sword from
the pavement. He'd only gotten in one good hit on that
demon, and its scales had protected it completely. The
fact that he'd gone into combat weak and starving hadn't
done his fighting technique much good.

Still, he couldn't simply walk away and leave the

woman in the hands of that demon without doing something.

The scent of her blood made his hunger that much worse. He swore he could almost taste her in the air.

His nose drew him to the fence she'd been climbing. There, clinging to the cold metal, were small smears of her blood. He touched it with his finger and brought it to his tongue.

Power lingered in that small taste, but along with it was the taint of demon blood, and something else he knew but couldn't place.

Ronan spat the tainted blood from his mouth and headed toward his van.

Headlights bobbed as another vehicle pulled in through the open gate. Ronan's first thought was that whoever was there might be blooded and able to ease his hunger. His second thought was that it could be human security coming to take him to jail for trespassing. As weak as he was, he wasn't sure he could fight off any attempts to capture him.

Ronan stumbled toward his van, holding his aching ribs. Before he'd made it the whole distance, a man got out of the other car and headed toward him in a rush.

Headlights hit the side of his face, and Ronan instantly recognized him as a fellow Sanguinar. "Connal. What are you doing here?"

There was a flicker of hesitation before he answered. "I should be asking you that. What happened?"

"I smelled blood. It led me here."

"Me, too. Here, let me help you." Connal shoved his shoulder under Ronan's arm and helped him to his van.

"There was a woman here. I think she was the bait in some kind of trap," said Ronan.

"I'm sure you're right. You must be more cautious in the future."

Ronan slumped into his seat. "I need blood."

Connal took a sudden step back. "I'm sorry, brother. I can't help you. I'm too weak."

He didn't look weak, but Ronan said nothing, simply nodded his understanding. "Go. I'll be fine."

"I could drive you somewhere, perhaps to one of the Gerai."

Ronan shook his head, declining the offer. He had too much to think about, and Connal had not yet learned the value of silence.

"The woman is gone, then?" he asked.

"Carried away by a demon. It was moving too fast to track."

Bitter regret pinched Connal's mouth. "I'll be on my way. Unless you have some other need of me?"

"No. Go. Thank you for stopping."

Connal turned and left, hurrying back to his vehicle as if demons were snapping at his heels.

Ronan didn't have time to puzzle out why Connal was in such a hurry. He needed to find this woman, but first, he needed to hunt and regain his strength. There was a nightclub not far from here that he frequented. Several blooded women went there regularly, and each one of them was more than willing to spend a bit of time alone with him. He took as much blood as was safe, and left them with memories of an incredible sexual encounter. The symbiotic relationship worked for both sides, and even if it hadn't, Ronan was desperate.

As he got behind the wheel, he realized what it was about her blood he couldn't put his finger on. There was an extra spark of power lingering within her, hiding beneath the Synestryn taint. Not only was she blooded, but she was pregnant, and the child she carried was also blooded. Whoever she was, she was capable of carrying a Synestryn child.

She had to be found. Immediately. And if he couldn't get her out of the hands of the demons, then he had to find a way to kill her before her offspring was full-term.

Jackie had no idea what she was doing, but she was smart. She could figure out how to tap into whatever magic Iain housed and use it to save him. Her sisters and the other women like them did it all the time. How hard could it possibly be?

She closed her eyes and focused on the luceria around her throat—the link to the power inside of Iain. Several of the scars around her neck were numb, due to severed nerve endings, but she had enough feeling to sense the necklace there, close to her skin. It vibrated, faster than Iain's pulse, but in time with it. It was warm, and seemed to be heating more with each passing second.

The vibrations sped, and a tingling formed along the inside of Jackie's veins. There was a thrumming in her chest, and a resonant kind of energy hovering all around her. It sparked along her skin, especially where Iain's fingers grazed her stomach.

She let the tingles enter her, gathering them up into a bundle. That bundle grew until it filled her, spilling out so that she was sure the trucker across the way could see it. Bright, throbbing heat beat against the air and shook the windows. The power continued to swell, but did nothing else. She didn't know how to make it do anything.

"Stop the poison," she ordered it, but nothing happened. Speaking out loud did no good.

The power started to become uncomfortable as it grew, bouncing around her insides until it was sparking off bones and organs. She tried to stop it, but that did nothing to slow the increasing strain she was feeling. More energy filtered into her through the luceria, and she could find no way to turn off the flow.

The bench seat beneath them trembled, and she heard change rattling in a cup holder. The keys dangling from the ignition jangled. Her hair stood on end, and there was a faint crackling of static electricity in the air.

If she didn't stop this soon, she was going to end up killing both of them.

She put her hands on Iain's naked chest and tried to visualize what she wanted to happen. Poison was just a chemical—a molecule of stuff in his body that didn't belong. All she had to do was find it, gather it up, and eject it out of some orifice or other.

No sweat. She could do that. It wasn't even all that complicated.

At least that's what she kept telling herself as she scanned his body for some way to find the poison.

A muscle in his chest twitched violently. She opened her eyes. The sight of her fingers splayed across something as beautiful as his bare body shocked her. The tree on his chest was so lifelike, she was sure she could feel the texture of the bark scratching her fingers. Heavy slabs of muscles layered his ribs, but his skin was too pale, and cold to the touch.

Three scratches raked across his shoulder, and they were red and puffy as if infected. He was no longer bleeding, but along those wounds were glowing smears of yellow.

Yellow, like the spit dripping from the demon's mouth. That was it. That was the poison.

Now Jackie knew what to look for, so she closed her eyes again and sent the power growing within her back into him, to scour his bloodstream for this glowing yellow invader.

She could feel something happening—some kind of shift in the hum of the power vibrating through her. It had a purpose now, and it arrowed in on that purpose, eager to do her bidding. In her mind, she could see glistening specks of energy scouring his veins, gathering up every glowing bit of poison it could find.

Beneath her grip, Iain shifted, his powerful body

arching under her hands. He sucked in a deep breath, letting it out in a hiss of pain.

The magical scrubbing bubbles had accumulated quite a bit of the poison now, and she had to send it somewhere. She really didn't want to make him puke for fear he'd choke on his own vomit, and she didn't think he'd thank her for using the other obvious exit. Instead, she guided the poison toward the cut she'd recently given him, forcing it to seep out through his capillaries until it was pooling on his skin.

Iain groaned and started to move beneath her. If he didn't hold still, the poison was going to go everywhere. She didn't know if it could be reabsorbed by his skin or not, but she wasn't about to find out the hard way.

She had nothing to wipe away the poison, so she stripped out of the leather jacket he'd given her, then her suit jacket, and used that to clean off the glowing demon spit.

Iain grabbed her wrist and his eyes popped open. His gaze went straight to the luceria around her throat, staring at it for several long seconds. He wore the strangest expression on his face—one of both reverence and regret. It wasn't exactly what she'd expected from a man whose life she'd just saved.

Then again, he'd nearly died, so he got a pass.

His fingers slid from her waistband, grazing her abdomen. She shivered at the touch, but tried to hide her wayward reaction.

He gathered the fabric of her jacket in his fist, pulling it from her grasp. Then he sat up and finished cleaning away the poison, wiping more from his bare arm. He opened the door and tossed the jacket on the ground.

She thought about complaining for a split second before she realized that she really didn't want to wear that jacket ever again, no matter how many times it was drycleaned.

When he turned back to face her, his black gaze was

steely, but there was a stark bleakness in his expression she didn't understand. "What did you do?" he asked her, as if she'd done something wrong.

Indignation made her straighten her spine. "I got rid of the poison that was killing you. You're welcome, by the way."

His eyes closed in regret before he regained control of his expression. "You think I'm going to thank you? Do you have any idea of what you've done?"

Now she was starting to worry. All this magic stuff was new to her. What if she'd done something wrong or broken some secret rule she didn't know about? "I don't understand. I did what Helen told me to do—what I thought you'd want me to do."

"You tricked me into bonding with you."

"Tricked you? No, I didn't."

"I was delirious. I thought we were under attack."

"We probably will be. I had to cut you. They can smell your blood, right?"

He gave her a grim nod, then scanned the surrounding area. "Maybe there's some way to take it back."

"Take what back?"

"Your vow. I heard what you said. I tried to stop you, but it was too late."

That was what was bothering him? "I'm sorry, Iain, but I don't know you well enough to promise anything even resembling permanence. I know that's what you men expect, and I know that's how it ended up for my sisters and the others, but that's just not how it's going to be with me. I have other plans."

His gaze settled on the luceria again, as if he couldn't keep his eyes away from the sight. "Then you should have spoken more carefully."

"What do you mean? I only promised to stay with you until you were better."

"No, until I was *good as new*. That's what you said. Those words. I'm *better* now, and yet my luceria remains around your throat." He reached out, tracing the necklace with his thick finger. His warmth sank through the band and into her skin, radiating out through her body. Her eyelids fluttered shut, and she had to stifle a groan of pleasure. Even through the barrier of the luceria, his touch still had the power to make her knees wobble with delight. It wasn't right. It wasn't what she wanted, but she couldn't help herself.

She forced her eyes open so he wouldn't know her secret shame. The look on his face was one of awe and regret.

Jackie thought back, reviewing her words. He was right. *Good as new.* That's exactly what she'd said.

"It's not a problem," she said, forcing false cheer into her tone to ward off the worry that was creeping in. "We'll just fix whatever else is wrong with you and it will all be fine." She hoped. "So what is the problem? Did I miss some of the poison? If not, it won't take long for those scratches on your chest to heal, right?"

His black eyes darted to the bench seat of the truck, making him look guilty as hell. "What's wrong with me is not something you can fix. No one can."

Understanding dawned and with it came a heavy dose of dread. It was his broken heart that was the problem, not his physical body. Losing Serena had hurt him deeply. He'd loved her, and now she was dead. Jackie couldn't expect him to be okay.

"You'll find someone else you can love again," she told him, her voice gentle. The last thing she wanted was for him to get all defensive and fight her every step of the way. If she had to find him a new girlfriend to free herself from this bond, then that's what she'd do. He wasn't exactly a cuddly guy, but he was hot as hell, built like a woman's favorite daydream. She could work with that—find some willing woman. Play matchmaker.

The idea of Iain with another woman grated against her, making her angry. It was ridiculous for her to suffer even a moment of jealousy, but she was too practical to lie to herself and pretend it hadn't happened. Twice now.

Iain's jaw clenched in frustration. "You don't get it, do you? This isn't a bit of heartache I'm dealing with."

"Then tell me. What's the problem?"

"It doesn't matter," he said. "There's nothing you can do."

Chapter 10

Iain struggled to keep control over his raging emotions. There were too many to count, too many to distinguish. He wanted to laugh and scream at the same time. He wanted to weep for all that he'd lost, and to sing with joy for the chance he'd been given to live the life he was supposed to have had. He wanted to strip Jackie naked so he could take her hard and fast, tying them together even closer, and he wanted to gather her up and hold her tight, where no harm could ever come to her. But mostly, he wanted to kill.

His pain was gone—taken away by Jackie—but rage pounded at him, demanding release. The monster screeched inside his skull, throwing itself at his thoughts until they were so jumbled he couldn't make sense of any of them. His entire body was clenched, dying for a fight, but the only one here was Jackie.

She'd bonded herself to him. He'd let it happen. Sure, he'd been incoherent at the time, but that was no excuse.

Good as new.

His soul was dead. He was never going to be good as new again.

He couldn't tell her. The shame went too deep. It was all he could do not to throw back his head and roar at the world for what had been stolen from him.

His monster was more powerful than ever. He'd been

so careful to keep it contained for so long, but it had seen Jackie now, and it wanted her. Iain could feel it stretching its wings and extending its claws, testing its cage. He had to get away from her before he did something violent and permanent.

Iain reached for the door, but Jackie's hands curled around his arm, stopping him. The feel of her slender fingers against his bare skin was nearly more than he could take. She was soft, warm, so vulnerable.

He turned to her to tell her to let go, that it wasn't safe to touch him. Before he could even open his mouth, the rage screaming inside of him quieted, as if eager to hear her speak.

She was beautiful. He hadn't really noticed it before. But he definitely saw it now. Her eyes were a soft, pale gray, and huge with concern. Her full lips were parted, and he got the strongest urge to run his finger over them and see if they could possibly be as soft as they looked. His luceria gleamed at her throat, filling him with a sense of pride and utter *rightness*. It didn't matter how big a mistake this was, or how much he knew she'd come to resent their union. For now, he felt a peace he hadn't known since he'd held baby Samson in his arms.

She was a gift, and somehow he was going to have to find a way to let her go.

She pulled in a breath, which pressed her breasts against her modest button-up shirt. His gaze darted down. He was obvious. He hadn't even tried to be anything else. As he watched, her nipples hardened beneath the thin fabric, making his mouth water.

She wanted him, too. He'd seen desire darken her eyes before, just as it was doing now. Her breathing sped, and a flush of pink swept over her cheeks.

He hadn't had a woman in a very long time. He hadn't even thought about sex until she came along.

His cock swelled against his jeans, aching with need. A sweat broke out along his spine and his body heated in a rush. The scent of her skin filled the cab of the truck, making his head spin. He needed more of her.

Iain leaned toward her, intending to nuzzle her neck and breathe her in. As soon as his path became obvious, she went stiff and froze.

"What are you doing?" she asked, her voice wavering with fear.

He looked at her face, seeing barely controlled terror hovering in her gray eyes. Her hand flattened to her throat in an unconscious gesture of self-defense. The fine trembling of her fingers made him want to crush whatever had scared her.

And then he saw the scars lining her neck and realized that he'd been the one to frighten her.

She'd been fed from for two years. Her scars attested to that. He could only imagine how his approach had looked to her.

He had to go. Now. While his emotions were quiet enough he could think and remember his honor.

"Leaving." Even that one simple word was hard to form. His jaw was clenched tight, his throat constricted around a scream he refused to let pass.

"You're leaving me here? Alone? I thought that was a big no-no. Helen is sending help, but I don't know how long it will take them to reach us."

Her mouth was so fucking pretty. He watched it move, reached up to touch it. If only he could kiss her once, he knew it would calm his raging emotions. He couldn't be expected to sit this close to her and not react. Not now, when she'd chosen to tie herself to him.

His finger slid over her bottom lip. It was smooth and incredibly soft. He could feel the slightest trembling beneath his fingertip, but she didn't pull away. Instead, her pupils grew huge and she licked her lips, sweeping her tongue across his finger in a hot caress.

He had to taste her, kiss her. Just once before the storm of anger came raging back, before his monster began howling again. He couldn't trust himself then. It was too dangerous. But now, in this precious moment, he was more man than monster, and that man wanted just one taste.

Iain leaned forward, closing the space between them. Her breathing sped, and he could see her pulse beating hard and fast in her throat.

He moved slowly, not wanting to scare her.

"Wh-what are you doing?" she whispered.

He didn't trust words. He'd say the wrong thing and ruin this chance to find out if she tasted as sweet as she looked.

Iain threaded his fingers through her hair, cradling the back of her head. His body shifted closer to her, until he could feel the heat of her knee touching his thigh. He leaned down and covered her parted lips with his own.

Jackie made a small sound of surprise, followed by a sigh of pleasure, which he greedily drank down. He'd meant to pull back after one quick kiss, but he couldn't. He wasn't that strong.

Her mouth molded to his, and he deepened the kiss, plunging his tongue past her lips. Her hands gripped his shoulders, and she leaned toward him, eager for more.

Iain lifted her to straddle his lap, and then let his hands move up from her narrow waist to pull her fully along his body. He felt her nipples harden against his bare chest, and cursed the fabric of her shirt for getting in the way.

She made sweet, needy noises as she kissed him back, tangling her tongue with his. She was like hot honey flowing over him, heating his skin. Her mound grazed his erection, sending a shock of lightning up his spine. She fit against him just right, but there were too damn many clothes in the way. If he didn't get her naked and drive his cock into her, it might actually kill him.

His hand moved to her collar to work the top button free. She went stiff in his arms, lurching back.

"No. I can't," she said. But her skin was flushed and her mouth was red and puffy from his kiss.

"You want this as much as I do," said Iain, his voice sounding barely human. His monster was waking, stretching its wings.

She swallowed and looked away, guilt and regret tightening her features.

How dare she deny him after what she'd done? She was the one who'd forced the union. Not him.

She began pulling her fingers from his bare arm, but he slapped his palm over them, holding her in place. He didn't want her to stop touching him yet.

She glanced down, then back up until she was looking him right in the eye. Her words came out precise and sharp. "Let. Me. Go."

Possessiveness washed through him, bringing with it another barrage of feral rage. The monster woke, ravenous and angry. She was his. She'd tied herself to him and she deserved whatever she got.

Wait. That wasn't right. A niggling of doubt wormed its way into his thoughts. He was supposed to protect and cherish her, not push her to do things that were against her will. Wasn't he?

There was too much going on inside of him. He couldn't sort it out. He couldn't figure out the difference between what he wanted to do and what he was supposed to do. And the monster would not shut the fuck up and give him a minute to think. It pounded at him, demanding to be set free. Everything was too jumbled and confused for him to have any hope of sorting it out.

"I need to go," he told her, his voice shaking with emotion. If she wasn't nearby, he couldn't hurt her. It was the only way he could think to protect her.

"You're sick. I can't leave you alone, but we can't do . . . *that* anymore, either."

"I'm fine." That was such a huge lie. He was being

crushed from the inside by the need to touch her again. "I just need to get out and clear my head."

Before she could stop him, he grabbed his sword from the floorboard, tumbled out of the truck, and slammed the door shut behind him. He walked a few feet away before the cold hit his bare chest.

It didn't matter. Chilly air wasn't going to kill him. But if he did anything to hurt Jackie, he'd kill himself.

He sucked in huge breaths of cold air and kept his back to her. He couldn't see any Synestryn, but that didn't mean they weren't there. Even though the traces of blood he'd wiped away were small, that's all it took.

Part of him wished they'd come. He wanted to fight, to kill. He needed to vent some of this rage before he did something horrible.

Iain paced like a caged animal. How could he have let this happen? She was supposed to have chosen someone else. Saved someone else.

He heard the truck door open and close again, but he didn't dare look at her. He kept his eyes on the trees in the distance, hoping she'd take the hint and go away.

"Are you okay?" she asked.

He could feel her presence against his back, like sunlight glowing on his skin. "You should go back to Dabyr."

"And leave you here? I don't think so. Get back in the truck. You're going to freeze to death out here."

He was still burning inside from that kiss, but he heard the shiver in her voice and was powerless to control his reaction. His leather jacket was on the seat. He went back and retrieved it, draping it over her shoulders, being careful not to touch her. If he felt the smooth heat of her skin, he might forget what was real and what wasn't.

She looked small and vulnerable, huddled in on herself with his jacket swallowing her up. It made him want to bare his teeth and growl at the world in warning to stay away from her.

"I think you should be the one wearing this, not me," she said.

He didn't trust himself to speak. He stared at her for a long time, watching the wind whip her dark hair around her face. Seeing her eased him somehow, quieting some of the chaos roiling inside him. He could have stared at her all night, but they were exposed out here. He was no longer bleeding, but there were traces of his blood on her jacket. It wouldn't be long before one of the demons picked up on the scent.

He grabbed the suit jacket, tossed it into a metal trash bin near the rest-stop bathrooms, and lit it on fire with a blowtorch he had stashed in the back of his truck. Hopefully that would keep the demons from coming here once they were gone. There were no guarantees, but it was the best he could do, given the situation.

It was time to get Jackie back home. He had never before trusted anyone enough to tell them about his soulless state, but he was going to have to now. He needed help figuring out how to get her out of the mess she'd inadvertently stepped in, and now that Gilda and Angus were dead, he could think of only one person who might have some answers.

"Time to go," he said.

Iain helped Jackie into the truck, and then slid in behind the wheel. He hit the highway, plowing through the miles at a breakneck pace. Jackie was silent beside him, splitting her attention between what was in front of them and what was behind. He could feel her anxiousness sliding through their newborn link.

He reveled in the connection even as he cursed it. This was how it was supposed to be. Being tied to her fulfilled his purpose in life. It was such a feeling of completion, it was hard to remember that it was utterly wrong for her—a depressing mix of useless and dangerous. And yet he couldn't deny the power of her gift to him. His pain was gone. Not all of it, but most of it had vanished when she'd taken his luceria and used his power to drive out the poison. The pressure that had built inside him had abated, leaving him feeling . . . light. After all those decades of agony, he was finally free. It didn't matter that it wouldn't last long. He soaked up the respite she'd given him, letting himself revel in it.

Iain hadn't felt true joy in a long, long time, but he remembered it now. It felt a lot like this, and he had Jackie to thank for restoring some of what had been lost to him. The restoration was temporary, so he was determined to enjoy it while it lasted. Once he went back to the way things had been, he might not even remember how he felt now.

As soon as he could, he took an exit to hit the back roads. The chances of getting pulled over by highway patrol were a lot slimmer out here, and if he had to stop and fight Synestryn, there were fewer people to see it happen, or to get in the way.

"Do you see anything?" she asked, her voice trembling with fear.

He hated it that she was afraid, and wished he could do something to take it away.

The thought hit him hard, triggering a memory of a dream—one he'd had while poisoned. Jackie had been afraid. Cold and desperate. Now that he was awake, he realized what that dream had been. It was the vision the luceria had chosen to share with him, but now it was hard to remember, with only bits and pieces of it flickering through his mind.

Jackie had been a prisoner in a cave, huddling together with a little girl for warmth. She was scared out of her mind and weak from the last round of feedings. Zillah had nearly drained her dry before tossing her back in her cell. Her arms and legs were cold and numb. She was shivering, and yet her thoughts were centered around the child next to her and how she was going to protect her.

That had been during the first few days of her captivity. How she'd endured another two years was beyond Iain. How she'd stayed sane was even more of a mystery.

But she had, and now she was here, bonded to him in a way she didn't understand. She hadn't meant for it to be permanent. She'd meant only to save his life.

How was he going to tell her that she was now tied irrevocably to a man with no soul?

She frowned and glanced at him. "Are you in my head? Reading my thoughts?"

He tamped down on the rush of fury her question caused. She'd said it like he had no right to connect with her in that way, as if the very concept disgusted her.

"No," he clipped out.

Iain had to get hold of himself and his raging emotions. He needed to find that blissful numbness he'd had for so long. It was simply a matter of discipline. All he had to do was exactly as he instructed the members of the Band of the Barren to do: pretend he was honorable as he'd once been. Pretend that the feelings battering him did not exist.

"I thought I heard something." She shook her head in confusion. "I'm just paranoid. Drake and Helen are always carrying on silent conversations with each other. She claims she likes having him in her head, but my brain has a very brightly lit *keep out* sign, okay?"

Iain nodded and took control of his wayward thoughts, just in case they were loud enough to leak through to Jackie. He didn't want her in his head, either, finding out what was wrong with him. At least not yet. Not until he had time to think and plan a way to free her. Right now the only way he knew to break their bond ended badly for him.

He wasn't ready to die yet. His brothers still needed him.

"Where are we going?" she asked.

"Dabyr."

"This isn't the way we came."

"I'm taking a back way."

Her head thumped back against the seat in frustration. "I'm never going to get out of there, am I?"

The misery he heard in her voice made him ache. The need to reassure her bore down on him, and he had to grip the steering wheel hard to keep himself from reaching for her. She wouldn't welcome his touch. She'd made that clear earlier. "You will. Just not today."

The temperature inside the truck had risen, thanks to a constant pouring of heat from the vents. Jackie stripped off his jacket and laid it on the seat between them. He knew the next time he wore it, he'd be able to smell her scent clinging to the lining. He looked forward to the intimacy as much as he dreaded it.

"I don't belong there, you know. I belong in my old world. It's the only place that makes sense."

"I know you think you don't belong with us, but you're wrong. You can't see it now, but one day you will be a fierce warrior."

She snorted as if she found the idea ridiculous.

"Helen is. Why would you be any less than your sister?"

"How is living my life, running a manufacturing facility, somehow less? What I do is important. I give people jobs and make sure they're safe while doing them. I keep the peace and settle disputes. Efficiency is up, accidents are down, and I make a shitload of money for my company, so everyone gets a nice, fat bonus."

"You *did*," he felt compelled to remind her. "You don't do that anymore."

She rubbed her temples. "Yeah. I did. And now I sit around a lot, being afraid to leave my room. I've fallen a long way down, Iain."

He loved the sound of his name on her tongue. It sent a thrill racing through him, making him eager to hear it again. Only next time, he wished there to be less regret in her tone and more joy. Or desire. He'd like that even more. "You're going to save lives now. Just like you did when you were held captive."

In his peripheral vision, he saw her body stiffen. "How did you know about that?"

"The luceria showed me."

"You had a vision?"

"I have memories of one, like it was a dream." Even as he spoke, more pieces of his vision became visible, like he was seeing something between shifting leaves on a tree. "You?"

She hesitated, and he could see her watching him from the corner of his eye. He wanted to look at her so he could better gauge her emotions, but he didn't dare take his focus off the pitted gravel road as fast as he was driving.

"I saw her," she finally said.

"Who?"

"The woman who broke your heart when she died."

Serena. Grief swept through him, leaving him cold and shaking. He hadn't mourned for her for a long time, and now that pain was back. Bleak, frigid grief pressed down on him, making his tone harsh. "I don't want to talk about her. Drop it."

Jackie fell silent, but he swore he could feel her curiosity sliding between them, through the luceria. It was mixed with a healthy serving of guilt, likely because he'd let his emotions come through in his tone.

Iain gritted his teeth in frustration. He was going to have to relearn how to control himself. It had been much easier to do when he'd been numb. He wasn't sure how he was going to find the self-control, but for Jackie, he'd try. That's what a man with honor would do.

"Thank you, by the way," he said, referring to her earlier statement. "For saving me."

She shrugged and continued to stare out the side window. "Anyone would have done the same thing."

She was wrong about that, but he didn't see the point in arguing. Jackie helped others, no matter the cost to herself. He could see that now as more snippets of his vision began to reveal themselves. Each one of them showed him another time that she'd taken care of a woman or child during her captivity, giving others her food, and even a precious blanket she'd managed to steal. She'd fought for them, begging snarling demons for water and scraps of garbage, bartering her own blood for their favors.

She was a noble, selfless woman—one who did not deserve to be tied to a soulless monster.

Iain had to find a way to break their union. She couldn't stay with him. It would destroy her once she found out that he was without a soul, destined to be sent to the Slayers to die if anyone learned the truth. She was far too precious to risk, and no matter how much she gave up, she couldn't save what was already lost.

That's what the luceria had been trying to tell him with the visions. If he didn't find a way to free her, she'd destroy herself trying to save him. He couldn't let that happen. No matter what it cost him.

There was a blur of motion from his right. He tried to slow and swerve to avoid it, but it was too late. The blur hit the hood of his truck and slammed into the window, cracking it.

At first he thought it was a deer. Then he saw the glow of its eerie green eyes. Synestryn eyes.

It clung to the hood of his truck. Its wide jaws were filled with pointed teeth, and at the end of its long limbs were thick talons that were dug into the metal. It was the same type of demon that had found them at the hotel. In fact, judging by the ragged patches of newly scarred, fur-less skin, this was the same creature Jackie had shot re-peatedly.

The demon shifted its grip, crawling closer to Jackie. Glowing yellow saliva dripped from its mouth and

smeared over the windshield, making it harder for Iain
to see. It scrambled closer, sliding around the hood as
Iain braked to a jarring halt. Its claws shredded the hood
with its hind legs while it began scratching at the spider-
webbed glass with its front claws.

Beside him, Jackie let out a single yelp, then fell silent. He could feel her fear beating at him through the
luceria, demanding that he remove the threat. To her
credit, she didn't lose her head. Instead, she reached
for her purse and the gun he knew she had stashed inside.

The monster inside of him roared for freedom, needing to kill. He tightened his control over it, fearing what
might happen if he let go in such a confined space. Jackie
was too close.

"You can't kill it with that," said Iain. "Stay here. I'll
be right back."

Iain slid the armored jacket on, and then jumped out
of the truck to lure the demon away.

The need to kill rose easily to the surface as he gave
the monster within him a bit of freedom. He felt no fear
of his own, only the distant screaming of Jackie's, held in
tight.

As soon as Iain was free of the protection of the
truck, the demon lunged for him, jaws gaping. A feral
light of recognition shone in its eyes, as if it knew who
Iain was.

Iain's sword was free and gliding in a smooth arc before the thing had time to land. His blade sliced across
one of the demon's arms, making it howl in pain and
fury. Black blood arced over the gravel road, sizzling as
it hit.

The demon fell back a few feet. It scooped up a handful of rock from the roadway and shoved it in its mouth.

Like hell he was letting that happen again.

Poisoned gravel flew at his unprotected face. Iain
dove under it, tucking as he rolled over the ground.

"There's another one!" shouted Jackie, from a few yards away.

The warning registered, and he took a split second to assess the threat. Another of these demons was loping across the ground on all fours, racing toward them. It was far enough away he still had six or eight seconds—not enough time to do this without help.

He had no choice. Jackie's life was on the line. As much as he hated letting her see this side of himself, it was better than letting her die.

Iain took a deep breath, begged silently for forgiveness, and then let go of his control, freeing his monster. It broke out, roaring in defiance, giving his body strength and speed. Moving on raw instinct and rage, he struck the demon, severing one of its legs. Before it had finished crumpling to the ground, his blade slammed down, lopping off the thing's head.

He turned to take out the next demon only to find that it was pinned to the ground, snarling and clawing at a dome of faint, watery light. Sparks spewed out from where its claws struck, but it couldn't free itself.

Jackie. She'd done this.

He stalked to the demon and struck it with his sword. The blow skittered off the light, vibrating up his arms.

His monster hissed in outrage. This was his kill and she was keeping him from it.

"Let it go," he snarled at her, barely able to form words.

The light flickered and died and Iain made quick work of the beast lying prone before him.

He scanned the area for more, his body shaking with the need for violence. Ragged breaths sawed in and out of his lungs, and his skin felt like it was on fire. He needed to kill again—to drive his blade into another creature and watch it twitch there until it died.

He was losing control. The monster was taking over, breaking free of the leash he'd tried to keep around it.

"Iain?" came Jackie's voice.

The monster spotted her standing less than ten feet away. She was so fucking pretty with her hair whipped about her face by the wind, and her gray eyes luminous with concern. Her nipples were puckered beneath the thin shirt she wore, and he wanted to strip it from her so he could see them, feel them against his tongue.

He took a step toward her with the intention of doing just that when he realized that he was no longer in control. The beast inside of him had protected her and now it wanted payment in return.

Iain couldn't let that happen. He regained enough control to close his eyes, shutting out the tempting sight of her so close. The monster threw its head back and let out an animalistic howl of frustration.

"Are you okay?" asked Jackie.

He could hear that she was closer now. Her tentative footsteps crunched in the gravel, drawing her closer to danger.

Iain turned and forced his legs to move, to put more distance between them. It did no good. She continued to draw nearer, ignorant of the threat he now posed.

"Stop." He mangled the word, but her footsteps ceased.

He could smell her on the wind—a light, tempting fragrance of warm woman mixed with a hint of spring.

Her hand settled on his shoulder. The beast grinned in victory and began to reach for her. Iain couldn't let her be subjected to what would come next. She'd end up on the cold, rocky ground, raped and bleeding.

Not his Jackie. Not while he still lived.

With a force of will he didn't think he possessed, he found the strength he needed to beat the monster back into its cage. It fought him, snarling and gnashing its teeth, but he managed to clang the door shut.

Iain was left sweating and shaking from the effort.

Her hands settled on his face, as gentle as butterflies. He opened his eyes and looked down at her.

Worry lined her brow and pulled her mouth tight. Iain let his sword fall to the ground and ran his finger over her forehead, hoping to erase whatever was bothering her. Her skin was smooth and warm, and her mouth relaxed at his touch.

He wanted to kiss her again, but knew it would be a mistake. Still, it was hard to remember his honor when he felt so battered, bruised, and weary. Battling himself had taken all his strength, and he didn't know how much more he had to hold himself back.

"Are you okay?" she asked.

He wasn't. He was so far from okay it was laughable, but he couldn't bear to burden her with his problems. "Yeah."

"Did you get any poison on you?"

He didn't feel the tingle of it, but there could have been some on his coat—the one that she was too close to.

Iain took a step back and searched his clothing for signs of blood or spit. There were none, except on his sword.

He grabbed his weapon and wiped it off on a patch of demon fur. "I can't see through the windshield," he said, hoping to find a safe topic to distract himself. "You'll freeze to death if we try to drive without it. We'll have to wait here for a new set of wheels."

He pulled out his phone and texted Nicholas with the details of their situation. That man was the most connected of all of them, with a love for technological gadgets that baffled Iain.

Nicholas confirmed he'd gotten the message, and called off the Sanguinar that was on the way to free Iain of the poison Jackie had already cured—the one Helen had sent.

"I could make a windshield. I just figured out how

Andra does her shield thing. I think I could use that same technique to keep the wind out."

"It's worth a shot." Anything that kept them from spending time alone out here in the dark together was worth a try. "Stand clear for a second."

She nodded, and he got inside the truck, using his feet to push the largest portion of safety glass out of the way.

"Okay. Let's give this a try."

Iain felt a tug on his power, then a steady stream flow from him as she placed a flat dome of energy over the hole the broken-out windshield had left behind. He wasn't sure how long she could keep it up, so he texted Nicholas with an update, fired up the truck, and headed out as fast as was safe.

Half an hour later, she'd fallen completely silent. He spared her a quick glance, and saw she was pale and sweating from the sustained effort.

"We'll stop here," he told her. "You need to rest."

"No. I'm okay. Keep going."

He almost argued with her, but he could feel her determination sliding through their link. She wanted to do this, and he couldn't resist giving her what she wanted.

The sooner she got away from him, the better off she'd be.

Chapter 11

Murak found the girl's house without effort. It was clustered around fifty other houses just like it—cattle in their pens.

Her bedroom was on the second floor, as if that were going to stop him from reaching her. Humans were such amusing, unimaginative creatures. It was no wonder they were beneath him on the food chain.

He summoned a breath of power and lifted himself from the ground to peer into her window. Darkness cloaked his presence, saving him the trouble.

The light from a TV cast a flickering glow over her spindly body. She huddled into herself, rocking, as she stared at a TV screen. He could sense the blood of his kind coursing through her, calling to him.

Retrieving her was going to be as easy as it would be enjoyable.

She lifted a cell phone, and her fingers trembled as she typed a text message.

Murak found it interesting that she'd begun to settle back into a normal human life so quickly. It showed a resilience that would serve her well in the years to come. Bearing Synestryn young was difficult on humans, and only a small number of them survived long enough to breed a second time. He was certain that this child would be one of those special creatures.

All the more reason to return her to her place beneath the earth.

He unlatched and removed the screen with a mere thought. Unlocking the window was effortless, though he took the time to do it slowly, allowing no sound to give away his presence. The girl continued splitting her attention between her phone and the TV, her knees pulled tight against her chest in a defensive posture.

As soon as his path was no longer barred, it was time to move fast. He flung the window up and sailed through the opening, knocking the lightweight sheers from his path as he went.

The girl saw him and immediately froze in terror. Her lips parted around a silent scream.

Murak landed on the floor by her bed, close enough to touch.

The poor, shaking creature shifted slightly, and a second later, a searingly bright light burned his eyes.

He hissed in pain and instinctively brought his arm up to shield himself.

A camera. That flash had come from a camera on her phone.

As soon as he realized there was no threat of sunlight, he reached for her. Her hair brushed across his fingertips as she rolled away, landing on the far side of the bed.

"Dad!" she screamed, a ferocious, wrenching sound of panic.

Murak had only seconds before the girl's father arrived, and in that time, he was going to have her securely in his grasp and out through the window.

He lunged over the bed, reaching out his long arm. She scrambled back like a crab, staring in terror at his clawed fingers.

The girl was quick. He'd give her that. But she was pinned against a dresser now, with nowhere else to run.

A grin stretched his mouth, displaying his teeth. The

girl began to shake violently, and he knew she had to be remembering all the times his kind had fed from her silky throat.

"Don't worry," he told her. "I won't drink too much. We need you."

He grabbed her arm, ignoring her ineffective attempts to pry his fingers loose. She struggled, kicking and clawing at him, but his skin was too thick for her to damage. All she was doing was wearing herself out, which would make the rest of his trip that much easier.

"Dad!" shouted the girl again, her shrill scream ringing in his ears.

The bedroom door flew open so hard, the wood cracked. A furious human man rushed in, pointing a double-barreled shotgun at Murak.

He swung the girl around, intending to use her as a shield so her father wouldn't fire, but before he could, she dropped to the ground, her deadweight nearly ripping his arm from his shoulder.

The gun went off. Pain splintered Murak's body, flinging him backward against the opening of the window. He could smell his own blood, and sudden, ravenous hunger washed over him.

It wasn't until the girl skittered away on her hands and knees that he realized he'd lost his grip on her arm. His prey was gone, and her father was preparing for another painful assault.

Murak tossed his weight back and fell through the window. He used his power to slow the fall, and then hid himself from sight.

The man peered out of the window, the barrel of his weapon preceding him. He stared into the dark for several seconds, scanning the area. "Are you okay, Autumn?" he asked his daughter.

Murak heard a whimpering, pitiful sound, but couldn't make out the words.

"Okay, sweetie. Don't you worry. He's not coming

back, and even if he does, we won't be here. Get your coat. We're leaving."

Which meant that not only did Murak have to take the time to heal from his wounds—he also had to find his prey again. But first, he had to feed, and there was an entire neighborhood of cattle just waiting to serve him.

By the time they reached Dabyr, Jackie was weaving in her seat. Exhaustion bore down on her, making it hard to keep her burning eyes open. Even so, the sense of satisfaction she'd gained in doing what needed to be done was one she'd almost forgotten. It glowed inside of her, pepping up her spirits and reminding her that she had once been a force to be reckoned with. She'd once been strong and capable.

She'd missed feeling like that, but until now, she hadn't realized just how much.

Iain turned off the engine. She tried to reach for the door to open it, but her arm was too heavy, her fingers too weak. Her whole body was trembling, making her wonder how she was going to make it back inside.

He came around to her side and opened the door. He stared at her, his face impassive. "You're too weak to walk, aren't you?"

"I'll be fine."

"I can carry you inside."

She hated the idea of being weak and helpless. Even more, she hated the idea of people seeing her being weak and helpless. "No. Please."

His chest expanded with a breath she knew would come out as a frustrated sigh. Instead, he leaned forward and cupped his left hand at the nape of her neck.

She felt the subtle click as his ring latched on to the necklace she wore. The heat of his bare hand sank into her skin, while a torrent of power flowed into her, driving away her exhaustion. A hot shiver wiggled down her spine and settled in her belly.

She let out a sigh of contentment and felt a smile tug at her mouth. "That's incredible."

"I should have done it while we drove, but I couldn't reach you, and I didn't think it would be a good idea for you to lie down in my lap."

It sounded like a lovely idea to her, but right now she wasn't exactly thinking clearly. Her head was fogged with warmth and a resonant hum of power. His touch was intoxicating, lowering her inhibitions and making her forget what was really important.

A moment later, he pulled away and all those tingly feelings were gone. She mourned the loss of his touch, but said nothing.

"Better?" he asked.

She nodded, not trusting herself to speak.

"You'll need to sleep now."

"I'm fine. Besides, I don't have time to waste. There's too much to do."

She moved to slide out of the truck, but Iain's big body blocked her way. His expression was hard and demanding. "You will sleep or I'll find a way to make you. What I did is temporary, and I only did it so you wouldn't be ashamed of your weakness. Don't make me regret that decision."

Arguing with him would have been foolish, so she decide to patronize him. "Fine."

"Good."

He followed her inside, tracking her footsteps all the way to her suite. On the way, she considered the wisdom of inviting him inside, but her decision was taken from her hands when she found Joseph waiting for them outside her suite. The look on his face was grim, and his shoulders sagged with weariness.

"What are you doing here?" asked Iain.

"Nicholas said you'd just arrived. I thought you'd want to be in on this."

"On what?" asked Jackie.

"Not here. My office."

Jackie followed behind, both curious and apprehensive about what was going on. Whatever it was, it wasn't good. With every step she took, some of the bubbling energy zinging through her began to fade.

Iain was right. Whatever he'd done wasn't going to last long.

They filed in to find Joseph's office already filled with people. Helen and Drake were standing in one corner, their heads close together, in quiet conversation. Nika sat on a corner of Joseph's desk with Madoc hovering over her. He seemed pale, and, if she didn't know better, afraid. Tynan lounged in Joseph's chair, his elegant fingers steepled under his chin. He was by far the prettiest person in the room, including the women, but Jackie admired him about as much as she had the demons who'd held her hostage. Any creature that lived on the blood of others was not to be trusted.

"Shut the door," ordered Joseph as he walked in.

Iain was the last one in, and he closed the door behind him. Jackie found herself inching toward him, seeking some kind of comfort in a room where none was going to be had.

"Two hours ago, I was contacted by Henry Mason. Synestryn tried to take his ten-year-old daughter tonight."

Jackie swayed on her feet as the meaning of his words sank in. A child—a little girl—had been attacked by the demons.

Iain's arm slid around her shoulders, steadying her. She couldn't help but lean against him. It made her a weaker person, but the horrors she'd seen in those caves came slamming into her, reminding her of just how much danger this child was in.

"Again?" asked Tynan, rising to his feet.

"What do you mean, again?" asked Helen.

Joseph's nostrils flared with anger as he nodded. "Autumn was one of the girls we rescued the night we found Jackie."

That little girl had been in that same system of caves? Jackie had probably seen her, though she hadn't known her name. There had been so many of them coming and going. After a while, she'd stopped wanting to know about them. All she needed to know was that it was her job to keep them as safe as she could for as long as she could.

She'd failed. Over and over she'd let them down. They'd been raped, killed. Eaten. She hadn't been able to stop it.

"We're leaving," announced Iain, his grip tightening around her. "This is too much to ask of her right now."

Iain was talking about Jackie—about her discomfort. She was so used to being on her own that it felt odd to have someone else defend her.

She looked up at Iain and took his hand. Her fingers threaded through his. They were thick and strong, callused from swordplay, and so incredibly warm. "I'm okay," she reassured him.

"You're pale, shaking, and scared out of your mind. I can feel it. And I can't let it stand."

"Autumn is smart. She snapped a photo of the Synestryn that tried to take her," said Joseph.

"A photo?"

"With her phone. Henry sent it to me." Joseph pulled a folder from his desk and held it out to Jackie. "Will you look at it and tell me if you recognize him?"

Iain snatched the folder away, glaring at Joseph. "What part of *this is too much to ask of her right now* did you not understand?"

Joseph was not cowed. "I could ask the children we found that night, but the Sanguinar have taken away most of their memories. All it would do is scare them."

Jackie couldn't let that happen. "I'll do it. I'll look at the photo. If it is him—Zillah—you can't make those kids remember anything he did to them."

Iain's entire posture screamed how pissed he was, but he handed over the folder. Jackie opened it, bracing herself to face the demon that had ended and destroyed so many lives. Instead, the face that greeted her was not Zillah's. He definitely wasn't human, with glowing green eyes and thin lips that barely covered his pointed teeth, but he wasn't what she'd expected.

There was something familiar about him. The candid shot was from a strange angle, pointing up, so that she got a good view of the inside of his nose. The skin of his neck was textured, as if he had scales of some kind. Maybe it was a trick of the light.

His bony hand was held up as if to block the flash, so she could see the veins under his pale skin were black and protruding from his wrists. The expression on his face was one of feral hatred and hunger.

That was it—the clue she needed.

"I remember him. He visited the caves where I'd been held. Zillah let him feed off one of the women as some sort of peace offering." It had been sickeningly polite, the way one would offer a guest a cup of coffee.

Jackie didn't care what politics went into the demons' ability to barter human life. All she knew was that what he'd done had scared her to death, thinking one of the children would be next.

"Murak," whispered Jackie, suddenly remembering what Zillah had called him.

"You know this demon?" asked Iain, his words lashing out cold and hard. "Did it hurt you? I'll tear its fucking head off."

"He was there only one time that I saw, but there was some kind of dynamic going on between him and Zillah. A power struggle? Negotiations, maybe? I can't be sure." Jackie looked up at Joseph. "Where is Autumn now?"

"I wanted her to come here, but her father feared for her mental health if they stayed in the area. Her family took shelter with relatives near Chicago. Only a handful

of people know about the move. I've got a pair of warriors on their way to guard the family."

Jackie thought back, trying to remember what she'd
seen and heard. Maybe it would help them find this
monster before he struck again.

"We could really use your help," said Joseph, looking
at Jackie. "You were held by them for a long time. You
know their patterns."

"Chaos has no pattern," said Iain. "You're reaching
for something that isn't there."

"Maybe," agreed Joseph. "But we're doing this. We're
going after him. With or without your help."

They'd find him underground, where he and his kind
lived. The idea of going into those caves made her skin
go cold and clammy with fear. "I don't think I can go
back there," she whispered in shame.

"Of course you're not going back there," said Iain.
"No one's asking you to."

"Actually, we are," said Joseph. "I am. This Murak is
after Autumn because of her age. They've done to her
what they did to Tori. They're feeding her their blood in
an effort to make her a viable breeding partner. I won't
let that happen."

Iain's expression grew grim. "I've been hunting for
these breeding caves for months, and only found a couple. How would we even know where to look?"

Joseph ignored Iain and spoke to Jackie. "All I'm asking is for you to go scouting. You might recognize something."

"Back off, Joseph," warned Iain.

Jackie tried to find an excuse not to do this. She wasn't
strong enough. "They moved several of us, but it was always at night in vans with no windows."

"Unless they drove the vans into the cave, you might
have seen something."

She had, but she'd been so terrified and weak, she
wasn't sure she even remembered it right, and what she

had seen wasn't any kind of distinct landmark—just tangles of brush and the slope of the land.

Jackie offered what she could. "The trips weren't long—a couple of hours. The caves were close to each other."

Iain shook his head. "I've searched those areas. The caves are there, and there's proof of Synestryn activity, but by the time I get there, they're mostly gone. Just a few stragglers are left."

If she didn't do something, more little kids would be taken from their families. More people would be used for food, left to suffer and die in the dark. Autumn's young life would be destroyed before it was cut short. Jackie had seen it before. She couldn't simply stand by and ignore the problem. She had to think of something she could do, but something that wouldn't put her back in the ground.

She hated what she was about to force herself to say—what she was about to force herself to think about—but it was necessary. "All you have to do is catch them at the right time. When they're unable to move."

"What are you talking about?" asked Joseph.

"They have these giant creatures. I saw one once. It was bigger than any animal I've ever seen." It was huge, pulsing with movement, like a maggot the size of a bus. "It's the thing that gives birth to some of their demons. I heard Zillah and his lackey talking about it outside of my cell, when they thought I was unconscious." She'd been so cold, so weak. Zillah had nearly killed her, taking so much blood her heart raced to keep her alive.

"You don't have to talk about this," said Iain, stroking her back with a soothing sweep of his hand. "Not if you're not ready."

She was never going to be ready to talk about her time in the caves, but it didn't matter. If demons were trying to steal more children, she had to help stop them. "It takes these things a few months to produce a litter, but when they're near the end of that time, they can't move. They're too big, and too valuable to abandon. If we can find the nest during this time, then they'll be trapped. Or at least they'll have to leave behind that thing for us to kill."

"How long?" asked Joseph. "Do you know any more details?"

She shook her head. "They were talking about not being able to move for another week. I don't know how long before that they were stuck."

"Where was this?" asked Iain.

"The second cave I was in. I was there the longest."

"Do you remember where it was?" asked Joseph, pointing to the map. "This dot is where we found you. All of the other black dots represent known Synestryn nesting sites."

Jackie stepped up. She tried to think back, but all she remembered was fear and cold. She hadn't yet accepted her fate and stopped using what little strength she had to fight them. That had taken her several more months of painful lessons to learn.

She cupped her hands in a circle around an area. "In here would be my best guess. Like I said, we didn't move far, so it has to be close."

"That area is riddled with caves, and it's near the Masons' hometown. It's possible we missed another nest. I'll have Nicholas gather up the images we have of those sites we did catalog for you to look through. He may have a photo of something you recognize. In the meantime, the rest of you need to gear up. You'll leave in a few hours. We need everyone focused on shutting these demon breeding grounds down."

"We can't go," blurted Madoc.

Joseph turned around and looked at him. "Why not?"

Madoc ran his fingers through his hair in distress. "I'm not sure I believe it, myself."

"Believe what?"

"You tell them, Nika."

Nika shook her head, making her white hair sway around her shoulders. A bright smile lit her face. "Nope. You know they all think I'm crazy. They won't believe me."

"Can you all please hurry this up?" asked Joseph.

"Sorry," said Madoc, looking sheepish. He cleared his throat. "We can't go because Nika's pregnant."

The room exploded in surprise. Tynan glided forward toward Nika. Helen's face split with a huge grin. Drake stood there stunned, and Iain went completely still and silent.

"How can this be?" asked Joseph, his voice filled with a healthy dose of suspicion.

"Well," said Nika. "When a boy Theronai and a girl Theronai love each other very much—"

"You know what I mean, Nika," snapped Joseph. "Did you cheat on Madoc?"

Madoc drew steel and started toward Joseph like he was going to kill him. Nika was faster and slipped in front of him, barring his path. "Down, boy. He didn't mean any insult."

"He should have thought better before calling you a cheating whore, then," growled Madoc.

Tynan held up his hands and his voice seemed to fill the room, drowning out all else. "The serum I gave Madoc to restore his fertility must have worked." He looked at Nika, then at Madoc. "May I?"

"May you what?" asked Madoc, his blade still out and gleaming with lethal warning.

"Confirm that it's true."

"Are you calling Nika a liar?" asked Madoc.

"No, of course not. This is strictly for my research."

Madoc's anger deflated. He looked at Nika. "He wants to touch you. Do you mind?"

Nika gave a negligent shrug. "Okay, but he won't be able to hear her."

"Hear her?" asked Tynan.

"Her?" shouted Madoc, swaying like he might actually faint.

"She's little. No heartbeat yet."

"That's okay," said Tynan. "I may still be able to sense her."

Nika shrugged again and pulled up the front of her shirt. Loose jeans bagged around her narrow waist, hanging on her hips. Tynan slid his hand over her belly, the barest tips of his fingers sinking beneath her waistband.

Madoc growled.

"Hush," said Nika. "Let him do this. It's the only way the others will believe."

Tynan's mouth lifted in a smile of pure joy. "She's right. She's pregnant."

Madoc's big body started tilting sideways, and Drake grabbed his arm with both hands. "Sit down before you fall over."

Everyone converged on Nika and Madoc, offering them congratulations and plenty of surprise.

Iain had said that all the men had been sterilized by Synestryn, but apparently that had changed. Tynan's serum must have cured whatever was causing the problem.

Jackie stood back, watching everyone fuss over Nika. She didn't know these people well enough to gush, but she didn't want to destroy what was clearly such a momentous event for them.

She slumped into a chair, trying to fight off the fatigue draining her.

They were so happy, especially Helen, who beamed up at Drake with a look of hope. He gave her a wicked smile and a blush spread down her neck. They hadn't said a word aloud, but the connection they shared was palpable and unwavering.

Jackie envied her sister for that.

Her gaze slid to Iain. He looked up and stared at her for a long time. His expression was blank, but emotion seethed in his dark eyes. Curious what he was thinking, she reached out, trying to feel him through their connection the way Helen had talked about.

She felt nothing, which left her feeling bereft somehow.

He came to her side and held out his hand. "You're tired. We should go."

"Just another minute," said Joseph. "Nika, Madoc, you two are to stay here and out of harm's way."

"But I can help," said Nika. "It's not going to hurt the baby."

"We're not going to take any fucking chances," said Madoc. "If I have to, I'll tie you up."

Nika grinned as if reliving a fond memory. "I think that's what got us into this condition."

Madoc looked at Joseph. "If we stay and listen, she'll want to help, so we're leaving now." He didn't wait for permission, simply gathered Nika under his arm and marched her out through the door.

Joseph's game face was firmly back in place. "Nika was instrumental in the last rescue, and no one can do what she does, so we're going to have to rethink our strategy."

"What does she do?" asked Jackie, wondering if she could fill Nika's shoes from a distance.

"She gets into the minds of demons, takes control of their bodies, and then makes their brains explode."

Yeah. Jackie wasn't going to be doing that. Not in this lifetime.

"We're spread thin with Zach and Lexi still working in Africa, and Gilda and Angus . . ." Grief tightened his mouth before he continued. "Everyone is going to have to do their part." He looked at Jackie. "You, too."

"She's not ready. She doesn't even know what she can do yet," said Iain.

"Apparently, she has a fair amount of skill with poison," said Helen, pride chiming in her voice. "She saved Iain's life."

"That will come in handy," said Joseph, looking at Jackie. "I won't make you go in the caves, but we need your help in whatever way you can give it. While we're working on details, you need to see what else you can do, but we can't wait long, so learn fast. By the lake, just in case proficiency with fire runs in the family."

"Let's go," said Iain. "We don't have much time." He looked at Tynan. "Can you come with us and check me out? I'm still not feeling like myself."

"Certainly," said Tynan.

"Did I miss some of the poison?" Jackie was horrified by the idea that she hadn't done a good job, and that he'd been suffering for the last couple of hours.

"You did fine," he reassured her.

The three of them left, shutting the door behind them. Iain led the way, walking swiftly down the winding halls.

"There weren't many people left in there to help plan the mission," said Jackie.

Iain glanced over his shoulder. "They'll make it work. What we're doing is just as important."

"What exactly are we doing?" she asked.

"I'm taking you to your suite so you can get some sleep. While you do that, Tynan here is going to make sure there's no poison left."

"And then?" she asked.

"Don't worry about that part yet. One step at a time." He said it like there was some other meaning there — one she couldn't figure out.

She feared that what he wasn't telling her was far worse than anything she might imagine.

Chapter 12

Iain followed Tynan to his suite in silence. It was all he could do to put one foot in front of the other without stopping to pound his fists into the walls, or draw his sword and start hacking.

As soon as the door shut behind Tynan, he let his facade slip.

Tynan reeled back, his hand straying to his hip.

"You've started carrying a sword?" asked Iain in angry disbelief.

"Having one's neck snapped has that sort of an effect on a man."

"I'm not going to hurt you. But before we go any further, I need your promise that you will never tell anyone what I'm about to reveal to you."

"Of course," said Tynan. "Secrets are no problem for me."

Sneaky bastard. Then again, that was one of the reasons Iain felt Tynan was the only one he could even consider trusting. "Say it."

"I promise not to speak of what you tell me here and now."

The weight of the man's vow hit Iain hard, making him snarl. It didn't matter that he'd asked for the promise. Logic was not playing a role in the stage of Iain's mind right now. He was all frantic rage and chaotic anger. Keeping his monster in check during that meeting had taken every ounce of his self-control.

"I don't know how long it will be until Jackie wakes, so I'll make this quick." He also wasn't sure how long he could keep from slamming his fist into Tynan's too-pretty face. "Jackie bonded with me against my will."

"That's not possible."

"It is when you're delirious from poison."

"You seem upset by the union. I would have thought you'd be pleased, or at least relieved."

He wasn't either. He was pissed, and that anger was growing fast with every second he was away from Jackie. Her presence seemed to still his monster enough for him to keep it caged, but now that she was gone, his control was slipping fast. "I want you to help me find a way to undo it."

"What vow did she offer?"

Iain stared out the window at the lighted landscaping. "To stay with me until I was as good as new."

"Ah. So you want me to finish healing you to complete the promise and free you. But why? Don't you want to be with her?"

He did. He wanted to soak up her spirit and selflessness. He wanted to revel in her beauty and be the kind of man who could offer her the pristine future she deserved. But none of that was possible. "Other men are in greater need than I am. She should be with one of them."

"She chose you."

"She chose wrong!"

Tynan held up his hands, his long, elegant fingers warding away some of Iain's anger. "I'll do what you ask, but there will be a price. I want blood in return for healing you."

"You still don't get it. There's nothing you can do to fix me. I'll never be as good as new. What I need from you is to find a way to sever the bond."

Tynan shook his head. "I'm sorry. I can't help you. And even if I could, I wouldn't."

"Why not?"

"Nika's pregnancy. That changes things. For both of us."

Iain still hadn't digested the news that Tynan's cure had worked. The implications of that were huge.

He could have a child.

While one corner of his mind swelled with joy at the thought, another snickered in derision. A soulless father. Is that what he wanted to offer a child?

"There are dozens of other men who can knock Jackie up. You don't need me for that."

"She picked you for a reason."

"Because she knew it could never work between us. All she wants to do is leave here and go live a normal life. She hasn't yet accepted that that is not an option."

"Then change her mind." Tynan said it like it was easy, like just willing Jackie to do something was going to make it happen. If that were the case, then his luceria would have already fallen from her neck.

Frustration grew inside of him, feeding off his rage. "I can't. I'm barely holding myself together. I'm afraid I'll hurt her."

"Madoc felt the same way with Nika. It worked out fine. Better than."

"I'm not Madoc," growled Iain.

"You could be. You could be united to a woman you love with a child on the way. What does he have that makes him more deserving of such a gift?"

"A soul," Iain spat out before he could stop himself. He hadn't wanted to admit it—not to anyone. He'd spent so many years protecting his secret, and now that Tynan knew, it was only a matter of time before others did as well. Vow of silence or not.

If he stayed tied to Jackie, eventually she would see the truth of it, bleak and festering inside of him.

Tynan's icy blue eyes went wide and he backed away,

drawing his sword with a quiet ring of steel. "You've turned?"

"I'm fine. I misspoke."

Tynan tilted his head. "No, you didn't. I can see it now. The empty hollowness within you. It's been there for a while. I don't know why I didn't see it before."

"I didn't let you. No one knows."

"I must advise Joseph."

"You can't. You gave me your word."

Tynan's mouth lifted in a sneer of contempt. "You tricked me."

"Just like Jackie tricked me. We both want the same thing here, Tynan. I just need you to help me make it happen."

"Your death would free her."

"I know. If that's the only choice . . ." He let his words trail off before the monster beat its chest, screaming that it would never surrender.

"What am I supposed to do?" asked Tynan.

"There's got to be something. All I need is to be whole again for one moment—that's all it will take to free Jackie."

Tynan's brows drew down in thought over his icy eyes. "If I agree, if I do this thing, I'll want payment."

"As much blood as you need for as long as I live."

"Done," agreed Tynan.

Iain's vow threatened to buckle his knees. He gritted his teeth and suffered through it. "Now," he told the Sanguinar. "Do it now."

Tynan smiled. "With pleasure."

Tynan wasted no time acting. He went straight for Iain's throat, sinking his fangs into the other man's flesh. He drank deep, willing the Theronai to sleep so there was no fear of violence.

Madoc had broken Tynan's neck not long ago, and that was not the kind of thing easily forgotten. Tynan took no chances now, especially not with a soulless warrior of Iain's skill.

Iain went limp, and Tynan eased his bulky body to the floor. Power roared inside of Iain, and as Tynan drank that power in, his hunger disappeared and his body expanded with strength. He took as much blood as he dared, knowing that combat was only hours away.

Then again, if Iain was too weak to fight well, he'd fall in battle with no one having to know about his soul's dead state. He could enter the Hall of the Fallen with honor, his life's work intact and unblemished.

As much as Tynan hated the idea of causing Iain's death, he wasn't above doing so. Jackie was the important one in this equation. She was the one he had to protect at all costs so that her children could come into this world and save Tynan's people from starvation.

He still hadn't had time to digest the news that his cure had worked. All of his people would rejoice at the news. More Theronai children changed everything.

Tynan forced himself to address the task at hand and see if Iain was as bad off as he feared. He closed the wounds on Iain's throat and ripped open his shirt.

There were several leaves left on his lifemark, but there was something wrong about them. They were still and hollow, as if dead. Perhaps it was the same kind of magic that had held Madoc's soul's decay in stasis for so long, giving him the time he needed to find Nika.

Tynan ran the tip of his finger over one leaf, concentrating on it. That's when he felt the metallic tinge of pigment.

The leaf was a fake—a tattoo meant to fool others.

Anger coalesced deep within Tynan's chest. How dare Iain endanger their lives by lying like this? He could have snapped and begun killing those inside Dabyr at any moment. The fact that he hadn't was a testament only to his stubbornness.

Tynan plunged into Iain's mind, not even trying to be

gentle. This man didn't deserve gentle. He was a danger to all of them.

He wove his way through Iain's thoughts, seeking out his intentions. Rage slammed into him, nearly knocking him back into his own body. There was so much of it, and it rose up in threatening waves, looming over everything, crashing around so violently that Tynan had no idea how Iain could stand it.

With a force of will, Tynan gathered that rage and shoved it aside, allowing him room to pass. What was left inside of Iain looked like the burned-out shell of a bombed building. There was no structure there, only charred clutter and chaos. His thoughts were a jumbled mass of greed, violence, and lust. It was a wonder that he hadn't already hurt the people around him.

Over everything was a shimmering film of something Tynan had never seen before. As he inspected it more closely, poking at it with a tentative thought, he realized what it was. Rules, order, honor.

Iain had indeed been holding himself in check for all this time, controlling his actions so that his emotions didn't come through.

And there was something else, too. A tiny, shining ribbon, as thin as a strand of hair, wove through the dark chaos, glowing wherever it passed. As he prodded it to see if this was some hint of a soul, he felt a distinctively feminine energy pass through him.

Jackie. This was her—the connection she had to Iain through the luceria.

Perhaps he could sever it here, freeing her.

Tynan funneled a small bit of power at the ribbon, testing it to make sure he wasn't going to hurt Jackie with his actions. As he sent that spark sailing into it, it flinched, jerking away from his touch as if he'd burned it.

Clearly, that idea was not going to work. He couldn't risk Jackie.

Iain was another story.

Before he made his final decision, he had to be sure of the man he was sentencing to death. There could not be so much as a flicker of his soul left, or what Tynan was about to do would be unforgivable.

He went searching deeper, letting his consciousness fan out in all directions, seeking out some hint of life left inside of the man. The deeper he went, the more chaos and rage he found. Dead tendrils of what had once been Iain's soul branched out, swirling and trying to wrap around Tynan's essence. He dodged the attacks easily, moving deeper until there was nowhere else to go.

A giant black mass loomed where Iain's soul should have been. Tentacles made of oily blackness snaked around, writhing in agony.

There was nothing left. No flicker. No spark. Nothing. All that was here was dead and rotten.

A thick tendril lurched toward Tynan as if seeking prey. He moved out of the way, and as he did, he saw a minuscule fleck of something. He wasn't sure what it was, but it glowed against the darkness, standing out in stark contrast.

He moved to get a better view and saw the ribbon.

Jackie's ribbon.

She wove herself through the tentacles, wrapping around and around until she was knotted about the pulsing, dark mass, binding herself to it. As he watched, she looped herself around yet another sinuous tentacle, spiraling around it as if she wanted to be close. Wherever she touched, the tendrils quieted, as if going to sleep.

Tynan reared back in shock, landing hard inside his own skin. He didn't know what that meant. Surely, if she was embedded that deeply, she'd have felt the dead thing rotting away inside of Iain.

Wouldn't she?

More important, if she was lodged that deeply, what would happen to her if Iain died?

Tynan looked at Iain's ring. It was snowy white, with only the faintest hint of gold moving within. Their bonding wasn't complete.

Good as new.

That was not going to be easy to accomplish. The few minor scrapes and bruises were easy enough to fix. Tynan did so with a mere thought, now that his body was fueled with the power of Iain's blood. When there was nothing left to fix physically, the only thing he could think to do was use peacebinding magic on Iain. It was common enough for his kind to force a promise from those they healed so they could never raise their hand against them in the future. The practice was useful for when the occasional wars between the races broke out.

Or for when one of the Theronai lost his soul.

If Tynan couldn't break the bond between them, and he wasn't sure what Iain's death would do to Jackie, then at least he could prevent the warrior from doing anything to harm him. That would give him time to work on the problem and research it. Perhaps this wasn't the first time something like this had happened.

It was Iain's rage that was the immediate concern. No man could walk around with that much anger and not act on it eventually. If he could get rid of the rage, then Jackie would be safe. At least for now.

So that's what Tynan did. He gathered up as much of the pulsing rage as he could, and drew it into himself. There was no other way to get rid of so much at one time. He was going to have to bear the burden and hope that his years of exercises in self-control would pay off.

Iain's fury hit him hard, making him cry out in pain. He felt like he was trying to swallow an electrified coil of razor wire. It lashed around within him, battering at its confines, seeking a way out.

Tynan reached for his power and did what he could to shove the violent anger inside as small a space as possible. The effort left him shaking and weak, lying on the ground, panting on his back, but at least he could breathe again.

Iain woke with a groan. He leaned over Tynan, his brow etched with confusion. "Did it work?"

Tynan could barely speak. His throat was tight and his insides felt ruined. "I can't break it. I'd hurt her."

Iain let out a long sigh of resignation. "I can't let you do that. I'll find another way."

There was only one other way. Iain's death. "Soon," said Tynan. "She's tying herself to you. If she grows close and you die, it may be years before she chooses another man."

The Theronai nodded his agreement. "I feel different. Better. What did you do?"

"Nothing," lied Tynan. "Go. I need to rest."

"You look sick. Did I hurt you?"

"Go!" he shouted, feeling the barrier around Iain's rage bulging under the strain.

Iain stood and left. Tynan pushed to his feet as soon as he was sure Iain was out of earshot, and began smashing furniture with his bare hands.

Chapter 13

Jackie flopped onto the bed and fell into a hard, fast sleep without even taking off her shoes. She jerked awake a short time later, sure that something was terribly wrong. It was as if someone had taken a cattle prod to her brain.

She had to be imagining things. There was no one around, and she was simply reacting to the excitement and stress of the past twenty-four hours. She'd tied herself to a man she barely knew, been attacked — twice — and walked away from a chance to help, like the coward she was.

Sleep was going to be impossible now. She didn't have to close her eyes to know that images of stolen children and ravenous demons awaited her.

Something was wrong. She could feel it. Iain was hiding something, and despite her request that he stay out of her head, she continued catching herself using the connection she had to him to poke at his mind, seeking answers.

Every time she realized what she was doing, she jerked back and scolded herself for being such a hypocrite.

In those few, small glances she'd had, she'd felt anger — so much of it that it overshadowed everything else. She wasn't sure what had happened to make him so mad, but whatever it was, he hid it well.

Which only served to make her wonder what else he was hiding.

Jackie found some fresh clothes sitting inside of her doorway. She didn't know how they got here, but she was grateful for something clean to wear.

She stripped out of her clothes, pausing when she automatically moved to take off her necklace. Of course it didn't come off, but it seemed odd wearing it in the shower—like she was toting a small piece of Iain along with her.

Then again, if he were here, she doubted she'd be thinking about much of anything beyond getting her soapy hands on his body. And if the man's kiss was any indication, she wouldn't be thinking at all—just feeling.

Even now, the mere memory of that kiss had the power to make her skin heat and her nipples harden. She wasn't going to forget that anytime soon, no matter how much distance he tried to shove between them.

She made quick work of her shower, dressed, and went in search of a distraction. Being around Iain was too much stimulus, but being alone gave her too much space to think. Now that she was spoken for, she felt like she could leave her suite and go in search of food. No more hiding in her room for fear of who might grope her.

Even though it was well before dawn, Jackie found a few people gathered in the open dining and recreation area. People at Dabyr kept odd hours in support of the Sentinels, making sure the place stayed running, even at night.

An elderly woman sat sipping coffee and reading a book, alone on one side of the room. For some reason, Jackie felt an instant kinship with her, as if they were both able to be alone even when surrounded by people.

"Can I sit down?" she asked the woman.

"I assume your legs function well enough. Or did you mean to ask if you *may* sit down?" The woman's mouth was painted red, with lines of lipstick fanning out into her wrinkles. A yellow pencil held her heavy bun in place at the nape of her neck.

Jackie tried to hide her grin. "May I sit down?"

"Please. Helen's told me a lot about you."

"You know Helen?"

The woman nodded. "I'm Mabel Hennesy. Miss Mabel to most people here. Your sister and I have been friends for a few years. She brought me here."

"Helen made you live here?"

"At first there was a bit of a fight, but I find it suits me. It's nice to be teaching again, though after all those years, I wouldn't have thought I'd miss it so much." She marked her place in her book with a silk ribbon and closed it. The pages were thick and yellow with age. The cover was worn leather, stained dark by the touch of many hands. There was no title, only an embossed tree sprawling across the cover.

"You teach? Here?"

"Someone's got to pound some sense into those teens' heads. I don't need my walker anymore, but I make sure the troublemakers know I still know how to use it."

Jackie wasn't sure what she meant, but it seemed rude to ask, so she let it go.

"I haven't seen much of you since you came to live with us," said Miss Mabel. "Helen said that Logan and Tynan weren't able to take your memories of what happened away, like they did with the little ones."

"I didn't let them. There's no way I'm letting anyone else have my blood."

"Oh, it's not so bad having an attractive man put his mouth on you. You should try it sometime. Made a world of difference for me."

The only attractive man whose mouth she didn't mind touching her was Iain, and they both knew that that wasn't going anywhere. "I think I'll pass."

A young, blond teenager came by the table with a small notepad. She set a glass of water in front of Jackie. "Do you want something to eat?" she asked.

"Sure. Whatever you have is fine."

The girl listed several choices, and Jackie picked one, not really caring what it was. She was hungry enough to eat anything, which hadn't happened in a long time.

Miss Mabel lifted her cup. "I'll take a warm-up when you swing back by. And then you need to get back to your room and study. There's a secret pop quiz on chapter seven tomorrow."

The girl smiled at the tip, and scurried off.

"She's so young," said Jackie. "What's she doing working in the middle of the night?"

"It's her turn to work the night shift. I make allowances for the kids' schedules, but they all have to learn to step up and take responsibility. This place takes a lot of effort to keep running, and we all have to earn our keep."

"But she can't be more than fifteen. She needs her rest."

"She makes do. Besides, she doesn't sleep much these days—not since her family was killed and eaten last year."

Jackie swallowed hard, her appetite fading by the second. "That's horrible."

"No more horrible than what you suffered, I'd wager. All the kids here have their share of nightmares. Sad truth is, they're the lucky ones. The Sentinels found them in time to save them."

Just like they'd saved her. And yet, here she was, refusing to help them find Murak for fear that it would force her to go back into a cave.

What about the kids that were trapped underground right now? Would they be found in time to be saved? Or would they be like so many others, dead before they'd even had a chance to really live?

"You okay, child?" asked Miss Mabel. "You went all pale."

"I'm okay. I'm just trying to make sense of things."

"What things? I've been here a while. I might be able to shed some light on the subject—whatever it is."

Jackie sipped at the water, feeling the chill of it slide all the way down. "I don't want this life. I don't belong here."

Miss Mabel nodded toward the luceria. "Seems to me you fit in just fine."

"This is just a temporary fluke—something I had to do to save a man's life. Once it comes off, I don't plan on putting another one on again."

"Are you sorry you did it? Are you sorry you put it on?"

"No. Of course not."

Miss Mabel nodded. "See. There's your answer."

"I don't see anything, especially not an answer."

The older woman sighed as if dealing with a stubborn pupil. "You were willing to change your life to save the life of another."

"Yes. So?"

"So, you've already made the choice once and didn't regret it. All you have to do is make that same choice and you won't regret that, either."

Jackie shook her head. "I don't follow your logic."

"It's simple. You're not the kind of person who walks away from responsibility just because it's hard. I've heard about what you did for the women in those caves. My guess is you did the same thing for the kids."

Jackie looked away, not wanting to think about that time. It was too grim, too disturbing to have in the foreground of her mind. "Please, don't."

"My point is you're a good person. You put the welfare of others before yourself. If you walk away from a job only you can do, you'll never forgive yourself."

"I'm not the only one who can do it."

Miss Mabel gave her a disbelieving glare. "You know

that's a lie. You're special. You might as well get used to it."

"I don't want to be special—at least not like that."

"And I don't want to die before I finish reading every book on the planet. We can't have everything we want. Heck, half of what we want isn't even good for us."

"I can't go back there," whispered Jackie. "I can't face that darkness again."

"Sure you can. There's some child out there right now, praying for a miracle. I hate to be the one to deliver the news, but you're that miracle. You have to be. No one else knows what you do and has the power to act on that knowledge."

The girl came back and laid a plate of pasta in front of Jackie, who stared at it like it was some kind of alien text.

"Is something wrong?" asked the girl.

"No, dear. Everything's fine," said Miss Mabel. "Jackie here is just having a moment. Let her work through it in peace."

The girl wandered off, glancing over her shoulder as if expecting Jackie to fall over.

"I'm not having a moment," argued Jackie.

"Sure you are. You're sitting there, deciding to do the right thing."

"You don't know that."

"The hell I don't."

Irritation made Jackie's words clipped. "How can you possibly know that?"

Miss Mabel's red mouth lifted in a sad smile. "Because I've spent a lot of time with the people who came out of those caves with you alive. They talk about what you did, said you always did the right thing, even when your choices were impossible. You'll do it again now, because that's who you are."

"You don't know me. We've never even met before tonight."

"No, but I know the body of your work, and there are several of those warm, tiny bodies safely asleep in their rooms tonight because of you. I have no doubt that you'll stay true to form."

Miss Mabel got up and left, taking her book, but leaving her declarations behind, hanging in the air.

Jackie was no hero. She'd done what anyone would have in her situation. Miss Mabel was wrong. And even if she was right and Jackie had been some kind of saint, then it was time for a vacation.

Wasn't it?

She stared out the huge windows, acutely aware of the life outside these walls passing her by. That was where she belonged. At least she wanted to believe that was the case.

She toyed with the luceria, sliding her fingers over the smooth band. It seemed to have its own living heat, vibrating slightly in response to her touch. She kind of liked it. Not that it mattered. Any second now, Tynan would patch Iain up and the luceria would fall away. She'd be back where she started, with men falling over themselves to get a chance to touch her.

Unless she gave Iain a new promise—one that would last a bit longer than only a few hours. Maybe one that would last long enough for her to kill Murak for daring to go after Autumn.

The mere idea of going back into the caves scared her to death, while at the same time it filled her with a vengeful thrill. Payback was the least those demons deserved. And who better to inflict a little justice on them than her?

But what about her real life? The one she wanted so desperately?

It was hard right now to picture herself in a boardroom, going over production figures and profit/loss statements. That was where she belonged, where things made the most sense, but that seemed so far away from where she was now. How was she ever going to get back there? And if she did, how was she ever going to put the past behind her?

She had no answers, and for now, it was a moot point. For as long as she wore Iain's luceria, she was tied to his world. And while she was here, her only real option was to kill as many demons as she could.

It was time to go and see exactly what she was capable of.

Iain wasn't sure what Tynan had done, but whatever it was, he was no longer screaming inside, fighting the constant need to kill. He could think clearly for the first time since Jackie had taken his luceria. The emotions he was feeling weren't gone, but they were quieter, giving him space to think. Even the monster slept soundly.

His first reaction was that he wanted to share his good fortune with Jackie, but then he realized that he couldn't say a word. Not even to her.

Tynan hadn't been able to break their bond, which meant there was only one way to free her. He was going to have to die. The question was, how long would he keep up this charade before he accepted his fate? How long would it take him to convince her to choose Cain?

He felt a tug on his power and knew that Jackie was awake. He followed that strand of power outside to where a pair of Sentinel Stones sat at the side of the training field. They were taller than a man and carved with intricate runes. One had been there a long time, and was covered in lichen, while the other had recently been transported here. It had been found in the basement of an old building in Kansas City, and there was a dark stain creeping several feet up from the bottom, where the Stone had been sitting in water.

These monoliths served as gateways between worlds, and keeping them safely behind the walls of Dabyr was vital in keeping the Synestryn from spreading their evil out beyond Earth.

Jackie was dwarfed by the Stones, standing still under the night sky.

"Why aren't you asleep?" he asked.

She kept her back to him. "Something woke me up. I couldn't get back to sleep."

The moon shone down on her glossy hair and highlighted her delicate bone structure. A long leather coat skimmed her curves, keeping her warm. She stood between the two Stones, staring up at the stars.

"What are you doing out here?"

"I like it here. I'm alone, but I don't feel lonely, you know?"

The idea that she was lonely bothered him. He took a step closer, catching her scent on the night breeze. "I'll keep you company, if you like."

She nodded absently, staring at something, reaching her hand up near one of the Stones. "Can you feel it?" she asked.

Iain looked and saw nothing. Felt nothing. "No. What are you talking about?"

She took his hand, curling her fingers around his palm. Then she guided it into the air. "It's warmer here."

"I don't feel any difference." Except the way his cells perked up at her touch.

"Neither could Helen. It must just be me." She sighed in disappointment and her hand fell to her side. Iain kept hold of her fingers, because he wasn't yet ready to give up touching her.

"Do you want me to have it investigated? It could be some kind of Synestryn weapon."

Jackie shook her head. "It doesn't feel sinister. It feels . . . familiar, like the hug of an old friend."

"Maybe that's what they want you to feel."

She gave him a pointed look. "I lived with them for two years. They wouldn't know what it was like to hug a friend even in their wildest dreams. They're not like us, Iain. They're evil, soulless monsters."

He barely stifled a flinch at her words. They shouldn't have hurt him—he shouldn't have even been able to feel hurt. But he did.

He untangled his fingers from her slender ones and shoved his hands into his pockets. If his true nature was ever revealed before he died, she wouldn't thank him for making her touch a soulless monster.

"You should go back inside. You need your rest."

"No, what I needed was to find my spine, which I have. I'm going with them."

"Going where with whom?" he asked.

"Hunting. With the others. Joseph is right. I know more about those caves than anyone. I should be out there, searching for the source of all this evil."

He started shaking his head before she'd even finished speaking. "It's too dangerous. You're not ready."

She held out her hand and a brilliant little flame sprouted up from her skin. "I'm ready. The magic stuff is simple. Exhausting, but simple."

"The connection between us is too new and small for you to do much."

"I feel it growing. Don't you?"

He did. Too fast. Soon, he wouldn't be able to block her from his thoughts and she'd know he was soulless. He didn't want that to happen. He wanted to die with what was left of his honor intact. "Have you been suffering any ill effects?"

She frowned as if trying to puzzle something out. "I keep getting this odd feeling, but it's not bad."

"What kind of odd?"

Jackie hesitated for a moment as if trying to find the right words. "It's like I'm surrounded by this black void, and every once in a while, a little light flickers to life. It happens right before I learn something new I can do."

Iain had never heard of such a thing, and that bothered him. She'd been at the mercy of Synestryn for so long, there was no way to tell what they might have done to her. "We should tell Joseph and Tynan. Gilda would probably have had some answers. . . ."

"But she's dead now."

He nodded. "She and her husband died the night we freed you. They were the oldest bonded pair among us. Now that honor falls to Helen and Drake."

"And they're not exactly experts."

"There's a couple in England and another in Australia. They've been together for nearly as long as Gilda and Angus were. They might know something."

Jackie shook her head. "I'm sure it's nothing to worry about. It's not like I'll be dealing with it for long."

At first he thought she knew of his plans to end his life, and then he realized she thought he only needed to get over a bad case of heartache. He couldn't lead her to false belief. It wasn't fair. She had to know the score. "Tynan wasn't able to break our bond. If he can't, I don't know of anyone who can."

She offered him a sad smile. "How do you mend a broken heart?"

The urge to blurt out that it wasn't his heart but his soul that needed mending pressed at his lips. "I don't want you to worry that you'll be trapped, tied to me."

"I miss my old life, and I really do want it back again, but first I need to do this. Being tied to you gives me more power than I'd ever imagined possible. And if you never get over Serena, then I'll learn to live with it, somehow. I'll move on with my life, and you can do the same. We'll go our separate ways. At least you won't die now, right?"

His gaze skittered away from hers. He couldn't look her in the eye while he lied. She deserved better than that. "What will you do when we're no longer bound?"

"Go back to my life, of course. I've never hidden the fact that that's what I want."

"What about the other men? Could you save one of them while you did so?"

Jackie's mouth flattened. "I don't know, Iain. I want to be the kind of person who would help, but I feel like I've already given too much of my life to the demons. If I accept another union, then what's to keep me from being pulled back into your world?"

"It's your world, too. You belong here."

"I know you think so, but I have to do what's right for me. I'm trying really hard to be a good sport about our accidental predicament. I didn't even freak out when you said Tynan failed to free me."

"Because you've already made up your mind to move on, with or without our bond."

"I'm going to help you find these breeding sites, but once the threat is gone, I have to move on. I'll go insane if my whole life ends up being a series of terror and pain."

Like it had been for the past two years.

He tried to hide his sympathy for her, knowing it would come across as pity. His Jackie wouldn't want anyone's pity. She was too independent for that.

"Are you serious about helping find these nests?" he asked.

"I am. We'll do this one thing together, and after that, I need you—all of you—to let me go."

This was likely the only gift he'd ever be able to give her, and he didn't want it to pass him by. "I will. I'll let you go." One way or another.

Chapter 14

Jackie went through the photos Nicholas gave her, searching for something that looked familiar. Many of the caves' entrances were shielded by brush, but only one of them was a gaping hole that went straight down into the ground.

As soon as she saw it, she remembered that—remembered staring over the edge, knowing that once she went down there, she'd never be able to crawl back up. The drop was too steep, her arms too weak from hunger and loss of blood.

"This one," she said, handing Iain the photo. "This looks right."

He nodded, his expression hard. "We'll need rappelling gear. And you'll need warm clothes. A cold front is moving in."

"When do we go?"

"As soon as you're ready. You should get some sleep first."

There was no way she was going to be able to sleep, knowing that as soon as she woke, she was headed back to the source of her nightmares. "I'll sleep in the car," she lied. "I just want to get this over with."

"I'll meet you at the garage in twenty minutes. You'll find everything you need in the storage room. I'll drop you off there on my way."

Twenty minutes later, she had an overnight bag packed with a change of clothes, toiletries, and a fully loaded gun with spare bullets. She stood by the door to the underground garage, watching Iain stride down the hall. His long, thick legs ate up the distance, and his arms bulged with the weight of the gear he carried.

He surveyed her up and down, his black eyes sparkling with respect. "You were fast."

"It's easy to pack when you own nothing."

Her flippant comment made him frown. "We'll fix that when we get back. You should have the things that make you happy."

"Things don't make a person happy."

"It'll make me happy to see you with them."

She tried to picture him smiling, and the only image she could conjure was the one of him smiling down at Serena, love filling his gaze. She would have liked to have him look at her with half as much emotion. Hell, even a fleeting grin would be miraculous.

"Why don't you ever smile?" she asked him as they went into the garage.

"Demons roam the earth. The people I consider family keep dying. Chances are I won't live to see summer. What's there to smile about?"

The idea of his death left her cold. Her voice came out in a wavering whisper. "Why do you think you'll die?"

"Shit happens," was all he said.

Jackie was certain there was something more to it than that. "That's it? Shit happens?"

He unlocked the doors of a big SUV and stowed his gear in the back. He took the strap of her bag from her shoulder and added it to the pile. "I've lived a long time. I've gotten lucky more than most. I may not grow old and die like humans, but I can be killed. Eventually, I will be. It's not something you need to worry about."

"Of course I'm going to worry. Especially when you talk like that. I . . . care for you."

His jaw tightened and his gaze went cold. "Don't," was all he said, and then he turned and got in behind the wheel.

Jackie got in and fastened her seat belt. "You know, if you don't loosen up and at least try to get over your past, then you're going to be stuck with me for a long time."

"You don't need to worry about that."

"Meaning I don't need to worry, or it's none of my business?"

"Take it whichever way makes you stop talking about it fastest."

Jackie wasn't willing to let it drop. Iain was cold, but it was only because he'd been hurt. He'd lost the woman he loved. That would make anyone a bit frigid. And if this were just about him, she might have respected his decision to wallow in his grief. But it wasn't. His wallowing directly affected her. Until he got over his heartbreak, she was going to be tied to him, and no matter how wonderfully scorching his kisses were, neither of them wanted that. She wasn't just pushing him for her sake, but his as well.

"I see why you loved her. She might have been the most beautiful woman ever born. And fearless, too."

"Jackie," he said in warning.

"In my vision, it seemed like you two had been together for a while, and yet she still hadn't taken your luceria. Why not?"

A muscle in his jaw bunched and his knuckles went white as his grip on the steering wheel tightened. At first, she didn't think he'd answer, but she waited, hoping the silence would expand until he had no choice but to fill it.

"Her mother," he bit out. "Her mother forbade it. I wasn't good enough for Serena, and her mother forced her to wait in the hopes that another compatible mate would present himself."

"It never happened," guessed Jackie.

Iain shook his head. "No, it happened. Two days before she . . ." He trailed off, then cleared his throat. "Another warrior came through the town where we were staying. His ring reacted, and Serena's mother gave her to him."

"Gave?"

"Customs were different then. Serena's mother had been alive for centuries, and followed the old ways. She felt Serena was her property and she could do with her as she pleased. So she did."

"But I saw her with you. It looked like the two of you were planning on . . . you know."

"Serena snuck out and came to my home. We decided to bind ourselves to each other that night. I didn't want to wait, but she wanted everything to be just right. I knew her. I knew the vow she gave me would be forever. She wouldn't have left any room for her mother to separate us, other than in death."

"But you were attacked," said Jackie, remembering the vision. "She never had time to give you any vow."

He gave a slight nod. "She died because of me, because I didn't have the courage to steal her away from her overbearing mother. I'd wanted her to accept me as a son, for us to be a family. I thought that's what Serena wanted, so I played nice. It cost Serena her life. If she'd had access to my power, she could have defended herself. She would have survived."

And he would still be with her, happy like all the other Theronai couples.

The loss of that happiness was as tragic as Serena's death. And yet, if he'd been tied to another woman, Jackie wouldn't have had the courage to choose any of the men. He was the only one she could have picked. All the others she would have let down. It had been Iain's lack of hope that had allowed her to take a chance, and yet that same lack of hope was also keeping him from moving on.

Maybe a man like him could never get over the death of the woman he loved. Maybe that was what had stolen his hope.

Her head flopped back against the seat in frustration. This situation seemed impossible, and the more she thought about it, the worse things got.

She was tied to a man who was in love with a dead woman, when what she really wanted was for him to love her.

Jackie froze in her seat as the realization dawned on her.

No. That couldn't be true. She didn't want his love. What the hell would she do with it, even if she had it? She was strong and independent and ready to take back her old life.

Wasn't she?

Did it even matter? There was no way a man like Iain could ever love her. She was no exotic beauty who went toe-to-toe with demons, armed only with a skinny sword and blindingly fast reflexes.

She looked at him, enjoying the sight. She knew she shouldn't stare, but they were too close for her to resist, and watching him calmed some of the fear vibrating inside of her. There was something reassuring in his obvious strength, in the thickness of his limbs and the width of his shoulders. At one time, she would have considered herself shallow for thinking such things, but after having seen what he could do in a fight, she realized the value of such assets as being more than mere eye candy.

His body filled the space, radiating heat and energy. She didn't have to touch him anymore to feel the pool of power he housed. It wove through their connection, widening the conduit more with every passing hour.

She wondered what he was thinking, but didn't dare reach out and try to read his mind. That was too intimate, too intrusive. If he'd done so to her, she would have been pissed, so she kept her mind to herself like a good girl, despite her curiosity.

"You can't blame yourself for Serena's death," she said. "If you want to blame someone, blame her mother and those archaic beliefs."

"I think it would be better if we didn't discuss this anymore."

"I need something to distract me from what we're about to do. I still can't believe I let myself get talked into going back to one of those caves. If the demons find me and drag me in—"

"They won't. I won't allow it." He said it like the words created reality, like he could control the outcome through sheer willpower.

"You may not be able to stop them. What if you get poisoned again?"

"You have my power now. You're hardly defenseless anymore."

That was true. Sometimes she was sure she could feel a new ability come to her out of thin air. Helen had struggled with learning fire. Lexi had trouble doing anything for a while. But unlike with her sisters, the knowledge seemed to pop into her head when she needed it, as if she'd been born knowing what to do. Even things she'd never actually tried before, she was certain she could pull off.

At least her confidence hadn't been destroyed with the rest of her life.

They rode in silence for more than an hour. Weariness began to drag at her. She hadn't slept much in days, and she feared it would slow her reflexes or hinder her judgment. She closed her eyes, hoping to get a nap, and fell into a hard, dreamless sleep.

The car's engine went quiet, jolting Jackie awake.

"Easy," said Iain, putting a comforting hand on her thigh. "Everything's fine."

She'd woken so many times to terror and tragedy during her captivity, it was hard for her to remember that she was safe now. In those few brief seconds before she remembered she was free, her body reacted, filling her system with adrenaline.

Her heart raced, and it was hard to pull in a full breath. She focused on the heat of Iain's wide hand on her leg, sinking through her jeans. That was real. Solid. He wasn't going to let anything happen to her.

Slowly, her jangled nerves relaxed, and she filled her lungs with oxygen to slow her breathing.

"Next time I'll make sure you wake more gently," he said, staring at her, unmoving.

That comment sent all kinds of interesting ideas floating about her head. His mouth was gentle. He could definitely use that to good advantage. She wouldn't mind at all waking up to find his mouth on her.

Not that that was going to happen, but it was nice to think about, and gave her something else to fill her mind that had nothing to do with fear.

They were parked outside a small house that had neighbors so distant she could barely see them. The sun was low in the sky, casting stringy shadows over the ground. She'd slept for hours, likely thanks to the soothing effect his nearness had on her.

"Where are we?" she asked.

"You wanted to visit Samson. This is his home."

Surprise and joy slid through her, warming her up. "You arranged this?"

He shrugged one heavy shoulder and pulled his hand from her thigh. "Joseph doesn't know, but Samson's foster parents are expecting us."

She was so excited to see him again and hold him close. He was so precious, and the fact that he was still alive after several weeks was more than a miracle.

She reached for the car door handle, and hurried toward the house. Iain slipped smoothly in front of her, blocking her path. "There's something you need to know before we go in."

Was something wrong with Samson? Was he sick or dying like all the other half-Synestryn babies?

Fear sat in her stomach, cold and hard. She wasn't sure she wanted to know. "What?"

"He's not growing normally."

She grabbed his arm to steady herself. This couldn't be happening, not after he'd beaten the odds and survived.

Denial rose to Samson's defense, protecting Jackie from her worst fears. "They can't know yet. He's only a few weeks old. There's no way they can tell he's not growing yet. Give him time."

Iain's hand smoothed over her hair in a comforting caress. "No, it's not that. He's growing, but he's growing too fast. He's not the infant you remember. I didn't want you to be shocked when you saw him."

"He's too big?"

Iain nodded, cupping her shoulder. "I'm sure he's exactly the size he's supposed to be, but it's not normal for a human. He may have been altered in some way so he would grow fast, or it may simply be a side effect of his parentage."

While he was touching her, her fear for Samson was manageable. There was something about being near Iain that made the worst things seem not so bad.

She nodded her understanding, and then reached for his hand, threading her fingers through his. She needed to be strong for Samson, and if that meant clinging to Iain like some lovesick schoolgirl, then that's what she'd do. "I want to see him, but we can't stay long. It's almost dark. I won't draw any danger to him."

"Okay. Let's go."

Hope spent all day hydrating and lounging in the sun, soaking up as much as she could. It sank into her cells, reviving them in a way she still didn't understand. By the time dusk fell, she hurried back to the suite she shared with Logan.

She stripped out of her clothes and crawled into the bed next to him. It was still chilly outside, and his living heat curled around her, making her shiver. Even as deeply as he slept, he must have sensed her presence and turned to wrap his arms around her.

Hope stroked his arm, marveling at how his body had changed from the first time she'd met him. He'd been all gaunt angles and sharp bones, starving for sustenance. He'd been heart-stoppingly beautiful, but now he was even more so. Dense planes of muscles stood out under his smooth skin, tempting her fingers to roam over him, memorizing every ridge and hollow.

His breathing was deep and even, but as the sky darkened, he began to stir and waken.

She had to time this just right. If he was too sleepy, he couldn't respond to her, but if waked fully, he would reject what she wanted. And Hope was determined to have her way in this. Grace's life depended on it.

She draped herself over his naked body and rubbed herself against him. His cock twitched and hardened, and he let out a low moan of pleasure. She was already wet, having plotted out her seduction all day. A low buzz of arousal suffused her, making her feel weak and powerful all at the same time.

Hope fitted them together and rocked her hips, sliding him into her in slow, clinging thrusts. His breathing sped, and his lovely eyes began to flutter as he woke more.

Any second now, his brain would engage and his need to protect her would kick in. He'd fed from her only two days ago, and she knew he'd resist doing so again so soon for fear of hurting her. No matter how hard she argued with him that she was fine, that all it took for her to recover was a bit of time in the sun and some water, he still refused.

But not tonight. Tonight she was getting her way.

She tugged on his shoulders, urging him to sit up. He moved slowly, lacking his usual grace, but he did as she insisted.

Hope lowered herself onto him fully, loving the feel of him buried as deep as he could go inside of her. She cradled his head, bringing his mouth to her throat. "Drink," she whispered.

Logan let out a low, animalistic growl, but kept his lips clamped shut.

What if she'd waited too long and he was already awake enough to know what he was doing?

It was hard to think with his erection stretching her, and the press of his body against hers. She'd thought she could keep her head better than this. They'd been together so many times since they'd met. It wasn't as if this was something new.

"Please," she said, using her fingers to ease his lips open. "I need it. Bite me."

The growl deepened, vibrating her chest. A second later, she spun around and landed hard on the bed. Logan's hips pumped, powering against her with deep, heavy thrusts. His teeth grazed her neck, and then a sharp pain made her gasp.

Logan's mouth sealed over her skin as he drank, the slight suckling sensation making her head spin. His cock continued moving within her, driving away the ability to think. She let go, giving in to her body's demands, and started moving in time with him.

Pleasure coiled inside of her, pulling tighter and tighter with each thrust, each suckling pull at her neck. She didn't even bother to try to stop it. She let go and let her orgasm come, ricocheting inside of her.

The sound of her cries filled the room and Logan's arms clenched around her as he drove deep. He let out a rough groan and came deep within her, filling her while the last pulsing waves of her own release eased.

Languid and sated, she lay there, enjoying the stroke of his tongue across her skin and the heat of their joined bodies.

"You manipulated me," said Logan. He'd levered

himself up on his arms and was staring down at her with a faint glow emanating from his pale eyes.

"Maybe a little. But I wasn't lying. I needed you to do it."

"Why?" His jaw was tense, bulging with anger.

"That woman I told you about? The one who sent me here? I remembered how to make contact with her using the Sentinel Stone, and I'm going to need your help."

"You didn't need to trick me to get it."

"I did, and you know it. All of your efforts have been going into healing those children, ridding them of the poisoned blood flowing in their veins. You're exhausted all the time. Don't try to pretend otherwise."

"I don't want you to worry," he said, stroking her hair away from her face. He was still hard inside of her, seemingly in no hurry to disengage their bodies.

He'd be moving away from her if he was truly mad, wouldn't he? Or maybe he was doing it to distract her. There was no way a woman could think straight in this position. It simply wasn't possible.

"You said messing with gateways was dangerous. I don't want either of us too weak to do this, so I spent the day in the sun refueling so that both of us could be strong."

His eyes scoured her face, looking at her with such love she still couldn't believe how lucky she was. She'd never expected any man to love her the way Logan did—certainly not one built like a god.

"Let's do this thing, then," he said. "And then we'll come back here where I can make love to you properly."

She grinned at that. "Properly? Is there something wrong with what we just did?"

"Yes. You need kissing and foreplay and many more orgasms." He moved off her and headed for the shower.

She didn't dare follow him for fear he'd make good on his promise and they'd spend the rest of the night in bed. The sad truth was Grace might not have that long.

A few minutes later, Hope led Logan outside to the Sentinel Stone that had been recently located in the old Tyler building. It had taken a flatbed truck and the magic of several powerful women to get it into place here, but it had been worth the effort. It looked right set among the trees and tranquillity here. It belonged.

"What are we going to do?" asked Logan.

Hope took the wooden amulet from around her neck—the one inscribed with her name. It had been the only item that had come through the gate with her. She hadn't even had her memories to guide her, only this one thing that had offered more questions than answers.

Until she'd met Logan. He'd helped unlock the door to her past, allowing her to know who she was for the first time in years.

She rolled up the message she'd written and wrapped it up in the leather cord holding the amulet. "We're going to crack open the gate and toss this in. With any luck, someone will find it and send help for Grace."

He tucked her hair behind her ear and slid his fingers down over her throat in a heated caress. "Are you sure this is worth the risk?"

Hope nodded. "Grace is worth it."

"She is, but are you sure that there's some hope of finding her help in this way?"

"If that woman who sent me here is as powerful as I think she is, there's a real chance she could create some kind of cure. All she has to do is toss it through the gate and we'll be able to save Grace."

Logan pulled in a deep breath and nodded. "As you wish, love."

Chapter 15

Iain felt Jackie's raging emotions pulsing through the luceria. She was excited and fearful, filled with hope and denial. She was no fool. She knew that Samson's odds of surviving were low—not only because so many children like him had died within hours of their birth, but also because if he showed even the slightest sign of Synestryn tendencies, he would be caged or killed.

Her fingers trembled between his, and it brought out protective instincts he'd thought long dead. It was one thing to know it was his job to keep someone safe, but another thing entirely to *want* to do so. That desire had been gone for so long, it was hard to keep it in check.

He had no idea what was happening to him—whether his own emotions were being restored, or if he was simply borrowing some from Jackie—but whatever the case, he was finding it difficult to remember his duty beyond where she was concerned.

There was a potential demon breeding site not far from here. That's where they should have gone, but he couldn't control the urge to make her happy—to give her a chance to see the child she'd saved with her insight.

If Jackie hadn't noticed that the sun seemed to drive away the Synestryn taint lingering inside Samson, chances were he'd already be dead. It seemed only fair that she get to visit with him and see with her own eyes how he fared.

Iain rapped on the door, and it opened to reveal a young man. He was clean-shaven, wearing a crisp button-up shirt and a loosened tie, as if he'd just gotten off work. "Yes?"

"I'm Iain Terra. This is Jackie Patton."

The man's face brightened with acknowledgment. "We're expecting you. Come in." He stepped back to make room for them to pass.

"I'm Will, and this is my wife, Dana."

Dana rose from the couch. She was also young, pretty, and wearing rumpled sweats and a stained T-shirt. Weariness hung around her, but also an air of happiness. She offered them a tired smile. "We're so glad you could come. Hold on. I'll go grab Samson. I'm sure he's awake by now."

"Don't wake him if he's not," said Jackie. "I don't want to disturb him."

Her fingers tightened around Iain's, and he tried to send her comfort through their link. He didn't know exactly how to do it, or if he was even capable of such things, but he had to try.

With every passing minute, anger grew within him. It wasn't nearly as bad as it had been before his meeting with Tynan, but he felt it creeping in, swelling as time passed. For now he was able to think clearly and offer Jackie what she needed, but he wasn't sure how long it would be until all he could think about was finding something to kill.

His days were numbered. He didn't want to spend the last few he had fighting his rage, when he could spend them trying to help Jackie see that their world wasn't so bad. That she belonged here.

"We're so happy that Joseph decided to let us keep Samson. He's brought so much joy to our lives," said Will.

"So there are no signs that he's evil?" asked Jackie.

Will hesitated. "He's . . . different than most kids. As I told Iain, he's growing fast. He eats a lot, and he seems to prefer meat to other foods."

"Meat?" asked Jackie. "He's way too young to be eating meat."

Dana walked into the living room. A toddler walked beside her, wobbling on his feet.

Jackie's shock blasted through their link, and a split second later, her body began to sag. He grabbed her around the waist and pulled her against him to keep her on her feet.

"He's so big," whispered Jackie. "How is this possible?"

"Please," said Dana, "watch what you say. He's smart and picks up on the emotions of others too easily. If you're upset, you're going to upset him."

"I'm sorry. I was just surprised."

Samson stared up at them with bright blue eyes. Iain thought he saw a few specks of black flitter through Samson's irises, but he couldn't be sure without staring.

"You've made sure he gets plenty of exposure to sunlight?" asked Iain.

"Yes. Just as Joseph said. Samson likes it, so we play outside a lot. Will built us a greenhouse so we could be out there in the winter, too."

Jackie looked at Dana, then back at Samson. The look on her face was one of awe and tenderness. "May I hold him?" she asked.

"That's up to Samson." Dana knelt down and asked the child, "Do you want to go see Miss Jackie?"

Samson looked at Jackie, then back at his foster mother. He nodded.

Jackie stepped forward, out of Iain's arms. He didn't like that she'd left, and he had to fight back a surge of irrational annoyance.

She held her arms out to Samson, waiting to see what he'd do.

He toddled into her embrace, and she hefted him up, grinning as she hugged him tight. A look of longing consumed her features, barely hidden by the joy beaming out of her. "You've gotten so big. I've missed you so much."

Samson pulled back, gaze somber as he studied her face. His chubby hands patted her cheeks, and then he pointed at her eye, then at his.

"He remembers you," said Dana.

"Of course he doesn't. He was too little."

"No, he's telling you that he's seen you before. It took us a while to work out his hand signals, but I've gotten pretty good at it now."

"Do you remember me, Samson?"

Jackie's eyes widened and she swayed slightly on her feet. Iain hurried forward and wrapped his arms around both of them so she wouldn't fall over with the child.

"He . . ." Jackie trailed off, shock whitening her skin.

"It's okay," said Will. "It's part of how he communicates. Don't be afraid."

"What did he do?" Iain demanded, struggling to keep his voice in control.

"I saw a flash from the night he was born. I saw my own face backlit by the sun."

Dana nodded and pulled Samson out of Jackie's grasp as if worried for his safety. "It's what he saw that night. I told you he remembers you. He seems to remember everything."

"Has he shown any signs that he's dangerous?" asked Iain.

A second later, his mind filled with an image of him scowling, towering over Jackie while she held newborn Samson. He'd threatened to kill the child, thinking he was a demon, but Jackie had stayed his hand.

That night, Iain had been the dangerous one. He realized now how that had to have looked to Samson, so small and helpless—how afraid he must have been.

"He's a good boy," said Dana. "He's different, but not evil. We're raising him right."

"I know you are," said Jackie. Then she looked at Samson. "I always knew you were a good boy from the moment I saw you. You're going to make us all proud."

Iain didn't like it. The child was a risk, or at the very least an unknown. He couldn't let Jackie linger here. Night was falling, and it was no longer safe. For any of them.

"We should go now. It's getting dark, and we still have work to do."

Jackie nodded and leaned over to kiss Samson on the cheek. She pointed at his eye, and then at her own. "I'll see you again soon."

They left the modest house and went back out into the cold. Jackie hugged herself, and he could feel a wistful sadness radiating out from her. He wanted to wash it away, but there was nothing he could think to do.

Once they were in the car, she said, "Thank you. For bringing me here. It's good to know that he's okay."

"It made you sad."

She was quiet as he pulled out of the driveway and onto the road. "It made me wish I'd been able to keep him. I've missed so much in such a short time. He's already walking. He'll be talking any day now, at this rate. I hate that I wasn't a part of that, you know?"

"He remembered you."

She smiled, shaking her head. "He did. It's hard to believe, but he did."

"He'll remember this visit, too."

"So will I." Jackie looked out the side window, leaning her head against the glass. "I'm not going to let Joseph stop me from seeing him again. I'm not going to let that child think that I don't want to be a part of his life."

"Even if it's dangerous? We have no idea what he's going to grow up to be, or what he's capable of now, even."

"I don't care. I understand that Joseph doesn't want to risk having him inside Dabyr, but he gets no say over what risks I take on my own."

"What about me? Do I get a say?" he asked, knowing it was stupid to even hope for such things.

She turned toward him. "Do you think he's evil?" she asked.

"Evil is not something you are—it's what you do." It had to be, or Iain was a giant hypocrite for not killing himself long ago, the way he did with other soulless creatures. "As long as his actions are good, then he deserves to live."

Jackie let out a heavy sigh. "He's never going to fit in anywhere, is he? Humans will know he's not normal, and your people will shun him because of who his father was."

"Our people. You keep forgetting that you're one of us."

"I'm a lot like Samson, you know? Both of us are screwed because of who our father was. He and I are going to have to stick together."

Iain bit back his comment that she wasn't screwed—she just hadn't accepted her fate yet. If aligning herself with Samson made her feel better, then let her think what she wanted. "How are you going to be part of his life and have your old life back?"

"I don't know, but I'll find a way. I'm smart. Samson is obviously smart. We'll make it work."

Like him, she wanted everything. He didn't have the heart to tell her that it wasn't possible. She could no more live a human life with Samson in it than he could breathe new life into his soul and be the man she deserved. They were both fooling themselves, and sooner or later, they were both going to have to choose between what they wanted and what was right.

He was pretty sure he knew how it ended for both of them. He only wished he was going to live long enough to see her come to accept her rightful place.

Logan hated taking risks like this with Hope. She had no idea how precious she was. And until today, he'd had no idea how easy he was to manipulate.

Still, he couldn't be mad at her. She was doing what she thought was right. He couldn't fault anyone for that, or he'd die a hypocrite.

He did exactly as she said, funneling his power at a specific set of runes carved into the side of the Sentinel Stone. They began to glow with blue fire, and a brilliant line of light spewed out, widening as he kept his focus on those runes.

"Keep going," she said. "Just for one more second." She tossed her amulet and the attached note into the light and stepped back. "There. Let it go."

Logan did. He released his power, letting it flow back into himself. He expected the gateway to snap shut, but instead, it stayed open those scant six inches.

And then it began to widen.

Fear took hold of him, and he grabbed Hope, shoving her behind him. He knew gateways were dangerous, and yet he'd let her stand next to him while he did this, risking her life like an idiot.

He focused on those runes and tried to funnel power away from them. "Go get help," he ordered. "I may not be able to stop it."

And there was no way of knowing what might come through. If Hope was right, then this place, this Temprocia, was rustic but not terribly hostile. But if she was wrong or he'd accessed the wrong runes, then there was no way to know what would soon be stepping into their domain.

Logan's efforts seemed to be doing no good. The crack continued to widen.

He stopped wasting his power trying to close it and readied himself for attack. Moments later, several Theronai came running out of the main building, swords drawn.

"Hope said there was trouble," said Nicholas, who came to stand beside him, blade in hand.

"Perhaps. I can't close the gate. I don't know what may come through."

"We'll be ready for it," said Nicholas, radiating confidence.

Joseph's angry voice sounded from behind him. "What the fuck are you doing?"

"It's not his fault," said Hope. "It was my idea."

"Yeah? Well, the next time you get an idea, ignore it."

Logan barely controlled the anger lashing inside of him. "Do not speak to her that way. It was my choice to participate. We are trying to save Grace's life."

"By provoking an attack from another world? Great idea," said Joseph.

There was a high-pitched, tearing kind of sound, and a moment later a figure appeared inside of the light. All he could see was a silhouette, but it appeared to be human, and alone.

The figure stepped through, and the light winked out, revealing a woman of indeterminate age. She was draped in shaggy layers of fur, leather, and rough fabric, all in muted, natural colors. Long, silver hair flowed over her shoulders and down past her hips. Her smooth face was a perfect mix of beauty and strength. The color and movement in her eyes reminded him of leaden waves kicked up by storm winds. Those eyes also gave away her origin. This woman was Athanasian.

She stood still, regarding the group of people that had gathered. As soon as her gaze fell on Hope, her lips quirked in a slight smile of relief. She opened her arms and Hope rushed forward before anyone could stop her, embracing the woman.

Logan shifted a protective step closer, unsure if he should pull Hope away or trust her instincts.

Hope turned and offered him a teary smile. "This is Brenya, the woman who raised me."

Brenya cupped Hope's face in her hands. "Are you well, child?"

Hope nodded. "Perfect. Everything turned out fine, just like you said it would."

"So you remember?" The woman's voice was soft and melodic, almost mesmerizing.

"Some things. Logan helped restore what I'd lost. More of my past comes back to me in bits and pieces, but I remember you. We need your help."

Brenya opened her hand, and in it was Hope's amulet and the curled paper on which she'd written her note. "I mustn't stay long. Time flows more swiftly in Temprocia, and every moment I'm away is one my people are in danger."

Joseph stepped forward. "I'm Joseph, leader of this place and these people."

"Then you shall lead me to Grace." Her tone was imperial, demanding obedience as her rightful due.

"First you tell me who you are," said Joseph.

Power seemed to radiate out from her, making her appear taller than she really was. "I'm a healer. That's all you need to know."

"No, it's not."

"Let her help," said Logan. "This may be Grace's only chance."

Joseph's mouth twisted with frustration, but in the end, he nodded. "I'm coming with you."

"Good. You may be of use," said Brenya.

"Logan, you and Hope come with us. The rest of you stay here. Make sure nothing else comes through behind her."

"I'll see to it," said Nicholas.

The four of them hurried to the room where Grace lay, barely alive. Torr was on the far side of the bed, but as they came in, he rose to his feet, his hand going to his sword. "Who's this?"

"My mother," said Hope. "She's here to see Grace."

"Not your mother, child. Serrien alone holds that honor. I merely took what she willingly sacrificed."

"I don't understand. Serrien is my last name."

"Your mother's name. She gave you to me so she could return to her world before the Solarc learned of her disobedience. But that is a story for when there is more time."

The Solarc ruled Athanasia with absolute authority. He was a megalomaniacal bastard by all accounts, and solely responsible for the starvation Logan's kind suffered. The Solarc was the one who ordered the gate shut, cutting off the source of blood the Sanguinar needed to survive—a curse handed down as punishment on the children of those who dared to defy him. If this woman worked against the Solarc, then she was likely more friend than enemy.

Brenya stepped up to the bed, watching Torr as she would a venomous snake. "Do you claim this dying woman?"

"I do. Hurt her and I'll make sure you regret it."

Brenya gave him a satisfied nod and rested her long-fingered hand on Grace's pale brow. She closed her eyes for a moment, and when she opened them, there was more than a hint of surprise in her gaze. "She did this for you?"

Torr swallowed and nodded, shame burning bright in his cheeks.

"Can you help her?" asked Hope.

"Perhaps. If she lives long enough. The time left to her can be measured in heartbeats."

Torr's voice was filled with demand. "Then do something. Now. Before it's too late."

"I can't. At least not here. It will take longer than one night to do what must be done, and the Solarc will know I'm here once the sun rises."

"Who cares what that fucking asshole knows?" Torr nearly shouted.

"You will when he sends his Wardens here to cut me down."

"Yeah," said Hope. "You definitely don't want to mess with those guys."

"She's right," said Logan. "One of them almost killed us."

"So what do we do?" asked Torr. "You can't walk away."

"I can and I will," said Brenya. "Whether I walk away with Grace is up to you."

"Me?" asked Torr.

"What you ask of me is dangerous. It could kill me."

"So could I," warned Torr.

Joseph took hold of Torr's arm and in a low voice said, "Threats are not exactly helpful here. How about you try a little respect for a woman who is likely more powerful than all of us put together."

Torr's jaw bulged, and he bit out, "What do you want me to do?"

"What are you willing to do?"

"Anything," said Torr too quickly. There was something about the way he said it that bothered Logan, making him wonder if his lifemark was still healthy as it had been a few weeks ago.

Brenya smiled, but there was no warmth there, only satisfaction. "Good. Remove your shirt and kneel."

Torr did as she asked, dropping to his knees in front of the woman.

"I'm going to mark you, and when I do, I will be able to summon you at any time from any place. You will pledge to me your sword arm and your fealty, vowing to defend me and my people in battle even at the cost of your own life. Do you so swear?"

"I do," said Torr with no hesitation.

Brenya laid her hand on his shoulder. Torr hissed in pain. She didn't let him flinch away, but held on tight, forcing the contact to go on for several seconds. When she pulled her hand away, there was an angry red mark in the shape of a crescent moon.

"You are mine now."

"Whatever," said Torr. "Just save Grace. Please."

"I will try. Bring her."

Logan said, "We can't disconnect her from the machines. She can't breathe on her own."

Brenya looked at Torr. "He will breathe for her."

"Before you go," said Logan, "there's something I need to know. Are there more women like Hope?"

Brenya's leaden eyes darkened with sorrow. "There are. Precious, hidden souls lost in a strange world."

"How do I find them?"

She shook her head, making her long, silver hair sway about her hips. "I do not know. I stripped them of their past and tucked them in among the humans to protect them. You will find them or not on your own."

"Did you give them each an amulet like mine?" asked Hope.

"The daughters of Celentia and Lahrien came through before you," said Brenya, a heavy sadness tugging at her mouth. "I gave them nothing, not even their names. That haunted me, so when I sent you away, I did so with your name, hoping it would give you some comfort to know that you were loved enough to be given the most basic of possessions."

Hope clutched Logan's arm, and he could hear her pulse speed. "I remember them. I played with them when I was little."

"Perhaps you can find them and see that they are safe? I would very much like to know that they are well."

"We'll find them," said Logan.

Joseph said, "And if you send any more people through the Sentinel Stone, they will come to us, safely behind our walls. We will protect them as we would our own."

Brenya regally nodded her head once in gratitude.

Andra busted into the room, her face red and her chest puffing with exertion. She looked at Brenya and froze. "Is it true? Are you a healer?"

"I am."

"You have to come see my sister. She needs you."

"I must leave. There's no more time."

"Please. Will you just look at my sister? The Sanguinar have tried to help her, but . . ."

Brenya eyed Andra, from the bottom of her combat boots to the top of her head, which was several inches above Brenya's. "Are you a warrior?"

"I blow shit up when I get the chance. Does that make a difference?"

"Do you claim your sister?"

Andra frowned, looking around the room for guidance. "Claim her?"

"Is she yours? In your keeping?"

"Yes. I take care of her."

Brenya looked to Joseph. "What is wrong with this woman?"

Logan spoke before Joseph could. "Tori was taken when she was eight. She was fed Synestryn blood for ten years. It's made her violent. None of us have been able to filter the taint from her blood."

"You've tried?" asked Brenya.

"Many of us have. She was with them too long. It . . . changed her."

Andra closed her eyes in agony. "I should have listened to Nika. I should have found her before it was too late."

Brenya looked at Joseph. "I will take this child."

Joseph seemed to count silently before responding, as if trying to rein in his temper. "Are you asking or are you telling?"

"I am doing this thing. Bring her to the gate."

"Do you have to take her?" asked Andra. "She's so fragile."

"Then she will not survive what I must do to cleanse her. Perhaps I should not bother."

"No," Andra hurried to say. "I don't mean that. She's strong. But her mind is troubled. I worry about her going anywhere without me."

"I have no time for this. I go now, with or without your sister."

"With. Please. Whatever it takes."

Brenya studied Andra for a long moment. "Remove your shirt and kneel."

Chapter 16

Jackie had hoped for something to distract her from missing Samson, but facing a cave was not exactly her first choice.

Iain drove the SUV over a rutted, barely discernible path and parked it. Even from inside the car, this place felt familiar. There had been leaves on the trees when she'd been here last, not only the first buds of spring. It hadn't been nearly as windy, and it had been much, much warmer.

"I've been here before," said Jackie. "It was the second cave they held me in."

"Are you sure?"

The things she'd seen were not those easily forgotten. Even from a few yards away, she could see the gaping hole in the ground, hidden only partially with brush. The slope of the land obscured it from anyone more than fifty feet away, making it an excellent place to hide.

They'd passed a collapsing farmhouse on the path here, and the skeletal remains of a barn. No one had lived here for a long time. Whoever owned this land probably had no idea it was infested with demons.

It made her want to research county records and make a few phone calls to warn people to stay away. Of course that was only going to make her sound crazy, and possibly even bring people here to check out her insane claims.

"This is a scouting mission only," said Iain.

"What does that mean?"

"It means we're not here to fight unless we have to. I'm going to go in and see if I can find that Synestryn breeding demon you were talking about, and then I'm going to come right back out."

"And what am I going to be doing?"

"Sitting in the car, all safe and warm. You've done your part already, identifying the cave. If you run into trouble, throw up a shield—which you know how to do—and I'll be here as fast as I can."

"How will you even know I'm in trouble?"

"I'll know. I'll feel your fear."

"You're in my head? I told you that I didn't want—"

"It's not something I'm doing. Your emotions flow into me. I can't help but feel them."

"I don't like it," she grumbled.

"I'm not exactly a fan, myself, but we're stuck with it for the time being. We're both going to have to learn to deal."

Iain got out of the SUV and went to inspect the cave entrance. As he was walking back, the headlights hit him, shining off his black leather jacket. He showed no fear, even though he was about to descend into a pit of monsters. His walk was steady and determined, his powerful thighs bunching beneath his jeans with every step.

He opened the rear hatch and started to rummage through the gear. Cold wind whipped through the SUV, sucking away all the heat that had built up inside. Jackie shivered, closing the front of her new coat to ward off the chill.

She didn't like this at all. She wasn't the kind of person who sat around and let others do the work. What if he ran into trouble? That cave could be filled with dozens of demons, even hundreds. There was no way he could face those odds alone and survive.

The idea of going down there scared her to death.

The things she'd seen were too horrific to face, and she knew that if she went down there, those memories would force their way to the front of her mind, demanding that she relive them.

She couldn't do it. She wasn't strong enough.

But she also couldn't leave a man she cared about to dive alone into a dangerous situation when her presence could mean the difference between life and death.

As much as she hated it, she knew what she had to do.

With a silent curse for having been dragged into this situation—into this world she wanted no part of—she shoved her way out of the car and stomped to the back of the SUV. "I'm going in with you."

"Like hell," he said, his tone flat and final.

No way was she going to let him make this decision for her. She was a grown woman, and in some ways more powerful than he was. He didn't get to boss her around. "I can go in with you, or I can wait until you're down there, and then go in. I don't know much about rappelling gear, so I could break my neck getting in, but I am going in."

He lifted his head from the ropes he was toying with and gave her a hard stare. "You were held prisoner here."

"I know."

"It scares you shitless to think about going down there. I've felt it."

"I know. I'm also scared to stay up here alone. I'm pretty much doomed to be afraid tonight, so I might as well do the right thing."

"There's no way to know what we'll see."

"I'm not a child."

"No, but there could be one down there. If there is, we may not be able to rescue them—at least not without backup. Are you going to be able to do that? Are you going to be able to walk away from a child in need?"

She knew that was beyond her, but it changed nothing. If she went down there, then any child in captivity would have a better chance of surviving with her help. "I'm going down there, Iain."

Anger tightened his jaw, making muscles bulge beneath his skin. "I could duct tape your ass in the seat."

"And leave me helpless to defend myself? You'd never do that."

"I can't risk your life letting you go down there. My brothers need you too much."

"It's not your life to risk. It's mine."

His nostrils flared and he shook his head, cursing beneath his breath. "Why are you being so obstinate?"

"Because you need me. Because despite the fact that you seem to have little regard for your own life, I happen to regard it very highly."

His gaze slid away as if he was trying to hide something. "Don't get too attached to me. We won't be working together long."

"So you've figured out a way to break our connection?" For some reason, the idea didn't seem as appealing as it had before. Maybe it was some kind of inherent magic in the luceria that tied them together, or maybe it was that she was no longer quite so appalled by the idea of sharing her emotions, but whatever the case, she was becoming used to having him around. She was getting used to having so much power as well, but even if she tapped into that of another man, she was sure it wouldn't feel the same. She wasn't sure she even wanted it to feel the same, as if that would somehow be cheating.

"I'm working on it," he said.

"How?"

"Don't worry about that right now. We need to focus on what we're doing here and now."

We. A jolt of victory shot through her as she realized she'd won. Then all she felt was dread, because she'd won. She was going down into that cave with him.

*   *   *

Iain kept careful tabs on Jackie, opening himself to let her chaotic emotions trickle into him. It seemed to feed his rage, but he couldn't tell if that was because he was somehow fueling his own feelings, or if it was a reaction to the trembling pile of fear she was putting off.

Either way, the monster within him—the one that Tynan had put to sleep somehow—was slowly waking and growing in strength. He could feel it happening and knew it wouldn't be long before he was right back where he'd been, fighting the constant need to kill.

He buckled Jackie into a harness, making sure that her face shield was in place. The magically enhanced trench coat she wore would protect her from some attacks, but he didn't plan to let her get close enough to need it.

They lowered themselves down. He kept tabs on her progress, staying by her side in case she started to panic. To her credit, she kept herself in control, even though he could feel how desperately she was fighting her fear.

Once this was done, he was going to inform Joseph that she needed to be kept out of combat situations. She wasn't ready for this. It was too much to ask of her, no matter how brave a face she put on.

They hit the floor of the cave. Jackie's breathing was shallow and fast, and he could feel little spurts of panic trembling through their link, beating in time with her frantic heartbeat.

He scanned the area, seeing no sign of demons this close to the entrance. During the day, it would be a dangerous place for Synestryn, so chances were they were deeper, where no light could reach.

Iain disconnected her line from the harness and cupped her face in his hands. She was so pretty, even though she was too pale and her gray eyes were wide with fear. He wanted to do something to ease her, but he was out of practice with such things, unsure what to do to comfort her.

The best he could offer was a distraction.

He lowered his mouth to hers, giving her the briefest, fleeting kiss. He knew if he let himself go further, he'd forget there was danger lurking nearby. She went to his head, driving out all rational thought.

Iain pulled back and tried to give her a reassuring smile. He couldn't seem to remember how to make those muscles move, or maybe they were weak from lack of use. Either way, all she got was what he was sure was a painful grimace.

"What was that for?" she asked.

"Luck," he said, hiding his true purpose.

Her cheeks had pinkened, and her pupils had dilated so she no longer looked so terrified. In fact, what he felt coming through the luceria now was a mix of confusion and the faintest hint of desire.

She wanted him, and that knowledge swelled within him, making him feel powerful.

His monster lifted its head as if scenting prey, but Iain ignored it. "We should go."

She nodded, licking her lips.

He was going to kiss her again. Not now, not when doing so could get her killed, but soon. He promised himself that he'd kiss her one more time before he died. That wasn't too much to ask in the way of a consolation prize.

Iain stepped away, shifting his focus to the job at hand. "Stay behind me and move as quietly as you can."

"I need a light."

"You can see in the dark. Just draw on my power and funnel it toward your eyes."

"Oh," she breathed. "Wow. That's amazing."

The speed at which she learned was what was amazing. It took most women weeks, sometimes years, to do what she seemed to be able to do almost instantly. He wasn't sure why that was, but if Tynan or one of the other Sanguinar found out, they might want to experiment with her.

Which would happen over his fucking corpse.

He ducked beneath an overhang of rock, following the natural opening in the stone. Jackie was at his back, so close he could feel the heat coming off her. The rough tunnel sloped down, hooking to the left around a giant stalagmite and stalactite that had been there long enough to meet and become a solid column. He moved to go around it when he felt Jackie tug at the back of his jacket.

Iain stopped and looked down at her. She was frowning, scanning the area as if confused. "I've been here before," she whispered.

"You said that."

"No, here," she said, walking to what looked like a crease in the rock wall. Instead, it was a narrow opening that led to another tunnel. "This way."

"Step back."

She did, and he squeezed through the gap, barely. He had to let his breath all the way out so that his chest collapsed enough to shove through. Jackie slipped through easily.

After a few steps, Iain could smell the fetid stink of Synestryn. It was cloyingly sweet and rancid, filling the tunnel like a fog. He tried not to gag, but the reflex was strong.

"Ugh," said Jackie.

A moment later, he felt a cool bit of power hovering over his mouth and nose. The air was clean, and he breathed it in.

"Better?" she asked.

Iain turned as he realized she'd done that. He'd never heard of such a thing, but then again, Jackie was nothing if not amazing. "I don't know how you did that, but it's handy." His voice came out slightly muted, as if he'd cupped his hands over his mouth.

Hers did, too. "It's necessary."

He continued down the tunnel, sword in hand. The rocks under their feet were loose, mixed with odd bits of bone. He heard Jackie stumble, heard the rocks shift suddenly and her quick inhalation of breath. Reflexes had him spinning before he could think about it, and he grabbed her arm to hold her up.

Her lips were parted in shock and the urge to kiss her again slammed into him out of nowhere.

This was not the time or the place. He knew that, but his body ignored facts, his fingers itching for the feel of her bare skin, his cock twitching in interest beneath his jeans. What he wouldn't have given for a nice, safe, quiet place where he could strip her bare and take his time kissing her from head to toe. Not that she'd want that, but Iain hadn't wanted anything quite this much for a long, long time.

Before he did something stupid, he let go of her slender arms and turned away.

The tunnel angled down, widening out as it went.

"I think we're close," she said in a faint whisper.

Her fear was no longer trickling into him—it was flowing, becoming more frothy and chaotic with each passing moment.

Iain tried to reassure her, forcing calming thoughts of safety and comfort through their link. He wasn't sure if what he'd done was working, or that he'd even reached her. Maybe there was something wrong with him— something about his dead soul that kept him from making the right connection. All he knew was that she was afraid, and the need for violence, the need to kill what was scaring her, was growing faster than he could control.

The monster pushed to its feet and began pacing the confines of its cage.

Iain moved forward cautiously. Inside his head, he got a momentary image of a cavern with three exits. One was lit, glowing with a faint golden light. In the next second, the image was gone, leaving him feeling oddly alone.

He ignored it, creeping round a bend in the tunnel. It

opened into a cavern nearly identical to the one he'd seen a moment ago.

Left, whispered across his mind, corresponding with the glowing exit.

Jackie. That had been her inside of him, guiding him forward.

The realization left him humbled and shaken. As much as she hated being part of their world, she was doing what needed to be done. He had to respect the hell out of her for that.

Of course it also meant that she was tying herself to him more tightly, or she never would have been able to communicate with him like that.

He was a fool for stringing her along like this. The closer she got to him, the harder it would be on her when he went to his death. What if she decided not to bond with another man, as Tynan had feared?

Iain turned to tell her to go back to the vehicle. He needed to end this here. Now. He didn't want her anywhere near the violence he was about to unleash, and he sure as hell didn't want her to witness his death.

From behind her, slinking along the path was a small, cat-sized demon.

He shoved Jackie aside and lunged at the beast before it could raise any kind of alarm. Its head flew through the air and hit the cave wall, tumbling until it bumped against Jackie's feet.

She let out a squeak of dismay and scrambled back, hitting her head on a section of rock protruding out from the wall.

Her body sagged, but she locked her knees and held herself up long enough for him to reach her.

"Are you okay?"

She pulled her hand away from the back of her head and her fingers were smeared with blood.

"Oh, shit," she whispered.

Iain didn't waste time echoing her sentiment. He

grabbed her arm and started hauling ass back out the
way they came. There was no wind down here to push
the scent of her blood around, but that hardly mattered.
They had only minutes, at most, to get the hell out of
here before every demon in the place came hunting for
a snack.

Jackie heard the demons coming. She remembered the
sound of their hunger all too well. The little ones made
these odd chirping sounds, while the bigger ones would
hiss or gurgle when they smelled a meal.

During her captivity, Zillah had commanded the demons, keeping them all at bay, allowing only those he
chose to feed from her. She hadn't realized until just
now how lucky she'd been.

They cleared a bend in the tunnel and came face-to-
face with at least a dozen pairs of glowing eyes. There
was no way they were going to make it out of this alive.

"I'll clear you a path," said Iain. "You run like hell,
shielding yourself from them."

She remembered the scar on the back of his hand—
the one that he'd gotten in a six-to-one fight. The odds
here were half as good as that, and he'd said he'd nearly
died that night. She refused to let that happen.

"I won't leave without you."

"You'll do what it takes to get out alive."

"With you," she insisted. Even the thought of climbing out of these caves alone left her shaking and cold.
She needed him at her side to stay strong and not break
down into a quivering mass of cowardice in pissed pants.

Iain let go of her arm and waded forward, as if he was
actually going to take on all of those things single-
handedly.

Before he could, Jackie yanked on his power and shot
a glob of fire at the closest demons.

Their fur burst into flames, and they screamed, leap-

ing back into their own numbers. Several more caught
fire, until it was one giant mass of singed fur and flame.

Iain pressed her toward the wall, shielding her from
the threat with his body. "We have to move. More are
coming."

Right. She knew that. She'd been so distracted by the
fact that her magic had worked that her brain had
stopped spinning for a moment.

The scent of burning hair and rancid demon filled the
tunnel. The magic she'd used to filter the air had failed
when she'd lost concentration.

She put that back in place, and then erected a thin
straw-shaped shield. The cylinder shot through the writhing mass of dying demons, glowing blue like at the heart
of a flame. She ordered that skinny straw to bend to follow the curve of the rock, then widen, opening up a tunnel for them to crawl through.

Jackie tried to send Iain an image of what she was
doing, but she wasn't sure if her message got through.
What she was sure of was that if she went through that
tunnel, so would he.

As soon as it was wide enough for his massive shoulders to pass through, she dove in, scrambling for the far
side of the tube.

Blood from her hand smeared against the wall she'd
created. Those demons that weren't being consumed by
fire clawed at the shield, trying to get to her.

Panic closed in around her, making it hard to breathe.
More demons were going to be waiting at the far end.
She didn't see them yet, but she knew they'd be there.

She couldn't let them take her alive. She couldn't go
back to being used by them, starved and tortured on a
daily basis. She'd rather die than live through that again.

"Don't you fucking quit on me," growled Iain from
right behind her. "Move!"

Until his roughly given order, she hadn't realized that

she'd stopped crawling. His words had her arms and legs moving, as if he'd simply taken control of them. She wasn't sure how he'd done it, but right now, she had other worries.

Namely, what would be waiting for her on the far side of the turn.

"Close it down behind me," shouted Iain. "They're following through."

Her head was throbbing, and a slow spin of dizziness had started to make it hard to balance. She hadn't thought she'd hit her head that hard, but now she was starting to think differently.

Maybe it was just all the slinging around of magic that was wearing her out.

Jackie tried to do what Iain said, being careful to err on the conservative side. She really didn't want to accidentally lop off his legs. They were way too nice for that.

She kept moving, slowing as she reached the turn. She was sure that one of the demons was going to fly through at any moment, clawing at her face.

As if in response to that worry, she felt power flow through her, and a faint blue glow filled her vision.

There was a barrier directly over her face shield—the one Iain had insisted she wear in case they ran into demons that spat poison. The barrier moved with her, rather than stopping her from progressing farther. It seemed to cling to her, which made her wonder if she couldn't simply wear it around like armor.

The stray thought clattered around in the back of her mind while she forced herself to make that final turn and face what lay ahead. As soon as she did—as soon as she saw what was waiting—she desperately wished that she'd let Iain go first.

Chapter 17

Torr followed Brenya out to where the Sentinel Stone stood. Grace was limp in his arms. Every few steps, he covered her mouth with his and forced a breath into her lungs.

He was terrified. She was so fragile, so light. Her body was even weaker now than it had been only hours before. He could see it in her pale skin and fluttering heartbeat. What if Brenya couldn't help? What if the simple process of moving Grace was enough to kill her?

Torr was never going to forgive himself for letting this happen. He should have seen it coming. He should have known that Grace had such a soft heart that she'd do anything to ease his suffering. He should have seen it the last time she came to visit him to tell him she was taking a vacation. It was there, shining in her eyes—her determination, her sorrow-filled farewell. All he'd had to do was pay attention and he could have stopped her from sacrificing herself for him.

But it was too late for that. All he could do now was carry her weakened body and give her the breath from his lungs.

It wasn't enough after what she'd given him. Not even close.

Brenya tilted her head to the side as if listening and then she turned to Joseph. "You have a visitor. Along the back wall. She's been waiting a long time for someone to free her from her prison. Apparently none of you could hear her cries for help as I did."

"What are you talking about?" asked Joseph.

"I have freed her. Go and learn for yourself."

Joseph nodded to a couple of the men, and they set out, jogging toward where Brenya had said.

Torr didn't care about visitors, welcome or not. His entire focus was on Grace and keeping her breathing. He held her close, trying to keep her warm in the chilly air. The blanket tucked around her body wasn't enough in this wind.

Andra had Tori by the arm, fighting against her sister's hold.

"I don't want to go," screamed Tori.

"I'm sorry, baby. You don't have a choice."

Tori snarled and tried to bite Andra's hand. Brenya must have seen it happen, because she pointed her finger at Tori and said, "Behave. This may be the last time you ever see your family again. Do you want this to be the way you are remembered?"

Tori spat at Brenya, who stepped smoothly out of the way so fast, she blurred. A maternal look of thunderous intent wrinkled the skin around her mouth, and she stepped forward, grabbing a fistful of Tori's hair. "You will tell your sister good-bye now."

Tori winced and bared her teeth at the woman.

"I'm sorry," said Andra. "It's not her fault."

"You treat her like a child. She hasn't been that for a very long time."

Tori seemed to calm down a bit at those words. Brenya led her by her hair to the Stone, and Torr was right on their heels, ready to go. He continued breathing for Grace, wishing his mouth were on hers for any other reason.

Her kisses had been so sweet, igniting his blood and making him want to be a better man so he deserved such a treat.

Those kisses were now all gone

Brenya lifted her hand and a white column of light erupted from the carvings in the Stone. It split the air, reaching up into the night sky. As the column widened, she turned to Torr. "Give her to me. We must go."

"I'm going with you."

"No."

Anger surged, but he bit it back, knowing that this woman might be Grace's only hope. "Someone has to carry her."

In the next moment, Grace became weightless and lifted from his arms. He grabbed for her, feeding another breath into her lungs before saying, "I'm going with you."

"I will not argue with you. This is the way it must be. She will live or she will die, but she will do it without you."

But what about him? He wasn't sure the same could be said for him. He loved her so much. How was he ever going to face the endless days without her in his life? "Please. Someone needs to breathe for her."

"I will do this. You stay. Do not remove the disk."

Brenya meant the disk fused into his flesh—the one that matched the one on Grace, the one that had magically transferred her perfect health to him and his poison to her. "Why not?"

"It could kill her. If it falls off, you will know I have failed and she is dead."

With that bit of news, Grace lifted out of his grasp completely and floated through the air toward the light. Torr watched the three of them disappear. The light winked out. The heat from where Grace's body had been only moments ago cooled. The crowd dissipated. Even Andra left, sniffing as Paul led her away in his embrace.

Torr stood there for a long time, feeling lost and empty. Grace was gone. There was no way to reach her.

He couldn't speak to her anymore. He couldn't touch her. Couldn't look at her.

He didn't even have a photo of her.

Ribbons of cold sank into his cheeks, and he realized he was crying big, fat tears of loss. Grace was gone, and the pain of that was worse than any he'd ever felt before.

There was no way for him to follow her, though he would have if he could. His future stretched out, bleak and desolate without her. He wasn't even sure if he wanted a future. Why live when he knew that he was destined to suffer for as long as he drew breath?

He had what he wanted, what he'd prayed for. His body was whole, and he was able to fight as he'd been born to do, as he'd ached to do for so long while stranded in his bed, trapped in his useless body.

But what was the point of fighting, when good people like Grace were just going to die anyway?

He went back to his suite, gathered a few things. Sorrow hung over him, making his steps slow and sluggish. There was nothing here for him. Not anymore. He wasn't sure if there was anything for him anywhere, but he couldn't stay here, with all the reminders of what was now gone.

Torr felt lost and utterly alone as he drove through the gates of Dabyr. He'd already left his cell phone behind, and dismantled the tracking device in his car so that no one could find him. He didn't want their pity or their company. All he wanted was to be left alone.

Grace was gone from the world, and there was nothing anyone could do to make that okay.

Iain heard Jackie's panic and knew what was waiting for them wasn't good. Impotent frustration seethed under his skin. He couldn't shove past her and face the threat first. There was no room. She was on her own for a few more seconds.

Smoke billowed into the glowing tubelike shield,

blocking his sight. It filled his lungs, making him cough out the acrid stench. His next breath was of clean, fresh air, but the smoke was still there.

Jackie's magic. She must have heard him cough and given him what he needed.

Iain surged to his feet the second he cleared the shield, lifting his sword. The screams of demons filled the cavern. He could see through plumes of smoke that several more demons were on fire, but he couldn't see Jackie. He couldn't tell if she was in danger.

The monster inside of him threw back its head, howling in rage. Iain bore down on it, telling it to shut the fuck up.

He could still sense Jackie, like sunlight glowing against his side, so he moved in that direction, making careful steps so he didn't bowl into her and slam her head into another wall.

Even the memory of the sight of her blood was enough to make his control stretch thin.

A dark shape leaped toward him, and he spun to attack, severing one of the demon's front paws. The thing hissed at him, and it wasn't until it was only a few feet away that he was able to see its face. It was human. Disturbingly so. The body of the demon was long-limbed and animalistic, but the face could easily have belonged to a teenage boy.

Iain hesitated—something he wouldn't have done a few days ago—and that hesitation nearly cost him his arm. The thing shot at him, latching its teeth just under his shoulder. Its jaws stretched open wider than was humanly possible, and its eyes rolled back in its head.

The warding on his coat kept the teeth from making contact with his skin, but he was going to carry a bruise from the crushing bite.

Iain jammed his blade down into the thing's neck and out the front of its chest. It went limp as its spinal cord was severed, and fell to the ground.

He kicked it away and moved closer to where he felt Jackie standing.

Iain found her finally, pressed into a deep crevice. Her hands were held up as if to ward off attack, and she was pale and sweating. Blood smeared her trembling fingers, and from her palms, he could sense a barely discernible flow of power.

He looked to see what she was doing, only to find at least twenty demons of different types fighting one another. They growled and bit, tearing flesh with their teeth. Beneath them, a pool of black blood spread out, widening as he watched.

"What the hell?"

She didn't say a word, but he could sense her fatigue. She was pulling more power from him than she had ever before, and the strain was too much.

Iain had to get her out of here.

"Put a shield up at our backs and run," he told her.

To her credit, she didn't stop to argue or question him. She understood instantly what he meant and he felt a shift in the power she drew from him as she did as he asked.

Iain took her arm and lifted her out of the crevice toward the exit. They still had to squeeze through that narrow opening, but if they could get that far, he could hold off whatever came their way.

Jackie moved too slow for his comfort, but she was wounded and exhausted. He couldn't expect her to go any faster and stay on her feet. He tried to take some of her weight, but as the tunnel narrowed, they had to go single file, and he had to leave her to her own power.

Anger coalesced in his gut. He never should have let her come down here. He should have taped her to the seat like he'd threatened. At least then she would have been safely aboveground.

Iain checked for danger on the other side of the crack, and when he saw none, he moved so Jackie could go through first. It took him much longer to squeeze through the narrow gap, and by the time he did, three more demons had found them.

That damn head injury was drawing them out, tempting them with the scent of her blood.

Jackie sagged. He could feel her drawing more power from him, but it was slower now, as if she was too weary to handle more.

Fire flickered out of her fingertips, sputtering as it went. Two of the beasts leaped out of the way, lunging toward them.

Iain stepped up and took them out with a couple of swift slices. It was nothing fancy, but he had no time for style right now. It was all about efficiency.

He took her by the arm again and sprinted toward the opening. As soon as he had a clear line of sight, his pace slowed.

Their SUV had been pulled down into the hole by the rappelling lines and was now crumpled and blocking their exit.

"Fuck!"

"Iain," said Jackie in that fearful tone he knew meant trouble.

He turned his head and saw the tunnel begin to fill with glowing green points of light. Dozens of them. Maybe hundreds. There was no way in hell he could take on so many at once, even if Jackie was at full strength.

"What do we do?" she asked.

Iain pulled her back, trying to offer her what cover he could. "I'll hold them off. You get yourself out of here."

"How?"

"Levitate, use wind currents, make a rope of magic. I don't know. Just do it. Fast."

"I'm so tired."

"I know. But you can do this," he said, trying to sound confident. "You *will* do this."

She didn't waste her breath talking. The weak tug on the luceria told him she was making an effort.

He took his off hand and cupped it around the back of her slender neck, letting the two halves of the luceria latch on to each other. It eased the flow of power between them, but he could only do it for a few seconds. The demons were closing in, and it was time to fight.

Jackie had never been as bone weary as she was right now. Every cell in her body ached with fatigue. Her joints felt brittle, and her skin felt like it had been coated with lead. Even breathing was hard.

The knowledge of how to lift herself and Iain out of this cave was within her, glowing with promise, but she could tell that it was no easy task. He was a big man, and moving him was going to take a monumental force of will—one she wasn't sure she had in her.

Of course, the only alternative was to leave him behind, and that she refused to do.

The heat of his hand at her neck soaked into her. Power slid through the luceria, pooling in her limbs, making them even heavier. She gulped down as much as she could as fast as she could, all the while eyeing the horde of demons creeping closer.

Iain stepped away to engage, but Jackie wasn't ready yet. She needed more time, more power to fuel her lift. It would do them no good to get halfway up to the fifty feet they had to go, only to drop onto a swarm of teeth and claws.

His body moved with lethal grace, his sword swinging in a silver arc. With each powerful swipe, another demon fell. But there were too many. One had slipped around the far edge and was trying to come at Iain from the side.

It was now or never.

Jackie unlocked the knowledge within her that showed her what she needed to do and let the power inside of her free. It lashed out, jerking her off the ground, propelling her upward at a nauseatingly fast pace.

Iain was right behind her. She could feel the drag of

his weight against her willpower and clenched her teeth to retain her concentration.

Halfway up, her body began to shake with exertion. She kept sucking Iain's power inside of her, channeling it directly to his weight. The sky overhead became visible, with stars twinkling cheerfully.

Below, demons began clawing their way up, scaling the walls toward the surface.

Even if she got them both out, there was no getaway car. They were going to have to run, and she knew that wasn't in her cards. She barely had the strength to breathe, much less run.

Dark spots began to blob in her vision, making it hard to see. She looked up, memorizing where she needed to guide them so they didn't bash into the rock walls.

A flash of dry grass passed in the corner of her eye. She was out. Now all she had to do was get Iain the rest of the way up.

Jackie angled herself sideways and plopped to the grass. Letting go of that effort gave her the remaining bit of strength she needed to haul his heavy ass up and over the edge of the pit. She heard him hit the ground with a grunt, and let go of the strand of power.

It snapped back into Iain like a rubber band stretched tight, leaving her feeling too weak to breathe. The demons were coming. She could hear their claws scraping on rock a few yards away, and yet she was too tired to care.

"Run," she panted, hoping Iain would at least save himself.

"On your feet," he snapped at her.

She would have laughed at him for such a ridiculous thought, but it was too much work.

He lifted her body and flung her over his shoulder. He broke into a dead run, her body flopping around against him hard enough to make her sick to her stomach. She couldn't even raise enough energy to complain.

"Get your shit together," he ordered. "They're right on our heels."

Her shit was as together as it was going to get. She was wrung out, dizzy, and struggling to simply breathe.

"Use me, damn it!"

A crazy part of her mind thought that sounded like a lovely idea. She could lay him out for her enjoyment, and take her time exploring his body. The few glimpses she'd had of his bare chest were enough to whet her appetite and make her want more.

Too bad she was too tired and dizzy to do anything about it.

Chapter 18

Iain swung around to face the oncoming demons. He put his back to what remained of the ancient barn and slid Jackie's limp body to the cold ground. He didn't like leaving her there, but it was safer than her staying slung over his shoulder while he waded into battle.

There were too many demons to bother counting. Mostly they were small, but all of them were deadly if left alive. Out here in the open like this, alone, he was too easy to flank. He'd faced worse odds than this before, but never with someone at his side who needed his protection. If it had just been him, he would have unleashed his monster and let it make him stronger and faster. But it wasn't just him, and every time he let that fucker out of its cage, it was harder and harder to put back.

What if he couldn't? The beast wanted Jackie. What if after the killing was done, it took what it wanted from her?

He didn't dare take the risk.

Iain moved forward to meet their charge, giving himself enough room so that he wouldn't step on Jackie, but not so much that any of the demons would have a chance to sneak in behind him to get to her. He started cutting them down, giving up all finesse for the sake of raw, brutal power.

The demons leaped at him, two and three at a time,

their serrated teeth bared and their claws extended. One
larger one with silvery spines started to vibrate to his
left, as if preparing to do something.

Iain wasn't taking the chance that it could launch
those spines—not with Jackie in jeopardy of being hit.
He left his right side open, hoping his coat would absorb
the worst of any blows, and cut the demon in half.

Silver spines exploded out in random directions,
bouncing off Iain's armored coat and hitting the rotting
wood with a hollow *thwack*. Three catlike demons got
hit in the bargain, skewering them, making them scream
and roll in pain.

While he'd been busy dealing with that threat, a pair
of larger Synestryn had slipped past him, zeroing in on
Jackie.

He was out of position, too far away to make it to
them in time.

Fear and rage detonated in his chest, and without his
permission, the monster inside of him broke free, taking
over his body. He felt muscles bunch, heard a roar tear
from his throat, saw the world blur by as he sped over
the ground. The first demon slammed into him, knocking him back. It seemed surprised that he'd appeared,
skidding on its paws to face the new threat.

The second demon was a split second behind and
jerked back in time to avoid a collision. Dried weeds
and clumps of dirt flew up from where its powerful claws
raked the ground.

Iain regained his balance and slammed his left fist
into the side of the demon's head. It spun around, yelp-
ing in pain. His body moved without thought, his blade
slicing through the air fast enough that it made a
whooshing sound. He cut through the thing's head, lopping off its eyes and snout. It continued to thrash and
claw as it bled out among the weeds.

The second demon was smarter, keeping its distance.

It waited for an opening as the smaller creatures threw themselves at Iain.

As fast as he moved, as strong as each strike was, there were simply too many of them. He couldn't keep them all away. One latched on to his leather coat and began crawling up his back toward his head.

That's when the bigger demon made its move.

There was no time to fight it off and remove the threat from his back, so he focused on the bigger one, urging his monster to hurry the hell up.

His body flowed through the moves easily, and for a moment, he enjoyed the sheer power he housed. The tip of his blade caught the foreleg of a smaller demon as it zeroed in on his real target. The slight hesitation in his strike that contact caused had been planned, allowing him to hit the larger demon in just the right spot. He severed an artery, and blood pumped out, arching several feet into the air.

Iain shifted his body and spun, letting the blood hit his back, rather than landing on Jackie. He couldn't feel the little demon on his back anymore, and as he glanced at Jackie, he realized why.

She had pushed herself up so that she was sitting against the barn's foundation. Her hand was raised, and smoldering at his feet was the corpse of the demon that had hitched a ride.

Weariness hung around her, making her shoulders droop and her eyes burn an angry red. She was panting with effort, but there was no sign she was giving up.

A potent wave of desire hit him out of nowhere. The monster forced Iain to inch closer. It wanted her. Iain's mouth was watering for a taste, his hands eager to feel her bare skin.

"Behind you," she gasped.

Iain swung around, instincts guiding him. He lifted his sword, and the demon flying toward him split in half on his blade as it hit, splattering his face mask with black, oily blood.

He whipped off the mask, which now prevented him from seeing anything, and searched the area for more demons.

In the distance, there were faint howls of hunger and excitement, but the ones that had left the cave to chase them were now gone.

"I've shielded my wound so they can't smell my blood," she said.

He tried to tell her how smart that was, but when he went to open his mouth, nothing happened. The monster was still in control.

He stalked toward her, hunger and desire growing with every step. The beast intended to take her here, on the ground, surrounded by leaking demon corpses. Iain could feel its intent as clearly as he could his own heavy pulse.

Iain struggled to regain control. Fear for Jackie made him desperate and the monster knew it. His head began to pound, and his steps slowed as their internal battle raged. Every time he thought he'd won, the beast would have a surge of strength and shove itself away.

"Iain? Are you okay?"

No, he was so far from okay it was laughable. It would be so easy to just let go. Let the monster win. He'd still be here, able to feel what it felt. He'd finally know what it was like to feel the heat of Jackie's body as he shoved his cock inside of her, over and over. He'd still get to feel the rush of orgasm and the thrill of conquest.

But what about Jackie and her feelings? She wouldn't want what his monster had to offer. It would be hard, fast, and brutal—likely exactly the kind of thing she'd been forced to witness while held by the Synestryn.

"Iain?" Her voice was worried now, tinged with growing concern and fear.

He couldn't let this happen, no matter how easy it

would be to simply let go. He had his honor, as dented and tarnished as it was. It was all he had left, and he wasn't going to shatter it by letting some fucking monster win.

With an audible snarl, he forced the beast deep inside of himself, burying it under the rubble of his soul. The monster howled and fought, but in the end, it was locked away, trapped. At least for now.

"I'm okay," he said, taking several steps away from her. He didn't trust himself to look at her again so soon. His cock was still hard, and his blood was still pounding with the need to take her. The adrenaline rush of battle wasn't helping matters, either. He needed a minute to gather his tattered control and mend it.

"We need to move. Help me up?" she asked.

He couldn't touch her now. Not yet.

"In a minute."

"I don't know how much longer I can hold them off. We need to move now."

Without looking at her, he asked, "Hold them off?"

"I put up a wall between us and the cave. It's keeping them away, but it's really hard to do, and I'm so tired." She was panting. He could hear that now, along with the strain in her voice.

He had no choice. They had to move now, before it was too late. His tattered control was going to have to be good enough.

Iain pulled her to her feet and stepped back. She wobbled unsteadily, threatening to fall over into the bloody grass.

With a curse under his breath, he hauled her up against his side, draping her slender arm over his shoulders. He wrapped his arm around her waist and took some of her weight off her feet.

"This way," he said. "I saw lights over there."

She nodded and did her best to keep up with the pace he set. Her body shivered along his side, reminding him just how vulnerable she was.

"Are you cold?"

"I'll be fine."

Which wasn't a no.

They hiked for about half a mile when he felt Jackie stiffen in his hold, and the constant tug on his power suddenly vanished.

"I'm sorry," she said. "I couldn't keep it up any longer. They're coming."

"If you can, try to keep your wound sealed. Maybe they won't be able to smell us." He wasn't counting on it, but it could buy them some time.

They came to a house with the lights on inside. He could see the colorful flashes of what he guessed was a TV screen, and saw a shadow moving around on the far side of the blinds. There was a beat-up car parked on the gravel driveway. Its paint had long ago lost its shine, and there was more rust than metal left, but when he looked inside, the keys were in the ignition.

He helped Jackie into the front seat, and put the car in neutral, pushing it toward what passed for a road out here. As soon as he was far enough away he didn't think they'd get shot if the owner caught them stealing his beater, he started it up and drove away as quietly as he could, keeping the lights off.

Jackie fumbled with the heater controls. "So cold."

"I know. Just give the engine a minute to warm up."

Worry nagged the back of his mind. It wasn't that cold, even for humans. Chilly, but not dangerously so, which made him wonder if she wasn't suffering from something else—maybe some kind of poison.

"Did you get hurt?" he asked, glancing her way.

Her eyes were closed and her head was lolled back against the seat. "My head."

"Anywhere else?"

She said nothing, so he reached out into her thoughts, despite her very explicitly stated instructions for him to stay out of her mind.

She was freezing, not just cold. Her muscles were tight, spasming in a futile attempt to create heat. Weariness weighed her body down, pinning it in place. Even speaking was difficult.

He didn't sense any pain besides that in her head, and some discomfort where his shoulder had dug into her stomach.

A glowing band of power streamed between them, much wider than he would have guessed. She was still using it to seal her head wound, despite how much effort it took for her to retain that level of concentration.

Iain turned up the fan all the way, which made a horrible whining noise before coming to a clunking stop. Smoke drifted out from the vents, smelling like burning rubber.

"Shit," he spat, then regulated his tone so it was more gentle. "We're not far from a safe place. Just hang in there and I'll get you warm soon."

She said nothing, so he stayed in her mind, gauging her well-being as he sped over the gravel roads.

She was struggling to maintain even the small flow of power needed to shield her wound. If he didn't do something, that was going to go down, too, and they'd be right back where they started, surrounded by demons hunting her blood.

"I want you to lay your head down in my lap, okay?"

"Why?" she mumbled.

"Just do it, please?"

She kind of toppled over, and he had to keep her from hitting the steering wheel, but he managed to get her safely settled, and wrapped his hand around her throat. The two parts of the luceria connected, locking together. He felt the flow of power ease, and heard Jackie let out an audible sigh of relief.

Her body shook violently, and he wished for a way to warm her up. They were less than an hour away from a

Gerai house, but he couldn't stand to think of her suffering for that long.

He pulled the car over long enough to strip out of his coat and drape it over her. The second he broke the luceria's connection, he felt her struggling to keep up the shield, so he hurried and settled her back where he could touch her again.

The miles seemed to drag by, no matter how hard he pushed the accelerator. Without thinking about it, he began to stroke her neck, reveling in the feel of her smooth skin under his fingers.

His body temperature kicked up, and he wished he could somehow channel that to her.

She was still shivering as he pulled into the driveway of the Gerai house. The porch light was on, and there were three other houses' lights visible in the distance. This area was heavily farmed, and the homes were spread out, leaving plenty of room for crops and grazing cattle.

Iain killed the wheezing engine, and lifted Jackie out of the car. The fact that she didn't tell him to put her down spoke volumes about how bad off she really was.

He lowered her feet to the porch, and found the key taped to the underside of the porch light.

The heat inside was on, but set low in the absence of people. He laid Jackie on the couch and turned the thermostat up.

There was no fireplace here—no way to get her warm fast enough to suit him. Except for the shower.

He went into the hall bathroom and started the water running. He made quick work of stripping off her coat and shoes, toeing off his own before he picked her up and carried her right into the tub, under the spray of hot water.

Jackie gasped and sputtered, clinging to him in shock. A moment later, she moaned in pleasure and leaned toward him, going limp against his chest.

A deep sense of satisfaction filled him, making him

feel stronger and more like the man he hadn't been in a long, long time. It was the same kind of feeling he'd had when she'd first taken his luceria—a kind of rightness, as if the universal order was all set straight.

It was only a trick of the mind, or of his biology. He knew that. There was no happily ever after for a man with no soul. It was best if he accepted his fate and simply enjoyed each moment for what it offered, rather than thinking of the future.

That was a bleak place for him, and one he was going to be visiting sooner than he wanted.

Jackie's fingers shifted along his skin. "Thank you."

"Better?" he asked.

He felt her nod. "Still cold, but I don't feel frozen solid anymore."

"Can you stand?"

"I think so."

He set her feet down, keeping a firm hold on her in case she was weaker than she thought. The water hit her head, cascading down over her body more fully now. Her dark hair went nearly black, and a pink flush began to replace the waxen paleness she'd had only moments ago. She turned inside his grip, facing away from him. He wrapped his arms around her, gripping her waist, enjoying the feel of her against his palms. Her head fell back on his chest, and as the water drops hit, he could see faint blue flickers of the shield over her wound.

"We can wash away the blood now. Turn around, and I'll tell you when to drop the shield."

She did as he asked, looking up at him, waiting for him to tell her when to act. Her gray eyes were so pretty up close. He could see pale silvery chips surrounding her pupils, which disappeared as her eyes dilated.

"Now?" she asked.

Iain forced himself to pay attention to where the water sprayed, guiding her head so that all the blood would be washed away as fast as possible. "Now."

She winced as the hot water hit her head. Most of the blood had dried, closing the wound, but some of it had worked its way into her hair.

"We should wash it, just to be sure."

She sagged at the idea, but leaned over to reach for a bottle of shampoo. Iain snatched it from her hands. "You stay under the water and get warm. I can do this."

The truth was he wanted to. He had no idea why, but the thought of tending her like this gave him a deep sense of satisfaction. He liked taking care of her.

It had been so long since he'd really cared one way or another about much of anything, finding enjoyment was as peculiar as it was welcome. He wasn't sure what it was about being connected to Jackie that had restored some of the man he used to be, but he was glad to be along for the ride, for however long it lasted.

He lathered her hair, being careful of her wound, while taking his time, stroking her scalp and down the tight cords at the back of her neck. The collar of her shirt irritated him, so he loosened a button and tugged it down in back so he could better feel her skin.

His fingers slid over her, lingering about the task, as he watched the minute changes in her expression to tell him what she liked most. The little frown at her mouth said he was hitting a tender spot, while the lifting of her brows and fluttering of her eyelids said he was doing it just right.

He rinsed the suds away, making sure they were all gone so none would get in her eyes. She looked up at him, opening her mouth to say something. The words seemed to die on her lips as she continued to stare. Her eyelashes were wet and spiky. Her hands were flat against his chest to hold herself steady. They began to creep up over his shoulders and around his neck. Her breasts rubbed along his chest, making his muscles clench with the need to shove her back against the shower wall and hold her there while his hands roamed her body. He could just imagine the feel of her hard little nipples beading up against his palm, or, better yet, his tongue.

He didn't know what she was doing, but with her body pressed flush against him, he knew she had to feel the stiff length of his erection against her stomach.

Honor dictated that he step back and flee this situation before he forgot himself.

Iain commanded his muscles to move, but they all stayed locked in place, rigid and unyielding. The monster inside of him salivated, dying for a chance to get loose and take what Iain's honor dictated did not belong to him.

Jackie would choose another man soon, and as much as he hated the idea, as much as it made his monster scream in rage, he knew she'd be grateful to him later for not giving in to his baser urges. She could go to her real mate—the one she should have been with now—with no guilt or regrets.

Before he had time to find the strength to take that long step back, she went up on tiptoe, and kissed him.

Iain's breath left his body in a surprised rush. Of all the things she could have said or done, that was not something he'd expected. Still, his reaction was visceral, swift, and uncontrollable. Everything inside of him, both man and monster, stood up and cheered as he gave in to her kiss. His hands slid around her, cupping her ass and pulling her up closer to his mouth. He flicked his tongue across her lips, begging to be let inside. She opened for him easily, as if eager for his taste.

Her sweet sigh of pleasure filled his mouth. He tilted her head back, taking as much from her kiss as she let him. The taste of her went to his head, casting out thoughts and concerns. All that mattered now was the feel of her in his arms and the scent of her skin, hot from the shower.

For the first time he could remember, both parts of him were in complete accord, working together toward a common goal.

Her fingers snaked beneath the soggy hem of his shirt. They were shaking, but whether from cold, fatigue, or something else, he couldn't tell. He knew he should stop and ask, stop and make sure she was well, but he couldn't seem to find the strength to pull away from her soft, sweet mouth.

She tugged on his shirt, making a faint noise of irritation. It took him a minute to figure out that she was trying to pull it off, but he wasn't cooperating, and the fabric was clinging to his skin, making the task impossible for her.

Iain stripped it off and went right back to kissing her. His earlier connection to her mind flared to life again, burning bright in his thoughts. He could feel her frenetic need, feel the empty ache low in her belly, and the swollen heat of her breasts. There was a franticness within her that went beyond lust. It was deeper than that, more desperate. She was barely holding on to her control, on the verge of collapsing into an emotional heap of despair and self-doubt. She'd been through too much, was holding too much emotion in. She'd decided to let it out, and he was going to help her.

If that's what she needed, he was powerless to stop himself from giving it to her.

In a heartbeat, he shifted gears, discarding his good intentions for better ones. He was going to give her everything she wanted, and then some. The fact that it was exactly what he wanted only made the task that much sweeter.

Jackie had worked the buttons of her shirt free, and slipped her arms out of the straps of her bra to bare her breasts. She rubbed herself against his chest, and the feel of her bare skin on his made his spine light up with sensation.

He let out a noise that was more monster than man and pinned her shoulders against the wall. He held her there so he could look his fill, watching as the water trickled over her flushed skin.

Her nipples were tightly beaded, her breasts swollen and begging for his mouth. He didn't even try to resist, lowering his head to flick his tongue over first one nipple, then the other. She sucked in a breath, and when he covered the tip of her breast with his mouth and suckled her, she let it out again on a long sigh of pleasure.

Her fingernails dug into his scalp, and the monster growled out his approval.

The water began to feel cool on his heated skin, and his protective instincts broke through the haze of lust long enough to remind him to keep her warm. He wanted her hot and relaxed for what he was going to do to her, not huddled up and shivering.

Iain turned off the water and unbuttoned her pants. The wet fabric clung to her legs, but he had her gloriously naked in seconds, then made quick work of shedding what was left of his own soggy clothing.

He wrapped her up in a towel and carried her into the closest bedroom. She kissed his neck as he walked, her tongue sliding over the skin where his luceria used to lie. It was ultrasensitive to the touch, making his whole body clench in desire. He barely had the sense to toss back the covers before laying her on the bed.

Jackie's gaze roamed over his naked body, her eyes darkening with lust as she worked her way down to his cock. He was harder than he'd ever been, aching with the need to slide inside of her.

A momentary flash of doubt flickered through him, but he couldn't tell if it was his or hers. He was too closely linked to her, too distracted by the sight of her glorious body, to separate the two.

She was so fucking pretty, all sleek, feminine lines and sweet, flowing curves. Her breasts were just the perfect size to fill his hands. Her narrow waist flared to womanly hips, and the damp patch of curls between her thighs made him want to spread her legs wide so he could see all of her, taste her. She wouldn't always be his, but for now, in this moment, she was, and he was going to make sure she knew it.

Iain slipped into the bed beside her. His cock rubbed against her hip, and he had to grit his teeth to keep from losing control. She turned toward him, shoving him back onto the bed. Her arms trembled with effort, but she held herself over him, staring down into his eyes. "It's been a long time for me. I may be out of practice."

"Don't fucking care," he managed to say, his voice rough with unsated lust. He could guarantee it had been even longer for him, since he hadn't been with a woman since long before she was born. Hadn't even thought about it.

"Good," she said, and then she kissed him, sucking his bottom lip into her mouth.

If the lightning storm going off in his brain was any indication, she hadn't forgotten what to do. His cock bucked against her stomach, and he could feel slick wetness gathering at the tip.

He'd never been more ready for a woman in his life, and yet he didn't dare rush this. She deserved his best effort, and he deserved to take his time and enjoy this as much as he could.

The monster wanted him to hurry the fuck up and shove his cock into her—make her take it all and fill her up with his seed, over and over. Iain told the beast to shut the hell up and enjoy the ride.

Her leg slipped between his, and she rubbed her mound along his thigh. He could feel the slick heat gathering between her legs as she rode him. The sweet drag of her flesh against his sent shards of electric current up his spine, making his balls tighten. It would have been so easy to come like this with her, but it's not how he wanted it to be. He wanted her to get off first, so he could hear her cries of pleasure while he could still pay attention enough to tuck them away in his memory forever. If there was one sound he wanted to remember when he died, it would be Jackie's sweet screams as she came.

Another option wove its way into his mind, but he cast it aside as impossible and selfish. Soulless men didn't deserve children, not to mention the fact that he couldn't have one even if he wanted—at least not without Tynan's help.

The hopeful echo of a child's laugh was not for him. But this—Jackie's soft sighs and the feel of her fingers stroking his skin—this was more than he could ask for.

She moved to straddle him, and he knew that if he let her sweet pussy anywhere near his cock, he'd forget himself and the monster would take over. Instead, he flipped her back onto the bed and pinned her there with his thigh while he kissed her.

He cupped her breast, letting his thumb slide over her velvet nipple. She arched her back and grabbed his head, pushing it down to her breast, while at the same time, his mind was flooded with the image of his mouth suckling her.

At least he knew exactly what she wanted. Now it was his turn to see if he could show her what he intended to do.

Iain created an image of his dark head between her thighs, his tongue stroking her, his fingers pushing deep. He propelled that thought through their link, and heard her quiet gasp of desire.

He took that as his invitation, and kissed his way down her body, licking hot trails over her ribs and around the hollow of her belly button. The farther down he went, the wider her legs opened to make room for his body.

Hot, pink flesh greeted him, and the scent of her arousal was nearly more than he could stand. He caught her gaze as he got his first taste, and then her eyes fluttered shut and her head flopped back onto the pillow.

So sweet, so wet for him, she drove him crazy without

even trying. He flicked his tongue across her clit, and her hips jolted off the bed.

Iain pinned her down with one arm while he slid his fingers along her folds, teasing her.

Desire grew between them, a needful, desperate thing. He wasn't sure if it was her desire or his own, but whatever it was, he wasn't strong enough to play around any longer.

He thrust two fingers inside her, feeling how tight she was around him, how wet. He tried to go slowly, giving her body time to stretch and adjust to his invasion, but lust was driving him on, compelling him to make her come. Once she let go, she'd relax and be able to take his cock much easier. Much deeper. He needed that closeness. He needed everything she had to give, because chances were, he'd never again feel the touch of a woman.

That thought spurred him on. He sucked her clit, and worked another finger inside of her body.

Jackie's muscles tightened down, and her movements became stronger as she bucked against him. Her breathing sped, and she started making a soft sound warning of her impending orgasm.

He sped up the pace. Through their link, he sent his desire to see her come, to feel it around his fingers and taste it on his tongue. That seemed to send her over the edge and her body began to shake as she came. He stayed with her, drawing her orgasm out until all that was left was the fluttering remnants of pleasure coursing through her body.

Iain lapped at her pussy, easing her back down. His own desire was clawing at him, but the satisfaction of watching her come gave him the strength to ignore it all. What he couldn't ignore was the rising need to make her do it again. Only this time, she was going to come around his cock.

Chapter 19

Jackie was shaking with pleasure. Her body trembled with it, until she was sure that it was radiating out of her pores.

No one had ever made her orgasm like that before, but the way he was looking at her, his dark eyes hooded and his cheeks stained with lust, she was convinced he was going to try to do it again.

She should have been too tired to care. Funneling so much power tonight had drained her. Fighting the cold had sapped her strength. And while she was limp and boneless, she wasn't even considering telling him to stop and let her rest.

Jackie could feel his need riding alongside her own muted lust. His was sharper, hotter, with jagged edges that tore at him until she wasn't sure how he could stand it. The fact that she could feel all of that should have been some kind of warning, but right now, with her body humming and warm, she didn't care to sort out what it meant. For now, it was enough to know that she had the most delicious man on the face of the planet naked in bed with her, lusting after her with a ferocity that shocked her, and she wasn't going to let that go to waste.

He crawled up over her, holding her legs spread wide with his body. The sheets beneath her were wet, but that was his fault as much as it was hers. Even now, she could feel slick heat easing from her as her body ached to be filled.

Jackie grabbed his head and pulled him down for a kiss. As his mouth met hers, a pulse of something dark and dangerous slammed into her through the luceria. It brought with it a rising tide of lust and physical need, and a hint of something...deadly. Illuminated for a split second, like from a flash of lightning, the feeling vanished, and all that was left was the thrumming beat of her own heart. It was like Iain had cut her off from himself, shoving her away.

And she didn't like it.

She pushed him back and stared into his eyes. "Let me in."

"No. You don't belong there."

Bullshit. It felt too right for her not to belong. He was hiding something, and she was going to find out what it was.

She grabbed his cock, sliding her fingers over it, spreading slick wetness down from the tip. Iain's jaw bunched as he let out a hissing curse.

"I want to feel what you feel again. Let me in," she ordered.

The tendons in his neck stood out, and his body shook as he braced himself over hers. "No."

She wasn't the kind of woman who took no for an answer. Her grip tightened, and she sped the pace of her strokes as she scooted to line their bodies up. "I want it. Give it to me."

Iain let out a pained groan and squeezed his eyes shut. "I don't want you to see it."

"See what?"

He didn't answer, so she slid the tip of his erection against her folds, covering him with her wet heat.

"Don't," he choked out, but whatever else he was going to say got swallowed up in a snarl. His eyes popped open and she felt the floodgates break between them.

Emotions surged into her in a chaotic mix of anger and lust, protectiveness and loneliness. It all swirled together until she couldn't distinguish one thing from another.

Iain let out a choked sound, but stared down at her as his hips surged forward. His cock slid into her several inches, and then all she could think about was the way he stretched and filled her. Physical pleasure blocked out the rest as he began to move.

His powerful body coiled around her, holding her close as his hips worked, rocking, forcing her to take more of him with each thrust. She tried to tell him to slow down, but there was no air to speak, and her own body was writhing, struggling to get even closer to him.

There was too much stimulus. Her body was shimmering with sensation. Her mind was stuffed full of thoughts and feelings not her own. Pleasure suffused her every breath, and with each shifting slide of him inside her, she inched closer to another devastating climax.

Words rattled through her head—low, frantic words of apology and regret. She couldn't understand any of them, but the tone stringing them together was clear. He was sorry for what he was doing.

She wasn't. Not even close. She was devastated by it, stretched in so many directions she had no sense of where she was going, but none of that mattered. The only things she cared about were the feel of his body moving against hers, and the deep, resonating satisfaction purring from his mind.

"It's okay," she panted. "It's good. So good."

A feral growl rumbled through him, and he lifted her hips, angling their bodies so he could slide fractionally deeper.

That was all it took. Her body coiled tight, then burst in an explosion of pleasure and light. Before she'd even had time to pull in a breath, she felt Iain tense and drive deep. His semen pumped inside of her, making her cry out as it pushed her even higher. She hung there, suspended in pure sensation and physical joy for what seemed like hours. Then finally, the storm eased and she went limp in his arms.

Iain continued moving inside of her in slow, steady thrusts that sent tremors streaking through her. She was shaken all the way to her soul, completely shattered and yet somehow restored.

She wasn't sure she'd ever have pleasure like that in her life again after what she'd been through. But now, with Iain still hard inside of her, and his powerful body draped over hers, she had hope that at least one part of her old life would be normal. Even improved upon, if what she'd just experienced was any indication.

It had never been that good before, and a part of her wondered if it would ever be that good with anyone besides Iain.

Iain watched Jackie sleep. Her skin was still flushed pink, and her lips were still swollen and parted as if waiting for another kiss.

He held himself in check, grateful that his monster had crawled back into its dank cage to leave him the hell alone. Iain felt . . . at peace. He wasn't fighting himself or demons or even his own kind. He simply existed in this quiet space where he could hear the faint sound of Jackie's breathing in time with his own heartbeat.

Holding Samson had been a lot like this—giving him a sense of rightness that he hadn't thought existed in the world. At least not for him, not anymore.

He still wanted her, but the raging need had been eased, and now he was content with being near her, knowing she was safe.

It wouldn't last. Whatever magic she'd wrought with her touch would soon be gone, and he'd be battling the forces around and within him once more.

Iain shifted his body closer, draping his arm over her

waist. She turned toward him, snuggling her face against his chest and letting out a happy sigh. He held his breath, trying to feel some shift in his lifemark, some subtle sway of branches that would tell him she'd somehow brought his soul back to life.

He knew it wasn't possible, but the longer he was around her—connected to her—the more hopeful he became. He hadn't cared about much of anything before. He did what he was supposed to do out of a sense of honor and duty, operating with little thought beyond what was the most efficient way to save his brothers and slay the demons. Like a robot, he did things without caring, moving from one task to the next without judging his actions.

Being linked to Jackie had changed that. He wanted things now—impossible, beautiful things. And while his emotions gave him the ability to be with her like this, in the aftermath of passion, they also made it hard to accept what he knew awaited him.

He could fool her for only so long. She'd learned to tap into his thoughts. She'd nearly seen his monster. It was only a matter of time before he could no longer protect her from what lurked inside of him—from what he truly was. She'd find out about his dead soul and everything they'd shared would forever be tainted with that knowledge.

He didn't want that. He wanted her to remember him with fondness, not horror. He couldn't stand the idea that she'd regret what they'd shared, or that, in doing so, she would look at his brothers with skepticism and mistrust. As much as he hated the idea, she needed to move on to find another mate—one who was whole and could give her everything she deserved.

Her fingers slid over his hip in a sleepy caress. Lust began to gather in him again, clouding his thoughts with how easy it would be to roll her back and fuck her. She was still slick from his seed. His cock would slide in easy.

She wouldn't even realize what he was doing until he had her where he wanted her, spread out beneath him, taking every inch.

It wasn't right. A man with honor wouldn't take advantage of a sleeping woman like that. A man with honor would get up and guard her sleep, ensuring that she was safe while she got the rest she needed.

So that's what he did. He knelt beside the bed with his sword laid out before him, and let himself drift into that meditative state where his throbbing cock no longer mattered. If danger came near, he'd know it. If she rose from the bed, he'd hear. But until those things happened, he would hover here, in this gray place, letting his body dissipate into the fog.

There was no thought here. No grief for what he would soon lose. It was as close to happiness as he was going to get.

While Logan drove into Kansas City, Hope scoured the Internet for signs of the women she'd played with as a child—the ones Brenya had sent through the Sentinel Stone. She knew what it was like to be utterly alone in this world, without a single friend or relative to claim you. Sister Olive had taken Hope in, but had anyone been as kind to these women?

Guilt weighed her down as her search went on. She couldn't even remember these girls' names, no matter how hard she tried. She could see their faces, and hear their voices, but that was all she could regain from her murky past.

Logan pulled into a parking lot and stopped the van. His hand curled over her shoulder, massaging the ache from her neck. "You've been at this for hours. It's time to take a break, love."

"You'd think it wouldn't be all that hard to find some kind of record of two women showing up in a city with amnesia."

"Be grateful that it is hard. I'm sure that their lack of attention has served to protect them."

She let out a long sigh and leaned her cheek against his hand. "We have to find them."

"We will. You and I will go into the city and find them ourselves."

"I don't even know where to start. The only articles I can find about women with amnesia are of people who have families. Most of them are elderly, and none of the pictures were of the girls I remember."

"Relax," said Logan, and she could feel a hint of power sliding through his voice, draining her muscles of tension. "We will find them. After I show you something."

"Show me what?

"I have a gift for you. I thought now would be a good time to give it to you, all things considered."

He was so sweet. Here she was worried sick, and he was working to find a way to make her feel better.

Hope gave him a smile that felt a bit sloppy. "I'm sorry I've been such awful company."

He stroked her cheek. "You're worried. I am as well. But we will find your friends. Trust me on that."

"I do." She knew he'd move heaven and earth to give her whatever she wanted. If those women were still out there, they would find them.

He grinned and, in an instant, became the most beautiful man that had ever walked the planet. "Look up, love."

Hope looked out the front window of his van and saw that they'd arrived at the Tyler building—the one that had once housed the Sentinel Stone, the one where she'd come through with no memory of who she was or why she was here.

"What are we doing here?" she asked.

"This is your gift."

"What? My gift?"

His smile widened. "I bought the building. I've already hired a construction crew to rebuild the interior, and a director to oversee the project."

"You bought me a *building*?" She had no idea why he would do such a thing.

"I bought you a homeless shelter—one to replace the one that burned down. I thought we could name it after Sister Olive."

The solid brick structure wavered in her vision as tears filled her eyes. She'd spent years working at the old shelter. It was like a home to her. Sister Olive had taken her in and watched over her when no one else had cared. And now she was gone—killed by Synestryn. The old shelter had burned to the ground. Hope had tried to move on, but her thoughts were often of the people left behind, of those who no longer had a safe place to go.

Logan must have known. And he wasn't the kind of man who could know about a need without working to fill it.

That was one more reason why she loved him so deeply.

"Thank you," she whispered, unable to speak clearly through gratitude clogging her throat. She unfastened her seat belt and leaned over, kissing him, trying to show him how she felt in the face of words that would not flow.

The kiss ended, and he cupped her face, staring down at her with eyes that pulsed with faint flickers of light. "I should buy you buildings more often."

She laughed at that. "You're ridiculous, but I love you anyway."

"So I didn't overstep my bounds?" he asked. "I know nothing can ever replace the void that Sister Olive left behind, but I thought this would honor her memory."

"It does. It's perfect. And so are you."

Jackie woke as the sky lightened. Her eyes opened to see Iain kneeling, naked, his eyes closed and his body relaxed. She stared at him for a long time, watching him breathe. The tree on his chest was mostly empty of leaves, unlike those of her sisters' husbands. Their trees had budded and sprung new leaves. She didn't understand the process, but she knew it had something to do with a woman taking a man's luceria.

Why was Iain's lifemark still bare?

Maybe it was because he knew they weren't staying together.

The thought bothered her more than it should have. She couldn't very well head back into her old life with a giant sword-wielding warrior following her to the office. And he would. She didn't doubt that for a second. Iain wasn't the type to leave her unguarded.

Even now, while there was a naked, warm woman lying right here, he chose to get out of bed and stand guard, rather than seeing to his own comfort. Men like that didn't exist anymore—or if they did, she'd never met one.

Jackie slipped out of bed and went to the bathroom and cleaned herself up. When she came out, Iain was standing in front of her, naked and glorious. His body was wrapped in muscles, covered in smooth skin, and completely delicious. As she watched, he became hugely erect. It made her mouth water and her knees weaken as she remembered just how he could make her feel. She couldn't help but stare.

Desire swirled around low in her belly, and she felt her nipples bead up, tightening in hopes he'd touch her again, or use his hot mouth to drive her wild.

"You should dress," he said, his voice rough and low.

"Later." When she was done with him.

She took a step forward and put her hand over his heart. The steady, strong beat soothed something deep inside of her, allowing a bit of tension she'd carried around for far too long to ease.

She curled her fingers into his flesh, enjoying the steely strength of his pecs. The scent of his skin filled the space between them, inflaming her senses even as it calmed her.

Outside of this place lurked monsters. Both real and metaphorical. She had big decisions to make that could alter the course of people's lives. But right now, right here, enclosed in this little house out in the middle of nowhere, she felt safe and happy. She knew they had to leave soon—that the outside world wouldn't wait forever—but she was in no hurry to make it happen.

Jackie stepped closer, pressing her naked body to his. He flinched and sucked in a breath, and then his eyelids fell shut in pleasure. Tingling bubbles soaked into her wherever his skin met hers. He was so warm, she couldn't stop herself from trying to get closer.

"We should go," he said, but she could hear indecision ringing in his tone. He wanted to stay as much as she did.

"We will." She pulled his head down so she could kiss his mouth, hoping to rid him of any more thoughts about leaving.

He gave in to her kiss with a groan, and then gripped her hips in his big hands. His erection throbbed against her belly, and she felt herself growing wet and slick in response. She needed to feel him inside of her again, but first, she wanted to show him the same kind of pleasure he'd given her last night.

She kissed his chin, and then his neck, lingering at the band of lighter skin where his luceria had once lain. Every time her tongue flickered over that patch, his body clenched and he sucked in a breath. A wave of feminine power swelled within her as she realized one more way she could make him feel good.

Jackie pressed her teeth to his neck, nibbling and sucking hard enough to leave marks. She liked the idea that others would know she'd claimed him—at least for now. It went against everything she was working for, but right now, she simply didn't care.

His hand snaked between them to cup her breast, his thumb rubbing across her hard nipple. Jolts of sensation arced into her womb, making her sway with the force of her growing need.

Sweat beaded up along her spine as she kissed a path down his chest and abdomen, until she was on her knees at his feet. He looked down at her, his cheeks dark and his mouth tight with lust. She could tell he knew what she wanted to do, and that he wanted it just as much as she did.

Jackie wrapped her fingers around his erection and licked across the wide end. His whole body clenched hard and he actually shook. He grabbed her head and pulled her away, staring down at her with a fierce, black gaze. "Don't. I won't be able to control myself."

She smiled up at him, victory coursing through her veins. She didn't want his control. She wanted him. All of him. "Good," she told him, and then she slid her mouth over his cock.

A low, rumbling groan vibrated through his body, into hers, tingling along her nerve endings. Without conscious thought, her mind reached for his, aching for that deeper connection she'd shared with him last night. It was against her principles to invade his privacy, but she couldn't help herself. She needed it, the way she needed the taste of him on her tongue and the feel of him stretching her as he filled her.

She felt his control—tight bands of it stretching through his mind. The effort was exhausting and painful for him. She tried to tell him to stop, but her mouth was busy, and the words flittering through her thoughts were too jumbled for her to have any hope he'd understand. The only thing she could think to do was reassure him that this was what she wanted.

Jackie showed him her desire, sending it through their link in hot, pulsing waves. The resounding echo that came back was darker and harder, tinted with an animalistic ferocity. And there was fear. For her. He was afraid of hurting her or scaring her, maybe. She couldn't be sure, but she was stronger than he thought. She could take whatever he had to give.

That's what she wanted.

Her message got through. She could feel the knowledge swelling in his mind, glowing like a beacon, lighting up all the dark urges he'd tried to keep hidden. She stared at them, groaning with need.

She pulled her mouth from his erection with a sucking pop, and looked up at him. "That's what I want—the real man within, not the one you show the world."

Jackie felt those bands of control tighten as he struggled to fight his urges. And then they snapped. Whatever he'd been trying to hold back was unleashed. She saw his body shift and stretch as if settling into his own skin. He rolled his shoulders in a powerful move and looked down at her. Those were not Iain's eyes. They looked like his, but she could tell the difference. The man gazing down at her in hunger was no longer Iain.

Chapter 20

The monster was out. It howled in victory. Jackie had freed it, and there was nothing Iain could do but pray he'd regain control again before she got hurt.

He grabbed the back of her head in one hand and his throbbing cock in the other. "Open," he growled, rubbing himself against her lips.

She smiled, and did as his monster asked, taking his cock into her sweet mouth once more. The hot suction drove him mad, making him fuck her mouth with short, shallow thrusts. She took him as deep as she could, but it wasn't enough. It would never be enough.

Pressure built in his balls as he watched her cheeks hollow out with every stroke. Her fingernails scraped over his sac, making him suck in a hard breath. It was too much sensation and yet still not enough.

Her hips began to undulate, and he saw she had her hand between her thighs. A moan of pleasure vibrated out of her throat, tickling his cock. He couldn't control his lust, he couldn't control his beast, but he could at least make sure that she was right there with him, spinning out of control.

Iain bundled up his desire and all the physical sensations and shoved them through the link, forcing her to feel what he was feeling. Her body went tense, and then melted with womanly softness as she accepted what he forced on her.

The monster mocked his efforts, and seemed to swell in power. "I'm going to come," the monster told Jackie, its voice inhuman. "And you're going to swallow."

Iain felt a shiver of excitement course through her. Her breathing sped, as did the hand between her legs.

Just the sight was enough to send him careening over the edge. His monster gripped her head tighter and held her in place while his orgasm exploded through his body. His semen pumped into her mouth and she went stiff. He was sure he'd disgusted her, but then he felt their link pulse with pleasure, and she sucked harder as she came.

The monster's gloating satisfaction grated against Iain, and he worked to regain control now that the monster was sated.

But it wasn't sated. It liked being free. It liked taking Jackie, and it wasn't going to stop until it had had its fill of her.

She lay crumpled on her side on the floor, panting to catch her breath. A rosy flush covered her body, and a slick sheen glistened along the inside of her thigh.

The monster picked her up and tossed her onto the bed. She looked up in surprise, not realizing that Iain was no longer behind the wheel.

Without permission or preamble, the monster parted her thighs and drove his cock deep.

Jackie let out a whimper, which turned into a sigh as he stretched her, filled her. "You don't need a minute?" she asked.

The monster growled in response and began to move.

Iain fought for control. She was so vulnerable like this, so trusting. She had no idea of the danger she faced if the beast decided to turn violent. Her actions had appeased it so far, but there was no way to know if she would continue to do so.

He gathered power into his body, tiny motes of it that

floated through the atmosphere. He wasn't strong enough to wage this battle yet, and he knew he'd have only one chance. The beast was distracted by the slick heat of her body, entranced by the way her breasts moved with every powerful thrust. Lust swelled within it, driving it onward with one single purpose.

It wanted to lay claim to Jackie. It wanted her for itself.

No fucking way Iain was going to let that happen.

He prodded at the monster's defenses, making it snarl. Jackie reached up and laid her hand on his face. "Are you okay?" she asked.

The beast shoved her legs up and quickened its pace.

She didn't deserve this—she didn't deserve to be fucked by a monster who cared for nothing but the pleasure it could find in her body. She deserved to be with a man who could love her.

That was beyond Iain, but at least he had enough honor left to know it. The beast didn't.

He waited until the pleasure swelled, until the monster was pounding into her, making her gasp with every heavy thrust. Then he struck.

Iain gathered all the energy sparkling in his skin and hurled it at the monster. The beast snarled, and Iain couldn't tell if the noise made it out of his mouth or not. The pleasure in his body raged, and as he regained a flicker of control, he nearly lost it in the wave of sensations buffeting him.

"Iain?" he heard Jackie say, both in his ears and in his thoughts.

She was reaching for him—prodding at his mind. She was going to see his internal battle and know that he'd allowed a monster to touch her. He couldn't let that happen.

With a monumental force of will spurred on by his panic, he beat the howling monster back into its cage and slammed the door shut.

A soothing presence filled his mind. Jackie. She was with him, but he had no idea how much she'd witnessed.

His cock was still inside her sweet body. His own was raging with need, so close to release he found it hard to breathe.

"I'm okay," he panted, hoping to reassure her.

He began to move away, sliding out of her pussy. She grabbed his hips to stop him, staring into his eyes. "It's you again, isn't it?"

He hated it that she knew. Shame bore down on him, and all he wanted to do was go somewhere where she couldn't see it. He let his gaze slink away like a coward, unable to look her in the eye.

"Whatever that was, it's gone now. I felt you fight it off. For me."

He couldn't stay here and talk about this. He had to get away.

One second he was shifting his weight to get off the bed, and the next, he was flat on his back on the bed with Jackie straddling him. She'd called on his power, used it to give herself a burst of strength. "I won't let you run away from me like this. You shouldn't be ashamed."

"You don't know what you're talking about."

"I'm not afraid of you. I'm not afraid of any part of you."

"You should be."

"Why? Because you could hurt me? Because I didn't like it?" She moved her hips, sliding herself against his cock. So slick and hot. He was dying to be inside of her again even as he hated himself for considering it. "I liked it. And if I hadn't, I could have shoved you into the ceiling with a mere thought."

She had a point, but Iain was having a difficult time making sense of it right now. All he could think about was the way she undulated atop him, the way her body curved and her breasts pouted for attention.

"You don't have to be afraid for me. I'm a big girl."

She trailed her finger across his throat, making the sensitive skin there tingle in delight. "And thanks to you, I have the power to take care of myself."

"It's a monster," said Iain, struggling to think clearly. All his blood was in his cock, starving his brain.

"It's part of you."

Iain wanted to deny it. He hated that she was right. This thing inside of him hadn't been put there by a demon or some Synestryn magic. It had been born there. Grown there. He'd fed it a steady diet of rage and fear, and it had become the only thing it could become: a monster. "I don't want it to touch you."

"Fine. Then you do it." She lifted his hands to her breasts.

He couldn't resist an invitation like that. His fingers curled around her, cupping her flesh, and he felt the velvet thrust of her tight nipples against each palm.

She closed her eyes and her head fell back in enjoyment.

The monster reared its head, but he shoved it back down and told it to stay the fuck away. This was his time, and he was going to enjoy every second of it.

Jackie angled her body and slid down, impaling herself on his cock. The snug grip was perfect, and he knew in that moment that he'd never get his fill of her, not if he lived forever.

She pressed her hands on his ribs and began to move, circling her hips in a way that teased his nerve endings and made his skin ignite. She stared down into his eyes, watching him carefully as if searching for signs of the monster.

"I won't let it come back," he told her.

She gave him a sultry smile so full of heat, he was sure his eyelashes were scorched. "Stop worrying and make me come."

He'd never been more eager to obey an order in his life.

Iain sat up and pulled her close, kissing her mouth. She moaned against his tongue and her fingernails bit into his back. His sweet little Jackie had turned fierce and demanding, showing him what she wanted in the sinuous moves of her hips, and the soft sounds of pleasure falling from her lips.

Their link flared bright, wider than it had been before. He could feel her need sinking into him, feel his own flowing back into her. The waves melded together, amplifying one another until there was no way to tell who was feeling what.

He couldn't get deep enough, couldn't move fast enough like this, so he laid her back onto the bed. Now he could slide nice and deep, hitting all the spots that made her breath catch in her lungs.

He leaned down, catching the tip of her breast in his mouth, sucking hard the way he knew she liked. Her pussy fluttered around him, and her back arched as she sucked in a gasp. She was close. He could feel it thrumming through their link, driving him forward with an urgent need to make her come again.

The monster screamed for a turn, but Iain ignored it, his focus completely on Jackie and the subtle signs of her impending orgasm.

He reached between them and found her tight little clit with his finger. She was so wet, it was easy to slide across it and make her cry out, over and over. She coiled tighter with each gliding touch.

Iain opened himself up, letting her feel everything he did. He knew it was dangerous, that he risked letting her learn of his dead soul, but he couldn't help himself. He needed this connection in a way he didn't understand. He needed to be a part of her, to exist in the same space while he gave her the ultimate pleasure.

She let out a gasping sob and then she exploded, her body pulsing with the waves of her orgasm.

Iain held his own back, watching her, soaking in the

sight of her pleasure. Her eyes were shut tight, her mouth wide open on a silent scream. The tendons in her neck stood out and a dark flush spread down onto her chest.

He rode her through it, keeping up the pace he knew she liked best. Finally, as the last fluttering waves passed through her, she opened her eyes and looked up at him with complete trust. So beautiful.

Iain lost his control. His body spasmed as his orgasm tore through him, strangling the breath from his lungs. Wave after wave pummeled him as his cock spurted inside of her, lodged deep, near the mouth of her womb.

She watched him the whole time, a contented smile playing about one corner of her mouth. He lowered his forehead to hers as he caught his breath, unwilling to stop looking at her. She hadn't shied away from him — not even after what she'd seen lurking inside. She was as fearless as she was beautiful.

Whoever was lucky enough to end up with Jackie at his side was someone to be envied.

He pulled back enough to stroke her cheek. His luceria glowed golden in the dim light, lovely against her throat. There was no more movement within the band, and not even the rough scars lining her neck could diminish the beauty of that sight. They were bonded. Completely.

If he'd had a soul, it would have rejoiced at the knowledge. Instead, he mourned for her and what she could have had by now if she'd been with a whole man.

"You're closing yourself off from me again," she said.

He had to. There was no other choice but to protect her from his secret. It wouldn't change anything if she knew. There was nothing she could do to save him. All knowing would give her was a responsibility to report him, or the burden of keeping his secret as well. He couldn't do that to her. She didn't deserve to have him dump on her like that when she'd helped him feel like the man he used to be for a few short hours.

Iain was sorry that he had to pull away from her. Being with her so close, touching her mind, was a joy he'd never thought to experience. And now that he had, he had to deny himself one more thing.

"I need to call in," he told her, rolling away to sit on the edge of the bed. "I'll report to Joseph and the others that we found the cave."

"We don't know it's the right one."

"It was filled with demons. It has to be cleaned out, one way or another."

"And then what?" There was anger in her voice. "You'll ask me to go hunting again? To find the real breeding site this time? I can't keep doing this, Iain. I'm no good at it, and it scares the hell out of me."

He couldn't deny her comfort, not when he could hear so plainly how upset she was. He didn't know what he could do to fix it, but he had to try.

Iain turned toward her. She'd pulled the sheet up to cover her nudity. The flush of arousal was still clear on her face and throat, but the languid pleasure shining in her eyes was gone. "We'll go back home. You'll stay there while the rest of us deal with the problem. You shouldn't have been asked to go back to where you were held. That wasn't fair."

Her chin angled up. "I'm not a coward."

"I know," he reassured her.

"But I'm not a fighter, either."

She was. She didn't want to admit it, but if she hadn't been a fighter, she wouldn't have survived captivity for so long. The fact that she wasn't comfortable in the role yet was likely his fault. He should have eased her into combat, taking her into safer situations, gradually working their way up to the big stuff.

If he'd spent ten minutes thinking about what she needed, that's what he would have figured out before now. Instead, he'd been too busy fighting his rage and trying to keep his fucking dead soul a secret.

He didn't know what to say to make her feel better. He wasn't even sure he was capable of such finesse. "When we're ... separated, you need to pick a gentler man. Someone who can take the time to train you right and see to it that you're comfortable in your power."

"When we're separated, I'm not picking anyone else. I'm going to live on my own. Besides, you don't seem to be making any headway with the broken-heart thing. How are we supposed to part ways?"

He ignored her question because he couldn't tell her the truth. At least not yet. "Cain is a good choice. He's patient. Kind. He'll see to it that you have a life that is as close to normal as one of our kind can get."

Her lips flattened in anger. "Cain? You screw me and then tell me to go into the arms of another man, like it's as simple as changing a shirt?"

The idea was appalling. Even now, he wanted to rip Cain's head off and kick it from a cliff. Iain had to take several slow, deep breaths before he could wade through his rage enough to even speak. "It had been a long time. For both of us. We needed the release. But it doesn't change things. Does it? Do you somehow magically want to be with me now?"

He held his breath, waiting for the answer to that question with more anticipation than he had a right to feel.

"No," she snapped. "I don't. I don't want to be with any of you. I think I've made that abundantly clear."

He couldn't let her think she had a choice. Her life depended on her accepting her situation. "Cain is the man you should be with. He needs you as much as you need him. Promise me you'll go to him when we're separated."

"I'm not making any promises to you or anyone else."

She was so damn stubborn. It was time to play dirty.

He dropped his voice to a low, coaxing tone. "I saw

how you were with Samson. I saw the longing in your eyes. Cain will give you the child you want."

If he hadn't been watching her so closely, he wouldn't have seen the way her eyes darkened with desire as he spoke the words. But he was, and he did.

And then desire turned to hurt as she looked up at him. "How can you even say that? How can you so calmly talk about another man giving me a child when I haven't even washed your semen from my body? Are you truly that cold?"

His gut clenched as though he'd taken a punch. "I haven't been administered the fertility serum. I can't give you a child."

She hugged her knees to her chest. "You don't even know if I want a baby."

"I've watched you. I've been in your mind. I know."

"You stay the fuck out of my head. I mean it." She jerked the sheet from the bed and wrapped it around her body as she stood.

He was losing her. She was slipping away, driving a wedge between them.

Desperation to see her safe spurred him on, searching for some way to make her see reason. "Cain will let Tynan give him the fertility serum. He'll pay the blood fee that I'm sure is associated with the cure. Whatever you want, he'll give it to you."

She stood next to the bed, quivering with anger. "Will he leave me alone? Will he let me live my life in peace?"

"He'll make sure you live. That's all that matters."

Jackie shook her head, and he saw tears sparkle in her eyes. "No, it's not. And if you cared for me at all, you'd see that."

She disappeared into the bathroom, shutting the door behind her. He tried to reach for her through their link, to make sure she was okay, but all he felt was a cold, hard wall blocking him out.

*   *   *

Jackie kept her mouth shut the entire way back to Dabyr. A couple of young men had come and picked them up, telling them that Joseph had ordered their return. From the way they said it, there was clearly something going on, but no one seemed to know what.

Frankly, Jackie didn't really care. Whatever it was, she was certain it would be one more thing getting in the way of her finding a real life for herself.

Part of her wanted to give up and accept her fate, but every time she considered that, a little sliver of her old self died. She'd worked so hard for so long to keep something of herself alive while facing the horrors of her captivity. She'd sheltered that deep, secret core of what made her who she was, and kept it hidden, protected. No matter how often they took her blood, starved her, or humiliated her, no matter how many children's screams she heard, or how many babies she saw die—that kernel of herself that made her who she was she kept locked away, shielded by the hope that she would one day be free.

And now that she was free, she realized that it wasn't truly any kind of freedom at all. She'd traded one cage for another. Sure, this one was more comfortable, but they still controlled her—with fear of what might happen if she left, or with guilt from the lives that would be destroyed if she didn't help them fight their war.

How the hell was she supposed to simply overlook those things and move on?

Every time they brought her back to Dabyr, she lost a little more of herself. They were slowly eating away at her resolve, sucking her into a world where she didn't belong.

It would have been easier to give in and surrender. Let them use her as a weapon. Be with Cain as Iain had suggested and simply conform.

Just the thought seemed to crush the soul from her body. She knew it was selfish not to jump at the chance to help, but she was terrified out of her mind that if she accepted her fate and threw her lot in with these people, she'd spend the rest of her life fighting and watching people she cared about die.

She'd done enough of that for one lifetime. She'd paid her dues to this war in blood and tears. She couldn't let it take any more away from her, or she'd have nothing left.

Joseph was waiting for them at the door, looking shell-shocked. His hair seemed to have a bit more gray in it than she'd remembered, and his shoulders bowed a bit further.

"What's going on?" asked Iain.

"Come with me," Joseph ordered.

He led them through the halls to an unlabeled doorway. Most of the rooms here were numbered to make them easy to find, but not this one. Unlike the other wooden doors, this one was metal. There was no peephole, and rather than the standard key-card reader, there was a number pad and some kind of screen.

Joseph placed his hand on the screen. A light slid over his palm. Then one LED turned green. He punched in a code, and the second LED turned green. The lock clicked.

"Brace yourself," he said, looking at Iain. "This may be a trick."

"What may be a trick?" asked Iain, scowling.

"Just watch what you say. We're not yet sure who she is, but we're hoping you can shed some light on it."

Joseph turned the knob and pushed the door open. The three of them filed inside. The room was dimly lit, plain, and painted in a dull gray. There was a counter filled with some electronic equipment on one wall, and a large window in the adjacent wall. The window displayed another room on the other side of the glass, painted the same dull gray, but with only a table and chairs bolted to the floor. Pacing around that table was the most beautiful woman Jackie had ever seen.

Serena.

Chapter 21

Iain stood there for a long time, staring, unable to believe his eyes. Serena, or someone doing a hell of an impersonation of her, was only a few feet away, on the other side of a two-way mirror.

Her long red hair had been cut at an odd angle, arrowing from her left shoulder down to her right hip. A large section of her skirt had been sheared off, revealing one long, shapely leg.

He remembered that dress. She'd been wearing it the night she'd been killed.

As the momentary shock of seeing this creature faded, rage took its place. How dare someone defile her memory by showing up here, pretending to be her? Serena deserved better.

"Who is she?" demanded Iain.

"She says she's your betrothed."

Jackie covered her mouth with the back of her hand and stepped away from the glass.

"It's a lie," said Iain. "She died. This can't be her."

"We had a visit while you were gone. An Athanasian woman ported here. Somehow, she sensed Serena's presence and freed her."

"Freed her? Where the hell did she come from?"

Joseph glanced at Jackie, then lowered his voice. "She says she's been held in some kind of stasis bubble for two hundred years. I think you should talk to her, see whether you can verify her story."

"Fine, but if she turns out to be trying to trick us, don't expect me to hold back," he warned.

"And if she's not?" asked Jackie. "What if she is who she says she is?"

"She's not," said Iain. She couldn't be. Because if she was his Serena, then he'd abandoned her, leaving her trapped and alone for two centuries. Even he wasn't that much of a bastard.

Iain went to the door to the adjoining room and walked in to face the impostor.

The woman saw him. Her face lit up with happy surprise, and she flew into his arms. Her slender body hit his, but he refused to hug her back, no matter how much like Serena she felt. Even her smell was the same—like new grass and lavender.

He disengaged himself from her grasp and took a long step back. "Who are you?"

Her smile faltered, fading as she stared at him as if he'd hurt her feelings. "You know me, Iain. I'm Serena."

He let his tone fill with the anger thrumming through him. "She died. Who *are* you?"

The woman stepped back. Her hands were shaking. "I was taken the night we were to bond. Snatched away by a bright light. It was Mother's doing. I could feel her touch vibrating through the magic, smothering me."

Serena's mother had never wanted them to be together. If she'd known their intention, she would have done something to stop it. But still . . . "If what you say is true, then how did you survive all this time?"

She bowed her head in weariness. "I don't know. I never grew hungry or thirsty. There was no pain, only endless boredom. I seemed to float around, tethered to the Sentinel Stone. Sometimes I could see things going on outside my cage. I saw glimpses of people. Heard voices and machines. I screamed for years for someone to find me, but no one came. *You* never came. I thought for sure you'd feel me and come find me."

He refused to believe it. He'd never once felt her presence, though he had searched for it. Every time he'd tried, all that had met him was blank nothingness. He was sure it was because she'd been killed. Even now, he felt nothing—no heat or subtle tug against his skin. He didn't know if that was because this woman wasn't Serena, or if his union to Jackie somehow blocked it.

But now, with Serena's double sitting there, so close, looking exactly as he remembered, he had to learn the truth. "Prove to me you are who you say."

"Let me take your luceria and you can see inside my thoughts. I'll be able to hide nothing." She rose and came toward him. Her eyes fell to his bare neck and she stopped dead in her tracks. Her throat moved as she swallowed, and grief pinched her lovely features. "I see. You've taken another."

"Convenient. Now you can't offer me that proof."

Her nostrils flared in rage and she grabbed his shirt in her fist. "Convenient? You think that being trapped for two hundred years only to be freed and find the man I love bound to another woman is *convenient*?"

The fire dancing in her eyes couldn't be faked. With every passing second, he was becoming more convinced that she was who she said.

Iain grabbed her wrist and closed his eyes. Once upon a time, he would have been able to feel her presence as easily as he could his own heartbeat. The luceria hadn't bonded them, but it drawn them together.

He felt a faint hum within his ring. It was muted—nothing like it had once been—but he didn't know if that was because this wasn't really Serena, or if his bond to Jackie was to blame.

"What was your favorite horse's name?" he asked.

She lifted her chin. "I never had a favorite. Riding always terrified me after that fall I took as a girl."

"What did your mother say to me when I first met her?"

"She said that you weren't good enough to clean her chamber pot, and that if you tried to steal me away from her, she'd unman you."

She'd also said she would put his head on a pike and nail his entrails onto a sign as a warning to other inadequate men.

Iain glanced at the mirrored glass, knowing Joseph was watching. So was Jackie, but he couldn't think about that now. His focus couldn't shift while he was dealing with a potential threat.

He gave Joseph a slight nod.

"Do I pass your tests?" she asked.

"Just one more thing. Show me your birthmark." He didn't elaborate. If she didn't know what he was talking about, then her lie was over.

The woman's mouth tightened in indignation, and a flush of color tinted her cheeks. Iain had always been amazed by how pretty her blush made her, and had worked to make it appear as often as possible. But right now, all he could think about was the sense of impending doom he felt now that she had returned.

She loosened the laces at her bodice and turned away from the glass as she leaned forward. There, on the smooth curve of her left breast, was the ring-shaped mark of a female Theronai.

He stared at it, trying to find something that reminded him of how he'd felt for her before—some hint of love he knew he should have for her. Love didn't just go away. It lingered. It left a mark, and yet Iain could find none.

Maybe it had died with his soul.

He turned and left the room, regret heavy on his shoulders. Not only had he let Serena down by abandoning her, but he'd also betrayed her by bonding himself to another woman. He was certain that Serena would be hurt by his actions, but truth be known, he was more worried about how Jackie would feel knowing that the woman he'd once loved had come back from the grave.

He closed the door behind him, unable to look Jackie in the eye. Instead, he kept his gaze on Joseph. "All of her answers were correct."

"Do you think it's her?"

He wanted to say no. It was selfish of him—not something an honorable man would do. It was easier to pretend she was dead than it was to face up to his utter failure of her.

"I do. My luceria reacted, though not as strongly as it once had."

Jackie backed into the corner, hugging herself.

Joseph nodded, staring at Serena. "We'll keep her here for a while yet, while I make arrangements for her comfort."

"I really need to go," said Jackie.

She was upset. Even though he was barred from her thoughts, he could see it clearly in her face. "I'll come with you."

"No," she said, a bit too forcefully, then in a calmer tone, "No. I'll be fine. I just need some time alone."

He started to follow her, but Joseph grabbed his arm. "Let her go. This is a lot to absorb. Give her some time."

He didn't have any time. Every second he spent away from her was one he'd never get back. With the clock ticking away the last of his minutes, he didn't want to waste them standing around with Joseph.

"Serena will need to be watched," he told Joseph. "Even if she is Serena, there's no way to know if her story is true. If she's been in Synestryn hands . . ."

"I'll see to it," said Joseph, his expression grim. "This changes things. With Jackie."

"It changes nothing."

"You're compatible with Serena. Jackie can be with anyone. You need to let her go."

"I know. I've already decided that. But please, give me the space to do this in my own way."

"Men are suffering."

Anger rose up, souring Iain's stomach. "You don't have to remind me. I'm acutely aware of what they're all facing."

"Then you'll do the right thing?"

It was starting to get hard to tell just what the right thing was anymore, but the part of him that had held on to honor reminded him of his course. "I will."

Joseph nodded. "Be quick about it. I want someone bonded to Serena as soon as possible so we'll know if she's planning anything."

That Iain couldn't help him with, but he pretended to agree and left the room.

He should have marched straight to the armory for a clean blade, and then headed out to meet his fate tonight. But he couldn't do it. Not yet. He had to see Jackie again and reassure her that all would be well. He wasn't going to abandon her for some other woman.

He was simply going to abandon her.

Jackie was a jumbled mess of irrational emotions. She hated Serena for showing up, even as she pitied the poor woman for her two centuries of captivity. Jealousy tore through her, but why should it when she didn't care what Iain did? He had already made it clear that he wanted her to be with another man. And none of this should have bothered her, because all she wanted was to be left alone to live her life. She didn't need Iain. Let him have Serena. It shouldn't have mattered one bit.

But it did, and that pissed her off.

She paced her empty suite, feeling the crackle of magic spilling from her fingers. Her hair stood on end, and the lights over her head flickered.

She needed to calm down. Act rationally.

The door to her suite opened and Iain walked in as if he owned the place.

"How did you get in?"

He held up a key card. "I thought you might not let me in, so I took precautions."

That made her stop in her tracks and stomp toward him. "You thought I might not let you in, so you went and got a key? Do you people not have any sense of privacy at all? Get the hell out."

"We have to talk."

"No. We don't. I know the score. The woman you love is back. You should go be with her. She needs you." Saying those words nearly choked her, but she forced them out.

"You don't understand. It's not that simple."

Jackie tugged on the luceria around her throat, trying to pull the damn thing off. "Serena is alive and well. Let this fucking thing fall off already, will you?"

He looked at the floor, his hands fisting at his sides. "If I could make it fall off, I would have done so already. You're the one who made that foolish promise."

Anger exploded inside of her and she got right in his face, going up on tiptoe to lessen the distance between him. "That promise saved your life, you ungrateful ass."

"You should have let me die." There was no heat in his words, only the even tone of acceptance.

That made no sense, so she instinctively reached through their link to see what was going on inside his head. There was anger, but none of it showed in his features. It was as if it wasn't even enough for him to notice. Beneath the anger was regret, guilt, and a sense of loss, as if he'd made some irrevocable mistake.

"What is it?" she asked. "What have you done?"

"So many things." He cupped her cheek, and she couldn't help but lean into his touch. Her traitorous body didn't care if she was mad at him, or that her feelings were clawed to pieces. It craved the feel of his skin on hers, and the bubbling tingles that sank into her, warming her. "I have to leave you. I'm sorry. I wanted you to hear from my own lips how much I wish things were different."

Jackie knew this was coming, but there was no way to brace herself for the blow. She rocked back, trying to keep the tears pooling in her eyes from falling. "It's fine. I understand. You love her. Of course you have to go be with her."

His eyelids lowered in regret. "Go see Cain. Please. I hate leaving you unprotected."

"I'll be fine."

"You will be as long as you have access to Cain's power. Promise me you'll go to him."

"No. I'm not making any promises to you."

"Please, Jackie. Just speak to him. Spend some time with him. He will keep you safe. He would never allow you to be taken by Synestryn again."

She was tired of this argument. What harm could there be in doing as he asked? Especially now, while she was already bound to Iain and unable to make any bad decisions. The one she'd already made circled her throat, preventing her from making another. "Okay. I'll go see him if it will make you feel better about doing what you need to do."

Jackie wanted him to be happy. She really did. Even as jealous as she was, as hurt as she was, she'd grown to care for him. He deserved a chance to be happy, even if she had nothing to do with making him that way.

He nodded, letting out a sigh of relief. His black gaze roamed her face as if memorizing it, and then he leaned down and placed a soft, quick kiss on her mouth. "Goodbye," he whispered, then turned and left her standing alone.

It was what she wanted, wasn't it? What she'd been asking for all along?

Jackie refused to cry, but she was going to end up doing just that if she didn't distract herself. She'd told Iain she'd go see Cain, so it was best to get that over with so she was free of her obligation. The sooner she stopped thinking about Iain, the easier it would be to get her shit together and move on.

Iain almost left without saying anything to Serena. He'd already caused her so much pain, and he couldn't think of a single thing he could say now that would ease any of it. Still, out of respect for what they'd once shared, he felt honor-bound to at least tell her good-bye.

He went to the interrogation room where she was being held. Joseph had had it built since finding out there was a traitor in their midst, and yet building it hadn't done anything to help root out the culprit. Not even Nicholas, with his electronic eyes and ears planted everywhere, had had any luck finding the traitor.

Iain wasn't going to have to worry about such things much longer. He'd caused enough damage, clinging to what he thought was honor, when it had really been hubris. He'd stayed alive thinking that he alone could save his brothers.

It was utter and complete bullshit. He realized that now.

Or maybe he'd just realized what he was doing to Jackie, tying her to a man with no soul. He'd nearly raped her. If she'd resisted, he would have. His monster had gone out of control, and he knew it was only a matter of time before it happened again.

He didn't just have a monster lurking within him — he *was* the monster, wearing a mask of civility, hoping no one would notice his claws and fangs.

The door was locked. Iain looked up at the camera and dialed Joseph. "I want to see Serena," he said.

"I don't know if that's a good idea. Tynan is going to take some blood and check it against family records. I want to be absolutely sure about her before we let her out."

"I'm not going to let her out. I just want to talk to her."

"Iain, I—"

"Damn it, Joseph! Just let me talk to her, explain about Jackie. I owe her that much."

Joseph sighed. "Fine. Give me a minute and I'll have Nicholas open the lock."

Iain paced until he heard the click and then went inside. There, on the other side of the glass, Serena sat, her head resting on her folded arms. As soon as he stepped close, she lifted her head. "Iain?"

So. She could still feel him the way she once had.

Iain went through the adjoining door, propping it open with a chair so he didn't get locked in.

She drew herself up, straightening her shoulders. Her regal beauty was still there, but its power over him had faded. Or perhaps it was his lack of a soul that had diminished his appreciation for her looks. Intellectually, he could see that her features were perfectly symmetrical and delicate, but when he reached inside to see how he felt about her, all he got was air and dust. There was nothing left there but the memory of what he'd once felt.

"How are you?" he asked. "Do you need anything?"

"I'd like some decent clothing. I don't like showing my limbs to any who walk in."

He nodded and sent a text to Joseph to see if she could get a change of clothes.

"What is that device?"

"A cell phone. A lot has happened since you were . . . taken."

"Taken," she said, a hint of mocking laughter in her tone. "What a kind way to phrase my imprisonment."

"I didn't mean to make light of what happened to you."

Her gaze moved to his throat, and grief flickered through her canted eyes. "How long am I to stay here?"

"It's not up to me."

"So, you're here to catch up on old times? I can't

imagine your woman would appreciate you keeping private company with me."

"I'm here out of respect. For what we shared."

"You mean you're here to tell me that you no longer love me. No need. I already determined as much the moment I saw you. You're different now."

He lowered his gaze for fear of her seeing right through him. "A lot has happened since you've been gone."

"Nothing has happened. At least not for me."

"I'm sorry, Serena. I truly am. I wish things could be different."

"So do I."

"You'll be safe here. Cared for."

"But not by you, you mean?"

"I can't change that," he said.

"Do you love her?" asked Serena. "Do you love her the way you did me?"

He wished he did, but the truth was that love was beyond him now. Both for Serena and for Jackie. "Talking about this is only going to hurt you."

She jolted to her feet, her skirts spinning around her. "Don't you dare speak to me of pain. I'm not a child for you to coddle. We were in love. I was willing to abandon my family for you. I deserve to know if you love the woman who has replaced me."

He stood, searching for a way to lessen the pain he saw glittering in her eyes. "Jackie and I have only known each other a short time."

She shook with anger as she grabbed his hand, holding his luceria in front of his face. "Your ring speaks differently. And your lifemark ..." Before he could even realize what she was doing, she grabbed the front of his shirt and tore it open. Buttons clicked on the floor.

She looked down at his chest, and her face went pale, her eyes wide. She pressed her hand against his lifemark, staring in horror. "Why has your tree not been restored?

Where are the leaves? I see only three, and each one of them is a lie."

Iain gathered her hands in one of his and tried to close the tattered remains of his shirt. "Serena, let me explain."

"Explain?" she whispered. "You can't explain away this." She looked up into his eyes as she backed away. "Now I know what it was I saw—what was different about you. You're not just colder. You're . . . soulless."

"No," he hurried to say, struggling to think of something to appease her and wipe away the fear vibrating through her.

As he stepped forward, she moved back, pressing herself into the wall.

The monster inside of Iain began to strain inside its cage, demanding to be set free. It wanted to kill Serena to keep her from spilling his secret. Then Iain could lie and say she was an impostor, that she'd turned on him. No one would ever question his decision to protect the people here.

He didn't even have the chance to fight the beast before Joseph busted into the room, his sword drawn. "Is what she said true?"

Iain reached for his blade. He could beat Joseph in battle. The man spent more time behind a desk than in the field. He'd gone soft, was out of practice. It wouldn't even be that hard to cut him down.

The monster cheered him on, clanging against the bars, chanting encouragement. *Kill, kill, kill.*

It would be so easy. So fast. He could be out of here in seconds, and no one would ever know his shame.

He felt Jackie's presence brush his mind, as if something had disturbed her. She was concerned. For him. He'd just dumped her, and yet she was worried what happened to him.

If he killed Joseph, she'd find a way to blame herself for his actions—for not having seen what he really was.

Iain drew his sword. The steel felt good in his hand. Right. The monster let out a hiss of encouragement.

Kill, kill, kill.

Iain couldn't. The only thing he had left was his honor, and an honorable man would never kill his brother or a defenseless woman.

He opened his fist. The sword fell to the ground in a clang of steel, and Serena scrambled to pick it up, pointing it at his chest.

He raised his hands slowly and looked at Joseph, knowing he no longer had a choice. "I won't fight, but do what you need to do fast. I don't know how much longer I can stay in control of myself."

Joseph stepped forward and slammed the butt of his sword into Iain's temple hard enough to make his world go black.

Chapter 22

Jackie felt something odd, but when she reached out to Iain to see what was the matter, he shut her out.

Fine. She really didn't want to know what was going on with him and Serena anyway. It was none of her business. She just wished the damn luceria would hurry up and fall off already, so she wouldn't keep getting tortured with glimpses of the man she . . . what? Was fond of? Cared for? Loved?

No. It was simply a matter of attachment—artificial feelings that would go away as soon as the luceria did. For now, however, it was going to be handy having Iain's luceria on for what she was about to do.

Jackie found Cain in the workout area. As chilly as it was, he was still shirtless, drenched in sweat. Huge amounts of weight were attached to a barbell, which he hoisted as if it were empty.

He was a big man, with gigantic hands, and a thick, heavy build. His eyes were dark green, and they watched her steadily as she approached. It was only when she was standing right next to him, making it obvious that she'd come to see him, that he stopped what he was doing.

"Can I talk to you?" she asked.

"Of course." His voice was deep, gravelly, and rough.

"Alone?"

His eyes darted to her necklace, then back to her face. "Yes, my lady."

Jackie had heard that term used before in reference to the other Theronai women, but she wasn't sure if it was some sort of ceremonial title, or a term of endearment. Either way, she ignored it so that she could have this chore over with as soon as possible.

She led him out to the vacant open area where they practiced with swords. The other men watched, not even pretending they weren't.

She let out a long sigh. "I've come to the realization that if I don't want to become a victim of the Synestryn again, I'm going to have to accept my disease."

"Your disease?" he asked.

"Yes. The one my father passed on—all this magic bullshit."

"I see. And what exactly does that mean?"

"It means that I'm going to have to wear one of these damn necklaces so that I can kick the ass of any demon who dares come after me."

"An exercise of sound judgment."

She snorted at that. "The problem is, I don't want the job that comes with it. I want to have as normal and *human* a life as possible. I'm not cut out for monster-hunting crap."

"Unless those monsters bring the fight to you."

"Exactly."

A cold breeze swept through, and she tried not to shiver. She had no idea how Cain could stand around shirtless, though she had to admit that it was a nice view. Not nearly as nice as Iain's bare chest, but . . .

Before that train of thought could completely derail her, she forced herself to concentrate. "Iain and I aren't working out."

"I hate to disagree, but the solidification of colors in your luceria tell a different story."

"Serena is back."

Cain shook his head in stunned silence.

"It's true. Iain confirmed it's her. She was apparently trapped in limbo somewhere, but she's out now, and there's no way I can compete with her. Even if she wasn't drop-dead gorgeous, Iain loves her." Speaking the words aloud made them too real, too devastating. She wasn't supposed to care who Iain loved, but she couldn't seem to help but be jealous. But it wasn't the jealousy that was the worst part. The worst part was the deep ache in the pit of her stomach that didn't seem to go away. As much as she'd fought their union, she was starting to get used to having him around. He was cold sometimes, but then he also burned hot, making her feel more alive than she'd ever felt before. And deep down, her gut told her that he needed her. As conceited as it was to think that she had anything to offer that Serena couldn't give him, she still felt . . . something.

Whatever that something was, she couldn't even explain it to herself, much less anyone else. She had to find a way to let go, and the only way to do that safely was to pick another man so she wouldn't become demon food again.

"My question to you, Cain, is whether or not you could let me live my life in peace. Iain seems to think that you could."

"What, exactly, are you asking me?"

"If I agree to take your luceria, it would be in exchange for your promise to let me live a human life. You can do whatever you want to do, but so could I. I'd get a house, a job . . . you know, a normal life."

"We wouldn't work together?" he asked as if the concept was too foreign to understand.

"I suppose we could, but whatever we did wouldn't have anything to do with the war, magic, or demons."

"Why? Why would you want such a mundane existence when you have the power to fight true evil?"

"Because I can't stand waking up every morning

wondering whether I'm going to live through the day. Because I can't deal with the terror of combat. But mostly because I can't stand seeing the horror those monsters cause. It'll kill me if I have to face that every day."

He nodded slowly, a deep sadness darkening his eyes. "I understand."

"Do you? Do you understand that I'll never get over this—that it isn't just some phase—or do you understand that I just need some time to come around to your way of thinking? I'm never going to want to be a part of your world."

"I understand that you mean exactly what you say. I'm unconvinced, however, that you will always feel this way. When you live as long as we do, it's hard to *not* change your mind about things."

"I'm not willing to keep fighting with someone about this. My question to you is whether or not you think you could be the kind of man to get the hell out of my way and let me live, even if we were connected by some magical necklace."

He was silent for so long, she was beginning to think her search was not yet over. "Okay," he finally said. "So long as it doesn't jeopardize your life, I could give you what you want."

"That is kinda the point—to keep me from risking my life on a daily basis."

"Fine, then."

A wave of relief settled over her, but she knew it was too soon to celebrate just yet. "There's one more thing."

"What?"

"Not now, but soon, I think I'm going to want a baby. It doesn't have to be yours, if that freaks you out, but I need to make sure that doesn't change anything for you. We're not going to be a real couple or anything, but a kid is a pretty big deal, so I thought you should know."

A look of intense longing crossed his rough face, and

she was sure he swayed on his feet a little. "It does change things. Immensely."

Damn it. She'd been so close. She let out a heavy sigh. "Thanks anyway."

As soon as she turned to walk away, he grabbed her arm. "You misunderstand me."

She turned back around and looked at him, waiting for him to explain. "How?"

"For you, I'd give up my dreams of being mated to a woman willing to fight the cause to which I've dedicated my entire life. For a child . . . I'd give up much, much more."

"Oh." She hadn't expected that, but it worked for her. "Okay, then. It's settled. As soon as Iain's luceria falls off, I'll call you. I don't want another session of grabby hands from all of the other men, so I'd appreciate it if you'd keep this to yourself."

He nodded, his throat moving as if he was unable to speak.

She hated it that she wasn't as thrilled with this idea as Cain was, but at least being abandoned by Iain made one person happy.

Jackie scolded herself for being so dramatic. Iain wasn't abandoning her. Besides, only a couple of days ago she'd been hoping he'd free her. She was getting exactly what she wanted—or at least as close to it as her magical parentage would allow. She was supposed to be happy about this. The normal life she wanted so badly— the one she'd dreamed about for two long, terrified years—was just around the corner.

If it was what she wanted so much, then why the hell did she feel like crying?

Jackie's phone rang, and Joseph's name showed on the screen. She looked up at Cain. "I'll call you soon."

"I won't leave the compound until I hear from you."

She walked away, answering the call.

"Where are you?" asked Joseph.

"Right outside of your office windows. Why?"

"We need to talk."

"That doesn't sound good."

"It's not. You need to brace yourself, Jackie. It's about as bad as it gets."

Jackie hung up and ran through the halls to his office. Her mind filled with images of her sisters dead or injured. In those brief few seconds, she saw Helen's body charred beyond recognition and Lexi bleeding into the ground. She didn't bother to knock on his door, but flew inside.

Helen was there. Her face was grim, but she was alive and whole.

The momentary flicker of relief she felt was short-lived. "Is it Lexi? Is she hurt?"

"No," said Helen, taking Jackie by the shoulders. "Lexi's fine. I talked to her last night."

"Then what? What's this awful news?"

"It's Iain," said Joseph.

Jackie's stomach sank, and she reached for the necklace to reassure herself it was still there, while simultaneously reaching out with her mind. Iain was there, greeting her with reassurance and comfort. "What about him? I know he's alive. I can feel him."

"This is so hard to say," said Helen. "You need to sit down."

"He's okay," insisted Jackie. "I told you I can feel him." If she hadn't been able to, she would have totally freaked out, but he was still there, in her thoughts, whispering to her that everything was going to be okay.

"His soul is dead," said Joseph, his tone cold. "I'm taking him to the Slayers tomorrow to be executed."

The world spun out from under her, and if Helen hadn't caught her, she would have fallen.

Drake was there, too, easing her down into a chair. "Way to be gentle, Joseph."

"There's no easy way to tell her what's going to happen, so get off my fucking back, Drake." Joseph looked at Jackie, then lowered his voice. "I'm so sorry, Jackie. If I'd known this had happened, I wouldn't have let you get so close to him. It's a wonder he didn't hurt you."

She looked around the room. Everyone was so sober, as if he were already dead. "Of course he didn't hurt me. What the hell are you talking about? He'd never let anything or anyone even get near me. If he told you that he hurt me, he's lying. I'll testify under oath, or whatever it is you people do."

Joseph's face was stony. "There's nothing you can say to change what's going to happen."

"Like hell there isn't. I won't let you convict an innocent man to die."

"You don't understand, Jackie," said Joseph. "There is no trial. His soul is dead. He'll be put to death tomorrow."

"What has he done to deserve this?"

"Didn't you hear me? He's soulless."

"So fucking what?" she nearly screamed. "Who did he kill?"

"No one. Yet."

"So you're telling me that you're going to execute him for something he hasn't done yet?"

"He will hurt someone. It's only a matter of time."

She raised her hand toward Joseph. Electricity arced between her fingers, snapping in the air. "Yeah, well, I'm about to hurt someone, too. Are you going to kill me?"

Joseph's jaw bunched with anger. "You have a soul. Iain doesn't."

"How do you even know that? From where I'm sitting, you look like the soulless bastard here."

"He knows, Jackie," said Helen, her voice gentle. "Iain's lifemark is bare. He hid it with tattoos of leaves, but Serena knew him too well. She saw right through him."

Jackie's hand fell, the electricity dissipating with her shock and pain.

Serena had known him well enough to see he had no soul after being with him for all of five minutes, and yet Jackie had been naked and intimate with him for hours and never sensed a thing. Maybe she wasn't as close to him as she'd fooled herself into thinking she was.

None of that mattered right now. She had to find a way to make these people see reason. "You can't kill a man for something he might do. If we did that, then all of you would have to kill yourselves, too. It's barbaric."

"It's our way," said Joseph.

"And you wonder why I don't want any part of your fucked-up world." She turned to Helen. "Surely you see how insane this is."

"I've seen through Drake what harm can come from letting Iain live. I have to trust that they know what they're doing. They've been dealing with this for thousands of years. If this is the safest way, then we should accept that."

"You all are fucking nuts. I want to see him."

"No," said Joseph. "He could hurt you."

With a thought and more force than was probably necessary, she used a slab of air to slam him back into a wall. The swords mounted behind him tumbled to the ground and papers swirled everywhere. "I can protect myself. Now where the hell is he?"

"Let her see him, Joseph," said Helen. "Iain's lies are over. He's not going to try to hide anymore. She'll see him as he really is now."

"Fine," Joseph gritted out between clenched teeth. "But I'm not letting you go alone. Helen, Drake, you go with her."

Jackie released the air holding him up, and he caught himself as he fell.

She didn't bother to thank him. She was not about to thank the man who wanted to kill Iain.

Cain hurried through the halls toward Tynan's suite. He pounded on the door with the side of his fist. "Open up."

Tynan cracked the door open, scowling at Cain. "The sun has not completely set. Go away until it does."

Cain couldn't wait, and he didn't have time for the scheming maneuverings that would gain him entrance. He needed this done. Now.

He shoved the door open. Tynan backed up, unable to stop him from barreling in.

"What is so important?" asked Tynan, his words clipped with irritation.

"I need the serum."

Tynan frowned, the wrinkles marring his pretty face. "You found a woman?"

Cain was shaking from the inside out. He still couldn't believe what Jackie had offered him.

Well, technically, she hadn't offered. She'd told him. She wanted a child. She hadn't said she wanted it to be his, but he wasn't taking any chances. If he got the opportunity to have a child of his own, he was taking it. And her.

"Will you give it to me?" he asked, unwilling to tell Tynan about Jackie, for fear that if he said it out loud, he'd jinx it and she'd change her mind.

Tynan stared at him for a long time, his pale, icy blue eyes steady in their scrutiny. "You seem desperate."

"If someone had offered you the chance for a child of your own, how would you feel?"

The Sanguinar nodded and left the room for a moment. When he returned, he held a syringe in his hand. "This comes with a price."

"Of course it does. I expected no less. What do you want?"

"Blood. And a peacebinding."

Cain instantly rebelled at the thought. If Tynan subjected him to a peacebinding, then he'd never again be able to hurt the man—even if they were to become enemies.

The syringe glinted under the overhead lights of

Tynan's suite, glowing with promise. Held inside that small vessel was the potential answer to his prayers. All he had to do was make a deal with the devil.

Jackie wanted a child. She'd have one with or without his involvement.

There was really no question. Losing Sibyl was killing him—literally. He couldn't help but reach out and grasp this opportunity, no matter the cost.

"Done," said Cain.

Tynan smiled and bared his fangs.

Chapter 23

As soon as the sun went down, Ronan rose from his sleep. He'd taken refuge in the basement of a Gerai house, locking himself inside, away from the sun.

He was anxious to continue his hunt for the blooded woman. Last night's hunt had brought him to this area, but the trail the scent of her blood left behind had grown cold. He didn't even know if she was still nearby, or if he was suffering from a case of wishful thinking.

Hunger twisted in his guts, driving him upstairs.

He smelled the presence of another person before he saw her. Light perfume or perhaps the soap on her clothing mingled with the scent of human woman. He found her in the kitchen, reaching into a sack of groceries.

She froze, her dark eyes widening with surprise.

"I won't hurt you," he told her.

She was in her fifties, he guessed, with a plump figure and kind, brown eyes. She covered her heart with her hands and breathed out a sigh of relief. "You surprised me."

On one hand was a wedding band, and on the other was the silver ring of the Gerai—a smooth band with a single leaf etched into the metal. Ronan glided forward and extended his hand to shake hers.

The ring of the Gerai vibrated against his skin, validating its authenticity. This woman was one of the rare

humans who possessed enough Athanasian blood to be
a true Gerai—a human who aided in the war against the
Synestryn.

"I'm Ronan. I'm sorry I scared you."

"It's okay." A dark blush colored her cheeks as she
stared, but he was used to that. His kind was beautiful,
and even the humans he'd known for years had a ten-
dency to let their gaze linger a bit too long.

He released her hand and stepped back. The predator
in him was urging him to pounce, to drink her blood and
sate his hunger. Instead, he lifted another sack of groceries onto the table and began removing items from the
bag.

"I'm not used to running into anyone here," she told
him.

"I was hunting in this area and needed to take shelter
from the sun."

"Are you hungry? I could fix you something to eat."

His hands froze in the act of removing a can of peas.

She stammered, hurrying to correct herself. "I'm
sorry. I wasn't thinking. You probably don't want real
food at all."

Her innocent offer made his hunger grow, drowning
out all other sensations. "I eat," he said, hoping to calm
her. "Real food, that is."

She caught his gaze and was trapped. He hadn't
planned to feed from this woman, but she was here, and
he was starving.

He let a small stream of his dwindling power slide out
of him to wrap around her. Her eyelids drooped and her
body slumped slightly as she relaxed.

"But what I need right now is blood. You want to give
that to me, don't you?"

His prey nodded.

Ronan kicked the refrigerator shut and lifted her into
his arms. The couch was nearby and perfect for his needs.
He let her head fall back, exposing her throat. "Do you

want to remember what I'm going to do to you?" he asked.

"No," she whispered. "My husband . . ."

That was for the best. The poor dear probably felt some kind of attraction to him and thought it was a betrayal of her vows. It wasn't. She couldn't help her reaction to him any more than he could help his reaction to her. He needed her blood, her power.

Ronan made quick work of his meal, drinking until she was hovering on the edge of losing too much blood. Her power slid into him, easing the ravenous hunger enough to allow him to concentrate.

He erased all memory of his presence and filled her with the compulsion to rest and hydrate before getting back behind the wheel of her car. No marks remained to show what he'd done, and he left her napping on the couch.

Before he left, he finished putting away the perishable groceries and set a glass of water on the table beside her. With his conscience eased, he backed his van out of the garage and drove off with the windows down, hoping for some hint of the trail that had gone cold.

For the first time, Iain knew exactly how his monster felt, being caged and trapped, impotent to act.

He clutched at the bars of the cell, pulling and pushing against them for some sign of weakness. There was no window here. The walls were concrete, and several feet belowground. And while he knew letting himself be taken into custody was the right thing, he was regretting it now.

Jackie was hurting. He could feel her shock and anger pouring through their link. Denial overshadowed her grief, making him wonder if she had yet accepted his fate the way he had.

He needed to be with her, to tell her that everything was going to be okay. Reaching out to her through the luceria wasn't enough. He wanted to see her face and know that she believed what he said. There was no way he could go to his death in peace if he knew she was left behind, confused and hurting.

The lock at the main entrance to the detention cell buzzed open. Iain strained to see who it was, but the angle was too sharp. "Who's there?"

"It's me," said Jackie, her voice washing over him like warm, clean water.

He let out a long breath and reached out through the bars for her.

"Hands to yourself," said a man. Then a second later, Drake walked into sight. "I'm here to make sure things stay nice and civil. Do you understand? If I see any sign of danger, I'm dragging her out of here."

Iain nodded and stepped back. He was going to be a good little boy if that's what it took to see Jackie again before he died. Besides, the idea of Drake touching her made his monster want to come out and play.

Jackie came into sight, so fucking pretty it took his breath away. Her gray eyes were shiny with unshed tears, and she chewed on her bottom lip in anxiety.

"Is it true?" she asked, inching closer. "What they said about your soul?"

His gaze dropped to the ground in shame and he nodded. "I couldn't tell you. I'm sorry."

"But you don't seem . . . evil."

"I hide it. Control myself. But it's there, lurking inside of me, growing stronger every day."

"That's what I saw, wasn't it? When we were . . . together."

He still couldn't look her in the eye. "I didn't want this for you. That's why I wanted you to choose another man. I knew I'd never be whole."

"And why the luceria won't fall off. Because you'll never be as good as new."

Her fingers slipped between the bars, so delicate and

beautiful. He remembered just how they could make him feel, and he wanted her touch again so badly it nearly drove him mad resisting the need to step forward so she could reach him.

"That's not safe," said Drake. "Don't make me force you to leave."

Her head snapped around to glare at him. "Try and see how well that goes."

Helen's voice came from out of sight, but nearby. "He's only trying to protect you."

"Just leave us alone for a minute, will you? We deserve some fucking privacy."

"I'm sorry," said Drake. "That's not going to happen."

Jackie pulled a burst of power from Iain, and then waved her hand. Drake slid out of sight as if he'd been pushed.

"He's right," Iain told her. "It's not safe for you to be around me."

"Not you, too. I'm sick of hearing the bullshit. I want you to tell me what I need to do to save you."

"There is one thing you could do."

"Name it."

"I need you to deliver a message to some men for me." He gave her the names of the other men in the Band of the Barren. "Tell them that I sent you, what's happened to me, and then tell them that the Band is compromised, and they need to go into hiding."

"I don't understand."

"Just tell them. They'll know what you mean."

"How is this going to save you?" she asked.

"It won't, but it may save their lives."

"I'm not concerned about their lives. I'm worried about yours."

"There's nothing anyone can do to save me. You can't bring my soul back to life any more than you could bring back the people who died in those caves."

She flinched, her brows pinching together in grief.

"Don't say that. There has to be a way—some magical spell or something?"

"Dead is dead. We both have to learn to live with it. I'm just sorry that you'll still be connected to me at the end. I'll try to keep my thoughts to myself, but you may have to keep me out. It shames me to admit it, but I may not be able to control myself and keep from reaching out for you."

A tear slipped down her cheek, but there was fury lurking beneath the sadness. "I won't leave you to die alone."

"I don't want you with me then, Jackie. I don't want you to feel the life drain out of me. It will haunt you forever. I'd rather you remember whatever it is you saw in me that makes you care enough to be standing here now."

"Of course I care about you. How could I not when you've thought of nothing but the people around you since the night we met? You must have known that this could happen—that you could be locked up and sentenced to death. That's why you were cold, shoving me away so I wouldn't end up right here, angry and devastated that you're just going to let them kill you. You haven't done anything. You can't let them do this."

He bowed his head, unable to look at the hurt radiating out of her eyes. Only, even looking away, he could still feel it pulsing into him, pounding at him through their link. "It's the only way now."

"What? There was another way before? A better one? Because if there was, let's do that instead."

He reached for her, wrapping his hands around her fingers. They were cold, shaking. "I knew the only way to free you was for me to die. As soon as we went into the next battle with people there to watch over you, I was planning to end it."

"You were going to *kill yourself*? That's no option."

"It was for me. It was an honorable way to go—one

I'd chosen. Certainly better than being sent to the Slayers in shame."

"I don't want you to die."

His fingers tightened around hers, trying to warm them. "You'll be fine without me. You're strong. Just promise me that you'll stay away at the end. I don't know how they'll kill me, but I have to know that you won't suffer alongside me. Promise me."

She shook her head, making more tears spill out. "I won't make this easy on you. I won't make it easy on any of you. If you do this, you do it without my support."

"It must happen."

"It's just more proof that I don't belong in your world. How could I belong with people who kill their own because of what *might* happen?"

"If you'd seen what someone like me is capable of, then you'd understand."

"I don't want to understand. I just want to wake up and find that this was all a bad dream."

His hands slid up her arms, cupping her shoulders. His eyes roamed her face, memorizing every little detail. He would put that picture in his mind when the time came, and let it comfort him. "Give me your belt and I'll end it now, so you don't have to suffer for as long as it takes them to get me to the Slayers."

"My belt?" she asked, confused.

"They took mine. I have no sure way of killing myself in here." He'd considered slamming his head into the concrete wall, but that was no guarantee of death. He had to do it right to limit Jackie's suffering. If he simply maimed himself, she'd still be tied to him. Permanent brain damage could trap her for eternity. "Help me and this will all be over in a matter of minutes."

A look of horror crossed her face and she pulled back, shaking her head. "I won't help you kill yourself."

"It's what I want. I'd rather die by my own hand than by someone who now calls themselves our friend. Think

about my future executioner. How would you feel if it
was your job to kill someone you didn't even know?" He
couldn't think of a way to make her understand that he
didn't want to tarnish what was a mostly noble life by
causing others pain as his last living act.

"No."

"Please. I want to end my life in the most honorable
way possible. Help me do that."

"I can't. I won't." She turned and ran, the sound of a
stifled sob echoing behind her.

Serena paced the room, her stomach twisting violently.

Iain had turned. The man she'd loved for so long was
dead.

Her heart wept for what she'd lost. If only she'd ignored her mother and bonded with him sooner, none of
this would have happened. She would have saved his
soul.

Hatred for her mother coursed through her body,
making her tremble with its power. For two hundred
years she'd sat trapped in that bubble, unable to speak to
anyone, catching only fleeting glimpses of the world as it
passed her by.

She didn't belong in this place. She understood none
of what she saw around her, not the glowing tubes of
light overhead, or the warm draft of air sliding through a
grate in the ceiling. The table was carved from metal
rather than wood, and she was almost certain that people
were watching her from behind the large mirror in one
wall.

Things were different now. Too different. Even the
brief trip she'd taken from outside this castle to this
room had shown her a world of wonders just waiting for
her discovery.

She'd trade every one of them in for one single leaf
clinging to Iain's lifemark.

The door opened, and a large man with a hideously

scarred face walked in. He offered her a smile, but the web of scars crossing his mouth twisted it into something ugly. She tried not to flinch, but her nerves were strung so tightly that she was certain she hadn't covered her insult.

His smile faltered. "I'm Nicholas Laith. Joseph sent me here to release you."

Instantly, she began to panic. She was in an alien world, devoid of the knowledge she'd need to navigate it. "Where shall I go?"

"Go?" he asked, seemingly confused. "You're not going anywhere. I just meant that you can get out of this room now. You can stay here with us. I had a suite prepared for you."

He opened the door for her to proceed, and led her out into a long hallway. "What are your orders regarding me?" she asked.

"Orders?"

"Your leader told you to come and fetch me, correct?"

"He said to make sure you were comfortable and to get you settled."

"So I'm not a prisoner here?"

Mr. Laith shook his head. "No."

"Then I can leave if I wish?"

He looked down at her, and despite his scars, his vibrant blue eyes were stunning. "Do you know how to drive a car?"

"I can ride. I can't yet pay for a horse, but I promise you I'll find a way to earn the money if you'd be so good as to extend a loan." She hated riding, but she'd do what she must now. At least she was free to do so.

He smiled again, and this time, she was accustomed to the odd puckering enough that it didn't startle her. "We don't have horses. We operate motorized vehicles, and they can go a hundred miles an hour, so until you learn how to drive one, you'd likely kill yourself."

Surely he was lying about traveling at such speeds.

Then again, he seemed completely genuine. "How long does it take to learn to operate one?"

"Depends on how chicken you are."

She wasn't getting anywhere like this. As much as she hated the dent to her pride, she had no choice but to be honest with him. "I can't stay here. Iain . . ." She swallowed back her grief, trying to keep her tears in check. "I need to be alone to grieve."

Mr. Laith's mouth flattened, but she couldn't tell if it was in sympathy or irritation. "It's safe here."

"I can protect myself. If you give me a sword."

"This world is different from the one you left. How will you cope?"

"I simply want some solitude. To heal."

"We have some cabins out back. They're rustic, but solitary. I'll have one of them cleaned up and prepared for you."

It was likely as good as she was going to get for now. "Thank you for your gracious offer," she told him.

Serena had always learned quickly. She'd set herself to the task of learning how to navigate these strange times, and then, once she'd learned to drive one of their motorized vehicles, she'd set out in search of a new life — one that would distract her from the pain of losing the man she loved.

Chapter 24

Jackie released Drake and Helen from the shield she'd put around them as she sprinted out of what she couldn't help but think of as a dungeon. She raced up several flights of concrete steps, and ran into Joseph's hard chest. He grabbed her upper arms and didn't let go.

"The security camera caught what you did to Helen and Drake. You can't go using your power irresponsibly like that."

She looked him right in the eye. "Fuck. Off."

His expression pinched with anger, but his voice was modulated and even. "You're suffering. It's understandable. I've already made arrangements for you to fly to Africa to visit Lexi for a few days. She misses you. The distance may help . . . mute your connection to Iain."

"While you kill him."

"We're only doing what we have to do. One day you'll see that."

"Bullshit. And if you think I'm going anywhere, you're wrong. I'm going to be with Iain through every second of his death. I'm going to soak it all in, memorizing every detail, every ounce of fear, every scrap of suffering. And then, when he's dead, I'm going to take all of that and find a way to shove it so deep in your brain you'll never be able to sleep again."

His eye twitched and his face darkened with rage.

"Do you think I want this? Do you think that if there were any other way of protecting the people who depend on me that I wouldn't do it?"

"You could . . . oh, I don't know . . . *not kill him*. That would be a good start."

"You have no idea how much damage he's capable of doing. He could kill dozens before we were able to stop him. He's fast, deadly, and without a soul, he must be put down."

"Then do it yourself. Don't send him to strangers like a fucking coward."

"I know you don't understand our customs, but they're in place for a reason. This is the way it has to be."

She used a burst of Iain's power to jerk from his grasp. "I don't accept that."

"You'd better learn how to find some solace fast, then, because this is happening, even if I have to have one of the Sanguinar drug you out of your mind so you'll behave until it's over."

He would, too. She could see it in his eyes. There was no mercy there. Regret, but not a hint of compromise.

Joseph's phone rang. Jackie pushed past him and started up the next flight of stairs.

"Where is he?" he asked.

Jackie paused. Something about the way he said it told her it was bad news. Big, bad news.

"Tell Ronan to hold off. We're on the way."

More steps echoed in the concrete stairwell.

"Iain isn't fighting this," said Drake. "I don't think you're going to have to worry about him hurting anyone so long as we do it fast. I don't know how he kept himself under control for so long, but it's a hell of a thing to see."

"I wish he'd fight," said Helen. "It seems so barbaric to kill him when he's not . . . rabid."

"We'll deal with Iain later," said Joseph. "Ronan found a human woman in Synestryn hands. You two go help him free her."

"We're on it," said Drake.

"What about Iain?" asked Helen.

Joseph let out a heavy sigh. "Henry Mason called and said they found proof of demons sniffing around his sister's house last night. He's bringing his family here as we speak. Finally. As soon as I see Autumn safely settled within our walls, I'll take Iain to the Slayers. There's no kindness in prolonging the inevitable. Especially for Jackie."

"She'll never forgive you for this," said Helen.

"I know. She can join the fucking club, because I'm not sure I'm ever going to forgive myself."

Their steps grew louder. Jackie didn't want them to know she'd been listening, but if she moved now, they'd hear her.

Knowledge of what to do sprang into her head as another flickering light glowed in the vast black landscape at the back of her mind. She funneled Iain's power into her and shifted the light around her until she was no longer visible.

She pushed herself flat against the wall and held her breath as the trio passed by her, exiting through the door at the top of the stairwell.

Elation trilled through her as she realized what she'd done. They couldn't see her. That meant that the security cameras probably couldn't, either.

Now all she had to do was collect a few things, and she could get out of here. First she'd get some supplies, some weapons and protective clothing. And then she'd get Iain.

There was no way in hell she was going to let his own people murder him. She'd find a way to get him out of here. They'd run and hide, and if anyone came near him with the intent to kill, she'd make sure they regretted it.

Joseph didn't know how much longer he could hold himself together. He was supposed to be leading these people, and yet how could he do that when he was beginning to question his own choices?

Executing Chris had nearly killed Joseph, and there had been nothing left of the man he'd grown up with. All that had remained of Chris was a ravening beast posing as a man. He'd beaten and raped a human, nearly killing her.

His death had been justified, and yet it still haunted Joseph. How the hell was he going to kill Iain when there was no outward sign that he'd turned? How was he ever going to come back from that kind of pain and guilt?

Joseph wasn't fit to lead these people. His term wasn't yet up, but he needed to leave his office and get out from under the decisions and paperwork and remind himself of the man he was born to be.

But who else would do his job? No one wanted it.

Someone had to do it. Too bad the someone doing it now was slowly having the life sucked out of him.

A tentative knock sounded on his door. He looked up to see Lyka standing in his doorway, all golden and glowing like a ray of sunshine. Seeing her eased the pressure behind his eyes and quieted the pounding in his head.

She was a Slayer. The only one under his roof. She'd come to live here as part of an agreement with her brother, Andreas. He'd left Lyka here and taken Carmen, the young woman Joseph had claimed as his daughter. The exchange encouraged both parties to be civil and respect the agreement, ensuring neither side rushed back into their war hastily.

He'd rarely seen Lyka since she'd arrived. Whenever he went to the dining hall and she was there, she seemed to disappear moments later. He didn't know if it was coincidence or if she was avoiding him, but her appearance now was a much-needed distraction.

"Come in. Have a seat."

She hovered by the door, her long, lean body completely encased in clinging black fabric. Even her hands were curled up and tucked inside her sleeves as if she were cold. A soft hood covered her slightly pointed ears and most of her sunny hair. Her canted golden eyes were veiled by thick lashes, her head angled downward, avoiding his gaze.

Her posture and demeanor now were nothing like the first time he'd met her, angry and hissing at her brother. She'd been all claws and teeth then, but now she seemed quieter, more subdued.

Lyka said nothing, just stood there as if hovering on the edge of a decision.

He could have stared at her for a long time, enjoying the curve of her body and the intriguing tilt of her eyes. Her presence was calming to him, allowing the frustration and anger to slide by, leaving less of a mark on him. But sadly, he couldn't spend the day staring. He had other, less enjoyable things to do. "I'm pretty busy. Is there something you need?"

"Sorry. I didn't mean to bother you. I just . . . I heard someone say one of your men has turned. I'm truly sorry for your loss."

He wanted to shout at her that Iain wasn't dead yet, but that seemed pointless. His soul had died a long time ago. The rest was a mere formality. "Thank you."

She pulled in a deep breath, and he couldn't help but notice the way it molded her breasts against her shirt.

Joseph felt a stirring of lust he hadn't had in a long time. His skin warmed, and his blood began to heat. Even his cock seemed to wake up, swelling inside his jeans.

Maybe he just needed to get laid to get out of his funk. Not that he'd ever even consider thinking about thinking about sex with Andreas's sister. He knew exactly how he'd feel if that fucker looked at Carmen as anything more than a precious treasure under his protection—one who was going to keep her pants all the way on.

Sex with Lyka was not an option, and sex with anyone wasn't likely to fix his problems, or do anything more than give him a few fleeting moments of pleasure.

She hadn't left yet. She stayed hovering in his doorway, watching him with her pretty eyes, wringing her hands.

He ignored his inappropriate feelings for a woman he knew he could not have, and rose from his chair. "Is there something else, Lyka?"

She saw him approach, and he thought she started to back away before catching herself. The movement was so quick, it was hard to tell if it had actually happened. Her gaze darted around warily, as if she expected him to pounce.

He had no idea why she was so skittish, but it pissed him off that she would seem worried he might hurt her. She was under his protection. He'd give his life to keep her safe if necessary, which, given the growing state of anger and unrest inside Dabyr, wasn't entirely out of the realm of possibility.

When she spoke, her words were breathless and rushed. "I was wondering if whoever you send to take your man to my people might take me with them. So I can see my family again for a visit. I'd come back here afterwards, of course."

Joseph had been so wrapped up in his own matters, he hadn't even considered her feelings. She was thrown into a place filled with five hundred strangers—a hostage to guarantee her brother's good behavior. She hadn't been allowed contact with her family to prevent any rumors of spying. She hadn't spoken to them in weeks and was probably homesick.

He took a step closer so he could better see her face. He didn't sense any signs of deceit, but that didn't mean he trusted her. "This trip isn't going to be a happy one. Are you sure you want to go?"

She nodded, scooting back a few inches. "I don't know how long it will be until I can see my family again."

Her gaze met his, finally, and he felt it like an electric jolt all the way to his toes. He wanted to get closer, but every time he inched forward, she moved back. She was out in the hall now as it was.

"Do you?" she asked. "Know how long it will be?"

He didn't, but he didn't want to tell her that. She already seemed so lonely. He couldn't bear to tell her it could be years before the Slayers and the Theronai truly trusted each other. Until such a miracle happened, she would be a virtual prisoner, albeit a comfortable one. He would make sure of it.

"I don't," he said. "You can come with me."

She paled and her little pink tongue swept out nervously over her lips. "You? You're going?"

"I couldn't ask someone else to sentence one of my men to death. It's my job. I'll do it."

"Oh. I thought you'd send one of the humans." She swallowed. "Never mind. I'll wait for another, better time. I'm sorry I bothered you." She turned to leave.

Something was going on here, and Joseph was going to find out what it was.

He raced out into the hall and caught up with her. He'd almost grabbed her arm when she whirled around, crouching in a fighting stance, baring her teeth.

So, she wasn't the weak, defenseless kitten she'd pretended to be a moment ago. This was more like the woman he'd first met—the one who'd come to him naked, wrapped in only a sheet, and seething with rage, ready to fight the whole gathering of men for one single swing at the brother who'd pissed her off.

"Do not touch me," she warned him. "Don't *ever* touch me."

The venom in her tone shocked him, but not as much as it confused him. Had someone hurt her? Or was it simply a case of her not wanting one of his kind to touch her? "Why not?"

"I don't like it. You keep your hands off."

Joseph shoved his hands into his jeans in the hopes it would appease her. "See. No hands. Now tell me why you suddenly changed your mind when you found out I was going."

"Maybe I find you abhorrent."

"*Maybe* you do, or you do?"

"All of you Theronai think you're so much better than us. It's disgusting. I wouldn't sit in a car with any of you."

"Not even if you got to visit your family?"

A hint of sadness flashed through her golden eyes before being replaced with anger. "It's not worth the stench of your kind."

"Wow. And here I thought you were all about making peace."

"Andreas wants peace, and he always gets what he wants."

Joseph knew it was a mistake, but it was one he was going to make. Her behavior was too suspicious, and he was going to find out what she was hiding, one way or another. A few hours trapped in a vehicle might be enough to get her to spill her secrets.

"Is that so?" he drawled, feeling a smile curve his mouth. Anticipation trickled through him, and for the first time in a long time, he was actually enjoying himself. "Well. I bet he also wants to see that you're safe and sound. Pack your bags, kitten. You're coming with me."

Lyka should never have opened her mouth. She knew it would get her in trouble.

She'd been so good, too, keeping to herself for weeks, coming out of her room only to eat and play with the kids. They were harmless. They couldn't ruin her world the way the Theronai could.

The way Joseph could.

But she missed her family, her sisters and brothers. She wanted to see them again and let them know she was safe and sound.

The ring-shaped birthmark on her arm burned, reminding her of the mistake her Slayer mother had made. One night. One single sexual encounter with a stranger, and Lyka had been cursed to straddle two worlds. She didn't fit in either one, but she'd chosen the one she'd wanted. And the one she disdained.

Andreas knew her shame. He knew what their mother had done, what Lyka really was. That's why he'd sent her here. He knew, in the end, they'd never kill her, even if they chose to break the peace treaty he believed in so desperately.

All it would take was one touch from one of these men to give away her secret, and she had to keep that from happening at any cost. None of them could know what she was.

None of them could know that she was a Theronai, too.

Chapter 25

For the first time in his life, Iain knelt to meditate without his sword gleaming in front of him. The concrete floor of his cell chilled his knees, distracting him and making it harder to slide into the peaceful quiet.

His monster was growing stronger by the moment, ever since Jackie had left. It knew it was to be put to death soon, and it did not want that. It wanted to be free, to roam the earth and kill and fuck and eat until it was too exhausted to move. Knowing Jackie was out there, alone and unprotected, inflamed the beast, making it more vicious and angry.

Meditation usually helped calm his monster, but right now, Iain was having trouble slipping into that quiet state where his body fell away and he simply existed, floating and numb.

Jackie was upset. Angry. Sad. Afraid. So many emotions were sliding into him, it was hard to concentrate. And while her emotions were uncomfortable, they were part of *her*, and he cherished them because of that alone. He'd find the bliss of nothingness soon enough. For now, it was best if he didn't waste the few moments he had left, even if that meant risking freeing his monster.

Without thinking about it, he reached out for her, working to send her what comfort he could. He felt her sink into that comfort, wrapping it around herself as if she were cold and it were the only thing that could warm her.

She was planning something. He could almost hear the wheels of her scheme grinding away.

Something bad had happened. He didn't know what it was, but it churned up old memories of her time in the caves. Every few seconds, he got another glimpse of a memory—a mere flash in time, when things for her were dark, cold, and terrifying.

Hours passed. He wasn't sure how many. Every few minutes, he could feel a tug on his power as Jackie pulled it into herself. He could feel her wearing down, growing tired, but her resolve was firm and unwavering. He didn't even think it would be possible to stop her.

A huge rush of power left his body, though he had no idea what Jackie was doing with it. In her current state of mind, it could be anything.

Stand still, he heard her order, as clearly as if she'd been in the room.

He froze, more in shock than obedience, and a second later, there was a string of light dangling down one side of his cell. It widened, growing fatter and fatter until Jackie stepped out of the portal.

Surprise rattled him, and he stood still, unable to believe his eyes. Most women had to work for years to learn to wield that kind of power, and yet Jackie had executed it perfectly, landing exactly where she wanted, rather than lodged inside a wall.

Fear and protective instincts rose up, crashing into one another, making his voice come out hard. "Do you have any idea how fucking dangerous that is?"

She bent at the waist, panting and holding her stomach. A moment later, she reached out her hand. "Don't care. Come on. I can't keep this up for long."

"I can't leave," he told her. "I'm a danger to you and everyone else."

"I'm not fighting with you about this. Give me your hand."

He could feel the strain of wielding so much energy, but he couldn't let her do this. "No. I could hurt you."

"*I'm* going to hurt *you* if you don't give me your damn hand."

Her fingers were extended toward him, her palm up in expectation. She trembled with weariness, and the desire to ease her began to swell, demanding that he do his duty and see to her needs.

If he went with her, he could save her a mountain of suffering and end this quickly. He could do what he should have done years ago, making his death as fast and painless for her as possible. If she was going to be trapped with him until the bitter end, it was the least he could offer.

He slapped his palm against hers and curled his fingers around her slender wrist. "Let's go."

Jackie teleported them to the car she'd packed and driven a few miles away from Dabyr. Her head spun, and she collapsed to the ground, gripping the dry weeds in an effort to pin herself down so she wouldn't fly away with the spinning of the earth.

She'd channeled more power in the past hour than she had since she'd met Iain, and the strain was beginning to spread through her body. Her joints ached and her muscles throbbed in time with her heartbeat. Her eyes burned as if she'd spent all day under the blazing sun, staring directly at it.

"Where are we?" asked Iain.

She couldn't speak yet. Her breathing was too labored.

He came to where she clung to the ground and slid his hand around the nape of her neck. The two parts of the luceria locked together with an audible click. Power flowed into her, soaking into her cells, restoring them.

Tingling bubbles filled her up and spread through her

veins until she was warmed from the inside out. The spinning stopped, and she leaned against his hard thigh, enjoying his touch.

"Better?" he asked.

"Much. Thanks."

He held out his big hand and lifted her to her feet. She rose, practically inside his embrace, and couldn't resist the need to be closer. Her arms wrapped around his neck and she pressed herself against him in a hard hug.

His scent sank into her, steadying her rioting nerves and soothing her worry. She laid her cheek to his chest, hearing the steady, hard pounding of his heart.

He was still alive. She'd succeeded in freeing him in time—a feat she wasn't sure she'd be able to manage. But here he was, alive and well, and she was nearly overcome with relief.

With his arms wrapped around her, she could almost fool herself into believing he was safe, and that everything was going to be okay. It was a gargantuan lie, but one she desperately needed right now.

She was no fool. She knew he was going to try to find a way to end his life. His resolve to do so vibrated between them, making her heartsick. She was going to do everything in her power to stop him, but she knew better than to think that just because she'd rescued him, they were out of the woods.

Jackie blinked back tears. She refused to spend even one moment of their time together crying. Later she'd indulge herself and wallow in misery, but for now, they had a job to do.

"Where are we?" he asked again.

"A few miles south of Dabyr. I packed the car with food and clothes and weapons."

"My sword?"

She shook her head. "No. That was in Joseph's office, and I didn't want to risk it. This one came from one of the storage rooms."

"The armory. Good. It's a clean blade, then."

"It seemed clean to me—all shiny and new."

He shook his head slightly. "No, clean as in it hasn't been used to kill demons before. Our swords gather power from the things we kill, and in the wrong hands, a warrior's sword could be broken, freeing that power. It would be like undoing one's entire life's work."

He caressed her cheek with the back of his hand. "When I'm gone, I want my sword—the one I've fought with all my life—to rest in the Hall of the Fallen, not to be used by our enemy."

She couldn't think about that now. She needed to stay strong. "I won't let you kill yourself. Don't you even dare try it."

"I'm sorry," he said. "I've upset you again. Let's talk about something else. Tell me how you managed to get out of Dabyr."

He hadn't denied her accusation, which only strengthened her belief that he was even now searching for a good way to die.

"I lied," she told him.

It hadn't been hard to bluff her way out through the gates. Her sob story about wanting to be far away from Iain when they killed him worked like a charm. Nicholas was a sweet guy, and completely unable to say no in the face of her tears.

The fact that the tears had been real didn't hurt.

"I see. Aren't you afraid to be alone with me?"

She looked up into his black eyes. "I've spent hours alone with you, and you haven't hurt me yet."

"But I could."

"Yeah, well, I'm fairly confident I could hurt you back, so how about we don't try it?"

He cupped her face and his thumb brushed her cheek. "There's a monster in me. If you see it come out, don't hesitate. It will hurt you."

She didn't believe that for a second, but there wasn't

time to argue. They needed to put more miles between them and Dabyr so that no one would find them.

Jackie nodded, pretending to agree, and handed him the keys. They jangled in her trembling grip. "You drive. I'm too shaky right now."

"Where are we going?"

"Somewhere safe. Somewhere they can't find you."

"Joseph and the others will find us. You know that," said Iain.

"No, they won't. I found the tracking device and melted it. Neither of us has a cell phone. Unless they plant trackers in our clothes or weapons, we're on our own."

His tone was grave. "You won't be able to call for help."

"I know." It was a risk she had to take. Even though there was a chance that something would go wrong and she wouldn't know what to do, she wasn't going to let Iain get thrown back into that dungeon again to await his death.

"This is reckless and dangerous. You're risking your life for nothing."

"For you. I'm risking my life for you, and that's not nothing. Now shut up and drive."

He let out a heavy breath and nodded. "This is a gift, and I won't let you regret it."

They got in and hit the road. Jackie tried to relax and regain some of the strength she'd used, but her mind kept wandering back to the one thing she didn't want to think about.

Iain was going to kill himself. She knew that was his intention when she busted him out of the dungeon. As much as she'd hated the idea of being tied to him, the thought of not having him close to her seemed impossible, unnatural, and wrong. They hadn't been together long, but in that time, she'd come to care for him. Everything he'd done had been with the thought of her in mind. He'd nearly died trying to help her find a normal life. He'd gone against orders and taken her to see baby Samson because he'd thought it would make her happy. He'd made love to her like no one else ever had, giving her the kind of pleasure that most women only dream about.

She didn't care that they said he was soulless. She saw the man he'd once been—the man who put the safety of others above his own, and gave up his own desires so that others could have theirs. It was a good life. A noble life. And she was glad she'd been a part of it for at least a little while.

If she could keep him from killing himself, she was sure that she'd find a way to prove to him that he deserved to live. She just didn't know how.

Weariness bore down on her. She'd used too much power, and her body wasn't used to the strain. She needed to sleep, but feared that if she did, she'd wake up to find him dead.

"Rest," he told her, as if sensing her thoughts. "I won't leave you without saying good-bye."

For once, she didn't mind having him in her head so much. It wasn't nearly the invasion of privacy she'd once thought. It was comforting.

When he was gone, she was going to miss that feeling almost as much as she missed Iain.

"Promise me," she insisted. "Say the words."

"I promise I won't seek out my death until after you wake."

The weight of his promise settled over her, reassuring her, making her body grow heavy. Despite her bleak thoughts, her eyes drifted shut and she eased into a light sleep.

Guilt weighed heavily on Autumn. Her whole family had been uprooted because of her. Her older brother wouldn't even speak to her because he had to give up his leading role in the high school play. Her mother cried all the time, and her father never slept anymore.

She was ruining their lives.

Part of her wished the Sentinels had never rescued her. As much as she hated being a prisoner of demons, at least then her family had been safe. Now not only was she still afraid all the time, but she'd dragged everyone down with her.

They were moving to Dabyr. That's what her father had called it. She'd heard whispers of the place, but no one she knew had ever seen it—not even her Gerai parents.

She stared out of the car window, curled up into the smallest space possible. The sun was going down soon, and as soon as it did, the fear would set in, crawling into the deepest part of her thoughts. Her brother said she was paranoid, but she knew better. She had the demons' blood inside of her. It had changed her. She could feel them now, lurking nearby, eagerly awaiting sunset.

Especially him. The demon who'd broken into her bedroom was different. Stronger. She'd felt him before at the school play. She hadn't seen him, but she knew how he felt—the chaotic way he made her veins vibrate. She'd thought it was all in her head, right up to the time he'd lunged for her.

Autumn's mouth went dry and her palms sweated enough to leave damp spots on her jeans. She hugged her legs closer, trying to remember that the sun was still up. He couldn't hurt her right now. They'd be safely inside Dabyr before dark. She didn't need to worry.

Dad pulled into a gas station and started filling up the tank. They still had hours to go until they could stop, and after it was dark, she wasn't getting out of this car until they were safely behind Dabyr's walls.

"Mom, I'm going to go to the bathroom."

"I'll come with you."

Mom took Autumn's arm and pulled her close. Before her capture, Autumn would have been too cool to let Mom do that, but not anymore. She'd spent months crying for Mom, and now that she had her back, she wasn't going to do anything to push her away.

Autumn took care of business and came out of the stall. A young man in a hoodie had Mom in his grasp, his hand clamped over her mouth. He pressed a funny-looking, long handgun against Mom's ribs.

Shock rooted Autumn in place as she sorted through what was right in front of her, trying to make sense of it.

"Autumn Mason?" asked the man.

"Y-yes."

A smile split his gaunt face and made his sunken eyes light up.

"Good."

The gun went off. Mom let out a sharp cry of pain and crumpled. Her head hit the sink, and she landed on the ground, unmoving on the filthy bathroom floor.

Terror and pain exploded in Autumn's chest. She lurched toward her mom, but didn't even make it to her knees. The man wrapped a skinny, incredibly strong arm around her waist and dragged her through the door.

She screamed and called for her dad. She clutched at whatever she could reach, knocking over food and displays of chips and snacks. The man behind the counter lay bleeding on the floor, his throat cut and his blood spilling onto the cracked tile.

"Dad!" Autumn screamed louder. She could see her father outside, pumping gas, but he couldn't hear her. The wind was howling, and the highway traffic was racing by.

She fought against her captor, kicking and clawing at him. Nothing helped. He kept moving toward the exit on the opposite side of the store—one out of sight of her father.

Autumn grabbed a twelve-pack of soda from a shelf as they passed, and slammed the heavy box into the man's face. He grunted in pain, but kept moving. "Behave, bitch, or I'll tell Murak to feed you to his pets."

Murak.

Oh God. She knew that name. She'd heard it before. He was the one who'd come after her.

Whoever this man was, he was working for the demons, taking her back into her nightmare.

A rush of strength filled her skinny limbs, and she twisted around enough to dig her thumb into his eye. He screamed in pain, and a second later, Autumn's world came to a shocking halt. The strike of his gun against her head barely had time to register before her vision winked out and she descended into darkness.

Chapter 26

Iain stared straight ahead, watching the road pass beneath them, so he wouldn't be tempted to watch Jackie sleep. He was free, thanks to her. Free to find a death of his choosing.

He hated the idea of leaving her. There was also a momentary twinge of guilt over leaving his brothers, but that paled in comparison to the way he felt for Jackie.

He'd let himself get too close to her. He'd become attached.

His monster paced inside its cage, testing the bars for weakness. Iain refused to let him out. He just had to hold on a bit longer.

Iain had no idea where he was going. He simply drove, following where his instincts led him. Eventually, he ended up at a Gerai house nearest the caves where he'd found Jackie. Andra had used her magic to collapse the cave entrance, preventing other Synestryn from using it as a nesting site. Gilda and Angus had died not far from here, crushed under tons of stone. Their bodies had been recovered and buried at Dabyr, but there was still a sense of loss hanging over everything nearby.

Those caves seemed like as good a place as any to die. At least there, he wouldn't taint another place with sadness, should anyone care enough to mourn him.

Jackie would. She already did grieve for him in some ways. Her heart was too tender not to feel bad.

The pain he caused her was his fault for letting her get too close. He never should have left Dabyr with her. He should have seen what a risk to her it had been. At the time, all he'd known was that he could keep her safe until she decided to choose one of his brothers. He never could have predicted that she would end up tying herself to him. *Until you're as good as new.*

Which he'd never be, but his death would free her soon.

As soon as the sun went down, he'd leave Jackie here. He'd walk to the caves, cut himself to draw the demons. Then he'd go down fighting.

The sun sank lower, inching toward the horizon. It was a pretty day, with a clear sky and a light breeze. He'd never really cared enough to notice such things before, but he noticed everything now, knowing it was his last chance to do so.

Jackie's sweet scent filled his lungs. Her skin was soft and warm under his fingers. Until now, he hadn't realized he was holding her hand. He could hear her steady breathing as she slept.

Her dark hair hid her face from him, so he brushed it back, soaking up the sight of her. So pretty. Her lips were parted, making his mouth water for a kiss, but he held back. She needed her sleep after all the power she'd handled in order to free him. There was no sense in waking her until the last minute, as he'd promised he'd do.

Iain simply watched her sleep, enjoying the sight, while the sun's color deepened to a rich, golden yellow that matched her luceria perfectly.

The Golden Lady. That suited her. It filled him with a sense of pride, while the monster in him let out a possessive growl of longing.

The beast wasn't going to go down without a fight. It didn't want to die. Iain was going to have to keep it in check until the very end, no matter what. If he didn't, the monster would fight its way free and go back to her.

She wouldn't be safe until both he and his monster were dead.

Jackie opened her eyes and blinked the sleep away. They were bloodshot—a sure sign she'd been wielding too much power.

She smiled at him, and then as reality set in, that smile faltered. Her gaze stayed fixed on his, unflinching. "You waited."

"I promised I would."

Sadness pinched her mouth and fell through their link, heavy and painful.

He didn't know how to make it better. It was his job to make her life a full, happy place, and he'd failed hideously.

"Don't be sad," he said.

Tears pooled in her eyes, gleaming in the waning sunlight. "I can't help it. I don't want you to do this."

He couldn't expect her to understand why he had no choice. She hadn't seen the violence and ruin that someone like him could cause. Before, when his emotions had been dead and cold, he hadn't cared if what he did hurt someone, so long as it helped his brothers, but now, staring into her eyes, he did care. The person he was most likely to hurt would be her, and that wasn't something he could allow himself to do.

"Hush," he told her. "Everything is going to be fine."

"I don't believe you."

Words weren't going to do any good. There was nothing more he could say that wouldn't cause her more pain, but there were still a few more minutes of sunlight left, and he wanted to spend every one of them with her.

"Let's go inside," he said.

She nodded, getting out of the car and gathering up some of the things she'd brought with them. Iain found the key under a flowerpot and unlocked the door.

He'd been here before once or twice. Like all the other Gerai houses, it was modest and unassuming, keeping people from poking their nose too close. Not that they'd find much. Stores of food and spare clothing. Maybe a sword tucked away in a closet. Clean linens, and sometimes, if they were lucky, fresh food was stocked in the refrigerator.

The furnishings were worn and out-of-date, but clean and sturdy enough to hold the weight of him and his brothers. This home had only two bedrooms, both with large beds and closets filled with clean clothes. Wood was laid in the fireplace, and he lit the kindling, hoping the warmth would help comfort Jackie.

He wasn't sure how he was going to slip away from her. She wasn't going to let him go easily. He could tie her up, but she would probably just burn through the bindings. He could knock her out, but that would leave her open to attack, and that was unacceptable.

There was only one thing he could think to do: call Cain to come and physically restrain her while Iain did what he needed to do.

Iain waited until Jackie slipped into the bathroom before he lifted the phone from the kitchen wall and dialed Cain.

"It's Iain," he said.

"Where the hell are you? People were turning Dabyr upside down looking for you. I got out just before they started checking lifemarks. Thanks for the warning, by the way."

"I need you to meet us. I'm going to do the right thing, but if you don't come and stop Jackie, she'll follow me right into the fight."

"I don't know," said Cain. "If I do that, she's going to hate me. It's not exactly how I want things to start out, you know?"

"She'll forgive you. Her heart's too soft not to. But I need you to do this. For her, and for me. I need to know she's safe so I can move on."

Cain was quiet for a moment. "Yeah. Okay. You're right. Her safety has to come first. Just tell me where you are."

"The Gerai house near where Angus and Gilda were killed."

There was a low exhalation of breath on the other end of the line, as if Cain was psyching himself up for an unpleasant task. "I'll be there as soon as I can, but it will be a while before I can reach you."

"I'll wait. And please, don't tell anyone where we are. I don't want this to be any harder on Jackie than it has to be. I'm in control."

"For now."

"Just hurry. I want this done tonight."

"I'm on my way now."

Iain hung up the phone just as Jackie opened the bathroom door. Her hair was damp at her temples, and her nose was red. She looked as though she might have been crying, but with her eyes bloodshot from overexertion, he couldn't be sure.

"Are you hungry?" he asked.

"No, but I should eat. It's been a while."

He rummaged in the fridge for something, but came up with only a couple of apples. The freezer held several labeled dishes that had promise. He pulled out some pot roast and popped it into the microwave.

Jackie plopped down at the table in exhaustion. Sadness radiated out from her in waves so strong they made his ring vibrate.

That was his fault. He should have stopped her from helping him escape, rather than going along with her plan. He hadn't realized just how hard this would be on her.

"You're going to be fine," he said, hoping to reassure her.

"No, I'm not. I want you to promise me you won't do anything stupid and kill yourself."

He ignored her request and started a pot of coffee.

"I mean it, Iain. This isn't a joke. If I have to, I'll lock you up myself." The venom in her voice would have been cute had he not believed every word she'd said.

"Let's not talk about that. Let's just enjoy a meal together."

"A last meal? How the hell am I supposed to choke that down?"

Frustration gripped him hard, chafing against his skin. The beast growled, clawing the bars of its cage. It would have been so easy to just let go and give in to temptation—set the monster free and let her see what it was he was protecting her from.

But he couldn't do that to her. She'd already suffered more fear and pain in the few years she'd been alive than she deserved. The sun would be down soon. Cain would come and restrain her. It would all be over in a few hours.

He knelt in front of her, taking her hands in his. Her fingers were cold and shaking. He rubbed them between his palms and looked into her eyes. He wasn't very good at erasing memories, but his connection to Jackie would make the task easier.

Iain slipped inside her thoughts as if he had been born for the task. He gathered tiny specks of power from the air and channeled them along his skin. His hands heated, and he whispered thoughts of calm comfort to her mind. After a few seconds, her eyelids drooped and she swayed in her seat.

If he could have, he would have erased all hints of himself from her memory, but that was beyond his skills. Instead, he dropped a filmy veil over her grief and worry, shielding her from them.

He searched for something cheerful to brighten her mood, and what came instantly to hand was the image of little Samson cradled in her arms, and the memory of them entwined in passion. He gathered those images and used them to hide her darker thoughts, making the happy things glow brighter so that her focus remained there.

At least for a while. He knew his fix was temporary, but for now, it would ease her and get her through the next few hours.

The microwave beeped. Iain set her now-warm hands in her lap and finished preparing their dinner. They ate in silence, her movements slow and methodical. He watched her the entire time, gauging the effects of his efforts.

Her gaze was distant, but calm. She seemed sleepy, but those distressing waves of grief were no longer seeping out of her.

Once her plate was empty, he said, "You should get some rest."

Her eyes jerked upward as he spoke, as if he'd startled her. She blinked a few times, looking around in confusion as if she didn't recognize where she was. "Rest?"

Iain rose from his seat and went around to her side of the table. Her head tilted back, and she gave him a dark, womanly smile that was filled with the promise of paradise.

He sucked in a sharp breath and tightened his control on his monster in the nick of time. It hurled itself against the bars, rattling Iain down to the soles of his feet. It wanted her. It wanted to hold her down and fuck her until the rage was gone. Which would never happen.

One single look, and the beast thought she should be his.

Iain stood there, gritting his teeth in an effort to maintain control. He closed his eyes, hoping that not looking at her would help.

It didn't. The monster simply formed its own image, remembering the way she looked naked and sprawled across the bed, her skin flushed, her lips red and swollen.

Her hands slid under his shirt, flexing against his bare skin.

Iain let out a low, animal sound that was part torment, part pleasure. Feeling her hands on him, feeling her touch his lifemark, was almost more than he could stand. He wanted her, too, but he was having trouble fighting both his own desires as well as the beast's.

Her fingernails bit into his skin, and he heard her chair scrape over the vinyl floor. The hem of his shirt dragged along his ribs, and her soft mouth pressed a kiss over his heart.

His abs clenched, and his knuckles popped under the strain of his tightened fists. He wanted to touch her so bad, to slide his fingers into her hair and hold her head while she kissed him.

He didn't dare move. Not his hands, not his mouth. If he gave even an inch, his control would snap and she'd end up bent over the kitchen table with her jeans around her ankles and his cock shoved as deep in her sweet pussy as it could go.

Another sound rose from his chest—a wordless plea for mercy—but if she understood it, she didn't listen. Instead, her tongue flicked out across his nipple, sending a string of chain lightning down his spine. His cock throbbed against his fly and sweat popped out along his hairline.

Her teeth closed gently on his nipple, and then she eased the erotic sting with her tongue.

Iain was fighting a battle on two fronts—fighting his own desires, as well as those of the beast. And he was losing on both. He needed to retreat, to get as far away from her as he could.

He shifted his weight to take a step back, but it was too late.

"Kiss me," she whispered, threading her fingers through his hair and pulling his head down to hers.

He tried to tell her how close she was to facing his monster, but his mouth wouldn't work. He scrambled for their link, letting her glimpse what he was protecting

her from. The violent need and lust hovering just inside
of him. It shamed him to let her see that part of himself,
but his feelings here were not important. Jackie's were.

Her body shook, and her grip on his head tightened.
He forced his eyes to open, sure he'd see disgust lining
her face. Instead, her pupils had grown huge with desire.
A fragile whimper passed her lips, and it was filled with
the sound of want, not fear.

Lust pulsed between them, tinted with feminine need.
Her lust, not his. She'd seen the beast and it hadn't scared
her away.

"You don't want that," he told her. "You can't want
that."

"I want you. All of you, even the darker parts."

She didn't know what she was saying. There was no
way she could truly understand what she would face.

He opened his mouth to order her to run away, but
before the words could come out, her mouth was on his,
hot and sweet and demanding. Her tongue plunged inside, and she fed him a soft groan of satisfaction.

Desire radiated out from her, filling their link with
her need. He could feel her skin warm and the flesh between her thighs grow damp and swollen. There was an
emptiness there that she wanted him to fill, a deep ache
of longing that only he could drive away.

Iain was unable to resist her need. He was powerless,
unwilling to let her suffer, unable to hold back anything
she wanted.

But he couldn't let the monster free. Not this time.
Not when it knew that he was planning to go to his death
tonight. If the beast broke free, it would protect itself,
and Iain might never be able to regain control. Whatever it took, whatever he had to do to control the monster, he'd do. For her. One last time.

Iain shifted his control, aiming every bit of effort toward keeping the monster caged. There was none left

for him, none left to keep him from giving in to his baser urges.

He kissed her back, slanting his mouth over hers, tasting her. Her fingernails bit into his scalp, lighting his nerve endings on fire. His cock swelled until he was sure he'd go insane with the need to shove inside her.

Her clothes had to go. He needed her naked.

Iain tried to unbutton her jeans, but his hands were shaking too hard. He couldn't seem to get the damn button out of the hole.

Jackie swept his hands aside and did the job for him. She stripped out of her clothes in a heartbeat, her gaze fixed on his, smoldering with desire. Her eyes had darkened to a deep gunmetal gray, and a flush was already spreading down her throat onto her chest.

The luceria glowed against her skin, and for a split second, he thought the scars lining her neck had faded. Not that it mattered. Scars or not, she was the most fucking beautiful woman he'd ever touched.

Her body quivered in anticipation as she stood there, her perfect breasts rising and falling with each rapid breath. Iain fumbled to rip his boots off, unwilling to look away from her.

The curve of her waist and flare of her hips drove him mad with the need to touch. The slim length of her legs reminded him of just how good they'd felt wrapped around his hips, and her rosy lips brought back every intoxicating second of his cock sliding in and out of her mouth.

As soon as he was free of his clothes, he reached for her. She crashed into his arms, her mouth landing on his in a kiss that stole his breath. The heat of her bare skin rubbing against his cock made the monster howl in frustration. It wanted to fill her, to take what it wanted without care for her pleasure.

Like hell Iain was going to let that happen.

He wrapped her up in his arms and lifted her onto the nearby counter, so he could reach her mouth easier. She hooked her ankles around his thighs and jerked him close, melding their bodies together from groin to chest.

Her tight nipples poked his chest. The slick folds of her pussy slid along his cock, making it pulse and throb for deeper contact. He needed to be inside her so bad he wasn't sure he'd survive the wait.

"No waiting," she breathed against his mouth.

Her fingers wrapped around his cock, and she lifted her body up, aligning them. Wetness welled from his erection, making the contact even slicker. As wide as he was, she was ready for him and he inched in nice and easy, driving a gasp from her lungs.

He was bathed in her heat, surrounded by her scent. Her feelings mingled with his, amplifying them.

The monster screamed for Iain to shove himself all the way in. To make her take it, make her like it.

If Iain didn't start moving, he was going to lose the battle with his beast and set it free. So he moved. He pulled back and surged forward, burying another few inches of himself inside of her. The slick glide against his skin made his body tighten as he fought to stay in control.

"More," she ordered, clawing at his scalp, wriggling her hips in an effort to lodge him deeper.

She wanted more. The beast wanted more. Iain certainly had it to give.

He lifted her from the counter with the goal of getting her to a nice, soft bed. He made it only three steps when she blasted him with an image of him fucking her against the wall.

His balls tightened, and he nearly came right there, feeling so much lust radiating out of her. She wanted this. She wanted this as much as he did, though he wasn't sure how that was possible.

Iain shoved her back to the kitchen wall, propping her up right between the telephone and a framed landscape painting. His leg hit a kitchen chair, sending it flying into the table. Something crashed to the floor, but he didn't give a fuck what it was.

Her breath came out in a rush, but he couldn't tell if it was because he'd been too rough, or because the act had completely buried his cock inside her. All he knew was her eyes fluttered closed in satisfaction, and her head fell back, displaying her neck.

Iain lowered his mouth to kiss her, lifting her body to make her ride his cock. Soft sounds slipped from her mouth, and her fingers dug into his shoulders.

He kept moving, filling her up with every dragging thrust. Her pussy fluttered around him, and her breathing sped. Then it stopped as she held her breath.

Her legs tightened around his hips a split second before her inner muscles clenched around him and she let out a long, high cry of release.

Iain rode her through it, keeping up the pace that made her tremble around him. He soaked up her cries and held back his own orgasm through a sheer force of will.

The monster roared in fury, and rattled the bars to be set free so it could take over.

As the rush of her climax passed, her body went limp, her arms draping over his shoulders, her head resting against his.

He wasn't done with her yet. He needed more from her—enough to fill the gaping void inside of him, enough to quiet the raging monster. There wasn't much time left for him, and he wanted to spend every second he could making Jackie scream in pleasure.

A bed was too far away. The couch was much closer. He carried her to it, held her close, and eased her back. The angle of his penetration shifted, and she arched her back, letting out a breathy moan.

He could feel what she felt. Their link was wide open, and the cascading pleasure seeping into her cells, making her limp and boneless, was his as well. The slide of skin on skin, the slick heat of their joined bodies. The heavy pound of his heart and the faster cadence of hers. He saw himself through her eyes, his own body compelling in this new light. Superimposed on that was the sight of her, spread out beneath him, her skin flushed, her body quivering with growing need.

It hit Iain that this was what it was supposed to be like. This was what his life should have been—joined to someone so tightly that it became hard to distinguish where one of them stopped and the other began.

It would have been easy to mourn what he was going to miss out on, but he couldn't stand to spend what time he had left grieving. He wanted to live. To love.

He couldn't love her. He was incapable of such things, no matter how much he wished otherwise. There was no room for love in a dead soul, so all he could offer her now was purely physical.

It would have to be enough.

Iain lifted her hips and thrust hard, angling himself in a way that made lightning shoot from her clit to her womb. He could feel the sensation flowing through her, rising between them, as easily as he could feel the slick glide of her body as his cock surged deep.

Her breasts ached, so he fondled and kissed them, suckling her nipples hard, just the way she liked it. The peak stood out, wet and red from his efforts as he moved to lavish attention on her other breast. His own body coiled tight, his muscles clenching and releasing as he pushed them both higher.

She was right there with him, her hips moving in time with his, her fingernails biting into his ass as she demanded a harder, faster pace.

The monster grew stronger, louder. Iain wasn't going to be able to keep it at bay for much longer. He didn't want to share this with the beast. Jackie was his. All his. No one else, nothing else, could have her.

It was time to make her come, time to let himself go and give in before it was too late.

Iain reached for her thoughts, needing to be as close to her as he could get. She liked it that he was nearly out of control. The idea that she could drive him to such abandon made her feel powerful and beautiful.

He wanted that for her. He wanted her to always be happy and know how precious she truly was.

He gathered up his desire, his need to make her happy, and put it on bright display, highlighted by his own ragged lust. She made a sweet noise, high and breathless. He recognized it from the last times he'd made her come. She was close, perched on the edge, trusting him to catch her as she fell.

That trust was Iain's undoing. Even as deep inside his thoughts as she was, even with the brutal face of the beast on display, she still trusted him to stay in command and keep her safe.

He wouldn't let her down, not in this, and not in seeing to her future.

Iain covered her parted lips with his and thrust his tongue into her mouth in time with the steady pace of his cock. She drank down his groan of pleasure, and held on tight as his orgasm slammed into him, rocking him to his core.

The first jet of semen made her body clench as she followed him into orgasm. Pleasure filled him, surrounded him, bursting from every pore, driving away every thought but the pulsing, radiant joy that wrung every drop of seed from his body.

Jackie trembled around him, holding him close and panting. A tremor shook her frame, and he lifted his head to make sure she was okay. Tears pooled in her eyes, but all he felt coming from her through the luceria was a gentle mix of happiness and satisfaction.

He couldn't stand the sight of her tears, happy or not. He cradled her head to his chest and stroked her hair, hoping the tears would pass.

His muscles felt wrung out and loose, but he was filled with a boundless energy, as if he could fight for days without stopping. Even his monster was soothed to sleep.

As his breathing slowed and his skin cooled, he committed every detail of this moment to memory. The smell of her skin, the sound of her heart, the feel of her arms wrapped around him, and the taste of her lips on his. This was the moment he would take into combat with him. This was the image he'd cling to as death came.

This shimmering moment of peace would ease him from this life. It would comfort him and appease the beast so that he could do the right thing. The honorable thing.

Jackie would be free to find joy with another man—one who was capable of loving her the way she deserved. And that thought made him as happy as his dead soul would allow.

Iain heard a car pull up outside.

He grudgingly moved away from her body. "Cain is here."

The contented look on her face merged into a steady, accusing stare. Rippling currents of betrayal filled their link. "Cain? You called him, didn't you?"

"Someone has to protect you once I'm gone."

She rose from the couch, her skin flushed. He felt the very moment that the veil he'd laid over her thoughts of his impending death lifted. Grief stabbed through their link, and she swayed on her feet. "I risked my ass to rescue you, and this is how you repay me? Calling another man to babysit me so you could go off and kill yourself?"

Cain was going to be walking through that door in a second, and she was standing there gloriously naked, still glowing with the remnants of pleasure. Iain couldn't stand the thought of the other man seeing her like this. She was his, at least for a few more minutes. Sharing her was not something he could tolerate.

The beast stirred, a possessive growl rumbling from its chest.

"There is no other way." Iain jerked a knit throw off the back of the couch and wrapped it around her just as Cain walked in.

His gaze swept through the room, taking in the sight in seconds. He lingered over the clothing on the kitchen floor, the broken plate, toppled furniture, and the slight indentation in the drywall.

His color deepened to an angry red, and his fists tightened at his sides. He swallowed. Once. Twice. "Get dressed. Fast. We have a situation."

He said nothing else, just turned and walked right back out, shutting the door behind him.

Iain had no idea what the situation was, but he knew he wasn't going to like it.

Chapter 27

Jackie was writhing with anger, so furious at Iain she could barely drag her clothes on. Her hands shook, and a sour knot had formed in the pit of her stomach.

He'd called Cain so he could kill himself, so she wouldn't chase after him like some kind of lovesick puppy.

After all they'd been through, after all they'd shared, he was just going to throw it all away because of some stupid custom.

She stomped out of the bathroom, to find Iain and Cain in a heated discussion. As soon as Iain saw her, their conversation immediately died off.

"Don't stop on my account. Anything you're going to say I can just rip from your mind if I want."

Iain's gaze moved up and down her body. His expression tightened, but she could feel a single throb of desire spill into her through the luceria.

As if he hadn't just finished making them both come so hard she nearly chipped a tooth.

"What's going on?" she demanded.

"Nicholas sent out word that a child has been abducted. It's Autumn Mason."

The breath left her body and all hints of anger fled in the face of her fear for the girl. Her legs wobbled, and before she could reach for the couch, Iain was beside her, easing her down onto the soft cushions. "She can't be gone. They moved her somewhere safe. Joseph said so."

"It wasn't safe enough," said Cain, his deep voice rough with concern. "Demons were sniffing around her in Chicago. They were on their way to Dabyr when she was taken. But we'll find her. Andra is already on the trail."

The way he said it told her he wasn't convinced.

"Cain and I are going to step outside," said Iain. "Stay here until he comes for you."

Cain held up his hands and took a long step back. "Like hell. I'm not doing it."

"You have to," said Iain.

Jackie looked between them, unable to figure out what was going on. There was some kind of tension there, but she had no idea why. Unless it was because Cain walked in on them. "He has to do what?"

Iain's gaze slid away, and she felt a twitch of guilt come through.

"He wants me to kill him," said Cain.

Jackie suffered through a malignant wave of revulsion that rocked her back on her heels. "Don't you dare," she breathed.

"I won't. Not only do I not have the stomach for it — you and I have an agreement. There's no way I'd ask you to be with me after I killed the man you've clearly come to . . . care for."

"We had sex," said Iain. "It doesn't mean she feels anything more for me than a momentary dose of lust."

His comment hurt, though she had no idea why it should. She knew what he was planning, and now that she was no longer crazed with desire, she could think straight enough to see that at best he'd been distracting her from trying to talk him out of dying, or at worst using her to pass the time until dark when he could go kill himself.

Cain stared at her, his dark green eyes steady and unblinking. "If she feels half as much for me one day, I'd count myself a lucky man."

Were they out of their freaking minds? "You're just going to stand there and let him talk about offing himself when he hasn't done anything wrong?"

"He will," said Cain, his deep voice ringing with certainty. "The urges are too strong to resist forever. I'm not as far gone as Iain, and I already struggle to remember the man I want to be."

"Listen to him, Jackie," pleaded Iain. "This is the only way."

She crossed the space, grabbed Iain's shirt in her fist, and gave him a hard shake. "You listen to me. You both are too wrapped up in this insanity to think clearly. A little girl is missing. We can't stand here and argue while those demons scare her, hurt her. You both are going to stop talking about all of this death bullshit and warm up those sword arms. We're going to need them."

"It's too dangerous," said Iain. "I'm too close to losing control."

"So am I, mister. If I have to teleport you back to that dungeon to keep you safe, I will. And then I'll come right back here—without you—and find Autumn by myself."

"I'd never let you go alone," said Cain.

"Yeah? Well good luck keeping up with me and my magical space-jumping power."

Cain's mouth tightened in frustration, but she didn't care how he felt. The two of them were going to help her.

"You can't do that," said Iain. "It's too dangerous."

"Says the man who's looking to die."

"*For you,*" he nearly growled. "My safety doesn't matter."

"But mine does?"

"Absolutely."

"Then come with me. Stop fighting. Don't make me go alone."

The men looked at each other over her head. She had no idea what kind of communication was going on, but she wasn't hearing a thing. Even their link was closed off, clamped shut so she couldn't get inside his head.

"Okay," said Iain. "Let's go find the girl."

"Just like that?" she asked. "What did I miss?"

Cain touched her elbow, and his ring vibrated so hard she could feel it in her skin. "Iain's not coming back from this. But you and I will walk out of there alive, with the girl."

She couldn't think about that. Not now. Before they found Autumn, she'd think of something to convince him to stop this foolish decision.

Iain cupped her face in his hands. This was the touch she knew, the one she craved. As much as she'd thought so only a few days ago, these men were not interchangeable. She wanted Iain. Only Iain.

"I don't want this to be any harder on you than it has to be. It's what I want. A noble death. My dying wish is for you to save my friend, my brother. Save Cain."

She shook her head in denial, but there was no breath for words.

"He's a good man. Better than I could ever be. His soul is dying, but you can save it. You can save him."

"I want to save you."

He stroked her face, his touch so gentle she couldn't believe there was any violence in him at all. "I know. I wish you could. But this is the way it has to be. Promise me you'll save him when I'm gone."

She couldn't. She couldn't even face the idea of a world without Iain in it.

"Don't push her," said Cain. "You ask too much."

"I can't let you die," said Iain.

Jackie couldn't listen. She had to get out of here—get some air.

She stumbled out the door, dragging the cold air into her lungs. Ribbons of tears cooled on her cheeks.

There wasn't time for this. A little girl was out there right now, alone and terrified. Someone had to find her. Someone had to save her.

Jackie hated that the job fell to her, even as she thanked God that the power to do so was in her grasp.

For two years she'd been caged and abused, starved and fed on. For two years she'd watched countless children die. She'd been powerless to stop any of it, but that time was over. Magic coursed through her body, trembling in anticipation of being summoned to do her bidding. She was going to find Autumn, and when she did, every evil creature that had ever even laid eyes on the girl was going to suffer. Jackie was going to see to it personally.

Ronan picked up the trail on his way to meet Drake and Helen. He wasn't as skilled at bloodhunting as some, but he was better at tracking than most. He knew this area. He knew the nests littered throughout the landscape — small, hidden dens and huge, gaping caverns alike. While he didn't spend much time cleaning them out the way the Theronai did, he kept tabs on his enemy in the hopes of locating the heavily blooded humans before the Synestryn did.

The demon that had been with the pregnant woman had left its scent behind, near a house where a strongly blooded newborn had just been brought home. It hadn't done more than sniff around, but it would.

Ronan was going to have to convince this family to move. Again. It was the only way to keep them safe.

He would deal with that later. For now, his focus was on the malignant scent of demon leading away, toward a nearby nest.

"Did you find something?" asked Helen. She sat in the open door of Drake's vehicle, watching him work.

"South," he said, pulling the scent deep into his lungs. It was sweet and rancid, like a stew of fruit juice and rotten meat. Now that he'd smelled it, he would not soon forget.

He got back into their vehicle and gave Drake instructions as to where to go.

They didn't have to go far. There was a narrow entrance underground, and it stank of demon. He couldn't smell the woman, but he wasn't sure if that was because she hadn't come this way, or if it was simply the stench of demon overpowering her lighter fragrance.

The three of them donned protective clothing and weapons and headed inside.

Chapter 28

Jackie had no idea how she found Autumn. It was as if she could see a trail of fear leading to the girl—a trail no one else could see. There was no proof that this was the place, and yet, somehow, she knew it was true.

"Are you sure she's here?" asked Iain.

"I am." She'd never been here before, but the faint flickering trail, glowing like sunlight on a wisp of mist, led right into a narrow, rocky opening.

Cain's headlights bobbed behind them as he pulled his truck to a stop. Both vehicles shut off, plunging the remote area into darkness. Jackie instinctively let a trickle of power flow to her eyes, letting her see through the thick, stifling dark.

Wind rocked their car. Iain put his hand on her knee, and the warmth of his touch sank through her clothes, making her shiver and long for more.

"You don't have to go in with us," he said. "Cain and I can find her. He'll bring her out."

"I can't let you go in alone." The way she knew she'd walk out alone.

"You've already been through so much pain."

"As if you care. You're forcing me to endure even more pain by killing yourself."

"I'm saving you. You can't see that yet, but I hope in time you will . . . when you're happy again."

Jackie couldn't imagine finding happiness while Iain lay cold in the ground. She'd grown to care for him too deeply.

No, it was more than that. She loved him.

She hadn't wanted to. She hadn't meant to. Loving him was going to ruin her, and yet she couldn't seem to stop. As cold as he could be, she'd seen the noble, selfless side of him no one else seemed to care about. He'd given her gentleness and passion. And now, he was freeing her in the only way possible by killing himself.

She didn't care what they said. His soul wasn't dead. No man who was willing to lay down his life for another could be called soulless.

Holding back her tears made her throat ache. "I don't want you to save me. I want you to save yourself."

Iain stroked her cheek, his black eyes steady as they looked into hers. "This is saving myself. If I end it before I do anything unforgivable, then my memory will live on, untarnished, my honor intact. If I try to defy the natural order of things any longer, I'll die in disgrace. I have too much to lose now. Please, let me do what I need to do."

He wasn't going to bend. She knew him and his honor well enough now to realize that. He'd decided that this was the safest course for her, and she could feel his steely resolve stabbing at her through the luceria. He was doing this. If she truly loved him, she would make his passing as easy on him as possible, rather than throwing a fit like a child.

If she spoke, she knew she'd break down, so instead, she simply nodded and got out of the car.

Cain slipped silently to her side. His expression was grim, but his watchful eyes were filled with a glint of hope.

Iain's death—his dying wish—was to be Cain's salvation.

Cain settled a clear face shield over her head and adjusted it into place.

She didn't want his touch or his attention. As kind as he was to see to her protection, it seemed . . . wrong, like some kind of betrayal.

She wanted to scream that Iain was still alive and standing right there, watching them, but if she let out even the smallest cry of outrage, her control would break and she'd fall into a sobbing heap.

Her grief was already hovering around her, slowing her steps and crushing her chest so that it was hard to breathe. In a few minutes, or a few hours, Iain would be dead, and there wasn't anything she could do to stop it. If she tried to save his life, he'd only find another way. And what if he did something he regretted because she tried to take his freedom of choice away?

He was still a good man. He'd worked incredibly hard to stay that way. What right of hers was it to ruin him, just because she selfishly wanted him to stay in her life?

A warm wave of comfort swept through her, like a long, hard hug. She could almost feel Iain's arms around her again.

He was the one going off to die and yet his thoughts were of her comfort.

She couldn't betray that goodness in him. She couldn't defy his wish to die. She had to let him go.

Jackie blinked away her tears, squared her shoulders, and gathered her strength. She was going to follow Iain's example and do the honorable thing, no matter how much of her it would destroy.

Beth huddled against the wall, shivering with cold and regret.

She'd nearly been free. After years of being here, trapped and tortured, she'd nearly escaped. If only she'd been stronger, maybe she would have made it over that fence.

Your blood is the key. . . .

She turned the words over in her head, trying to figure out what that man had meant. It seemed like he'd been trying to help her, but if he was, it did her no good. No matter how long she spent reaching for an answer to that riddle, none came.

Beth was never going to get out of here if she couldn't figure out what he'd meant. She was going to die in the dark, alone and afraid.

Her head pounded. She couldn't remember the last time she'd eaten. Days ago? Weeks? There was no way to be sure. She was too weak to think straight. Whatever reserves she might have had, she'd used them all up trying to get up that fence.

Still, she couldn't accept her fate. Inside, she was a fighter. Sure, she was a starved, wimpy fighter, but that person she'd once been was still alive inside of her somewhere. Wasn't it?

She didn't want to think about that now. She needed to sleep and escape this place for a while. Maybe she'd even dream of the sky again. Daylight. Sunshine.

Beth curled up on the cold ground and tried to remember what they looked like.

Iain split his focus between comforting Jackie, the path ahead, and keeping a tight rein on his monster. The beast was roaring in defiance, pounding and beating at its cage in an effort to escape. If he let the monster out, it would fight for its life. It wouldn't care who it had to kill to survive.

The cave seemed empty as they moved through it. Synestryn demons had left for the night to hunt and feed, returning here only once the sun forced them into hiding. They had until sunrise to find the girl and get out, or they'd have to fight their way free.

While Iain was content with dying, he wanted everyone else out safely.

Without effort, he slipped inside Jackie's thoughts, keeping tabs on the ethereal trail she saw that led to

Autumn. That trail wasn't of Jackie's construction—it belonged to another. If Iain's guess was right, Jackie was somehow seeing Andra's magic and her ability to find lost children. He didn't understand how it worked, but a fleeting thought made him wonder if Jackie wasn't somehow connected to Andra. Maybe that was how she learned to wield magic with so much ease—she was learning to do so from the women who'd already figured out how.

The longer he was in her thoughts, the more sense that theory made.

He wasn't going to be able to be with her like this for much longer, so he wanted to soak up every second of it, reveling in her inner beauty and strength. Just being connected to her like this made it easier to control his beast, as if her presence somehow soothed and quieted it.

The trail wound to the left, through a cavern filled with bones and bits of fur and refuse. As they entered, the stench of rotting meat and dung was nearly overpowering. Jackie made a gagging noise, and a second later, cool, clean air filled his nose and mouth.

"Wow," said Cain. "That's one hell of a trick. Thanks."

"I don't know how I stood that smell for so long."

Even as she spoke, he could see the horrible memories that smell brought back. Pain and death filled her thoughts, so vivid and frightening he actually flinched away from them for a moment.

His magic was extremely limited; he couldn't access any of the power he housed. He could only gather up what energy was around—hovering in the ground and dancing in the air—for immediate use. And that's what he did now, collecting tiny scraps of power that he used to shove those bleak memories away, warding them off. She'd lived that horror. It wasn't right that she should have to relive it again.

Jackie's hand settled on his shoulder in thanks, a brief, fluttering touch that ended far too soon.

Of all the things in this world, it was her company, her touch, he'd miss the most.

Their trail led west, thickening as it went. They were getting close. He could hear noises now—the skittering of claws over stone, the low, gurgling, wet sounds of demons feeding on whatever prey they'd found.

He hoped that the fact that the trail was still there, hovering in the air, meant that Autumn was still alive, and that the demons were feeding on something else.

Iain held up his hand, silently calling a halt. Without even thinking about what he was doing, he whispered directly to Jackie's mind that he was going to scout ahead. She should stay here. He felt her agreement and slid forward, moving quietly over the loose debris on the ground.

The pathway widened into an alcove about the size of a large living room. The ceiling here sloped upward, and rock formations draped down in limestone curtains. Water dripped from the tips, making the air damp and thick.

On the farthest side of the area, he could see bars set into the stone. Between him and those bars were more than a dozen demons feeding on human remains. One of the bigger Synestryn crouched over a severed human arm, growling at anything that got close. Its skin was black, slick, and hairless, looking like it was coated in some kind of oil. The smaller demons were covered in fur, with oversized heads and jaws filled with serrated teeth. Their limbs were heavily muscled, all tipped in thick, black claws. Their eyes flared a bright green as they fed, ripping meat from other human bones.

A white shoe bobbed on the end of a man's severed leg, splattered with red blood. Two demons fought over the prize, snarling and hissing at each other as they tried to drag it in opposite directions.

Iain's first thought was that he didn't want Jackie to see this. It was too horrific, and would serve only to remind her of what she'd suffered. His second thought was of the girl and the trail leading directly through the writhing mass of demons toward those bars.

They were going to have to cut their way through the group. There was no way around that he could see.

He went back to the others and told them what he'd found.

"I don't like it," said Cain, "but we don't have a choice."

"I'll go in first," said Iain. "Jackie, you hang back and lend a hand from a distance."

She nodded, but her skin had gone pale, her pupils constricted to tiny dots, and a line of sweat had broken out across her forehead. He hated seeing her afraid. He hated that the last time he was going to spend with her would be filled with fear and death.

Iain felt her gather her courage and watched as she squared her shoulders. A rush of power funneled out of him, and her game face was firmly in place beneath the clear face shield.

He gave her an admiring nod and moved in.

They stayed silent until the last second, before Cain and Iain charged the closest demons. The smaller ones were in front, and they hissed in surprise before springing to attack. Iain cut down two with one heavy blow. Their furry bodies hit the wall, where other demons scurried to consume them.

Ignoring those for now, Iain waded deeper into combat, fending off one attack after another, moving on animal instinct and centuries of practice.

Cain held his own beside Iain, protecting his flank and mopping up the wounded demons as they fell from Iain's blade.

A distant vibration of power rumbled through him. He could feel something building, but didn't dare pay it any attention right now. One single distraction and he could go down before they'd found the girl. He didn't doubt for one second that Jackie would charge ahead, with or without him, if he failed to complete their mission.

He heard a whisper in his mind, urging him to move left. It was Jackie's voice, her presence within him, so he obeyed, shifting his body a bit more with every step forward.

Seconds later, a wash of golden fire spilled out past his right side, so close it singed his sleeve. Every creature in its path was consumed by flames, screaming in agony as their hair and skin burned away.

The big demon in back jumped out of the line of fire, finally abandoning its meal. The thing was easily eight feet tall, even hunched over like it was. It lumbered forward, heedless of the creatures it crushed under its wide paws.

Its jaws dropped open, revealing chunks of bloody skin and ragged swatches of blue jeans between its teeth. A huge, hot roar blasted out of its cavernous mouth — large enough to swallow Iain in two bites. Spittle sprayed out, splattering against Iain's face shield.

Cain shifted, his blade cutting through a smaller demon that was only inches from Iain's shin.

He could feel Jackie pulling on his power, drawing it into herself for another attack. All he had to do was buy her some time — a few precious seconds. .

Iain showed her what he was going to do, thrusting the image through their link even as he propelled his body forward. He shoved his blade deep into the thing's thick arm and used that to vault himself onto its back.

It screamed in pain and reared up, trying to knock Iain off.

He stabbed the thing at the base of the neck, but all he hit was a heavy lump of fat.

The demon staggered back, racing toward the cave wall. Iain didn't have time to move. He was going to be crushed. If he dropped off, the huge paws would smash him just as dead.

That couldn't happen yet. The girl was still trapped.

Iain's mind raced to find a solution as he scrambled up the slippery body, reaching to cling to the thing's head. The demon slammed backward. It was too late. Iain hadn't moved enough. He held his breath, bracing himself for the pain.

Blue sparks spewed out from the wall, but there was no pain. Not even the chill of the stone touched him.

Jackie. She'd protected him.

Not that it would do much good. The burning sting of poison began sinking into his hands where he'd come in contact with the demon's oily skin secretions.

Let go! he heard Jackie shout in his head. Trusting her, he did as she asked, releasing his grip.

She caught his body, and he swore he could feel the warmth of her hands lowering him to the ground. Not that that was possible, since she was across the room.

His body rolled in the bottom of a faintly glowing bubble. He didn't try to fight his way free, because he could already feel her drawing in more power for another task.

Golden fire spilled from her fingertips, lashing out at the giant demon. The licks of flame wrapped around its body, setting its oily skin ablaze. It hissed in pain and fury.

Iain hit the ground hard, rolling over bones and filth to break his fall. His hands burned, and the tips of his fingers had started to go numb. He landed at Jackie's feet, and his world hadn't even had time to stop spinning before she locked her hand around his wrist and began pouring power into his arm.

Hot, tingling lightning erupted over his skin, burning away all traces of the poison. He felt something wet seep out of his palms, and then saw smoke rising as it evaporated.

The poison. It was gone, along with the burning, numbing effects.

There was no time for words, but he let his thanks

slide into her, along with the next pulsing glow of energy she was pulling from him.

She hadn't stopped slinging magic around since combat had broken out. He didn't know how much more she could do, but it was already more than he'd ever expected for such a short burst of time.

Cain was holding his own, keeping the demons off both of them, herding them toward the flames consuming the hulk they'd taken down.

Iain ripped off his shirt and wrapped it around his hand. The hilt of his sword protruded from the burning demon, and he made a quick grab to recover it. His shirt smoked, but none of the heat met his skin, so he shoved his way up to Cain's side, cutting a path through the few remaining demons scurrying about.

When the last one had fallen, he turned to find Jackie. She was slumped against a wall, breathing hard. A bright, pink flush covered her cheeks, and her bloodshot eyes glowed with a sense of accomplishment.

"Autumn," she panted. "Over there."

Iain wasn't letting her get more than a few steps away, so he wrapped his arm around her waist, taking her weight, and urged her forward.

Smoke wafted through the room, obscuring their vision. Jackie waved her hand, and the smoke parted from their path. Lying on the floor, on the other side of the bars, unmoving, was a young, scrawny girl.

"Autumn?" said Jackie, as if she found it hard to believe.

The metal bars were rusty, but not flimsy. Each one went into the surrounding stone at top and bottom. Iain grabbed one to test it and found it sturdy.

He was strong, but there was no way he was breaking those without some tools.

"I'll do it," said Jackie, weaving on her feet.

"Just unlock it," said Cain. "Save your strength to cover our exit."

She nodded and put her hand on the lock. Her eyes closed for a moment, and then he heard a faint metallic squeak. The door slipped open a scant inch.

"I'll get her," said Cain.

Iain turned to watch their backs, peering through the thick smoke. Smoldering demons lay scattered across the floor. The big one still twitched occasionally, its skin blistered and cracking.

Jackie's jolt of panic was his first sign that something was wrong. His head spun around to find the threat, his sword rising to destroy it.

Before, all that had been on the other side of the bars was a rock wall, but that had changed. Whatever illusion or veil had covered what really stood there, it was gone now, revealing a larger room stuffed full of eerily human guards. Each one was armed with a sword, and there were at least thirty of them, maybe more.

Standing in front of them, with his long, bony fingers wrapped around the throat of the little girl, dangling her unconscious body off the ground, stood another demon. He radiated power. Not a single creature behind him twitched, as if they wouldn't dare do anything without his permission.

He was so human looking that it took Iain a moment to figure out that he was Synestryn. The faint green glow to his eyes and the black blood pulsing beneath his pale skin gave him away.

"Murak," said Jackie, her hatred for the demon coming through both her tone and their link. Pulsing waves of anger spilled out of her, splashing against him, rousing the monster inside.

It wanted to kill this creature for her. It wanted to mount its head on a plaque and offer it at her feet as a tribute.

Iain tightened his control and shoved the desires of his beast aside.

"You're looking well," said Murak, his eyes lingering on her throat.

Cain shifted forward. Murak tightened his grip until Autumn's face began to darken with lack of oxygen. "I wouldn't do that. Not if you want the girl to keep breathing."

"What do you want?" asked Jackie.

"To bathe in your blood. For starters."

"Fine. Take me," said Jackie. "Let the girl go."

Iain growled.

Cain said, "Like hell."

Murak grinned and his gaze caught Iain's. "Judging by your bare throat, you're her power source, correct?"

Iain said nothing.

Murak continued to stare at Iain as a grin widened his mouth, displaying sharp teeth. "I'll take you in exchange for the girl."

"Done," whispered Iain at the same time Jackie screamed in denial.

"Drop the blade. Come here."

Leave. Take the girl and run, Iain told her silently.

He felt her resistance, but even as it formed, it crumbled. She knew his time was up. This was as good a way as any for him to go.

Iain stepped past Jackie and through the cage door.

Murak tossed Autumn at Cain, who caught her before she hit the ground.

"Go now, before I change my mind," ordered Murak.

Cain backed out, never taking his eyes off the demon. Tears slid down Jackie's cheeks, and she bit her lips as if trying to contain a sob.

Murak pulled a foot-long dagger from his belt and shoved it into Iain's chest. The strike was so fast he barely had time to realize what had happened before pain bloomed inside of him, shoving out all rational thought.

The blade ripped out of his body, and blood cascaded down his naked chest.

Jackie screamed in horror. He tried to tell her it was okay, but he couldn't gather his concentration enough to form words or thought. And even if he could, all breath had left his body, rendering him mute.

"Run, Jackie," warned Cain in a tone that screamed he knew what was coming next.

Iain fell to his knees, landing there before he recognized that he'd started to collapse. Blood seeped from his wound, wetting the waistband of his jeans. Strangely, he wasn't upset. He was freeing Jackie. Cain would protect her now.

He'd always wondered how it was going to end for him. At least now he knew his life had saved that of a little girl. It was a good trade.

Murak kicked Iain the rest of the way to the ground. There was a smile in his voice as he ordered his troops. "Kill the man. Bring the women to me."

Chapter 29

Beth woke up from her bleak dreams suddenly. Her heart fluttered in her bony chest, and a deep tingle spread out through her arms and legs. She kept her breathing quiet out of habit. The less attention she drew, the better.

An unfamiliar noise echoed down the stone wall to the small cell where she was kept. Voices. Words. Not the gurgle of demons. A woman's voice.

Someone was here.

Excitement trilled through her. What if whoever was out there could save her? It might just be another unfortunate soul being sentenced to this living hell, but she had to try.

Beth yelled, "Here! I'm here."

She strained against the bars, pressing her ear as far through the space between them as she could. Whoever was there, their voices faded, growing more distant.

They were leaving.

Your blood is the key. . . .

Her blood was her enemy. Every time she bled, the demons would come, hungry for a taste. The little ones would crawl through the bars, nipping at her until one of the bigger ones would come and chase them away.

Your blood is the key. . . .

It was her curse. The demons could all smell it—even the smallest cuts would draw them.

She pounded against the bars in frustration, yelling for those people to come save her.

Their voices were gone now. She could no longer detect even the faintest echo of them any longer.

Your blood is the key....

She didn't know what that meant. All she knew was that if she bled, the demons would come.

Maybe that's what these people were after. Maybe if she drew the demons to her, they'd come, too.

What did she have to lose? She wasn't going to last much longer in here. If they didn't kill her now, delivering the demon baby inside of her would. Her life was down to a few months at most. This was the best chance of escape she'd had since that fence had loomed high overhead, taunting her with freedom.

Beth brought her wrist to her mouth and dug her teeth into her skin. The grit and dirt coated her teeth, and the metallic tang of blood smeared over her tongue. She spat the muddy, bloody spit onto the ground and blew a breath across the seeping wound.

Fear curled around her, making her shiver. If this didn't work, if the little demons came fast, she had just become food.

Jackie stood in stunned shock as Iain fell to the ground. Rage and horror mixed together within her, swirling in a thick, black fog she couldn't see through. Her body was frozen, her voice locked in her chest. Pain sliced through her where the dagger had hit Iain as if it had struck her as well.

Her legs were weak, and the need to scream bubbled from deep within as she felt Iain fading from the world.

Cain tossed Autumn's limp body over his left shoulder. "Work fast, Jackie," he said. "Once he's gone, you'll have no power."

Power? That's what he was worried about? She didn't give a fuck about the power. She wanted Iain. Forever.

But that had been stolen from her, just like her former life. Everything she cared about, everything she'd ever wanted for herself, had been taken from her and burned to ashes at her feet.

It wasn't fair. It wasn't right. The pain and injustice that these demons had heaped on her was not something she'd earned. How dare they cause her more pain? How dare they even touch a man like Iain—one who'd devoted his entire life to helping others?

Jackie let the rage have her. She threw herself into the chaotic mass, letting it fill every cell until she felt like she would explode with the pressure. A high, ragged scream broke free of her mouth, vibrating her whole body with the force of it. The air shimmered, throbbing with her anger, seething in barely visible waves as it stretched out toward the armed, humanlike demons charging toward them.

The first three rows of soldiers clutched their heads, clenching and bowing over in agony. Blood leaked from their noses and ears as her scream stretched out, filling the cavern. Several demons fell. Those behind them trampled them under dirty feet.

Cain grabbed her arm and pulled her away from the charging horde.

She looked at Iain. He'd crawled aside to the base of a wall, and was struggling to regain his feet. One of the soldiers lifted a crooked, rusty sword to strike at him, but instead hit the flickering blue light of her shield.

She extended the protective wall across the barred door, preventing any of the soldiers from getting through.

"What are you doing?" asked Cain. "We have to run."

"I'm not leaving without him." She couldn't. Even if all she carried out was his body, she couldn't leave him here as food for demons.

He tugged on her arm, making her stumble. "I'm not letting you die."

"Then put the girl down and lift your fucking sword. I'm doing this, with or without you."

She didn't wait for Cain to agree or even respond. She jerked her arm from his grasp and sucked in as much of Iain's power as she could stand.

Fire. It poured out of her, roaring from her body in a golden cone of heat and light. It splashed through the bars, making them glow red. More solders fell, turning to ash before their screams had finished echoing off the cave walls. The stench was overpowering, but she didn't dare try to juggle anything beyond fire and shielding Iain from it.

The flow of energy coming from Iain stuttered, and the fire simply stopped lurching from her body. She fell to her knees, shocked at the sudden loss of what she'd become so used to having. The emptiness rang through her, leaving her feeling scraped hollow, brittle, and weak.

Jackie reached up, expecting her throat to be bare of the luceria, but it was still there, hot and trembling with the recent barrage of power.

There were still at least two dozen guards left standing, and a horde of smaller demons. They crawled over the charred corpses of their kind, scrambling to reach the bars. Beyond them, she saw Murak standing watch, his arms crossed over his chest, a grin on his ugly face as if he was enjoying the show.

Jackie was going to kill him. He'd hurt Iain, and she was going to see to it that he paid for that, even if it cost her her life.

The first soldier busted the metal door wide and leaped through it. Another followed behind, and another.

She reached for Iain's power, but all that was left was a weak, pitiful trickle.

He was dying, and there was nothing she could do to stop it.

*   *   *

The scent of the pregnant woman's blood slid into Ronan's nose, intoxicating him. She was powerful, even in her weakened state. And she was close.

He turned around, thumping Drake on the shoulder so he'd follow along behind. "This way."

The stone walls flew past him as he rushed forward, letting his nose lead the way. The stench of Synestryn grew heavier, sickening him. He didn't dare try to block it out for fear of losing the woman's trail.

Ronan spun around a corner and nearly ran headlong into a writhing pack of demons. They were all shapes and sizes, snarling and biting at one another as they piled high, trying to get to something he couldn't see.

The woman. There were bars here. She had to be on the other side.

"Back up," ordered Drake, pulling Ronan back by his arm.

A wave of flames washed out from Helen's hand, crashing against the demon pile. Demons hissed and gurgled as they ignited, scurrying away in an effort to douse the fire.

"There's a woman behind them!" Ronan shouted so that Helen wouldn't kill her.

Immediately, the flames backed off. The smaller demons curled up into balls of ash and cinder. The larger ones turned toward the threat and charged. Two of the biggest ones hadn't even bothered to stop and put out the fires consuming their fur. They simply charged in, teeth bared and ready for blood.

Ronan slipped aside, out of the path of the closest one. His thin blade slashed down, slicing through the beast's tendons, rendering one of its legs useless.

"Get the woman," shouted Drake. "We'll hold them off."

Ronan wasn't a trusting man, but when it came to combat, he'd grown used to putting his life in the hands of the Theronai. Outside of combat, things were much,

much different, but for now, he let trust reign and did as Drake said.

The bars were about ten feet tall, lodged deeply into both the rocky floor and ceiling. It was a standard setup for Synestryn captives, and one he'd seen used far too often for his liking.

Ronan inched his way around the smoldering pile of demons and kicked some aside so he could peer into the cage.

The woman was there, dirty and shivering. Her matted hair hung over her face, dragging the floor as she knelt, hugging herself. She was pressed into the farthest crevice she could find, rocking slightly and letting out a pitiful, low whimper.

Ronan's heart broke for her. He could tell by the length of her hair and the ill fit of her clothes that she'd been here a long time. Years, perhaps.

Behind him, battle raged on, but he ignored it, putting all his focus on the frightened woman crouched a few feet away.

"I'm Ronan," he told her, modulating his voice so that only gentleness came through—none of his anger. Within his tone, he embedded a hint of power, just a mere whisper of it, urging her to stay calm and trust him. Once she was in reach, he could do more, but for now, it was all he could manage. "We're going to get you out of here."

She looked up, her pale face covered in dirt save for two paths where her tears had run. Panic made her eyes wide, and he could see her heart fluttering wildly in the gaunt hollow of her throat.

She stayed there, frozen motionless, like a rabbit.

"I won't hurt you."

The bars blocked his path. He had enough strength to bend or break them, but then he'd be left weak and unable to help her further. And she was going to need help. She'd been starved. She was pregnant, likely with something inhuman. Bite marks covered her ankles, wrists, and throat. One was bleeding now. She was going to need him and his ability to heal her.

Ronan used his sword and boots to shove away the remains of the charred demons from the doorway. He pulled the leather sleeve of his coat down to cover his hand and pulled on the hot bars. The door was locked. Of course.

"Duck!" shouted Drake.

Ronan jerked toward the ground, making himself as small a target as possible. The severed head of a demon clanged against the bars, rattling them.

The woman looked up, her chin trembling. "The key," she whispered, her bony finger pointing behind him. Her hand shook, but she was still with him, thinking clearly enough to help.

Ronan looked to where she pointed and saw the metallic glint of a key hanging from a hook driven into the stone.

He skirted around the remains of combat, ducking the splatter of black blood flinging from the tip of Drake's sword. He grabbed the key and sprinted back, wasting no time in opening the door.

The woman was standing now, her clothing hanging from her frame. The sleeves were too short, as if she'd been wearing it for years. Her jeans were in tatters, held closed over her protruding belly with a bit of shoelace. The faint outline of a kitten was embroidered on one leg—a childish emblem meant for childish clothes.

Whoever she was, she'd been here a long, long time.

Ronan held out his hand, planting his feet solidly on the ground so that he didn't give in to the urge to race toward her.

She looked at his hand, then his face, then past him to what was going on outside the bars.

"We won't let them hurt you. Give me your hand."

She took a step. He could see her whole body shaking with the effort.

"That's right. Just a bit more and we'll have you out of here."

Another step, then another. She was close enough for him to extend his reach and take her hand, but he held firm, letting her come to him.

Her fingers settled against his skin, cold and clammy. The dirt caking her stood out in stark contrast to the paleness of his skin. Slowly, so as not to frighten her, Ronan closed his grip and offered her what he hoped was a kind smile.

All he tried to think about was getting her out, but thoughts of her captivity kept invading, distracting him from his goal. He couldn't even imagine the things she must have suffered. The fact that she'd trust him enough now to touch him was humbling.

"Come on," he said, sliding a bit of power through his words and touch, offering her his warmth and whatever slice of solace she could take from him.

Ronan tugged her forward and helped her over the corpses littering the area. Drake and Helen had taken care of the remaining demons, but there would be more. Her blood would draw them.

Without seeming like he was doing it, he shifted his grip to her bleeding wrist and healed the wound shut. It wasn't deep, and it was a relief for him to be doing something useful for her. Given her current state, he wasn't sure how much anyone could really do to help her.

"We need to go," said Helen. "Those out feeding will be coming back soon and block our exit."

They started back the way they'd come, but the woman tugged on his sleeve. "I know a faster way out. Go right up ahead."

Drake led the way, and did as the woman said. About a hundred feet down the corridor, it opened up into a large cavern. The sounds of battle rang out from the far side.

Ronan pressed the woman back, shielding her from

sight with his body. Fire flared, blinding him for a moment.

"Jackie," breathed Helen. "That's Jackie over there. With all those demons."

Indeed she was, fighting like a woman possessed, clearly heedless of her own safety. Cain was there, too, along with two unconscious bodies—Iain and a young girl.

The fight wasn't going well. There were too many of them. Cain was doing his best to keep the demons off both Jackie and the unconscious girl, but it was a losing battle.

Ronan wanted nothing more than to get the woman clinging to him out of this place, but he knew it would have to wait. Jackie was too valuable to lose, and there was no way Helen was going to leave her sister here to fight the demons by herself.

They were going to have to fight their way free.

Chapter 30

Jackie picked up Iain's sword and held off any demon who dared come close to him. The small trickle of power flowing into her held Murak in place, preventing him from leaving. The bubble surrounding his body wobbled every time he struck it, but so far, it had held steady.

Iain was fading. She could feel his heartbeat weaken with every passing second. If she didn't stop the bleeding, he wasn't going to make it.

With a silent apology, she demanded more from Iain, drawing more of his power into herself—just enough to shield her back.

Without letting go of Murak, she let Iain's power slide over her, cradling her close and protecting her from attack the way he would have done had he been able.

She fell to his side and pressed her hands against his bloody chest. The stab wound was deep, so close to his heart, she wasn't sure whether it had been hit. He was bleeding heavily, telling her that there wasn't much time.

"I'm sorry," she whispered, then ripped a thick ribbon of energy from him, causing him to groan. She closed her eyes and concentrated on finding the severed blood vessels in order to close them. Her hands slipped on his skin. Heat seared her fingertips, drying the blood beneath them. Iain sucked in a pained breath and his heavy muscles clenched tight.

The effort was grueling. She felt her cage around Murak falter, and had to let it go—had to let him go. Iain was more important.

Heat flowed through her. She could feel waves of it rising from Iain's body, hear the air crackling with it.

The stream of power began to waver, stuttering as she demanded more from it. The shield at her back fell, exposing her to dozens of demons hungry for Iain's blood.

There was nothing she could do. She knew instinctively that if she let go of the small thread of strength she'd managed to hold on to, she'd lose it forever. Iain would be gone. She'd be powerless. Both of them would die.

If she was going to die, she wanted it to be because she'd given her all to save him, not because she'd given up on him.

The sound of the demons behind her grew louder, closer.

They had realized her protection was gone and were closing in.

Cain fought his way toward Jackie. He couldn't leave Autumn unprotected, so he had to bring her along, fighting with her slight weight dangling over his shoulder. He told himself it was no different from protecting a brother's flank, but that was a fat lie.

Her limbs flopped around with every slice and thrust, forcing him to move carefully so as not to chop off her leg.

Jackie had stopped helping him kill the demons and instead knelt over Iain. She was trying to save his life. Cain knew that. He would have expected no less of her. But she seemingly had no care for herself or her safety. From the moment she'd dropped Iain's sword, Cain knew that her life was now in his hands.

Finally, after what seemed like half a year of combat, he was only a few feet away—close enough to see faint blue sparks flying off her back.

She was still alive.

The field holding Murak in place sputtered and then dropped. Cain closed the last few remaining feet toward Jackie, cutting down wave after endless wave of armed Synestryn soldiers and smaller, clawed demons.

The blue flashes sparking at her back began to fade.

Her shield was faltering, just as the one around Murak had done.

Cain was out of options. He lunged sideways, keeping his left side and Autumn out of the reach of swords and claws. His right arm moved with frenzied speed, making his muscles burn in protest.

A blade was headed right for him. He couldn't stop it. He couldn't dodge. It was angled to strike his right arm. He could already see his limb being severed, flying across the space to land as food for demons.

There was nothing he could do but watch as the blade fell.

The demon blade struck, but he felt no pain. Bluish sparks scattered in all directions. Half a second later, Drake was at his side, lopping off the legs of the demon who'd nearly ended Cain's life.

The girl's weight lifted from his shoulder. He grabbed for her, but as soon as he felt the faint, welcoming heat of friendly magic surrounding her, he let go.

Drake was here. So was Helen. She must have been the one to relieve him of his burden.

"Thanks," shouted Cain.

Drake grunted in response, going low to strike while Cain went high. Between them, two more demons fell.

Two down, another dozen more to go.

Jackie had managed to stop Iain's bleeding, but she was too late. He'd lost too much blood.

His breathing was fast and shallow, his heart fluttering in his chest. Tied to him as closely as she was, she could feel him trying to leave his body.

She couldn't let go. She loved him. She needed him to stay.

She knew it was selfish, but she didn't give a shit if it was. All that mattered was holding him close, so that's what she did.

Jackie wrapped her arms around him, pressing her cheek to his chest. She tightened her hold on his power, refusing to let go.

"Don't leave me," she begged him. "Not yet."

I have to go, she heard him whisper against her mind. *You're not safe so long as I draw breath. Soulless . . .*

"I don't give a fuck about that. I've seen your soul in your actions. You're a *good* man."

It's too hard. My monster has grown too strong.

The core of him—the part of him that made him who he was—began to lift out of his body. She could see it in her mind, feel it through the luceria. It pulsed with power, streaming with thick, black branches. Within that mass was a narrow, golden ribbon wound tightly around it. The ribbon glowed against the darkness, stretching back into Jackie.

His soul. That giant, powerful thing was his soul. She could feel the emptiness of it, the deep aching void that had once been filled with light and life. Gone. All of it gone now—dead and scraped hollow.

He was right. There was nothing left of his soul to be saved. Dead was dead.

Grief welled up inside of her, hot and fierce, clawing and tearing her apart.

She didn't want to live without him. Intellectually, she knew she'd eventually heal, but she'd already suffered too much. She didn't want to suffer through his death, too.

"I love you," she whispered. "I'll go with you."

No! He screamed it into her thoughts, shoving her back. She didn't go far. She was tethered to him too tightly, knotted around him too many times to ever be free.

Where you go, I go, she told him, content with her decision.

Something ferocious and deadly broke free, shaking its huge body and stretching its powerful limbs. She could see it in her mind—inside of him—the monster he'd spoken of. She'd felt its presence before, but seeing it now, she knew why Iain feared letting it free.

Giant, layered with thick muscle under tough skin that looked like stone, it towered in her mind, teeth bared, leathery wings spread, and clawed hands open and ready to grab her.

Go, it growled at her. *Leave us to die.*

She firmed her resolve, refusing to let something so insubstantial scare her away. *No.*

We won't let you die.

Then stay. Stay with me. Live.

No soul. No life.

Then take my soul.

The monster froze and then cocked its head to the side. It looked down on her with Iain's eyes.

No! she heard Iain shout from a long way off.

Done, said the monster, its pointed teeth gleaming behind its grin.

A horrific, wrenching pain ripped from her chest, stealing her breath. A dark presence shoved itself into her head, taking over her limbs.

Like a puppet, she jerked to her feet. Power roared into her, but she had no control—no idea what was happening.

Her feet lifted from the ground and she rose into the air above the battle below. Her head swiveled around until she sighted Murak slinking away.

Her hand reached out and an instant later, Murak

stopped. His body rose up and drifted closer until he was right over the crush of demons fighting her friends, her sister.

Another swelling spike of power funneled through her, and she watched as the skin peeled back from Murak's body. He screamed, but it did no good. His skin was stripped from him, ripping away clothing as it went. Blood rained down over the demons, distracting them from combat.

All that energy that had been rushing through her vanished, and Murak fell into the waiting jaws of his troops. His screams rose up as he was ripped apart by the teeth of his own soldiers.

Jackie fell to the stone floor, landing next to Iain. He was ghostly pale, unconscious, and unmoving. She tried to reach out and touch him—to make sure his heart was still beating, but her arm was too heavy.

Sleep, she heard the monster growl, only this time that voice came from within her. *You must live for me now.*

Chapter 31

Iain woke. That alone was surprising enough. Even more surprising was the sense of peace and the utter quiet within him.

There was no monster. No rage. He hadn't felt like this since the day his soul had died.

He was lying on a bed with Ronan staring down at him, concern lining his pretty face. Behind Ronan stood Helen and Drake. Cain was in the doorway. On the bed next to him was Jackie, lying far too still.

Panic made him sit up, and a rush of dizziness slammed into him.

"Easy," said Ronan. "She's fine. Just sleeping."

"What the hell happened?" he asked.

"I put both you and Jackie to sleep for a few days so you could heal," said Ronan. "I wasn't sure either of you would make it."

"We're at a Gerai house," said Helen. Her eyes and nose were red from crying.

Drake put his arm around his wife's shoulders and pulled her into his embrace.

"It wasn't safe to move you," said Ronan. "We almost lost you both."

"Where's the girl?" asked Iain, his voice rough and dry.

"Autumn is at Dabyr with her family, recovering at her mother's side. So is the other woman we found." Ronan's gaze darkened as he said that last part, as if it upset him to speak about it.

"Everyone's fine," said Drake, clearly more for Helen's benefit than Iain's. "We all made it out."

Ronan nodded. "And you woke up. I'm glad to see all is well. I wasn't sure it would be."

"What's that supposed to mean?" asked Iain.

Ronan glanced at Iain's chest. "See for yourself."

He looked down and half of his lifemark was as dead and barren as ever, but the other half was green and lush with a new batch of leaves. He stared at it in shock for a long time, trying to figure out if he was still dreaming, or if this was some kind of sick joke of the afterlife. "I don't understand."

"I don't, either."

His memories began to come back. The kidnapped girl. The caves. His inevitable death. Jackie refusing to let him go. He remembered feeling her tied so tightly around his soul that he knew if he tried to leave his body in death, she would have followed him.

His monster. It had bargained with her, accepting the gift she offered. Her soul. Iain had tried to stop it, but he'd been too weak. He'd had no chance of regaining control of the beast.

"Oh, God," he breathed, the impact of what had happened barreling down on him.

She'd given him her soul.

Iain reached for her, diving headlong through their link. He had to give it back. He had to force her to take back her offer.

The ethereal constructs of her mind seemed familiar to him now. He'd spent so much time connected to her that she felt like home.

He found her lounging by a sparkling blue pool, soaking up the sun. She seemed completely at ease, completely content. She looked up at him, shielding her eyes with her hand. Her sweet body was barely covered by a bikini, her skin dewy with perspiration.

The smile that stretched across her face drove the breath from his body with its beauty. "Care to join us?"

"Us?"

Her words made him notice that a few feet away on a lounge chair lay his monster, completely naked and sunbathing.

Confusion rattled him, but that seemed only to make Jackie's grin widen.

"He's not all that bad, you know," she told him.

Iain's mind sputtered as he tried to make sense of her words. "Not all that . . . ?"

She shrugged one lovely shoulder. "A little rough around the edges, but completely trainable."

The monster let out an affirmative growl. "At least she doesn't keep me locked in a fucking cage all the time."

This was all too surreal. None of this made any sense. Clearly he *had* died and this was what hell looked like.

As if reading his mind, she chuckled. "You're not dead. Neither am I. Neither is Stan."

"Stan?"

"I thought he should have a name," said Jackie.

The monster smiled. "Kinda manly, don't you think? Very human."

Iain had no words to express his feelings of *What the fuck?*

"You need to stop worrying," she told Iain. "Everything's fine."

"The hell it is. You gave me your soul. Take it back."

"I *tried* to give you my soul. You only took half. We're both going to be fine. I'm just going to sleep for a bit longer. Stan here had me use so much power to kill Murak that I'm still wrung dry."

"I'll fix that," promised Iain. "And then we'll talk."

She and Stan went back to their sunbathing, completely ignoring him.

Iain fell back into himself and opened his eyes. "Her soul," he whispered to the concerned group hovering over him. "She gave me half her soul."

"That changes things," said Ronan. "We didn't even know such a thing was possible."

"I'm going to call Joseph," said Drake. "Ronan's right. This changes things."

He and Helen left.

"I need to take her outside. Replenish her strength."

"You're too weak to carry her," said Ronan.

"I'll do it," Cain offered.

Iain nodded. As much as he hated seeing her in another man's arms, it was for the best. He needed to feel the ground beneath his fingers and draw upon its strength to drive away her weakness and his.

Ronan helped Iain stumble outside. He knelt on the cool ground and dug his fingers through the dry grass into the moist dirt below. Cain held her close enough for him to cup his left hand around her throat and allow the two halves of the luceria to connect.

He gathered up the power of the earth and let it trickle into her. It strengthened both of them, and soon, he felt almost normal.

Iain took Jackie from Cain's arms and cradled her against his bare chest just as she was beginning to wake. Her gray eyes looked up into his, so full of love he wasn't sure he could hold it all.

He heard Ronan and Cain walk away, leaving the two of them alone under the stars.

"We made it," she said, her voice faint.

"Thanks to you."

She smiled at him, and it warmed his very soul.

His soul. He had one again, thanks to her.

She laid her hand over his heart, and the branches of his lifemark swayed, stretching toward her touch.

Tears filled Iain's eyes and splashed down onto her wrist. "Thank you," he told her. "Thank you for saving my life. Thank you for sharing yours with me."

She shrugged. "You would have done the same for me."

He would have. He'd do anything for her. He loved her.

As that thought hit, his whole being swelled with the strength of it. He loved her. She'd not only saved his life but given him back the most basic of pleasures—loving another. That had been stolen from him for so long, he'd forgotten how good it felt, how restoring and peaceful it was to love.

Even his love for Serena was there, faint and watery by comparison with what he felt for Jackie, but still its own kind of gift.

"I love you," he told her, enjoying the ring of those words in his ears.

Her eyes shimmered with happy tears. "I love you, too."

A smile stretched his mouth for the first time in years.

Jackie pulled in a breath and grinned back. "I thought you were hot before, but when you smile, you're . . . breathtaking."

"I'll show you breathtaking," he said, and lowered his mouth to hers. He was going to spend the rest of his long, long life showing her how grateful he was, and just how deeply a man with half a soul could love.

Tynan's phone rang, distracting him from his thoughts. Project Lullaby was progressing well, but not nearly fast enough. They were going to have to pick up the pace if they were to have any hope of saving themselves from starvation.

"Jackie's pregnant," said Ronan as soon as Tynan answered. "Your cure has worked again."

Shock glued Tynan's lips shut for a brief moment. His world began to shift under his feet. Things he'd believed true were simply wrong, and he was struggling to adjust to the new data. "I never gave Iain the serum."

"Then how is it possible she carries a child?"

"I have no idea. Did she bed another man?"

"No. I walked her memories while she slept, searching for a way to save her. I saw no other man. I did, however, see something else."

"What?"

"There was this odd memory of a black field, like a starless sky. Lights flared into existence, one by one, as she learned how to channel Iain's power into different forms and uses. It was so bizarre that I poked around, searching for the source of such an odd mental image."

"What did you find?" asked Tynan.

"One of the lights had a familiar feel. It felt like . . . Lexi, whose mind I've touched. I inspected that light more deeply and found a connection there. Lexi actually called me to see if I was well—she said she'd suddenly had a bad feeling that something was wrong. I don't understand how or why, but Jackie is connected to Lexi. And to many others."

"Did you recognize any of the others?"

"Yes. Andra, Helen, and Tori also had lights of their own. But there were others as well—ones that were not at all familiar. There were, however, some things they all had in common."

"And what were they?"

"Every light felt feminine and was laced with power. It is my belief that whoever these women are that Jackie is connected to, every one of them is a Theronai."

"How many?"

"Six. And I saw each one flare to life as I walked her memories. More may well appear."

The implications of that were huge. It meant that there were more women out there just waiting to be found. Tynan's mind spun as he put this new information into place, forcing other pieces to shift and spin to make room. "How do we find these women?"

"I don't know. Jackie may be able to locate them. But there's something else this explains."

"What?"

"I believe this connection is why she's seemingly compatible with all male Theronai. If she's somehow tied to other women, it could grant her the ability to tap into any man's power."

"Do you think that this ability is something that can be learned?"

Ronan's voice dropped with disappointment. "I don't think so. My guess is that this is an inherent ability that only Jackie possesses. I will look into it further if I get the opportunity. Iain's awake now, though."

So the chances of Ronan spending time in Jackie's mind were slim.

"Do I tell them?" asked Ronan.

"Tell them about Jackie's gift, but keep the news of her pregnancy to yourself for now. Let me administer the serum to Iain first."

Ronan's voice was accusatory. "You want to take credit for this when it wasn't your doing?"

"Think about it, Ronan. If the Theronai have somehow spontaneously regained their fertility and they don't know it, the chances of procreation are higher, especially with human women. If they know they could have offspring, some of them may choose to use birth control. Do we really want that?"

"No. Of course not. We need all the blood we can get."

"Then we're in agreement. As soon as Iain returns, I'll give him a shot of saline and no one will be the wiser."

"Until the next woman turns up pregnant by one of the male Theronai."

A smile stretched Tynan's face. "There may be hope for our race yet."

*   *   *

Cain couldn't watch the lovefest. It wasn't that he begrudged Iain his happiness, but it was hard to see his chance for a future come so close, only to slip through his fingers.

Jackie had never truly been his. She never would have been his, even if Iain had died. She loved him, and Cain was thrilled to see her happy.

His own happiness hardly mattered by comparison.

Cain looked down at the cold, black ring on his finger. He was delaying the inevitable. Wearing this ring might even prevent him from finding the woman for him—assuming she was even out there. He didn't hold out much hope, but the thought of missing out on what might be his one and only chance left him cold and afraid.

It wasn't the pain. That he could stand, no matter how grueling it got. It was the loneliness. It was eating him up inside, chewing away at the few strands of hope he'd managed to hold on to.

The ring wasn't going to help. It was cheating. He'd lived his whole life by the rules. Skirting them now seemed . . . cowardly.

Cain pulled the ring from his finger and set it on the kitchen table of the little Gerai house. Iain would find it and give it to someone else.

He felt another leaf inch down his chest. The pain hit him hard, leaving him panting through it, gripping the back of a chair so hard he heard the wood creak. Slowly, the pain eased up to simply grueling, and his vision returned.

Things were changing, and Cain wasn't sure he could change with them. He'd been alive for far too long. As much as he loved his job of protecting humans and guarding the gate, a man couldn't live for his work alone.

Sibyl no longer needed him. Gilda and Angus were dead. Several of his brothers had found mates, and their ranks were once again growing. Even little Nika was pregnant, giving hope to all the other men.

Cain had never realized how much he loved having a child of his own until Sibyl was gone, and a great, gaping wound had opened up inside of him. She wasn't his by birth, but she was his daughter in every other way. Even now, all she had to do was call him and he'd run to her aid.

But he knew her better than that. She wasn't going to call him. She craved her independence too much. He was on his own and had to find a way to keep going, so that's what he'd do. For whatever time he had left.

Turn the page for a sneak peek at
the next Edge novel,

EDGE OF SANITY

Coming in December 2012 from Signet Eclipse

I t was the blood that woke him.

Clay Marshall's fingers were glued together, sticky and itching where the blood had dried. The heavy, metallic smell of it clogged his nose, choking him with the stench of violence.

He stared at his dirty hands, disoriented and numb from shock. Fatigue dragged at his bones. Pain pounded deep inside his skull, worse than any hangover.

The water stain on the ceiling was a familiar comfort, telling him he was in his own bed. Now, if he could only remember how he got there.

As the fog of sleep cleared, the meaning of the blood began to take hold. Concern gnawed at the edges of his numb haze, nibbling away at the false sense of calm. Reality squeezed around him, shoving out his breath like a giant boa constrictor.

Clay sat up, trying to control the fear before it became full-blown panic. His clothes were stiff and dark with drying blood, as if someone had splashed a bucket of it down his front. He searched for the source of the blood, seeking out the kind of physical pain this much blood loss would create.

He ripped off his shirt and jeans, only to find the skin beneath whole. His sheets were stained, but there was no pool lying where he'd been. Those smears were only from contact with his clothes.

Clay rushed to the bathroom on shaky legs, and peered into the full-length mirror on the back of the door. No cuts. No gashes. Only a collage of bruises of varying ages, and a body that was so thin he barely recognized it.

The blood wasn't his, and yet he could find no relief in that knowledge. It had to belong to someone.

The need to scrub it away rose up, compelling him to stumble into the shower. Cold water hit him hard, driving the air from his lungs before it slowly warmed. He lathered himself from head to toe, watching in disgust as the rusty suds spiraled down the drain.

Even though the hot water stung, he still felt detached from the world, as though he were covered by a thick layer of foam, preventing anything from really reaching him. His head was clouded with confusion—so much so that he was only just now realizing that he was confused.

He dried off and headed for his kitchen, where the coffee lived. After three cups and twenty minutes, Clay's brain finally began to function. And with that relative clarity of thought came fear.

There were stains on his floor in the shape of his boots, leading from the kitchen door all the way to his bedroom. He followed them to where the bloody pile of clothes lay on the rug.

There was even more blood on them than he'd imagined. So much that he knew someone had to be dead. The question was, who? And had Clay been the one to kill them?

A sick sense of dread settled over him, making the coffee in his stomach churn.

He had no memories of last night. The sun was streaming in through the windows, but he couldn't remember anything since lunch yesterday. As hard as he tried, there was simply a gaping black hole where that time should have been, as if he'd been asleep since then.

The blood proved otherwise.

Clay turned on the local news, barely breathing as the anchor moved from one story to the next. He wasn't sure what he expected to hear—reports of a building collapse or a giant pileup on I-35, maybe—but he knew what he feared: murder.

His hand shook as he surfed from one station to the next, seeking some sign of what he'd done. When they started repeating the same stories, he wasn't sure if he was more relieved or scared. Maybe he hadn't hurt anyone. Maybe he'd saved someone's life and gotten them medical attention. Then again, maybe they just hadn't found the body yet. Or bodies.

This wasn't the first time Clay had woken up with blood on his hands, but he had no way of figuring out how to make it the last time. The only person he could trust was his best friend, Mira, and he couldn't stand the idea of burdening her with his problems.

Still, if anyone could help him solve the mystery, she could.

Clay dug his cell phone out of his bloody jeans and wiped it clean before dialing Mira.

Her voice was so cheerful and bright it hurt his head. "Good morning, Clay. You're up early."

"Heya, Squirt. I need a favor."

"Sure."

"I need to know if anyone in the area was killed last night."

The line went silent for a minute. "Uh . . . what?"

He hated lying to her, but there was no other way. "I saw a ton of blood on the sidewalk outside a club. I was wondering if anyone was murdered. Can you find out?"

"Where was it?"

Shit. He hadn't been thinking clearly enough to consider even such a simple question. He was even worse off in the mental department than he'd thought. "I don't remember. I was drunk."

"Clay," she said in that voice that told him she knew he was lying. "What's really going on?"

"Can you find out or not?"

She let out a heavy sigh. They'd been friends a long time—since they were kids—and he was not easy on his friends. Especially Mira.

"Hold on." Disappointment weighed on her voice.

Clay heard the clicking of keys in the background before she came back on the line. "There was a drug-related shooting that killed three. One fatal car accident. Three deaths from natural causes. That's all I could find."

"Any John or Jane Does?"

"You want me to hack into the morgue? That's a little dark, even for you. What's going on?"

"Nothing. Really. Don't worry."

"How can I not worry? You sound awful. Did something happen?"

The lie nearly choked him. "No. I'm sorry I bothered you."

"You're not a bother, Clay. You know I love you. Whatever you need, I'm there, okay?"

An unexpected spurt of emotion clogged his throat. She was the only person in the world he really cared about. He didn't know why she stuck with him when he was such a mess, but he was glad she did. "I love you, too, Squirt."

"Then let me help you. The headaches, the blackouts—you need help."

The pile of bloody clothes popped into his mind, staring at him in accusation. Until he figured out what was going on, he wasn't safe to be around. "I'll be fine. But I'm not feeling so great, so I'm taking a sick day. Will you let Bella know?"

"Sure. Get some rest and call me if you need anything, okay?"

"I will," he lied.

*   *   *

Mira hung up the phone, feeling sick to her stomach. Clay was getting worse. The bruises, the split knuckles, the dislocated joints. And now he wanted her to check death records? Even if her IQ had been cut in half, she would have been able to figure out what that meant.

He thought he'd killed someone.

Clay kept pushing her away, making up reasons why they could no longer hang out together. The more she tried to help, the harder he pushed.

If he wouldn't let her help him, she had to find someone who could. And there was only one man Mira knew who even had a chance at getting through Clay's thick skull.

What she was about to do would piss her best friend off, but that was just too bad. She owed him her life— even if he didn't remember—and if she had to suffer through his anger, so be it.

With her decision made, she dialed the phone.

Clay had just shoved the last of the bloody fabric in a trash bag when his doorbell rang. He took his time washing his hands, hoping whoever it was would just go the hell away.

The chime rang again, followed closely by a sharp knock.

"I know you're in there," came a man's calm voice. "Mira called me."

Payton Bainbridge. His boss's right-hand man and all-around buttinsky.

"Go away," called Clay.

"Not going to happen. Open the door."

"I'm sick." He forced out a fake cough to add texture to the lie.

Payton's disbelieving tone said he wasn't buying Clay's story. "I'm immune. Open the door."

The sooner he got this over with, the sooner Payton

would leave and shove his nose into someone else's business.

Clay unbolted the triple-locked door and let the older man in.

Payton was in his late fifties, with the suave kind of good looks that made younger women take notice. Or maybe it was simply his ridiculously expensive suits that spoke to them. He walked in, spine straight, hair perfect, suit without a single wrinkle, looking like he'd just walked away from one of those celebrity makeovers. His pale eyes moved over Clay's rumpled clothes and mussed hair, but rather than seeing disdain for Clay's lack of grooming, there was guilt in his eyes—as if he were somehow responsible for the way Clay looked.

"You need a doctor." Payton shut and locked the door behind him, dimming Clay's already dingy living room.

"I'm not that sick. Nothing a bit of rest and some chicken soup can't cure."

"You're favoring your left knee and hunching over as if your ribs ache. No amount of soup will fix that. You need to be X-rayed."

Payton had looked at Clay for all of ten seconds and seen that? Shit. That meant he was going to have to take more time off work than just a day.

Clay straightened up, ignoring the throbbing pain in his ribs and shoulder. "My bones are fine."

Payton pushed past him and walked into the kitchen as if he owned the place. "Mind if I make coffee?"

"You won't be here long enough to drink it."

The older man ignored him and went about searching Clay's cabinets, putting a fresh pot of coffee on. "Mira says you're in trouble."

"Mira is wrong. Everything is fine."

"Your bruises say you're lying. Judging by the color palette you've got going there, you've been injured at least three times in the past two weeks."

"I joined a fight club. I would have told you, but you know the first rule of fight club. . . ."

Payton turned around, his face tight with anger and something else Clay couldn't name. "This isn't a joke. She said you were asking about dead bodies."

"Mira and I are clearly going to have to have another talk about oversharing information."

"She trusts me. You should, too. I'm not here to judge."

"Then why are you here?"

Payton's direct gaze slid away to the empty mug he was holding. "We all make mistakes, Clay. If you've made one, I can help set things right. All you have to do is tell me the truth."

The truth wasn't going to help him any more than it was going to help the person whose blood he'd been wearing when he woke up. "I've got it under control."

"Do you?"

"Yeah. So you can take your coffee to go. Keep the mug."

Payton stared Clay right in the eyes, daring him to lie. "Did you kill someone last night?"

In that moment, Clay's world began to close in around him. The panic he'd felt since seeing the blood exploded until there was no room left to breathe. The edges of his vision began to fade out into gray nothingness. Sound became muted until all he could hear was the rapid, out-of-control beat of his own heart.

He needed help. He needed to find someone who could make sense out of the chaos his life had become. Mira was too vulnerable and precious for him to fuck over with his problems. As far as she stuck her neck out for him, one of these times she was going to lose her head.

Payton stood there silently, patiently. He didn't move a muscle or blink a lash. There was no hint of reproach on his face, only the faintest lines of regret.

Clay swallowed, barely able to work up enough moisture to move his tongue. His choices were simple: continue on alone and wake up covered in blood again, or grab ahold of the lifeline Payton offered.

He didn't want to hurt anyone. He knew he was completely capable of killing and not remembering it. The mission in Arizona a few months ago had taught him that.

What if he killed again? What if this time he hurt someone he cared about? What if he hurt Mira?

That couldn't happen. He'd eat a bullet before he'd take that risk.

And yet he took that risk every day, never knowing when he'd lose another chunk of time and wake up bruised and broken, with no memory of what he'd done or where he'd been.

Today had to be his wakeup call. Mira was still alive and safe. That could all change so fast. She was like a sister to him—the only family he had—and he couldn't gamble with her life.

Clay met Payton's stare and told him the truth. "I don't know."

"How can you not know? Either you killed someone or you didn't."

"I don't remember anything about last night. That's how. I remember grabbing a burger at lunch yesterday. After that . . . nothing. Until this morning when I . . ." He couldn't even say the words. If he did, they would make this whole bizarre nightmare real.

"What happened this morning?" asked Payton, his voice gentle but insistent.

Rather than reply, Clay fetched the trash bag and dumped it out on his kitchen floor. Bloody sheets and clothes tumbled out in a stiff clump. The meaty smell nearly gagged him.

"This happened," said Clay.

A look of panic that mirrored Clay's brushed over Payton's aristocratic features. "Are you hurt?"

"Not enough to make this mess. It's someone else's blood."

"Or something's. It could be animal blood."

Clay hadn't even thought about that, and it brought him a sense of relief so heavy his knees buckled under the weight. He collapsed into a kitchen chair, dizzy and swaying. "You think?"

"It's possible. I'll have it tested."

"I don't want anyone else involved."

"I understand. I'll make sure the test is anonymous."

Clay's head was suddenly too heavy to hold up. He propped his elbows on the table and let it sag into his hands. "Things are all fucked up, Payton."

"I know. I'll help you sort it all out. But you've got to be completely honest with me. No more evasion. No more lies. Agreed?"

Clay hesitated. As much as he liked the man, he didn't trust anyone as much as he'd need to if he was going to spill his guts about everything. Instead, he let out a nondescript grunt that could be taken as agreement.

"This has been happening for a while, hasn't it?"

"The bloody clothes? Hell no. At least not like this."

"No, I mean the lost time—the blackouts. This isn't the first time you've lost your memory."

Clay debated lying, but Payton didn't seem too freaked out by the possibility, which gave him the boost to say what needed to be said. "It's been going on for months now."

"How often?"

"Not very, at first. These last few weeks . . . at least four times that I know of."

"What do you mean by that?"

"There were a couple of times that I woke up and things weren't where I thought I'd left them. Once I was wearing clothes, when I was sure I'd stripped down before going to bed." He lifted his head and forced himself to confess. "I think I'm going insane."

Payton's mouth turned down and a haze of regret

dulled his eyes. "You're not. I won't let that happen. I'm going to see you through this. If you do what I say, everything is going to be fine."

"I don't see how. Once Bella finds out, I'm going to lose my job."

"Bella won't find out. We're going to fix this. I swear it."

For a glittering, hopeful second, Clay believed him. He clutched on to that hope and held on tight. "How?"

"First, you need to give me your phone."

"What?"

"Your cell phone. If I'm right, then it's dangerous for you to carry one."

Clay had no idea what to make of that, but he shoved his hand into his jeans and pulled out his phone. He set it on the table.

Payton stowed it in his pocket, his demeanor changing to one of all business. There was no more emotion showing through—just the get-it-done attitude that Clay had come to recognize. "I'm going to send you someplace safe. Isolated. I want you to take my car and go there right now."

"Why?"

"I'll explain everything once I'm sure, but for now, I need you to trust me."

"Why send me away?"

Payton pulled a key from his ring and wrote an address on the back of his business card. "The farther you are away from here, the better. Don't tell anyone where you're going. Don't speak to anyone along the way—not even a clerk at a gas station."

"Payton, you're freaking me out here. Why go to all the—"

"When you get there, unplug the phone. Don't bring any electronics with you. No laptop, no games, no GPS. Nothing, understand?"

"No. I do not."

He shoved the key and the card at Clay. "I need a couple of days to gather some information, but you shouldn't be alone. I will send someone to stay with you."

"I don't need a babysitter."

"You do. If you don't want to hurt someone else, you do. Trust me."

"I don't want anyone to know I've gone off the deep end. I have to work with these people."

"It won't be someone from the Edge. I'll have your guardian show up at the back door at exactly six thirty-two. If anyone but me shows up at any other time . . ."

He trailed off as if debating his options, leaving Clay hanging.

"What? What crazy thing do you want me to do along with all this other cloak-and-dagger bullshit?"

"If anyone else shows up at any other time, kill them."

Payton waited until Clay was behind the wheel and on his way before he left in the other man's car.

First order of business: burn the evidence. He didn't need to keep a sample to see if it was human blood or not. He knew it was. The things Clay would be used for had nothing to do with animal control.

The suggestion about it being animal blood had been a strategically timed diversion to keep Clay from breaking. The man was already on edge. There was no way to know how long he'd been suffering with his secrets. He'd said months, but chances were even Clay wouldn't remember everything.

Payton was counting on it.

After a quick stop at one of the houses Payton kept set aside for extreme circumstances, the clothes and sheets were no more than a burning ball of ash. He watched the glowing embers while he made the call.

Dr. Leigh Vaughn answered on the sixth ring, leaving Payton biting his nails.

"This had better be good. I'm in the middle of something."

"I'm sorry for the interruption, but it's important."

"It always is," she said on a sigh. "What is it this time? Another secret gunshot wound I can't report?"

"No. It's a much bigger favor than that."

"Spit it out. I don't have all day. Patients are waiting."

"Send them home."

"What? No way. If your emergency is that serious, then take them to the hospital."

"If you do this, I'll get you in to see Garrett."

The line went silent for too long.

"Leigh? Are you there?"

"Yeah," she said, her voice thick with emotion. "I just . . . You're not joking, are you? Because if you are, you should know that I'm really good with a scalpel, and you have to sleep sometime."

"No jokes. I wouldn't do that to you."

"Okay," she said. "Whatever you need. Name it."

"Be sure. Because once I drag you into this mess, you're in it for good. Understand?"

"I don't care. If you can promise me a visit, then I don't care."

"Good." Relief poured over Payton like cool rain. Until now he hadn't been sure exactly how he was going to keep Clay safe while he took care of his mistakes.

"What do you want me to do?"

"Pack as fast as you can. Bring your medical supplies. And a gun. Make sure you pack a heavy sedative. Chances are you're going to need it."

NATIONAL BESTSELLING AUTHOR

SHANNON K. BUTCHER

*They are the Sentinels: three races descended from
ancient guardians of mankind, each possessing
unique abilities in their battle to protect humanity
against their eternal foes.*

THE NOVELS OF THE SENTINEL WARS

Burning Alive
Finding the Lost
Running Scared
Living Nightmare
Blood Hunt
Dying Wish

**"Enter the world of Shannon K. Butcher
and prepare to be spellbound."**

—*New York Times* bestselling author Sherrilyn Kenyon

Available wherever books are sold or at
penguin.com

FIRST IN A BRAND-NEW SERIES FROM

Shannon K. Butcher

LIVING ON THE EDGE
An Edge Novel

After a devastating injury, Lucas Ramsay knows he's finished as
a soldier. But when the general who saved his life asks him for a
favor, he says yes. All Lucas has to do is keep the general's
daughter from getting on a plane to Colombia—which is easier
said than done…

Independent to the core, Sloane Gideon is a member of the
Edge—a group of mercenaries for hire. But she's not on the
clock for this mission. Her best friend is being held by a vicious
drug lord, and Sloane must rescue her—no matter how many
handsome ex-soldiers her father sends to dissuade her.

With little choice, Lucas tracks Sloane to Colombia—where she
reluctantly allows him to aid her in her search. But as they grow
closer to the target, they grow closer to each other. And before
the battle is over, both will have to decide just what they are
willing to fight for…

**Available wherever books are sold or at
penguin.com**

Can't get enough paranormal romance?

Looking for a place to get the latest information and connect with fellow fans?

"Like" Project Paranormal on Facebook!

- Participate in author chats
- Enter book giveaways
- Learn about the latest releases
- Get book recommendations and more!

facebook.com/ProjectParanormalBooks

Penguin Berkley Jove ACE NAL Signet Obsidian Signet Eclipse RoC W